the G·I·R·L who RACED

FAIRYLAND

All the Way Home

the GIRL who RACED FAIRYLAND
All the Way Home

CATHERYNNE M. VALENTE

ATOM

First published in the US in 2016 by Feiwel and Friends
First published in Great Britain in 2016 by Atom
This paperback edition published in 2017

1 3 5 7 9 10 8 6 4 2

Text copyright © 2016 by Catherynne M. Valente
Illustrations copyright © 2016 by Ana Juan

The moral right of the author has been asserted.

A CIP catalogue record for this book is
available from the British Library.

ISBN 978-1-4721-1284-2 (paperback)

Printed and bound in Great Britain by
CPI Group (UK) Ltd., Croydon, CR0 4YY

Papers used by Atom are from well-managed forests
and other responsible sources.

For everyone
forever.

Dramatis Personae

SEPTEMBER, a Girl
SUSAN JANE AND OWEN, her parents
MARGARET, her aunt
AROOSTOOK, a Model A Ford
SATURDAY, a Marid
A-THROUGH-L, a Wyverary
AUBERGINE, a Night-Dodo
HAWTHORN, a Troll and a Changeling
TAMBURLAINE, a Fetch and a Changeling
BLUNDERBUSS, a Combat Wombat
SCRATCH, a Gramophone
THE STOAT OF ARMS
JACQUARD, a Mantelet
AJAX ODDSON, a Dandy
MERIDIAN, an Ancient and Overgrown Library
GREENWICH MEAN TIME, a Security System
FIZZWILLIAM, a Bathysphere
HUGGER-MUGGERY, an Octopus Assassin
SEPIA SIPHUNCLE, a Cuttlefish
BROTHER TINPAN, a Monkfish
BRUNHILDA, the Greatvole of Black Salt Cavern
CONKER, a Wombat
BLUESTOCKING, also a Wombat

TUGBOAT, a Tobacconist

HEMLOCK, a Troll

HYSSOP, a Troll

LYE, a Golem

MAUD, also a Shadow

THE WATCHFUL DRESS

DEATH

PAN

CHARLES DARWIN, an Englishman

REBECCA, a Human Girl

Racers

CHARLES CRUNCHCRAB I, King of Fairyland

THE MARQUESS, Deposed Ruler of Fairyland

PRINCE MYRRH, her Son

GRATCHLING GOURDBONE GOLDMOUTH, a Clurichaun
(formerly a Baseball)

MADAME TANAQUILL, Prime Minister of Fairyland

TITANIA, a Fairy Queen

HUSHNOW, the Ancient and Demented Raven Lord

QUEEN MAB

HALLOWEEN, a Shadow and Queen of Fairyland Below

WHIPSTITCH, the Elegant Emperor

THE HEADMISTRESS

CURDLEBLOOD, the Dastard of Darkness
PINECRACK, the Moose-Khan
PENNY FARTHING
THRUM, the Rex Tyrannosaur
CUTTY SOAMES, the Captain of the Coblynows

Winds

THE RED WIND, a War Wind
THE BLUE WIND, a Sneaking Wind
THE SILVER WIND, a Following Wind
THE BLACK WIND, a Fierce Wind
THE GOLD WIND, a Blustering Wind
THE GREEN WIND, a Harsh Air

Large Animals

IMOGEN, the Leopard of Little Breezes
IAGO, the Panther of Rough Storms
CYMBELINE, the Tiger of Wild Flurries
PEASEBLOSSOM, the Puffin of Sudden Blizzards
BANQUO, the Lynx of Gentle Showers
CAPULET, the Jaguar of Soft Showers
Numerous Gorillas, Orangutans, Flaming Badgers, Wombats,
Octopi, Toads, Spaniels, Ponies, and one Polar Bear

CHAPTER I

The Queen of Fairyland and All Her Kingdoms

In Which We Begin Just Precisely Where We Ended, Far Too Many People Talk All at Once, an Emperor Gets Himself Stabbed, Queen September Makes Her Inaugural Speech, and a Wondrous Race Is Scheduled for Thursday Next

Once upon a time, a country called Fairyland grew very tired indeed of people squabbling over it, of polishing up the glitter on the same magic and wonder and dashing dangers each morning, of drifting along prettily through the same Perverse and Perilous Sea, of playing with the same old tyrants and brave heroes every century. Because she was quite a large and opinionated country, and because she was as old as starlight and twice as stubborn, and because she had a mountain range on her left border that simply would *not* be bossed about, Fairyland decided to do something about it one day in March just after her morning tea.

A vast and hungry country takes tea somewhat differently than you and I. Fairyland's teatime consisted of a dollop of rain in the Autumn Provinces, a particularly delicate icing of clouds over the Painted Forest, a healthy squeeze of blazing sun in the Hourglass Desert, and a fresh, green wind blowing wild through the streets and alleyways and secret corners of Pandemonium.

The Green Wind sailed through the tufted wool cupolas and brocade bridges and taffeta towers of the capital city. He banked off felt and bombazine memorial statues, twirled on his left toe on the copper silk tip of Groangyre Tower, and stopped to kiss every black lace gargoyle on every rooftop and balcony in the place. He was a handsome thing, with a neat little pointed green beard and dancing green eyes. He was dressed in a green smoking jacket, and a green carriage-driver's cloak, and green jodhpurs—but he had left behind his green snowshoes in his flat in Westerly and swapped them out for green winklepicker boots. Fairyland is warm in March, which is not called springtime, but Bideawhile, for Fairyland has not four seasons, but five and one quarter. In Bideawhile, the bare winter trees put forth tiny paper buds, and on these buds are written secrets, memories, tales only trees can tell.

The Green Wind finished freshening up every curtain and front stoop in town. He straightened his green cravat and soared over the Janglynow Flats, through Hallowgrum and Seresong, stopping only for a short coffee at his favorite crinoline café, and then, without further dawdling, straight through the satin green of Mallowmire Park, to a certain window in a certain palace. The certain palace was called the Briary; of all the lovely towers and castles in Pandemonium, it alone was not made of silk or wool, but of living vines, briars, trellises, and flowers that bloom all year long. The certain window belonged to the Queen of Fairyland.

Pink and yellow peonies chased each other round the window frame. A bluish yellow light fluttered over the walls of the Queen's bedroom, where wild dahlias of every color crowded together, as close as wallpaper. The light came from a hard-working hurricane lamp on the Queen's table. The room stood quite bare except for that humble table, two armoires, and the Royal Desk. The Royal Desk was carved out of a single enormous crystal tree that some brave window-maker cut down long ago in the Glass Forest. It still glowed with fiery hot colors though it was a thousand years old and counting. Rich green and violet and scarlet and orange blankets towered on a small thin bed like an embroidered mountain, for the work of a Queen often takes all night long, and even monarchs need naps, from time to time.

But the Queen was not asleep in her bed or at work at her desk. In fact, the Queen had not yet even seen that bed, nor jumped up and down on it even once. The room stood quite empty and prim and full of anticipation, waiting to be useful. The Green Wind made his apologies and sailed out into the sunny sky. He swirled down the buttercup and begonia walls of the Briary, past the tearooms and the coffee-rooms and the saucer-rooms, to quite another window.

This window was round the back, very tall and thin and serious, like a church window, but it offered a far more interesting view than an empty desk and a hurricane lamp at the end of its oil and its wits. The Green Wind put his green eye to the window and saw several alarming things inside: a broken Dodo's Egg (along with its Dodo), an enormous scrap-yarn wombat, a talking gramophone, a great red Wyverary, a Marid, a troll, a girl carved out of wood, a Redcap, and about a hundred people, animals, Fairies, and other assorted creatures with the power of frowning and shouting, all drenched in jewels and velvet, all expressing those powers of frowning and shouting as hard as they could.

In the midst of it all stood the Queen, looking as baffled as a goose in calculus class.

And so the final dish in Fairyland's tea was a heaping, hideous, unruly platter of shouting, stomping, and rather unskilled fisticuffs.

"*You* shut up!" screeched Hushnow, the Ancient and Demented Raven Lord, who collected all the bright and shining things from all the worlds and hoarded them in Fairyland before the days of the week had names. Warm sunshine danced through the blooming walls of the Briary's great hall. Light bounced off the Raven Lord's onyx-armored wings.

"Emperors do *not* shut up!" roared Whipstitch, the Elegant Emperor, who ruled Fairyland with a silken fist five hundred years before your grandmother learned to dance. The golden buttons on his peacock-blue cloak trembled in fury.

"Has anyone got a rowan branch?" trilled Titania sweetly—and I'm sure I needn't tell you who *she* is. She stared down a certain pale giant by the name of Gratchling Gourdbone Goldmouth, with angry red stitches running all up and down his tattooed skin and SPALDING written on his back in a lovely hand. "It's *just* the thing for giving jumped-up sporting equipment a good hiding."

Goldmouth bellowed rage at the palace hall.

"And you I'll have for a coat," Titania purred to Reynaud

the Fox, a King so old the word hadn't been invented when he pounced upon the crown.

"*What* did you say to me?" the fox snarled, his tail puffing up ferociously, the smell of his wrath filling the crowded room. The room was so crowded, in fact, that some Kings and Queens and duchesses and lords and presidents and empresses and sultans and ancient foxes from before a noun was a noun had begun to spill out into the street. They all wore such fine clothes and finer voices and the very, very finest of tempers that it hurt to look at the great, rude, noisy lot of them all crammed together like a pack of businessmen trapped in an elevator. Everyone who had ever ruled Fairyland, even for the littlest moment, poured into the grand hall of the Briary. More and more came all the time, some still wearing the robes they'd been buried in, others, respectably retired, caught in their dressing gowns, still others, like Reynaud and Horace the Overbear wearing no more than their own good fur.

"You are all despicable fools and if you do not cease your whining I shall cease your faces," seethed Madame Tanaquill, Prime Minister of Fairyland, and, to her mind, the only one in the room with half a right to speak. The buckles and horseshoes and blades of her iron dress clanked against one another.

"Please!" cried a girl in a blue dress, wearing a crown of glittering jeweled keys. "Everyone please be quiet!"

We know this girl awfully well, you and I. She was born in May, and she has a mole on her left cheek, and her feet are very large, but no longer ungainly at all. Her name is September. She is seventeen years old. She was born in Nebraska, she has not seen her parents in ever so long, and she rather wishes her dress was orange.

She is the Queen of Fairyland and All Her Kingdoms.

In short, everything was just as you and I left it not so very long ago. The world had gotten itself turned on its ear and couldn't hear itself think for the braying and honking and *see here, young goblins* of the royal mob.

The trouble was, only a few moments ago, September had been a stately middle-aged woman languishing in a prison that looked very much like a rum cellar. A Moon-Yeti had taken the years of her youth from her. A Dodo had given them back. And somewhere between the Yeti and the Dodo, she'd forgotten what it was like to have a seventeen-year-old voice, a voice that didn't know its own strength yet, a voice that Grown-Ups felt very safe ignoring completely. No one paid her the mind they'd pay a bus ticket.

"A-Through-L, would you?" September said, looking up, with the impish sort of love that occurs between a girl and a reptile, into the shimmering orange eyes of a towering scarlet Wyvern.

"Oh yes!" A-Through-L cried. After all, he was aces at *shhh*ing, being only half Wyvern. His father was a Library. A powerful *shhh* is the final test of any Great Librarian, and Ell had been practicing.

The Wyverary opened his long red jaws and roared fit to deafen the moon. A stream of indigo fire erupted from behind his wicked teeth, twisting and crackling over the heads of the furious Kings and Queens of Fairyland. Thrum, the Rex Tyrannosaur, roared right back in Ell's face. But as he was merely an extinct lizard and not a Wyverary, his roar had no fire in it. No one else so much as took a breath between insults. Half of them had gone red in the face, the other half green, and at least a third had begun to cry.

A great stone strode up to the rear of the crush of Fairies and foxes and gnomes and ravens. It had legs and fists but only the barest beginning of a face. It did not even have a name. It was the last to arrive, but the oldest and strongest of them all—the First Stone of Fairyland, laid down before one seed of glowerwheat, before the first luckfig root went searching in the soil for water.

"HELLO," said the First Stone politely. It sat on the grass, carefully trying not to crush the violets.

September, Queen of Fairyland and All Her Kingdoms, waved back shyly. She hadn't the first idea how to be a Queen. She could be a Knight, or a Bishop, or a Criminal, or a Spinster, but what could she possibly do with *Queen*? She thought of the Marquess and Charlie Crunchcrab. She thought of the Whelk of the Moon. She thought of everyone she'd ever met who was in charge of anything. She thought of her mother bossing around her engines, of her father keeping peace in his classroom—and September knew what to do. After all, in chess, the Queen does whatever she wants.

Queen September put her hand straight up in the air as though she meant to ask a question in class. She waited. It always took a while when her father did it. The Changelings Hawthorn and Tamburlaine understood right away, having been in middle school only last week. They raised up their hands immediately. Hawthorn's huge, mossy troll fingers and Tamburlaine's dark, slender wooden palm shot up into the air. Saturday extended his long blue arm. Scratch and Blunderbuss, being a gramophone and a wombat, respectively, could not quite work out how to manage it. They sat up as straight as they could instead, stretching scrap-yarn nose and gramophone bell toward the ceiling.

It was no good. September was not as tall as the First Stone or Gratchling Gourdbone Goldmouth, or even the Quorum of Quokkas wrenching their tails in anxiety.

"May I?" she asked Blunderbuss. The scrap-yarn combat wombat was nearly the size of A-Through-L, made of a hundred different colors of leftover yarn, and, September judged, quite comfortable for standing on. A Wyverary's back is rather knobbly and pointy—good for riding, but a terrible podium.

"You'd do my fuzzy heart happy," chuffed Blunderbuss, and got down on her huge knees to let September up. Saturday thatched his fingers together to help her hoist herself. He kissed her cheek as she put her toes into his hands. "Ha!" barked Blunderbuss, when September was safely aboard. "I always thought a Queen would weigh more! I could carry a hundred of you, if you'd all sit still, which you wouldn't, but I'd make you!"

Once again, Queen September put her hand into the air. She did not say a word. And now, slowly, the others began to notice September and her friends and their funny fingers pointing at the sky. A duchess here, a pharaoh there, a brace of congressional banshees in the corner.

"What's she doing?" asked Pinecrack, the Moose-Khan. "She looks quite, quite stupid. I shan't have the first pang of guilt about impaling her with my doom-antlers."

"Perhaps it's some new gesture of power at court. We had many in my day," considered Curdleblood, the Dastard of Darkness, a shockingly handsome young man dressed like a minstrel, if only minstrels wore all black and had long, sharp teeth hanging from his hat instead of merry bells.

"Your day was a thousand years ago," snapped the Headmistress, who had ruled only a short while before King Goldmouth swallowed her whole, and was extremely unhappy to be teleported from her tidy ghost-crosswords into this intolerable clutter.

"And it was a *wretched* day, I must say," said a sweet young lady with candy-cane bows in her hair and a dress all of butterscotch and marshmallows. When she conquered Fairyland, folk called her the Happiest Princess, though at the moment she felt quite cross. But she didn't stop smiling, even as she spat at Curdleblood: "You painted the whole country black! I was still scrubbing behind the mountains when I lost my crown!"

"Still," the Moose-Khan mused, "we shouldn't like to appear *ignorant*. Much may have changed since the age of hoof and snow. I don't want the Queen to think me old-fashioned."

Pinecrack sat back on his haunches and lifted one hoof into the air. The Headmistress, ever conscious of manners, followed suit.

"Her?" snarled Charlie Crunchcrab, who had been King Charles Crunchcrab I only ten minutes ago. It's very hard to make such a quick adjustment, and we ought not to think too harshly on him for behaving as poorly as he is surely about to do. "*Her?* She's not the Queen. That's just September! And that name is a Naughty Word, you know. She's the Spinster. She's a troublemaker. She's a revolutionary and a criminal and a dirty *cheat*. She's a human girl! She hasn't even got wings! If she's the right and proper Queen, then my hairy foot is the Emperor of Everything!"

"Sir, I beg your foot's pardon, but *I* am the Emperor of Everything," a young boy in a dizzying patchwork suit interrupted. Though he was a child, his voice rolled deep and sweet across the floor, like cold chocolate poured out of a dark glass. "At least I was," he finished uncertainly. And he raised his hand in the air.

"Oh, I see, you're trying to show me up!" cried Cutty Soames, the Coblynow Captain who sailed Fairyland across the Sea of Broken Stars to its current resting place. He stuck one sooty, filthy arm up with a sneer.

Others did the same, one by one, more and more, paw and hand and hoof and talon. No one wanted to be singled out as a country rube or an unfashionable cretin who didn't know the wonder and mystery of the Raised Hand. Finally, the grand hall stood quite silent, filled with all the Kings and Queens of history politely waiting, like schoolchildren, for the teacher to be satisfied with their manners.

"Thank you," said Queen September, lowering her hand. "Now, you must stop behaving like a stepped-on sack of scorpions or we'll be here till Christmas, at least! And I don't think any of us would really like to holiday together, so let's all serve ourselves a nice big plate of hush."

"HELLO," said the First Stone from the long lawn of the Briary.

"Hello!" answered September brightly. "See, isn't it nice to act like somebody raised us well?"

"Who the devil are you?" hollered a mermaid soaking in the Briary's saltwater fountain, resting smugly in the arms of a silver statue of herself.

"You're a human being! You're not even allowed to look half of us in the eye!" howled a man in a waffle-cone hat and doublet and hose made all of mint ice cream. Have a care not to laugh—once, centuries ago, every soul in Fairyland feared the Ice Cream Man. "Get down off that wombat so I can break your neck, there's a good girl."

Madame Tanaquill swept through the throng, her head held high, striding forward with the sure knowledge that the sea of kings would part before her. It did. The train of her iron dress steamed and sizzled behind her, burning the floor of the Briary and several unfortunate toes, any Fairy thing it touched, for none could bear iron but Madame herself. She glared at Hawthorn and Tamburlaine as she approached, but turned her sweetest smile toward September. And it *was* a sweet smile, the sweetest since the invention of kindness, full of patience and love and understanding. It chilled September to her toes. Madame Tanaquill put a hard, cold, possessive hand on September's foot.

"My dear friends!" she sang out. "Most beloved and respected jewels of Fairyland!" The way she said *beloved* and *respected* sounded very much like *rotten old rubbish* and *not worth the rust on my décolletage*. "May I present to you this marvelous morning, the brave and bold September, our darling monarch, our hallowed Queen! I'm sure you will soon come to love and admire her as I do."

September wondered if every word Madame Tanaquill said meant just the exact opposite of what actually came out of her rosy, prim mouth. The Prime Minister did not love or admire her any more than she loved or admired a glass of spilled wine in her dancing hall. This same woman had dropped September and Saturday and A-Through-L in prison and promptly forgotten about them. But just now the great Fairy was looking up at her with every ounce of affection and joy a face could wring out, her wings fluttering demurely, a blush riding high on her glorious cheeks.

"You needn't worry," September said flatly. She didn't

like to say things flatly, but sometimes it is the perfect antidote to someone trying to convince you the noose in their hand is a lovely silk ribbon for your hair. "I don't want to be Queen. I didn't ask to be Queen. I shan't be Queen any longer than lunchtime if I can help it! I daresay a kitchen chair would make a better Queen than me."

Madame Tanaquill's smile grew even deeper and more genuine, even more like a mother filled to bursting with pride. But the bottom fell out of her dark eyes; hateful lightning flashed within.

"I don't have a care what you want, you horrid little insect," she hissed through her smile. "The Crown chose you. You *are* Queen of Fairyland. It's about as appetizing to myself personally as a pie full of filthy, crawling worms, but it's a fact. You can pull and pry and blubber, but that Crown won't come off until you're dead or deposed. I could cut you down in a heart's-breadth, but the rest of these ruffians would have my head. They take regicide *terribly* personally. Make no mistake; this present predicament is *entirely* your fault, you and your wretched Dodo's Egg. You will want my help to sort it limb from limb. You are a stranger in Fairyland—oh, it's charming how many little vacations you take here! But this is not your home. You don't know these people from a beef supper. But I do. I recognize each and every one. And if you show them that you are a vicious little fool with no more head on her shoulders than a drunken ostrich, they will gobble you up and dab their mouths with that *thing* you call a dress. You may not like me, but I have survived far more towering acts of mythic stupidity than you. I am good. I know what power weighs. If you have any wisdom in your silly monkey head, from this moment until the end of your reign—which I do hope will come quickly—you and I shall become the very best of friends. After all, Queen September, a Prime Minister lives to serve."

Madame Tanaquill turned her shining face to the assembled Kings and Queens of Fairyland, some of whom still had their hands up.

"You must forgive her. She is only a new Queen, and new Queens are like baby horses: They do not know what their legs are for yet, but they are perfectly adorable while they try to work it out! All of us remember our first days in the Briary, I'm quite sure. We were all then grateful for the patience shown to us as we searched for the necessaries and put down rebellions and turned our enemies into flamingoes. Ah, memories! Let us now extend that patience with both hands to the newest member of our very exclusive club."

She clapped her shimmering hands together—and applause filled the hall.

"It's perfectly clear what's happened—an illicit Dodo's Egg was brought onto the premises by persons of dubious intent and cracked open on the floor like the world's worst breakfast. Some of you may recall that a Dodo's Egg restores what was lost. This is a very dangerous magic, for it can get rather overexcited and run wild where other magics would sit nicely with their eyes on their own paper. This is why we Fairies only used them privately, in the safety of our own homes, and after working hours. But some people haven't got the class a Fairy holds in her handbag, and so, here we are. All the lost Kings and Queens of Fairyland, dead and alive and other, found and rounded up and come round for supper with no notice at all. It's *very* awkward for all of us, I'm sure! But we must make the best of an absurd situation." Madame Tanaquill held one hand delicately to her forehead, as though all that had thoroughly tired her out. "Goodness! There's enough out of silly old me! You'd think I had the Crown! I shan't say another word until we've heard from the lady in question."

The Prime Minister looked expectantly at September.

In chess, a Queen can do anything she wants, September thought. *No one else is going to come and tell me what to do, so I had better get on with doing for myself.*

"Good afternoon!" September cried out in her best Queenly voice. "I'm very pleased to meet all of you, even though I can tell by the fire coming out of a few of your noses that almost none of you are pleased to meet me. Except the big rock in the back, and I've got to tell you: At the moment, he is by far my favorite. Um. I think, for my first decree, I had better insist that no one maim or murder anyone else for at least a week. You can all hold out that long. I know better than to ask for longer. Some of you have *very* sharp claws." September took a deep breath. She remembered the Blue Wind—she who blushes first, loses. If she let them think they awed her, she was lost. "For my second decree, I shall have to ask that you all wear name tags. I know you were all very important once upon a time, but you might as well be portraits in a museum to me." September thought she'd done that quite well. Having spent a little time being forty years old helped a bit, when it came to scowling down Grown-Ups and saying wicked things so that they didn't sound wicked, only a bit bored.

A young girl in a black dress and a black hat as tall and tiered as a wedding cake looked up at September from the throng. Her hair glowed deep, angry red.

"You know me," said the Marquess softly—oh, but how sound carries in the Briary! Her hand fluttered to her fine hat, as if everything might be all right, might be just as it was, if only she still had it.

"Yes," answered Queen September. "I know you." A look both dark and bright passed between them. "Perhaps you'd better stay where I can see you."

Hawthorn the troll reached into the satchel he still wore slung over his huge, mossy shoulder. He pulled out a notebook and a handsome silver pen with indigo ink inside. He had a moment of panic, for he loved his paper and pen. He'd named them Inspector Balloon and Mr. Indigo back in Chicago, where he'd been a child and a Changeling, stuffed into a human body like a thousand-pound crystal into a brown paper bag. But trolls are canny creatures, and Changelings love little so much as making trouble, and out of both of these together, Hawthorn had stitched an idea. He stepped forward with authority. He was only thirteen, but a troll's thirteen is a very serious age. Hawthorn didn't know it, but he sounded awfully like Nicholas Rood, the psychologist who'd raised him. Nicholas had quite the bossiest voice he'd ever heard, and Hawthorn had once done Madame Tanaquill's laundry.

"Step right up," he bellowed, and if you have ever heard a troll bellow, you will understand why even Kings and Queens found their feet obeying before they knew what had smacked their eardrums. "Tell me your name and I shall write it out very nicely for you and pin it to your chest with one of your brooches or cloak-pins or, if you are a dinosaur or a bird or a rock or a slice of cheese, we'll just sling it round your neck on somebody's spare jewels. Do remember to spell it out for me if anyone's got runes or umlauts or apostrophes or extinct letters in! Who's first?"

The Marquess stepped forward. She spelled her name through clenched teeth. M-A-R-Q-U-E-S-S. A sour and sneering titter bubbled up from the royal horde.

"Oh, *darling,* that's not how you pronounce it," clucked Titania. "And anyhow, don't you know that's a *boy's* title?"

"How embarrassing!" chuckled Madame Tanaquill, covering her mouth with a shimmering hand. "Who raised you, child?"

The Emperor of Everything wrinkled his noble nose. "I suppose they're letting anyone wear the big hat nowadays. Look around; this room is half bumpkins and half barbarians. I'd wager she's never so much as dog-eared a page of the Whomsday Book!"

"Or stayed up till all hours reading Ichabod Lurk's *Peerage, Spearage, and Fearage* under her blankets!" smirked the Headmistress.

The Marquess flushed horribly, redder than her hair and blacker than her dress. "If I had my lions, you wouldn't dare say such things!"

Whipstitch waved his ringed hand in the air. "If wishes

were dishes we'd all tuck in, lovey! If I had my Button-Down Guard, you'd have a poleax in your eye! We all have our disappointments."

"*Have* you got lions? Or have you got a wee brace of kittens you just *call* lions to puff up their chests a bit, the way a dirty little wastrel calls herself a Marquess and thinks she's somebody?" Titania asked, tilting her shining head in sympathy.

Hawthorn didn't pause. He kept writing out name tags, one by one, tearing strips out of Inspector Balloon, wincing with each tear. Tamburlaine pinned them to chest after chest like particularly unhappy medals.

"Shut up," hissed the Marquess. "I chose it, you miserable, rouged-up idiots! Why shouldn't I have a boy's title? People listen to boys! They fear boys—they fear a King and hope a Queen will show them mercy! Why shouldn't I be a Marquess? I rule the world! *I* say how things are pronounced! *I* say what belongs to boys and what doesn't!"

"You don't, though," interrupted September calmly. The calm came up from inside her, pooling into her heart, smoothing everything clean. It had been so long. She had done so much—faced down a Yeti, shot her own shadow, seen the world from a prison cell, raced up to forty years old and back to seventeen again. September found she no longer feared the Marquess much at all. She even looked a bit short and sorry to her now. "You don't rule the world. You don't rule anything but yourself. You can still be a Marquess, if you like. But it means nothing more than saying you're somebody's old Auntie they only see once a year at Easter. You're just like everyone else. It's your turn to hope there's a box of mercy in the pantry." September sucked in her breath. The words formed in her mouth but she didn't want to say them. She needed to think. She needed half a moment to breathe. But you couldn't breathe in front of this lot. Breathing showed weakness. She didn't need Tanaquill to tell her that. "*I* rule Fairyland—"

"No!" squawked a voice from the rear of the assembly. Not one voice, but eight, all speaking together in perfect harmony. "Nope! Nope! No! Don't say another word, Missy! Make way!"

The Stoat of Arms barreled through the grand hall, the seal of a nation come alive. If you have ever seen a passport, try to remember the strange tangle of animals stamped on the cover, for all nations have them. Now, imagine them all leaping off that little leather book and yelling and squawking all together. The Stoat of Arms was not one creature, but a blue-skinned, black-horned unicorn rampant and a little girl in knight's armor standing upon the backs of two enormous golden stoats. A rainbow of silver stars, black roosters, and sunflowers arched above their heads, and a tiny, twinkling Fairy balanced on her right toe on the tip of the topmost silver star. Applause greeted the miniature zoo—everyone there, save September and her friends, had known the Stoat of Arms long and well in their day.

"Yes, thank you, cheers," said the two stoats, the girl, the unicorn rampant, the black roosters, and the Fairy altogether in one voice. "Hortense, kindly refrain from petting us, how many times have we had this discussion? In four hundred years you might have learned to control yourself." A lady in a samite gown and a hippo's head snatched her hand back guiltily. "Well, I think we can all agree this is an unprecedented and completely intolerable situation! I know you all far too well to think you will play nicely with the other children! Oh, come now! Has the Knapper stabbed someone already?"

"Nope!" called a cheerful-cheeked man wearing a cloak of knives. "He's fine!" He waggled Whipstitch's hand in the air, but the Elegant Emperor looked very pale and woozy.

"You see?" cried the stoats and the girl and the unicorn and the chickens and the Fairy. "Be honest, ladies and gentlemen, how many of you have spent the last quarter-hour fomenting rebellion, plotting to murder, or thinking of how nice the city would look if it were on fire?"

CHAPTER I

Many, many hands raised up, some sheepish, some defiant, some rather bored.

"Fortunately," continued the Stoat of Arms, all eight of its voices filled with disgust, "you won't get the chance. Fairyland is very well acquainted with all of you and has had quite enough of your nonsense. She is frankly exhausted by the last several thousand years of shenanigans and cannot imagine why all of you are so obsessed with who sits on a certain chair and wears a certain hat. However, if you will insist on treating her as a prize in a silly game, so be it." The two golden stoats smacked the floor of the grand hall with their front paws twice, in just the same way as a judge might bang her gavel. "In three days' time, which will be Thursday, for those of you who lived before calendars became sentient, let all who wish to rule Fairyland gather at the Ghostloom Gate on the north side of the city. Thursday shall be known far and wide as the day of the Cantankerous Derby! All hopefuls, thoroughbreds, long shots, cheaters, townies, speed demons, and dark horses shall commence a Wondrous Race, beginning in Pandemonium, and ending at Runnymede Square in the ancient city of Mummery! The winner shall receive the Crown, the Sceptre, and a nice blue ribbon with #1 written on it. All are eligible! Ravished, Stumbled, Changelings, Fairies, Gnomes, Rocks, and Trees! Participation comprises a binding contract to accept the results of the race. Sandwiches and coffee will be provided!"

"That's all?" cawed Hushnow, the Ancient and Demented Raven Lord. "Then you shall all certainly be calling me Your Grand High Such and Such by Monday morning! I'm faster than any of you sorry lot!"

"I beg to differ," scoffed the Piebald, the Stallion of Time. His mane was all of clock hands, and his tail was a long pendulum.

"SANDWICHES AND COFFEE WILL BE PROVIDED!" roared the Stoat of Arms. "And that is most certainly not all! You must present yourself at Runnymede Square in the ancient city of Mummery bearing the Heart of Fairyland, or be disqualified! The Cantankerous Derby is a Race with a Hunt hidden inside! In the meantime, the Briary has ample room to accommodate you all in comfort and safety, from inclement weather, privation, but most importantly, from one another. Please proceed in as orderly a fashion as you are capable of to the Second-Best Parlor, where you will find the Scuttler, who keeps the running of the Briary. He will show you to your room and present you with a schedule of meal times, exercise hours, and social activities divided by who is least likely to eat one another before Thursday. Are we understood?"

A murmur of mixed doubt, eagerness, muffled outrage, and longing for lunch passed through the gathered court.

"But I *am* Queen of Fairyland," September said softly. She nervously touched the crown of jeweled keys upon her head. Now that it was about to be whisked away from her, suddenly September did not feel quite so sure she wanted nothing to do with Queenery. "Why can't it be me?"

The Stoat of Arms turned toward her with several haughty gazes—which is the same thing as apologizing to somebody who has been in government as long as the Stoat. "Indeed you are, madam. For three days. And Fairyland is very glad to have you. But please—such things are to be discussed in private, Your Majesty. You and I will adjourn to the Royal Closet, which I have already certified as ruffian-free. As for the rest of you, go! It'll take the poor Zinnias weeks to make the grand hall livable again!"

The Zinnias, since our Stoat will certainly not deign to tell you a thing about them, are the Royal Guard of the Briary, a platoon of very stern armored emu-birds with zinnia flowers blooming all over their breastplates and their helmets. This might make them look silly to you or I, but Pandemonians know that each of those flowers can fly free like an assassin's throwing star, and they are sharper than they seem. Flowers are always more serious than they appear.

You would not think a room could empty so quickly, but given the chance at a bit of cake and a place to plot in private, few creatures will dawdle. Half the Kings and Queens of Fairyland vanished in the space of a hiccup, blinking out of the grand hall and appearing in the Second-Best Parlor before anyone could tell them not to drink all the brandy. A quarter flew or hopped or bolted straight to the Helledoors, the blooming doors of the Briary proper, each violet petal etched with scenes from reigns long forgotten—though perhaps not quite so forgotten today as they were yesterday. The stragglers slipped through halls and secret nooks and trapdoors they knew like their own best beloved brothers and sisters. And the Stoat of Arms, with all its many and varied limbs, pushed, prodded, nudged, and jostled September away from her friends toward a long, slender hallway with no splendid flowers or decorated door. It looked dark and lonely. September protested loudly, but Stoats have won several prizes for stubbornness over the centuries, and you would have better luck protesting the sun.

"I *want* them to come with me!" she cried.

"You haven't any right," snarled Saturday.

"I'm not afraid to roast a stoat *or* a unicorn," warned A-Through-L.

Hawthorn and Tamburlaine exchanged looks, not at all

sure what they ought to do or say, having only met September a few hours before. Perhaps they were not included in her protests. Perhaps they ought to have slipped away with the rest.

"They absolutely may *not* come with you," insisted the Stoat of Arms. "And thank you for encouraging them, young lady! A coronation is a private affair! You might as well ask to watch her dressing in the morning! It's shameful! Go to your rooms, sit down, be quiet, have a bath or play a bit of pooka poker, do try not to turn anyone into kangaroos, and I'm certain Her Majesty will attend you as soon as she is able!"

September disappeared down the dark and lonely hall, pursued by a Stoat. Saturday, A-Through-L and Blunderbuss, Hawthorn and Tamburlaine and Scratch were left suddenly alone to find their own way. The Briary was not their old friend, full of familiar spots and happy memories. It was their new and wild and unknown maze, and they had no bread crumbs to mark their path. They all stood very still for a moment, glancing at one another uncertainly.

A clicking, scuttling, businesslike clatter saved them from simply bedding down in the center of the grand hall: the smart, swift footsteps of a broad, polished, black-and-white-checkered crab. He looked up at them with glittering crustacean eyes and snapped his great fore-claws.

"Hullo, misters and missuses! My name's Spoke, and I'll be your Scuttler this fine evening. First visit to the Briary? I can always spot first-timers . . ."

When all the glittering mob had gone and the floor of the grand hall stood empty of all but their boot-scuffs and discarded gum wrappers and magic cloaks and loose change and lost hair combs, a figure peeped in from the sunny afternoon. He had cloven feet and shaggy fur upon his legs. He had horns upon his head and a devilishly handsome beard. He looked all round the grand hall, but there was nobody left to greet him.

"Am I late?" said Pan.

CHAPTER II

SOMETHING NOT SO GRAND AS A GRYPHON

*In Which September Collects Herself, Meets an Iron Lady,
Acquires Her Regalia, Finds Several Lost Items,
and Discovers an Old Friend Lying in Wait*

The Briary is not alive in the way you and I are alive. But it *is* alive. Its roots, if I may be forgiven for discussing such things in public, go all the way through Fairyland and come out the other side as a small hut covered in black tulips. This is a very secret place, so I'll thank you not to tell anyone about it, or else I shall be sacked. Think of the Briary as a very large, very old Burmese python in whom you can very happily live; a python tastefully furnished with gilded couches and fringed lamps and a great lot of paintings in every imaginable style. The Briary can squeeze up and in until it is almost unnoticeable if no one is at home. It can stretch up and out and twist round and about if guests have arrived for supper and more room is needed. It is quite an understanding Royal Residence.

Through all these snakelike halls and ways, the left-hand stoat of the Stoat of Arms pushed her velvety nose at September's back. The left-hand stoat was called Gloriana, the right-hand, Rex. September hopped a little, walking faster up a long, rose-patched hall winding its way to the heart of the Briary.

It was the first quiet September had held in her hand since that ridiculous, astonishing wombat had barged through the walls of her prison cell. Sunlight drifted through the green walls like a breeze, chasing shadows, brightening their edges, and running off again down staircases and laundry chutes and dumbwaiter shafts. She remembered the first time she set foot in the Briary, a thousand years ago and a thousand more, it seemed to her now. How frightened she had been! And all she'd done was stand very still while the Marquess sneered at her and say no when she tried to have her way. September had never even thought to wonder what that polleny palace looked like further in and farther out. All she could see then was the Marquess and her terrible smile.

But now, it was *her* house, at least for a little while. September tried to pull that thought over her head, to get her arms in the sleeves, to smooth out the skirt of it. *This is my house. I live here.* But it wouldn't smooth. All she could think of was her own dear house in Nebraska with her father and mother in it, only now she pictured the creaky old farmhouse covered in far too many flowers, their small and amiable dog jumping up on everything and snapping at visiting bees. *I probably have my own bathroom,* she thought idly.

That did it.

It all came rushing in at her: escaping prison and falling backward into seventeen again and the terrible look in Madame Tanaquill's eyes and the crown on her head and how much she did, finally, miss home and her parents and that silly, daffy dog and the big rude roan at the Killory farm and her school with its nice, safe, quiet essays to be written and equations to be solved. The smell of flowers in her nose got so thick and heavy that September couldn't breathe. She wanted to sit down. She wanted to sleep for a hundred and fifty years. She wanted her father. She wanted to have nothing to do today but fix an old fence. She wanted her mother to appear and fix everything for her, to just take it all over and make the decisions and sweep up all the nastiness into a bin. *Her mother would make a good Queen,* September thought. Her mother wouldn't blink.

But the Stoat of Arms would not let September rest. Her mother did not appear. The stoats nipped at her heels; the human girl pushed at her back; the unicorn whinnied softly; the chickens grumbled; and the Fairy on top kept tossing shimmers from her tiny wand to mark the path. September squeaked, trying to breathe in the perfume and the gloam, but the chickens squeaked louder.

Finally, they came to a plain, round door in the lush wall. It didn't have a knob in the shape of a magical flower. It didn't have any copper or gold or little rubies in it. It was just a few birch-trunks slapped together, hardly even a door at all. It reminded September of the janitor's closet in her old school, full of mops and bleach and napkins, never meant to be noticed among the classrooms.

The Stoat of Arms bowed slightly. It couldn't manage more than a slight bow, being made of two stoats, three roosters, three silver stars, a little girl, a unicorn, and a Fairy. More than a little bow was simply too much choreography. "If you please, madam. The Royal Closet will only open to the hand of the Queen."

September's curiosity swept aside her worry. Her curiosity had always lorded it over most of the rest of her, and by now, it was mightily accustomed to getting its own way. September put her hand flat on the pale birches. She didn't know whether to push or pull, and didn't want to make a fool of herself by getting it wrong. But in the end, the door swung inward as soon as it felt her fingers land. Within, she saw only a wide, soft darkness.

"We shall wait here for you, Your Majesty," said the Stoat of Arms, and all of the creatures that made up the Stoat of Arms bowed as one.

September reached out one hand and scratched Rex behind one ear. Rex felt quite, quite humiliated, but he did not protest, for a Queen has the right to pet anyone she likes. "You don't have to be so formal with me. We have met before, you know." Which was how she knew he hated being scratched.

"Have we?" The Stoat of Arms wrinkled its several noses doubtfully. "I'm sure we would remember."

"Oh, I'm terribly easy to forget!" September said airily, and smiled a much older woman's smile, the sort of smile a girl learns on the back of years of holding her tongue. "When Madame Tanaquill and Charlie Crunchcrab locked me away in the Redcaps' cellar, you were having a cup of punch and chatting up an undine. Come now! You *must* remember! It was the night of the Summer Sabbat and I'd only just come back from the Moon. My friend, the Vicereine of Coffee, swiped an invitation for me. I do have so many friends in Fairyland these days, it's quite extraordinary! Saturday and I drove across the Wishbone Wastes in my darling Model A Ford Aroostook while Ell flew gaily overhead. It was our favorite way to travel. We all arrived at the border of the Candelabra Desert just as the sun set. How the lanternweeds blew in the summer wind! How the absinthe cacti bubbled and overflowed! How beautiful all the Fairies shone and spun! They were everything I could have imagined. Their wings glittered like all my old dreams. And I saw *you* nibbling on a great huge slab of saguaro cake, surrounded by Fairies who laughed at every joke you made. I'm sure they were really wonderful jokes, Sir Stoats! I should love to hear them someday. Yes, the night we met, I wore orange; you wore chickens. The brass band struck up 'The Kraken's Waltz.' Saturday and I took to the desert dance floor. He put his arm around my waist. Ell let a gout of indigo flame erupt into the air for the delight of all the gathered lords and ladies. My love and I saw the violet sparks reflected in each other's eyes. And then—oh, I just can't recall what happened next! You must help me, Sir Stoats! What was it? You do remember now, don't you?"

The Stoat of Arms, for perhaps the first time in its long, long life, looked distinctly embarrassed. "Then you were arrested by Madame Tanaquill's personal constabulary and buried in a cellar for two years. The car was impounded, I believe."

"Yes, *that's* it! How silly of me to forget." September quirked her eyebrow and laughed quite deliberately, a hard, barbed laugh she had learned long ago from the dancing, dastardly Blue Wind. "She who blushes first loses," she said in a gentler voice, and tapped the Stoat on the nose.

My darlings, I am quite as surprised as you! A narrator looks away from her charges for half a tale and returns to find they've gone wily and wild in her absence, and learned all manner of new magics she intended to teach them much later.

September straightened up and tugged on the (rather oversized now) long blue dress she'd worn when she was the Spinster and hatched her plots from the depths of a rum cellar. "This is where I'm to be coronated, is it? Well, Stoats, we'd best get it over with. Will you be all right on your own? I wouldn't want you to get bored."

"We have brought a magazine, and our pipes." The two stoats, three cockerels, unicorn, Fairy, and human girl that made up the Stoat of Arms each produced handsome churchwarden pipes and waved them at September.

"Very well, then!" said the Queen with a deep breath, and stepped inside the great round door.

It shut behind her with a satisfied *clunk*. September calmed her hammering heart. She was not so wily or wild that it did not terrify her a little whenever she had to pull on *haughtiness* like a party dress and whirl about in it.

Within the Royal Closet, lamps bubbled to life all along the walls, glass goblets filled with liquid light of blue and gold, like cups of punch at a birthday party. September stared—the room yawned on forever. She could see neither ceiling nor walls. A beautiful velvet floor spread out before her so that her feet fell without the littlest sound. Everywhere she looked she saw splendid clothes hanging neatly, or displayed on dress forms, or laid out for mending, or soaking in laundry tubs. Hatboxes towered up into the shadows beyond the goblet-lamps. A sea of shoes lapped at the hems of the hanging gowns and suits and cloaks and trousers. Umbrella stands bristled with swords, canes, scepters, staves, wands, and the occasional umbrella. The ranks of shining clothes were only broken by mirrors here and there, mirrors taller than a Wyverary and framed in gold, in ice, in green flame or indigo, in ancient oak, in unicorn and narwhal horns, in ships' ropes, in curious, blinking eyes, in gemstones September could not name, in pocket watches, in brocade, in lost love letters. In the center of the vast wardrobe stood a little podium with a large and beautiful book lying open on it, along with a pot of scarlet ink.

September could hear her footsteps echo wildly as she crossed the hall to peer at the book. At the top of each thick, parchment page, she read:

GUEST BOOK.
PLEASE SIGN IN.

And below that, a number of neat columns with titles like NAME, SPECIES, and TIME IN/TIME OUT, each one brimming with magnificent signatures. She ran her fingertips over the last two entries in the lovely ledger: *The Marquess. Human. 2:15 p.m., April 2nd, the Year of the Yellow-Tongued Hobgoblin/ Deposed via Ravished Girl, 10:58 p.m., May 24th, the Year of the Valiant Teacup. Charles Crunchcrab. Fairy. Midnight, August 9th, the Year of the Unhappy Hippogriff/Deposed via Dodo's Egg, Tea-time, March 15th, the Year of the Emerald Acrobat.* September searched for a quill pen—under the edges of the book, on the ledge of the podium. She felt a little like the older kids who scratched their names—and other, bolder things—on the bathroom walls at school. Surely, someone would come along and scold her any moment now. But she found nothing.

"Oh, I'm terribly sorry," came a brisk, tidy voice, a voice like snug seams and straight hems. "How unprofessional of me! Wait just a moment."

September whirled round. A creature clattered forward through the rows of wonderful clothes. Her slender limbs were made all of wrought iron, curling and twisting in lovely patterns like the ones in a fine old gate. The wrought-iron girl stood much taller than September, her long legs bent backward like a heron's, her hair forged in a crown of leafy iron vines round her dark skull. As September stared, the lady opened her wrought-iron rib cage like the lid of a secretary desk. A sewing machine unfolded out of her, kept hidden where her heart might have been. She reached down and pulled a coil of plain linen from a scrap basket sandwiched between an Elizabethan gown and a motorcycle jacket and fed it through her machine heart. The needle moved up and down merrily and when the linen emerged, it had become a graceful quill pen with a sharp bronze nib. The quill was a real quill, too, a sturdy turkey feather with gold and red speckles.

September pulled it free and dipped the new pen into the scarlet inkwell. She bent down to the guest book, trying to make her face as brave and bold as the one she'd shown to the Stoat of Arms, and she only hesitated a moment before writing: *September Bell. Human. A Bit After Teatime, March 15th, the Year of the Emerald Acrobat.* She frowned at her handwriting—it looked rather plain next to the dashing flourishes above, the *t*'s crossed with rapiers and *i*'s dotted with alchemical sigils of the other "guests."

"Most excellent. Now we can begin!" said the wrought-iron lady, folding up her black rib cage again. "I am the Archbishop of the Closet, the Sartorial Seneschal. You may call me Jacquard. Jack, if you are lazy and cannot manage two whole syllables. I'm here to help with your fitting."

September smiled broadly. "You didn't call me *Your Majesty* or *Your Grace* or *Your Highness.*"

Jacquard shrugged. Her eyes were the only part of her that wasn't smelted out of iron, but delicately etched silver with warm sunstone irises. They glittered like real eyes when she blinked. "Oh, I don't trouble myself with that sort of thing. I've seen so many of you under my tape it would be like bowing to a buttonhole. But I can try to remember if you'd prefer."

September sighed with relief. "I wouldn't, at all! Really, I don't see why anyone does! I didn't ask them to! Anyway, it seems to me that whenever a person says: *Your Majesty*, they mean: *I would rather drink a glass of gasoline than spend another moment with you.*"

Jacquard grinned. Her lips had ribbons carved into them, all tied in smart bows. "Good girl. Perhaps you'll last longer than the soup course in your supper tonight."

"I don't want to *last* at all. I don't want to be Queen. I keep telling people that, but no one listens to me. I just want to be left alone."

Jacquard chuckled. She produced a measuring tape from her metal arm the way a lady might produce a handkerchief from her sleeve. "Young miss, if you didn't want to be Queen, perhaps you shouldn't have kept whacking every monarch you met with *quite* such a large and pointy stick. The trouble with upsetting the applecart is that you've got to clean up the fruit when you're done."

"How do you know what I've done?"

Jacquard wrapped the tape round September's waist. "If you had to mend the trousers of Fairyland's masters, you'd learn the name *September* quick as a stitch, my humble hellion. I've heard your name along with the most dreadfully impolite language—you'd blush if I repeated it. I've heard it hissed, hollered, snarled, cursed, and flung against the wall. You're quite famous, I'm afraid. Public menace number one. I'm just fiendishly pleased to meet you! I would shake your hand, but Fairylanders are quite allergic to me. Now, we have a great heaping basket of decisions to make and not much time, so why don't we buckle down to our task?"

"Why don't we have much time? If I'm Queen, surely I can take as long as I like to decide whatever it is that needs deciding."

"The Cantankerous Derby begins in three days' time. Unless you are much faster and cleverer than you look, your reign will go down in my book as precisely seventy-two hours long. Not the shortest—that honor goes to the Blessed Bonk, a hobgoblin who lasted all of fifteen minutes before falling down a flight of stairs, hitting his head on a china cabinet, and drowning in a mud puddle. The mud puddle turned out to be the very river nymph who succeeded him. But three days is not quite long enough to stretch out in. No, you must choose your regalia quickly. You must get ready for the Race. If the Queen stood at the starting line in her street clothes, I would die of shame."

"My regalia?" September had to admit her Spinster dress no longer fit her. It was too long in the arm and the hem. But *regalia* did not sound like the sort of thing you could ride a Wyverary in.

"Oh yes!" cried Jacquard. "A ruler must have regalia, just as a businessman must have his suit and briefcase, just as a soldier must have his rifle and his cap, just as a flying ace must have her aeroplane. How will anyone take you seriously as a Queen if you do not look like one? It is the dearest duty of the Archbishop of the Closet to assist you in choosing all the tools of your trade." The wrought-iron girl spread her long arms to indicate the vast reaches of the Royal Closet. "Your name, your scepter, your costume, your shoes, and your steed. You have your crown already." September touched the circle of jeweled keys on her head. She hardly felt its weight anymore.

Jacquard led September to a row of drawers with glass tops, like a jeweler's case where engagement rings might be kept. Inside lay ribbons of every color and fabric, olive lace and copper silk and crimson damask and orchid rope. Each one had tiny words woven into them, winding round and round the ribbon like lengths of black thread. "Firstly, you must choose a name."

"My name is September."

"No, no, you misunderstand, my dear! You must choose a *dynastic* name. You can be anything you like—a Queen, a Sultana, a Caesar, a Marquess, an Empress, a Baroness—any sort of Ess you can think of." Jack opened the drawers and pulled out a length of ribbon for each title. "You could even be a King, if you liked—Fairyland is wonderfully modern on that point. If you don't care for old-fashioned courtly ranks, you could be the Sheriff or the Cannoneer or the Dark Horse, the Alewife or the Tobacconist or the Hydronaut—oh, we haven't had a Hydronaut in *centuries*! And it needn't be so plain as one word. You might be the Princess of Pluto or Lady Ironbones or Count Fortune or the Wintry Warlord. The choice is yours—your first choice. Your name goes before you—it tells everyone what you're about. Names are awfully old magic, older than the monarchy, older than me. Your name is the armor you wear in the Battle of Everyday. Hardly anyone gets to pick their own. It is one of the privileges of your position. When your parents choose your name, they make a little wish for your future and fold it up inside your heart forever. When you choose your own, you make your own wish."

"What others call you, you become," said September softly, remembering the words a Yeti had once spoken to her.

"Oh yes. If you were to choose Lady Brightbat, for instance, I daresay you'd find your vampire teeth half grown in by bedtime. If you wrap Warlord round your shoulders, soldiers a thousand miles away will wake up with a start."

September considered. She had been a Knight and a Bishop and a Criminal and a Spinster—so many titles for a girl from Nebraska with the smell of chicken feed and dish soap still on her! But she never stayed in any of them long, always running out of one name and into another. Would she really transform into whatever she called herself? Perhaps it should be something big and powerful, then. The Gryphon or the Valkyrie or the Giantess. But if she became a Giantess, she would have a devil of a time explaining to her parents why she suddenly needed a horse-acre bed instead of her sweet old pillow. And now that she was free, she would go home when her hourglass ran out, wouldn't she? Those were the rules. Even being Queen did not change them. The Marquess knew that and so did she. Would her parents know her at home, if she came back a Giantess? Something not so grand as a Gryphon, then. And thinking of home, September's heart ran ahead in front of her mind, and before she knew it, she had decided.

"Could I . . . could I be the Engineer? My mother's one, you see. And for a long while I didn't think much about anything except Fairyland—getting here and being here and staying here. But I haven't seen my mother since before I went up to the Moon and I miss her. I miss her so much. And she fixes things. Mends things. Makes them good and sound and flyable again. Even if I'm only Queen for a little while, that's the sort of Queen I'd like to be."

"Done," said Jacquard, and drew a great length of sturdy grass-green suede from the drawer. "Next, you must select your Royal Scepter. You will use it to make Decrees, which is

a jumped-up way of saying Get Your Own Way at Once."
Jacquard pointed at the crowded umbrella stands. Ivory-
handled canes glimmered, as well as golden staves topped
with opals and tiger's eyes, shoehorns and fireplace pokers and
rapiers and bullwhips and parasols. "A Royal Scepter is not
quite so blunt as a sword, nor quite so fancified as a magic
wand—though of course you could choose a sword or a
magic wand if you wanted to bore me half to tears. You
might have seen Royal Scepters and never known what you
were looking at. Your predecessor used a crab hammer."

"What did the Marquess use?" September said quietly. If
she had to be Queen, the most important thing was to be
nothing like the Marquess, she felt.

"She lost hers. She replaced it with a Spoon, I believe. I
should mention, in the event of loss of any regalia, you must
provide your own replacement. The Royal Closet is not
responsible for articles lost or damaged in the process of monarchy or other shenanigans."

A thought occurred to September. "Could I . . . could I
have my old wrench? The one I pulled out of the casket in the
Autumn Provinces."

The wrought-iron lady rummaged through the umbrella
stands, pushing aside raccoon caps and woolly scarves and
sealskin kirtles. Finally, she produced, from a blown-glass

stand half squashed beneath a pirate's chest full of spare buttons, the long, sturdy wrench September had won from the Worsted Wood so long ago.

"Everything ends up here, sooner or later. At least, it ends up here if it's any good. Many of the gowns and suits and winter coats and waistcoats and shoes you see in the Royal Closet belonged to some King or Queen once upon a time, was worn and loved and twirled about in."

"What about the rest?"

"I made the rest. I am a Mantelet. I must make something, or I will die. Mantelets were one of the first beasts to crawl out of the cauldron when Fairyland was new and could not yet sleep through the night. We looked around us and saw trees, rivers, deserts, fields, even the Perverse and Perilous Sea—all the things that grew and lived according to their own cantankerous nature. But nothing *made*. Nothing woven or hammered or erected or distilled or sculpted or painted. We yearned to be the ones to weave and hammer and erect and distill and sculpt and paint. We saw visions of a Made World alongside the Wild World. I was born in the Houppelande Hills before the calendar learned to count to thirty-one. My father was a printing press with kind letter-block eyes. My mother was a blacksmith's forge with warm, molten arms. But I? I loved to sew. Every kind of stitch looked like scripture to me, scripture and starlight! Anything I could get my hands on I put under my needle—until I became so skilled that I didn't need anything under my needle to make a pair of seven-league boots, or a dress of fondest hopes, or Groangyre Tower with its silk balloon. The Elegant Emperor asked me to come and live at the Briary long ago. No one can touch me, on account of my iron, but I touch everything that touches them. Between fittings—which is what a Mantelet calls a coronation—I make the regalia of the future. A thousand skirts for a thousand Queens to come. I even made the Marquess's hat." Jacquard smiled modestly. "There is nothing here that is powerless. I've soaked even the smallest lace ruffle and fleece lining in magic, in every kind of magic. This kimono?" She pulled a glittering white-and-black robe free of its cousins. "This kimono can call down the snow no matter how hot and high the sun rides. My chartreuse tuxedo can turn you into a lightning-breathing bird of paradise. This purple petticoat forces the wearer to tell the truth no matter how much they may wish to lie, while the black one compels them to sing a song for everything they do. I must have a *little* fun, after all. You may choose your Royal Costume from anything you see, or I will make you something new out of your name and your scepter and your longings and your needings. And perhaps . . . perhaps I can make you something to help with the Cantankerous Derby. Something swift and armored and full of tricks."

September did not need to look through the racks of beautiful clothes. She had been thinking hard all the while the Mantelet spoke and knew already what she wanted.

"Jacquard, I do not want anything in this wardrobe. It's all more wonderful than anyone could ask for—Cinderella would take one look in here and lose her entire mind, I think. And perhaps I ought to think practically and let you sew me a Racing Suit that would let me cross the world in two steps. But what I want, what I really want, isn't here. I want everything back, Miss Jack. Everything I've had and lost—my wrench and the Witch's Spoon and my Watchful Dress and my emerald-green smoking jacket. The Red Wind took her coat back and I suppose that's her right, so I can do without as I only borrowed it. For my steed, I want Aroostook with its ratty old potato bag over the spare tire and its sunflower steering wheel, and for my shoes I want my old mary janes, both of them, on both my feet. I want all my things back again and in one piece, for when I have them, *I* shall be all one piece!"

The Archbishop of the Closet blinked her wrought-iron eyelids over her silver eyes. "Queens never listen," she said. "I've told you: Everything that's any good is here. You must understand, September. Today is not your coronation day. It is more like your wedding day. A Queen weds Fairyland, and though Fairyland is a tempestuous spouse, she keeps a very fine house." Jacquard wrapped the length of green ribbon round September's finger like a ring—and in a moment it had become one, a cuff of plain, rough, green stone clutching her finger. The stone felt warm and alive. "And if it is your wedding day, you ought to have your own dress."

Jacquard opened up her black rib cage into a sewing machine once more. The needle whirred to life, pounding the presser foot furiously. But there was no fabric beneath it, no silk, no goldcloth, no wool, no linen. Just air. For a moment the needle pattered against nothing. And then—a scrap of orange appeared against the Mantelet's black heart like the first crocus of Spring.

It all came roaring out of her in a rush: the orange explosion of her own Watchful Dress, stitched with droplets of gold, garnets hanging from its familiar neckline, its skirts dimpled with black rosettes, its green silk rope circling the waist, even the twin pocket watches dangling from the bustle. The warm wooden handle of the Witch's Spoon, the gleaming patent leather of her dear old mary janes, somewhat larger now, for she no longer had twelve-year-old feet. Hello, shoe!

September has missed you so! And finally, a green velvet cuff shot free of Jacquard's chest. The emerald smoking jacket flew off the needle joyfully, flinging itself toward September and wrapping her up safe in its plush arms, tying its sash round her waist with a great sense of personal satisfaction.

Somewhere far away from the Royal Closet and far below the towers of the Briary, September could hear a horn honking.

"Thank you! Oh, thank you, Jack!" cried September, hugging herself tight so as to hug the smoking jacket. For the first time since she fell off the Moon, she felt quite herself again. Such feelings rarely last long, for the meaning of *oneself* changes as quick as clouds skipping. We ought to let our girl roll around in it while she can, don't you think?

When she had quite recovered, September went to Jacquard and held out her hand. "I am a human girl. I am not allergic to you."

The Mantelet took her hand, hesitantly, as though she expected the Queen to yank it away at any moment. Though September could not know it, no one had touched Jacquard in two thousand years. So you understand why, without either of them understanding how it happened, the handshake turned, as if by magic, into a long embrace.

"Are you quite certain you don't want to be Queen?" Jacquard whispered into the jeweled crown of the one girl in all the world who could hug her and live.

Just then, September was not certain at all.

. . .

September closed the birch-trunk door of the Royal Closet. She looked round for the Stoat of Arms, but the crotchety old menagerie seemed to have abandoned her.

In its place stood a man with a neat green beard, wearing a green carriage-driver's cloak and green jodhpurs, and smart green winklepicker boots. Beside him, a large and handsome Leopard sat on her haunches, licking one paw with casual interest and purring loudly.

The Green Wind had found his moment. A Wind always looks for his moment, knowing it will come and the whole of the world will be better for his having waited. Hamlet arrives on his cue, and not a moment before. The Green Wind leaned casually against the wall of the Briary, green out of green, shining from his shoes to his cap, as though he'd been there for a hundred years.

"You seem an ill-tempered and irascible enough child," he said with a grin. "How would you like to be stuck in the middle of a hopping grand mess?"

"Green!" September cried, and dashed across the copper and jade floor to throw herself into his arms. "I thought you'd got lost forever!"

"A Wind never gets lost. Only distracted," he answered, and squeezed her tight. "You mad little thing. I leave you alone for one minute and you go and make friends with a wombat!"

CHAPTER III

An Audience with the Queen

*In Which September Has Her Supper, Learns a Number of Rules
(One Involving a Kraken), Beds Down in a Wyvern's Nest,
and Receives an Unusual Invitation*

"Now," said the Green Wind, when he and September and the Leopard of Little Breezes had turned thirteen corners, run down six blind hallways that led nowhere, and opened three doors onto scenes they certainly ought not to have witnessed, and come at last to a curtained archway in the viny walls, "there are important rules in governing Fairyland, rules which cannot be broken, jostled, or teased. Oh, I suppose you *will* break them, being yourself and not another. And in fact, if you want to win the Derby, you should probably get to breaking them sooner rather than later. But I gave the Stoat of Arms the night off on the condition that I would look at you *very* sternly and shake my finger most emphatically whilst laying it all out. *We have always been aces at rules, that girl and I,* I told him. *While you are mainly aces grumbling.* So let us pretend for a moment that you, September, cannot break these rules, even though you have never met anything so small as a leg nor so large as a moon that you could not break in two."

Two Zinnias guarded the archway, their flowered helmets shading steely, determined eyes.

"Tell me the rules," said September, laughing as she leaned her head against the Leopard of Little Breezes's spotted fur. She felt she would never stop laughing now the Green Wind had come back. Nothing could go too terribly awry when he was about.

"Firstly, dinner is served promptly at six o'clock in the evening in the Moonwort Pavilion," answered the Green Wind, and drew aside the rich curtain onto a vast and lovely room that looked as though it had been waiting all its life for a motley gang of Changelings alongside a Marid, a gramophone, an outsized red reptile, a Queen, and a woven wombat the size of an overambitious elephant. A great cheer went up from all of them when they saw September, who gasped as Saturday and Ell barreled toward her across the bright floor.

Saturday called: "September! I thought we'd never find you in this place!"

"The Scuttler said you'd come," trumpeted A-Through-L. "Do you know, he's a Taxicrab! Our Taxicrab! Do you remember Taxicrabs? I don't suppose there was much work on the Moon after we finished with it. Oh! You've got your jacket back!"

The place felt like the common room of a particularly unhinged college or a particularly well-behaved madhouse. September supposed it had once been a billiards room. Someone had stacked six colorful feather mattresses on a stately old pool table to make a kind of nest—a nest considerately furnished with river rushes, silk batting, and old bones. Just the thing for a Wyvern's nap. Beneath a bank of green glass windows stood a marvelous brass soaking tub big enough for ten or twelve dolphins and a few of their friends, filled invitingly to the brim with salty ocean water, cold enough for a Marid who had not seen the sea in ever so long. A round, dark table stood in the center of the room, set for one. One plate, one goblet for water and one for wine, one knife, one fork.

"Dinner is served promptly at six o'clock in the Moonwort Pavilion," said the Green Wind again. "Though we'll make an exception, just for tonight."

Saturday held her tight.

Chessboards and checkerboards and brownie backgammon and pooka poker lay on twisted, tangled tables fashioned out of ivy and willow whips and marigolds and fig flowers. And there lay Blunderbuss, the combat wombat, rolling and snorting in a huge tangled burrow along the east wall. Raspberry vines and old eucalyptus leaves and banksia flowers like orange ice cream cones thatched together over a patch of rich, dark dirt as thick as a Persian carpet.

"Oh! Oh!" cried the scrap-yarn wombat, scrabbling in the dirt with both front paws. "I never thought I'd get to *dig* again! I thought I'd got so big I'd never again know the joy of hiding underneath the brush and waiting for someone startle-able to come wandering by! Don't bother me, darling dimwits! I washed up to go exploring, but now that's done, I'm gonna get good and *dirty* again. How's Queening? Is it marvelous? Do you like it? Have you spat out any good laws yet?"

Hawthorn the troll grinned at his friend. He was sitting on a pistachio flower stool beside a handsome cinnamon-wood desk, which he knew was meant for him, as it said HUMPHREY! in a fancy cursive hand on the left-hand corner. He touched the edges of a stack of fresh notebooks and the points of nine pencils sticking out of an old-fashioned inkwell. He kept pulling them out and smelling them when he thought no one was looking, the wonderful scent of anything freshly sharpened.

"The Zinnias wouldn't let us leave once they stowed us here," explained Tamburlaine, who lay dreamily on her back before a sweetstone fireplace of every color, plus two the Briary had invented just for its own use. It took up the whole west wall of the room. "They're being very strict with everyone—I suppose they don't want anybody getting strangled in the hallways with all these old devils creeping about."

Fire roared cheerfully in the hearth and the silver woodrack groaned with glittering fresh logs brought all the way from the Glass Forest. Beside the fireplace rested a glorious golden cabinet filled to bursting with records of every size and sort. Scratch hopped and clattered like a newborn horse, using his needle to flip through albums with a thrill only a gramophone can know. Tamburlaine laughed, but not cruelly. Her hair was blooming brighter and thicker than it ever had in the human world, not only plum blossoms now but pomegranate and wild lobelia, too. The Leopard of Little Breezes stretched out beside her to soak up the fire.

"Hey! What's yours, Tam?" Hawthorn asked suddenly. "The old house put out presents for everyone like it's making up for a hundred Christmases. But I don't see any paints or books for you. I didn't even think."

"It's the fireplace," Tamburlaine said softly, sinking to her walnut-wood knees beside the hearth. "Of course, I would *like* paints and brushes, but the Briary knows what I am. I'm a Fetch. My heart is a little burning coal. I tried to tell you that once, but I don't think it came out right. Fire calls to me and I call to fire. It was all I could do not to burn the house down when I was little. Not because I didn't love my house, but because I'm built to burn, and to love things that burn." She tore her eyes from the blazing glass logs and laughed a little, wiping her eyes. "You all got the sort of things an auntie would give you, if she were specially rich—but me? The Briary's telling my secrets. Naughty thing!"

Several pots of paint and long pearl-handled brushes appeared guiltily out of the top of a blackberry-bramble sideboard.

Down below the wide windows, September could see the lights of Pandemonium swirling. She could see Groangyre Tower and the Janglynow Flats and even the movie theatre where she and A-Through-L had eaten lemon ices together. Suddenly, glasses and plates rose up out of the table-for-one in the center of the room like apples bobbing up out of a pail of water: a glass of golden-colored milk, a snifter of bright green liquor with emeralds floating in it, and a stack of magenta cakes with coppery butter melting on top.

The Green Wind quirked one green eyebrow. "I'm afraid you're going to have to eat breakfast *and* dinner, as Mr. Crunchcrab had a very busy day being deposed and forgot his flapjacks."

September smiled at all of them, safe and happy and in one place for once. She looked up at the Green Wind. "Why should I have to eat Charlie's breakfast? I'm sure it's gone cold by now."

"You are the Queen of Fairyland. Everything you do echoes in Fairyland, one way or another. If you do not have the milk of a dun cow, a snifter of liegelime cordial, and a short-stack of magnamillet flapjacks each morning, the Greatvole of Black Salt Cavern will wake from her thousand-year slumber. I only hope we're not too late!"

September sat down. Pandemonium floated up to her on one side, in smells and in the sounds of a million voices, belonging to a million people she had never met. On the other side crowded round the faces she knew best in all the world, save her own mother and father. Ell seemed very curious about the flapjacks. She sipped the liegelime cordial; she cut into the magnamillet flapjacks. It all tasted like limes and pancakes ought to, and she said so. Certainly nothing tasted like the defeat of a Greatvole.

The Green Wind went on. "And every night for dinner, you must dine upon roast legislamb cutlets, gruffragette salad, and wash it down with hot regicider, or the Wickedest Whale will rise from the deeps and swallow us coast-first. This is the Second Munificent Mystery—as Queen, even your snacks are a spell."

"Are all the rules about what I'm meant to eat?" asked September between mouthfuls. The moment she finished her milk, the plate before her vanished and another appeared, piled high with glistening blue-black meat, something that looked a bit like eggplant and a bit like eggs, and a wooden mug of steaming cider that smelt of apples and anxious dreams.

The Green Wind laughed and floated up into the air, turning a somersault in the firelit air. "Certainly not!" he cried. "But it is a *bit* important to avoid Greatvoles and Wickedest Whales, don't you think?"

"I've never met either of those things, but they sound like dreadful houseguests. I'd wager they don't do a lick of washing up!" agreed Blunderbuss.

The Green Wind stood on his head by the draperies. "Now! Rule the second! You may only oppress the people horridly on Wednesdays, Fridays, Sundays, and public holidays. Thirdly, the use of magic mirrors, dragons, and popes is strictly prohibited. Fourthly, you must swim in the Parliamentary Pool one hour after eating every day in order to prevent hurricanes in Brocéliande. Fifthly, all monarchs are required to give two weeks' notice before any significant act of tyranny. Sixthly, war is like a dress in a department store. It may look very tempting on the rack, but once you've got it on it's nothing but a mess. Seventhly, tax collection occurs on second Fridays. Eight, you may do mostly as you like, but so may everyone else, only you get to do it in a nicer house. The ninth rule is, be nice to Fairyland. She is old and tender of heart and when her feelings are hurt, she cries volcanoes. Ten, you may not abdicate. You may only be deposed, transmogrified, or killed. Or outraced on Thursday, if you're not careful! And eleven, though this is less a rule than a public service announcement—there is a kraken with a rather unpleasant personality living in the cellar. Good luck!"

"That is a lot of rules," Saturday said with a frown.

"Don't worry, there's plenty more! She'll need to braid her hair in a Titan's Knot to keep down the infinite furious kobolds that dwell beneath Lake Hobble-on, that sort of thing. You'll find a diagram on your bedside table, September. Oh, my sweetest of scalawags, I'm afraid it's ever so much more complicated to run Fairyland than to run off to it. I have never sought after power, myself. You've got to set an alarm clock to be a powerful man and I won't have it. I never even meant to be a Wind! I thought I'd marry a girl named Jenny Chicory, and that was all my ambition in the world. But I tripped and fell into the sky instead, ring-o the bluebells! Do you know how your friend Blue got to be the Blue Wind in the first place? She stole the old Wind's skates! That's how it's done for Blues. Single combat for Reds. I think the Goldens have singing competitions. But not a one of us went seeking our lots."

"I didn't seek after anything! The Crown just . . . well, it ran me over like a squirrel in the road. I shall be glad when the Derby's done with and I can braid my hair as I like!"

The Green Wind put his head to one side. "Will you? I have kept an eye or six on you. It seems to me that wherever you've landed, you've gone straight at whoever was in charge like a bull at a matador and knocked them right off their particular chair. Not that I'm not proud! I could fairly burst. But you do have your little habits, my autumnal acquisition. I think you like bossing around a world or two. You've been doing it all along, only now you've got a very fine hat. Of course, it is always easier to fight the powerful than to wield power yourself."

And that is the last lesson of childhood: You spend all your years fighting against the injustice of big folk and their big rules until you are ready to rule yourself.

September finished her meal. She felt quite sore from eating, and her belly let it be known that it wanted nothing more to do with her. She stared out into the soft, breezy night. Perhaps she wouldn't be glad when the Derby was over and she lost—for of course she *would* lose, that wasn't even a question. She liked folk talking to her as though her answers mattered as much as anything ever had. She liked her crown. But her heart felt very still. "Green, if you've kept all those eyes on me, you must have seen all the things I've done. In Fairyland-Below and on the Moon and . . . just everything. You saw my father become the Alleyman and how lonely I was sometimes and how often I spoilt things when I was trying so hard to do well. You must have seen me with the Yeti. You must have seen me grow from fourteen to forty in the space of an hour. You must have seen us all locked away with the Redcaps and their rum. Green, why didn't you help me? I got so lost and you didn't help me."

As if in answer, the gramophone spun his handle gleefully. A black and bright record slid out from its friends. It was called *Siren Sings the Greens*. On the cover danced a real siren, kicking her long heron-legs, spreading her great blue-green wings round a lovely lady's face, with long red hair full of starfish and sapphires. Beside her howled a dark, curly-haired hound, which, if September had been the one choosing music, she might have recognized, for she met that very dog on the Moon not so long ago. The Black Cosmic Dog has a surprising number of hobbies.

Scratch had played hundreds of records in his life, for he needed them to speak, having no mouth or tongue or lungs of his own. But this one was different. This was a *Fairy* record. No one would call anybody baby on this record. No one would forget to hire a bass player. Maybe Fairies had never even *heard* of those blasted C, F, and G chords that humans loved so well. (All gramophones have strong opinions on popular music, though they cannot tell anyone what they think of jazz.) Tamburlaine laid *Siren Sings the Greens* carefully onto Scratch's turntable. He spun his crank and an achingly beautiful voice poured out of his brass bell, a voice both deep and sweet, raspy with loneliness and late nights and seaside air, but bottomed in bronze and moonlight.

The greens ain't nothin' but a fire in your heart
A spark in the dark when you and your song have to part
I know I ain't nothin' but a hawk without a home
But I got the greens on my side so I'm never alone

The Green Wind turned a lazy backflip in the air and drifted down to the table. He sprawled out on it, crossing his legs before him. The Leopard of Little Breezes yawned by the fire. "Miss September, who do you think I am? Nothing but a Wind in a green handbag, that's who."

Perhaps he would have said more. Perhaps he would have told September that he had no more power to save anyone than a green balloon, unless what that anyone needed most was a gust of air or a well-timed cloud. Perhaps he would have told her that he had been busy with his own adventures, his own loves and losses and prisons and Yetis. Or perhaps he would simply have kissed her on the forehead and winked and flown off, for that is what most adults do when they don't want to answer a question straight. But the Green Wind did not get a chance, for as soon as he called himself a handbag, a knock came at the door.

Hawthorn ran to the fireplace, ignoring it, speaking urgently to his friend: "You know, Tam, I've been thinking—"

"Yes, so have I," Tamburlaine answered.

"Only that we must do it together. Tom and Tam, like it was back home."

"But do you think she'll be angry?"

"I don't know, shall we ask the dragon?"

"Pardon me," said A-Through-L, looking up from fussing

with his nest, a bit of batting stuck to one horn. "But in the first place, I am not a Dragon, and in the second place, it's very rude to hatch plans without including your new flatmates. Unless you're hatching *schemes* rather than *plans,* in which case it's downright mean."

"You'll just have to get used to it, Big Red! They do it all the time," groused Blunderbuss, buried gleefully under half a foot of moss and dirt. "Only include me when they decide their little plots require an armored combat wombat, or at least a good roar. And he's a Wyvern, dum-dums! Count the feet. Get your taxonomy straight, you're embarrassing all of us!" Hawthorn and Tamburlaine hung their heads. "My favorite dum-dums! Best dum-dums since sliced tomfoolery."

Tamburlaine began: "We only wanted to know if September would get mad at us if—"

"How could I be mad at anybody?" interrupted September. She stood up from the table, so full of feast and feeling she thought she might pop like a soap bubble. For a moment she stood there, a bit stiff, for Queens are not meant to tumble headlong around a room and tackle their favorite people in it. She didn't know much about being a Queen, but she knew that. And they'd all seemed quite happy and at home without her. The room hadn't made anything to welcome her, after all, except a bit of supper. Perhaps she *wasn't* welcome.

CHAPTER III

But she tumbled anyhow, while the knocking at the door sounded again and no one paid any more attention than they had the first time. September darted across the lovely carpets and leapt into Ell's nest. As she jumped, the Watchful Dress folded itself out of being a ball gown and into being a knockabout orange shift with sturdy stockings. She landed against the warm scarlet flank of her Wyverary, giggling madly. It was so nice to leap and land without the littlest creak in her bones. She held out her arms for Saturday and he leapt, too, all three of them ending up in a pile of laughter and mussed hair.

"How could I be mad at anybody? I started out today in prison and now I'm Queen! And it's hardly past eight o'clock! By midnight I expect I'll have turned into a basilisk and started a career in the ballet!" She looked round the wonderful room and pressed her lips together. Perhaps it was bad manners to feel jealous when you were a Queen.

"There's nothing for me here at all," said September, a prickling of hurt in her voice.

"Well, it's not your room, is it?" said Hawthorn. He sat back in a great, soft troll-sized armchair. "Oh, I don't mean it like that! You can come by whenever you want! But you're the Queen! I'm sure the house has got something better for you. Something really spectacular."

Saturday put his hand on hers. "Let's go find your room. We can repaint it—I'm sure Crunchcrab wallpapered in barnacles or something. Let's go find it and spill food on the floor and break all the lamps and stay up all night together like we used to do in the rum cellar. Did you know Blunderbuss can shoot passionfruits and horseshoes out of her mouth? It's fantastic!"

"Yes, let's!" agreed Blunderbuss heartily. "And maybe on the way we can find a library for Ell to nosh on? Castles always have libraries, usually with Forbidden Tomes in them. It's the law."

And September felt quite as though she had skipped several chapters in her favorite novel and opened it up again only to find everyone much further along than she.

"Come in!" sang Hawthorn and Tamburlaine together. Scratch gave a jaunty little squeak with his needle.

The Scuttler cleared his throat and opened the door with a grand sweep of his claw.

"SPOKE!" hollered September, clambering down from the nest to greet him.

"Miss! Oh, it is lovely to see a familiar face, isn't it? I hardly meet a soul from the old lunar days anymore. Came down from the Moon when the quakes cracked my shell a good one. Good thing scuttling is almost exactly like taxiing!

Come when you're called, show company around the place, know what's needed before it gets to needing, take the occasional trip below stairs and forward in time—just like home! Ah, I should say something fancy, shouldn't I? How's about: Greetings to you upon this fair evening, Your Highness?"

September wrinkled her nose.

"Naw, you're right, it don't fit me any better than a pair of pants. Anyhap! I've come to deliver an invitation to you and deliver you to the invitees." Spoke held up one black-and-white claw with an elegant calling card snared between the pincers. "Your Most Grand High Tip-Topping Such and Such, You Are Cordially Demanded to Attend the First Meeting of the Reconvened Once and Future Club at Nine in the P.M. This Very Night in the Rex Tyrannosaur's Room Because His Is the Biggest. Bring Your Own Brandy and Ancient Resentments."

"A club? Already?" Tam said.

"Can we come this time?" Ell pleaded. His great, orange, hopeful eyes loomed above them all like lanterns.

"Invitation is for one, lads," Spoke answered with chagrin. "And arguing with that lot is like arguing with the Code of Hammurabi."

"I don't know what that is but it sounds very boring," snorted the scrap-yarn wombat.

"I'll come back soon," September said. "We'll throw passionfruits at my bedroom walls, I promise."

September followed the former Taxicrab out of those cluttered, cozy quarters and the circle of her dear ones, where, it seemed, she could not be allowed to stay for a moment. But a moment later, she ducked her head back round the edge of the door.

"What did you think would make me angry?" she asked Hawthorn and Tamburlaine.

"Oh," he answered her. "We wanted to know . . . if it would upset you. If we entered the race on Thursday. Since you don't want to rule Fairyland and we . . . well, we do."

The Green Wind began to laugh. After a moment, the Leopard of Little Breezes joined in, and even her laughter had spots.

CHAPTER IV

The Once and Future Club

*In Which September Is Inducted into a Secret Society,
Meets a Number of Nefarious Ne'er-do-wells, Interrogates
a Dinosaur, and Comes to a Decision*

Imagine a room where George Washington, Queen Victoria, Ivan the Terrible, Montezuma, Cleopatra, and Eleanor of Aquitaine were sharing brandy and cigars and making splendid jokes at one another's expense, demanding that Emperor Qin let them all have a slice of his poppy seed cake, Charlemagne put a pot of coffee on, and Artemisia of Halicarnassus tell the one about that time she defeated the Greeks at sea. Now, imagine standing outside that room, knowing just who was in there and how fiercely and strangely they all would behave once the door opened and you had to squeeze in between Caesar and Queen Isabella and hope you knew which fork to use for poppy seed cake.

September could not decide how to knock. It had come upon her suddenly and frozen her to the spot. She had never thought much about knocking before. But, knowing what lay on the other side of that door, she could not decide whether one decisive knock was more monarchical, or a polite two raps, one after the other, or perhaps three casual whacks—how did she knock at home? How did normal people knock? What if they could hear in her knock that she was just a human girl, not even so much as the Spinster anymore, just a terribly quick and easy midnight snack for a Rex Tyrannosaur?

September read the sign hanging on the door a few more times while she considered the question. It had been written in red pen on the back of a takeaway menu from one of Pandemonium's more elegant noodle houses. There seemed to have been some disagreement about the rules.

The Once and Future Club

Est. ~~1000 Years Ago 2000 Years Ago None of Your Business~~
About Two Hours Ago

You Must Have Ruled with ~~an Iron~~ ~~Golden~~ ~~Velvet~~ SOME KIND
OF FIST for at Least ~~5 Years~~ ~~1 Year~~ a Solid Week to Enter

No Casual Dress, Cussing, Dairy Products,
or Commoners Allowed

The Watchful Dress shivered and wriggled and writhed, shaking itself out of a shift and into a lovely long tangerine-colored evening gown with a green sash. It had read the dress code instantly, and knew what was expected of it. The emerald smoking jacket felt it was already quite formal, thank you very much.

Do Queens even knock at all? September supposed they didn't. All doors were open to a Queen. All doors belonged to the Queen. And besides, this was her house now. She shouldn't be any more fearful of it than of her own bedroom door. But she had not ruled for a solid week yet. Not even a solid day. But surely some exceptions must be made for the current monarch? In the end, though her manners shuddered and hid behind her heart, September turned the knob and entered the drawing room without announcing herself in the least.

She half expected the Once and Future Club to be as crowded and noisy as the grand hall had been, with Kings and Queens hanging out of every window and dueling over dessert. But a pleasant, hushed, and half-empty room greeted her instead. Several lounge chairs and sofas had been hauled in from other parts of the Briary, for a Tyrannosaur has little need of footstools and tastefully plush pillows. Dinosaurs do, however, have great need of high ceilings and room to thrash a tail about. September could hardly see the chandelier; it hung so far up in the shadowy rafters that it looked like a distant moon. Someone had set up a slapdash bar on one end of the enormous parlor. Fringed lamps made little pools of soft, friendly light here and there, polished end tables hoisted drinks and sweets, and there was even a hastily hung portrait over the fireplace, slightly skew in its heavy silver frame. September recognized it—the portrait of Queen Mallow she had seen in the grand hall the first time she had ever set foot in the Briary. Only someone had painted Fairy wings onto her and pasted antlers cut out of another portrait onto her golden hair. The whole place looked like an illustration from an old detective novel involving men who smoked elaborate pipes.

September recognized several club members: There sat Madame Tanaquill, smoking a cigar in a black leather armchair, her iron dress swapped out for a graceful gown the color of lime juice. She turned and whispered something to old Charlie Crunchcrab, who'd dug up his old Ferryman's peacoat and shoved his wings through it once more. He glared at September, but neither of them said a word to her. Hushnow, the Ancient and Demented Raven Lord, preened on a mahogany perch. The Headmistress bustled about, clearing glasses and plates, her stern cobalt dress still buttoned all the way up to her throat. Pinecrack, the Moose-Khan, drank from an elegant copper soaking tub full of mulled wine while Cutty Soames, Captain of the Coblynows, straightened his cravat in a long mirror. Curdleblood, the Dastard of Darkness, stoked the fire with a long, cruel-looking poker. Thrum, their host, the Rex Tyrannosaur, stood gallantly by the fireplace, his teeth and green scales glinting in the ruddy light. He was deep in conversation with a large panther.

"Iago!" September exclaimed, louder than she meant to.

The panther turned toward her and purred. He padded across the floor of the Once and Future Club. The Rex Tyrannosaur looked much insulted, and went to fetch ice.

"Hullo, September," rumbled Iago, the Panther of Rough Storms. He jostled her shoulder with his great dark head. "I presume you know everyone?"

September wanted to hug him, but she was not sure it would come out right. You never could be sure, with Iago. "But you've never ruled Fairyland. How can you be a member?"

"Cats go where they like. Besides, I was thinking of racing myself on Thursday. I do love a good lope. I like to get a good whiff of my competition before I commit to anything."

"You? You want to be King of Fairyland? I thought you belonged to the Marquess."

"I belong to no one. I let her stroke me when I was in the mood for scheming. I carried the Red Wind when I wanted to stretch my legs. I hunted cloud-mice and pounced upon lightning bolts and enjoyed my own company when I couldn't stand either of them. A cat's love gets bored easily. But we are naturally suited to leadership. Most people obey us without even having to be hissed at. Would you like a drink?"

"HELLO," said the First Stone, who had installed himself behind the bar, fixing drinks with more grace than you might think a boulder could muster.

However, few seemed interested in his concoctions. The First Stone pushed a brandy snifter at September. She peered inside. Water so cold it had begun to turn to ice at the edges, ancient gray moss, several small fern and snail fossils, and a half-burnt stick still smoking at the tip. The First Stone beamed at her with his rough half-hewn face, clearly feeling that he had given her a great gift worthy of a Queen. Perhaps these had been the most precious things in the world once upon a time, in the primeval age before even dinosaurs: water, the first baby plants and animals, fire. But Madame Tanaquill and Cutty Soames clearly preferred brandy in their brandy snifters. September sipped it politely.

"Mmmm!" she said, even though it tasted mostly like very wet dirt and unfathomable secrets from before the invention of dreams. The First Stone beamed even more broadly.

"So you're her," said the Headmistress, eyeing September appraisingly. "I am the Headmistress. I reigned eleven centuries ago, before I was deposed by the bint with the cigar over there. I was very good at it—I am sure I would have much to teach you."

"Oh yes, terribly good," cooed Madame Tanaquill, seeming to take notice of September for the first time. "Go right ahead. Teach little September all about the Caged Wood." The Prime Minister of Fairyland glided across the drawing room to September's side. Her lime-juice gown trailed invitingly behind her; her violet hair floated round her head in a delicate bob. She draped one long arm around September's shoulders. "My friend here put each and every Fairy into an iron cage and hung us up on the boughs of a babbling baobab forest. She left us there for a hundred years with only the kindness of crows to feed us—and crows are vicious little cretins, you know."

"Oy!" squawked Hushnow, the Ancient and Demented Raven Lord. "I'm right here!"

"Fairies were rather shy and curious creatures before she got ahold of us," Madame Tanaquill continued, ignoring Hushnow entirely. "A hundred years of listening to babbling baobabs and begging crumbs from crows will drive even a doctor mad."

"Now, *that's* a lie," snorted Pinecrack, the Moose-Khan. "How do you fit such a big lie in your mouth, Tansy? She put you in cages because you and yours couldn't stop stealing the wings off a dragonfly's back and the horns off a goat and the tusks off an elephant! Let me tell you, kid, tusks looked a thousand kinds of stupid glued to frogs."

"How *dare* you," Tanaquill hissed. "How dare you call me a frog? You're nothing but a ruined horse."

And the Prime Minister of Fairyland flicked her fingers at Pinecrack. A sizzle of ultraviolet bubbles snapped, popped— and the Moose-Khan's antlers turned to ash, falling from his head and into his bathtub of wine in a fine gray spray. Thrum roared in reptile rage.

"Lovely. Lovely behavior. Ever been bitten by a moose? I know how you like new experiences." Pinecrack turned on her, his eyes gone molten blue with hatred and rage.

"Put them back or you'll have my cutlass for a spine," snarled Cutty Soames, who had crept up on her, even in a pair of marvelous high-heeled boots covered in shells and jewels.

September had seen him moving on Tanaquill, but had kept her mouth shut.

"Come now," sighed Curdleblood, tamping a long black pipe. "This is unworthy. One does not behave this way in a gentlemen's club. We agreed to refrain from magic and other weapons while the club is in session. I know some of us are very cranky, having only recently come back from the dead, but reanimation is no excuse. Tanaquill, put his antlers back. September, good evening. I'm pleased you accepted our invitation. Welcome to the Society of Tyrants."

"I'm not a tyrant," protested September.

Madame Tanaquill smirked. "Only because you don't know how yet." She flicked her fingers again and two bony nubs appeared at Pinecrack's temples, growing quickly into new antlers. It did not look like a comfortable process.

"I'm not a tyrant because I don't want to be a tyrant."

"Who wants to be a tyrant?" asked the Headmistress, sipping a glass of champagne. "I certainly didn't. Did you, Hushnow? You, Cutty? No? And yet—Hushnow stole the sun and held it hostage. Cutty Soames stole the three most precious things from every house in Fairyland. Yes, the Headmistress put all the Fairies in cages—but Pinecrack outlawed magic except for those in the Cervidae family—that's anybody who's part deer, love. Hushnow forced all of Fairyland to grow wings whether they liked it or not, Thrum ordered anyone herbivorous to present themselves at the palace every morning for convenient devouring. And I expect you know about Madame Tanaquill already. Even our quiet friend Mr. Q. Humdrum there cast a terrible spell so that everyone could only repeat the day he came to power over and over, so that nothing would ever change and he would never have to suffer surprise. And yes, me too. Fairyland was such a disorderly place when I deposed the Happiest Princess and ascended the throne. I had to make it better. I had to make it right. You see, sweetheart, nobody wakes up in the morning and thinks: *Today I shall be a wicked murderous tyrant and crush something nice under my boot.* It just happens to you. Like catching a cold. It starts the first time someone says no to you and goes on and on until everyone is saying no and saying it so loud you can't sleep for the din."

"What about him?" September asked, pointing at the First Stone, who had just finished adjusting a paper umbrella on a goblet of mud.

"The Stone?" the Headmistress asked, nonplussed.

"Yes, the Stone. Was he a tyrant?"

"I don't suppose there was anyone *to* tyrannize, except ammonites and will-o'-the-wisps."

"HELLO," said the First Stone amiably.

"See? He wasn't a tyrant, so it's possible not to steal and crush and outlaw and cast terrible spells. Not that I shall have time to do any of those things. I've only got two more days as Queen. Which I think is *awfully* unfair. You all got to be in charge as long as you could hold on to it. I still don't understand why I can't just keep on being Queen."

"I thought you didn't want it," said Madame Tanaquill coolly.

September's cheeks burned. "I didn't want to do my mathematics homework back home. Or mend the fence or mind the chickens. But I did it anyway. Just because a person doesn't want to do a thing doesn't mean they ought to shirk." The words came out before September could stop them. She tripped and fell into honesty at the worst times, and came up with the truth all over her dress. The crown felt suddenly warm on her head.

"It's hardly a usual situation," the Elephanta said.

"Be grateful, girlie," huffed Cutty Soames. "Fairyland likes you. She's doing you a favor. Because, if not for the Derby, one of us would probably have killed you before you even got to meet our Jack. I think Titania already had a plan involving a mud puddle."

"Where *is* Titania?" September asked, choosing to ignore the threats of a goblin in a pirate coat. "And all the others?"

"We didn't invite *everyone*," Hushnow, the Ancient and Demented Raven Lord, crooned. "Only people who've decided to race already. Oh, and of course, only people we can stand to share the air with. Goldmouth is a brute and the Knapper would murder us all inside a minute and never spill his drink. Titania's halfway to Buyan by now. She had enough of Queening before Tansy there was even born. Oh! How she and her man used to fight! Sank half of Fairyland underground by the time they got themselves tuckered out. A lot of us feel that way. Getting cast down by some young upstart once was quite enough."

"So this is it? You're the only ones racing?"

"Two more days, child," said Curdleblood softly. "Everyone must decide in their own time."

"Well, I oughtn't to be here at all, then," said September, setting her snifter down. "I haven't decided yet. Whether I'm going to race in the Derby."

This caused some uproar among the members of the Once and Future Club.

"See?" bellowed Charlie Crunchcrab. "*See?* She doesn't even *want* it. She's a disgrace! Why did the crown pick her when she's just a little nobody with no ambition?"

"Come off it, Chuck," Madame Tanaquill snorted. "You hired those two kids to find a way for you to abdicate. We all know it. You didn't want it, either."

"Well, I do *now*. I didn't abdicate! I meant to, yes, but I didn't! The crown was taken away from me. There's nothing like a robbery to sharpen your priorities."

"And *I* didn't depose you on purpose, Charles!" snapped September. "I don't know why you're so cross with me. It's not like you were doing such a marvelous job at it, you know."

The Panther of Rough Storms interrupted them. His golden eyes gleamed in the lamplight. "I'm sorry, September, but you have to race. Hasn't anyone explained it to you? The Derby won't work if you don't compete. You cannot abdicate, remember. We must *take* Fairyland from you. You are the Queen; you have the crown. It is only half a Race. The other half is a Hunt. And I suspect we will end up with a Duel as our third half before it's all done. It's hardly a Derby without Duels. We are Racing one another. We are searching for the Heart of Fairyland. We will Duel to determine the strongest. But we are Hunting you. You are the fox, and we are the hounds."

"Well, that is the oddest way to run a government I have ever heard of," September said stubbornly. "It's just absurd to elect a leader with a race or a chase or a hunt for a heart!"

"What's an 'elect'?" asked Hushnow, the Ancient and Demented Raven Lord.

"It's how we decide who's in charge where I come from. Everyone in the whole country votes for the President and the man who gets the most votes wins."

A chorus of gasps went up from the club. Madame Tanaquill held a handkerchief over her mouth.

"That's ghastly!" cried the Hushnow, the Ancient and Demented Raven Lord.

"What if everyone chooses the wrong man?" gawped Pinecrack. "And if it's *always* a man and never a moose or an octopus or a spriggan I think that's just obscene, and prejudiced, and you ought to leave right now."

September frowned. "Well, sometimes people do. But it's only for a few years, and then there's another election."

The Rex Tyrannosaur looked nauseous. "Quite, quite horrid," he whispered.

"Yes, I think we'd all better collect ourselves," said the Headmistress. "Nothing like that could ever happen here, of course. Perish the thought."

"Well, it could, you know . . . ," began September.

"*Perish the thought!*" the Headmistress roared. She cleared her throat and composed herself, wiping her hands on her skirt.

"Please." September held up her hands. "I didn't mean to offend. Let me ask a question instead: Why do you want to rule Fairyland? Why are any of you so riled up to get the crown? It seems like a bit of a raw deal to me, if I'm to be honest. Assassinations and intrigue and eating the same thing for every meal in case a Greatvole comes to tea and on top of it all you can't ever quit, even if you want to. Yes, I understand it's devilish fun to be in charge of things and tell everyone what to do, but I can think of at least three things that I like better! And one of them is being left well enough alone!"

"Well, it's hard to get anyone to let you eat them if you're not King," said the Rex Tyrannosaur thoughtfully.

"If you're on top, you can make certain you and yours never have to live in a cage again," Madame Tanaquill said through clenched teeth. "And, even better, you can fill those cages up again with everyone who ever hurt you."

"Or, if certain folk are gobbling up the whole world for themselves, you can stop them so there's something left for everyone else," snarled Charlie Crunchcrab.

"It's the biggest heist there is." Cutty Soames sighed dreamily. "The big score, the last hit. When you're King, you've won."

Tanaquill couldn't leave it at one answer. She tapped her glass with one long fingernail. "You can make the whole world look just like you, and never have to look at anything frightening or different ever again."

"And when you see something dreadful, something that needs mending, something that cries out in pain, you can fix it. You can make it right and no one can stand in the way of your rightness," the Headmistress said softly.

"Yes, that's the main thing," crowed Hushnow, the Ancient and Demented Raven Lord. "No one can stand in your way. No one can talk back to you or call you a stupid crow or make you feel small ever, ever again. You get to feel big forever."

Cutty Soames nodded. His cutlass shone. "*Not* being King is like a chain round your neck. It's the only way to be sure you can always do just as you desire."

"But what do you desire that you can't have without a crown? None of you are starving. You all wear jewels and smell wonderful and live in splendid houses. What do you want to do that you cannot?"

"Nothing just *now*," admitted Cutty. "But there could always be *something*."

The members of the Once and Future Club left the knot that had formed at the First Stone's bar and settled into a number of chairs and sofas. September sat gingerly on a pale blue-and-gold seat that looked like it had escaped from someone's dining table.

"So." September sighed, tucking into her water and moss. "I have to race."

"Obviously," sighed Madame Tanaquill. "The Stoat of Arms ought to have told you. I shall strangle all of them when I see them next. I haven't strangled the Stoat for centuries. It'll be just like old times."

"Please don't strangle anyone! I'm sure they meant to tell me. It's been a busy day! I can hardly keep my feet under me I'm so tired! All right then. I have to race the ancient Kings and Queens of Fairyland this Thursday morning at eight o'clock, which is before breakfast. I don't suppose any of you would tell me where the Heart of Fairyland is? Just to make it fair."

"I haven't the first idea," said the Prime Minister of Fairyland, shrugging.

"They don't even know *what* it is," yawned Iago, who had snoozed through their quarreling, curled up by the fireplace.

"Well, that's the trick of it," said Cutty Soames a bit guiltily. "If we knew, it wouldn't be much of a race. I suppose it could be anything: a doorknob, a bag of wind, a jeweled necklace, a rhinoceros . . ."

"A hot air balloon, a spinning wheel, a tear from the eye of a phoenix, a bicycle pump . . . ," added Pinecrack.

"An egg with a needle inside, a book that reads itself, a golden ball, a golden toad, a golden sword with a golden toad's soul in the blade . . . ," Thrum growled. "Or a great lot of things scattered all over the blasted place."

"We don't know." Madame Tanaquill silenced them all with a glance. "Some of us have ideas—some of us have *moronic* ideas—but we don't know."

A small shadow fell over Iago's green-yellow eyes and the glowing hearth. A girl's shadow.

"I know," said the Marquess. She stepped into the room imperiously, as though she had never for a moment ceased to own those chairs, those lamps, that fireplace, even the glasses and plates.

Madame Tanaquill rolled her eyes. "Oh, *do* shut up."

The Marquess knelt beside Iago and stroked his ears. He purred in delight. "I *do* know what it is. Perhaps the rest of you spent your time in the Briary counting your gold or your servants or your toenail clippings, but I did not. Even before my first reign, Queen Mallow's reign, I was a student of Dry Magic and Dry means books. I know more about Fairyland than any of you could scrape off the floors of your glitter-rotted minds. Even you, Foxy. I'll meet you all at Mummery with pots of tea and a footbath ready, and when you've had a nice rest, you can all go hang. Coming back the first time was so hard, so difficult. But this? This is easy. This is nothing. This is a postmistress's work. Get the package, deliver it, collect postage fee, which, in this case, is my crown." She looked straight at September. "You wicked little *thief.*"

"It's sweet when humans try to lie," Crunchcrab sneered. "They're such amateurs. You're nothing but a filthy farmer's daughter and the only thing you know is what to feed a cow. I don't know why anyone is pretending we don't know what will happen on Thursday. Tanaquill will win and grind all our faces into the dirt, and we'll have to call her Your Highness for a thousand years. That is how the world works. The worst wins. I wasn't bad enough, that's where I went wrong. And you? You're not even on the books, Missie Marquess."

The Marquess's hair flushed deep cerulean blue, like the underside of the sea. She smiled. It was a smile that grew in the grinning, deeper and wider and kinder and brighter, until September shuddered. She remembered that smile. It froze her bones.

"And you are a Ferryman who abandoned his boat. You ought to be ashamed. Do you even know where she's anchored? I do. Starfish have chewed halfway through the hull, giant seagulls have pecked out the portholes, and there's a family of sea lions living in the captain's cabin. That poor ship. I've half a mind to mend her myself."

Anyone else might have ignored her, or scoffed at her, for it would never list among the immortal lines of villainous banter. But Charles Crunchcrab the First flushed deeply, horror and shame flooding his face. His eyes filled with hot tears. The Ferryman of the Barleybroom said no more.

"Now," said the Marquess cheerfully, her hair brightening to gold. "I should very much like a drink."

But as September watched her stare down the First Stone until he put a little sand in a cup and dropped it in front of her, she thought that the Marquess had no better idea than any of them. After all, she knew a little about pretending to be brave when the fear in you has eaten up half your heart.

September left the Once and Future Club exhausted, hardly able to stand in her mary janes. The Green Wind was not waiting to guide her to her bedroom, nor the Stoat of Arms nor Saturday nor A-Through-L nor even the stuffed wombat. She stood alone in the Briary. All she could hear was its quiet, steady blooming.

"Sleep, Briary," she whispered. "Show me where I sleep."

For a moment, the hallway remained a hallway, long and green and silent. Then, a slender row of pale silver flowers sprang up beneath her feet. It whirled forward, each blossom sprouting as September put her foot to it. She laughed and ran along the silver path, her tiredness all gone, racing the flowers down staircases and round pillars, under buttresses and through doors wide and small. Finally, the silver blossoms came up short in a wine cellar deep within the Briary, at the edge of a trapdoor with a bronze pull-ring bolted into it. September felt very uncertain that this was meant to be her bedroom, but the flowers seemed insistent, waving back and forth all round the door in the floor.

"All right, all right!" said September, and pulled up the ring. She saw nothing inside but a soft half-light. She thought, for a moment, of climbing through all the dark doors of Fairyland Below until she found a Minotaur. She thought of wriggling into the hole at the top of Moonkin Hill. September took a breath. "All of that turned out reasonably well, I suppose!" And she crawled down into the light, toes pointed like a dancing girl's.

There was a moon in September's bedroom. It shone down on a lush green valley full of long grass and glowing lacy mushrooms and more of those tiny silver flowers growing everywhere. The night sky soared overhead, black and full of stars like city lights, but somehow she knew she was not really outside. A little green hill on one side of the valley peeled back like covers of a delicious soft bed, inviting her to lie down. There was a stone well nearby; its pail sloshed with warm milk. Night birds whistled lullabies—lullabies she knew, involving biplanes of paper and ink. The air hung warm and sleepy all around her. This was Fairyland, some secret, loving heart of Fairyland where she was meant to sleep safely, where the strange wedding of a country and its Queen would take place.

September, though she did not feel at all sure about sleeping inside a hill, crawled into the grass and the silver flowers. She wished she were in the grand billiards room with Ell and Saturday and the rest. But she pulled up the hill over her shoulder. She did not feel squelchy mud on her toes and her knees, but soft, familiar sheets. September rested her head on a pillow of moss and slept the deepest sleep she had known since long before the Green Wind came to her window and showed her how to ride a Leopard.

SISTERS OUGHTN'T KEEP SECRETS

In Which Certain Ladies Make Their Own Way

L et us leave September to sleep for a little while. She has learned it—it's ever so tiring to be suddenly in charge of a story when you have become quite accustomed to the story happening *to* you, rather than you happening to *it*. And besides, Kings and Queens are the most trying of people. There are far too many of them about for anyone's comfort and peace of mind. Why, we have hardly gotten to catch our breath! Let us sit down together for a moment, and I shall pour you a glass of whatever you like best. You may hold my hand if you wish, I don't mind. I shouldn't want you to feel alone.

Now that we have made ourselves quite comfortable, I must tell you—we have forgotten about something important.

I'm sure you did not mean to, and I certainly did not. It is only that so many exciting things have happened that we did not notice. Let us peer beneath the sofa cushions and beneath the bed for it. Let us jostle the curtains and lift up the tablecloth. We shall get ourselves into trouble if we do not find it. For this tale began in Nebraska, and we have not so much as glanced Omaha-way in ever so long. It is hard to remember to go knocking at a farmhouse door when so many palace doors await—but a door is a door, and a door is always an adventure.

In this particular farmhouse, which I expect you know nearly as well as I do by now, two women were standing in the kitchen. They looked terribly alike, as they always had, even as children. The same dark hair and dark eyes and fierce set of their jaws, just the same as September's eyes and hair and jaw. Their names were Susan Jane and Margaret. They were sisters. And one of them had just said something very odd indeed. Margaret touched her sister's cheek gently. She smiled, a smile that startled and teased and danced.

"Listen to me, Susie," Aunt Margaret whispered, so that only they two could hear. "I know where September is."

"How could you? Why wouldn't you tell me at once?" said Susan Jane.

"Listen to me very carefully. Whatever I say, you must believe me, even if it sounds like the most ridiculous thing a person has said in the whole history of the world. Do you promise?"

"Yes," said September's mother.

Margaret found herself suddenly very afraid. There were words she had never said aloud to her sister before, or even to anyone in the state of Nebraska or the country of America. Words she knew weren't safe to say, words more powerful than thunder. Aunt Margaret had led a life filled with secrets, and that is a very hard habit to break, even if you badly want to break it. So for a good while she said nothing, because she could not make herself say the thing she had kept hidden at the bottom of her heart for so long. Finally, she let a long breath out through her nose and wrestled her secret out into the little midnight kitchen.

"September is in a place called Fairyland. It's very far away, farther away than any place you can think of, and then farther away still. It's a storybook place. A place that's met magic and shaken its hand. Now, I know this because . . . because I've been to Fairyland, too. All those times I said I was going to Paris or Turkey or Morocco or Mongolia? I've been lying up, down, and all around, Susie. Where would a woman like me get the money to visit Paris? No. I've never been to France. Never been to much of anywhere. Except this place. And I think you remember. I think you remember when I was little and I would run off into the woods and you couldn't find me all day and into the night, even though you knew I'd run into the woods and the woods weren't all that terribly big to begin with. I think you remember green shadows under the kitchen window, and the sound of a cat far bigger than ours purring at the door."

"Fairyland. A real place called Fairyland." And it seemed to Susan Jane that she did remember, a little. She did remember her sister whispering in the dark, chasing butterflies that weren't butterflies at all, the shape of a man at the window in green jodhpurs and green snowshoes . . .

"Very, very real. The realest. The first time I went I was nine years old. A man all in green flew up to the second-story window in our old house on a flying leopard and said: *You seem like a mad and mischievous enough child, how would you like to come away with me on the Leopard of Little Breezes and be delivered to the Tattersall Tundra that lies near the pole of Fairyland?* And once he said it, I did feel mad and mischievous, and I did want to see what a Tattersall Tundra was, and I jumped out of that window as fast as you can say your own name."

"Weren't you afraid of a strange man at the window?"

"Well, I reasoned later that anyone who can win the love of a flying leopard has to be mostly all right. And he was. I rode on the back of a great arctic fox and wore trousers and fell in with the Tobogganeers, a band of snowy Stregas who keep their freezers stocked with magic. I learned to change myself into a polar bear and a manticore and a snow-scarab. And that was only the first time. I know it sounds mad but you promised to believe me. Time's got its hat on funny over there, so I could play in Fairyland for months and still come home for dinner with new ribbons in my hair. Only it wasn't play, exactly. I have another name when I'm there. I have a little house in the mountains. I've . . . done terrible things and I've done things so grand I wish I could throw a parade down Farnam Street in my own honor."

"Has September done terrible things?"

"Oh, I'd imagine she has. And wonderful things. Fairyland has a weakness for the dramatic. I don't know exactly; we've never been there at the same time. But I've heard her name whispered and hollered. I suspect she's been there a few times by now. I know the look in her eye. It's the look in my eye."

"And is that why? Is that why September's gone to this Fairyland, because you went? Did you take her there?"

"Oh no, Susie. That's not how it works. Fairyland comes to you. I didn't have a thing to do with it. It just happened that way. There's . . . there's a weak place in the world, I think. Near here. More people go through than you think. I used to always worry you'd stumble in somehow and I'd have to share. Oh, that's terrible of me, I know, but all little girls are terrible, sometimes. Anyway, I always came back. September's always come back, too, because you have to come back. Humans don't much get to stay. They don't even get to say when they come and go. Except me."

Susan Jane looked at her sister as though she had never met the woman before. "Why you?"

Margaret smiled softly. A smile full of pride that didn't want to seem proud. "I did Fairyland a favor once. I was rewarded."

Aunt Margaret touched the ring on her right hand. It was an interlocking silver puzzle ring she'd brought back from Turkey when September was only little. It had four rings with ridges and engravings and patterns on them. If you turned and twisted them just right, they snapped together to become one single, complete ring.

"I promised I would believe you. I promised I would believe you." Susan Jane said it a few more times, so that it would become true.

"Do you want to go to Fairyland, Susie? I should have asked you before, I know. Sisters oughtn't keep secrets. Only it was *such* a good secret."

"Oh yes," breathed September's mother.

CHAPTER V

THE CANTANKEROUS DERBY

In Which the Race Begins

Before anything else can happen, I must tell you a few things about Fairyland races. Fairylanders are simply mad for games and contests and races of all sorts, and thus, everyone knows the rules and nobody will bother much explaining them to one another. But I am rather kinder than most sportsmen and all referees, so I shall bring you up to speed while the early Thursday morning shadows and a few centaurs gather together all the things a healthy, happy race needs to grow up thrilling and swift.

Have you ever been to a racetrack? In the world where you and I keep our galoshes, they are very odd places. Someone fires a gun and a number of horses or cars or people run as fast as they can in a great long circle, and they go round and round and round and everyone cheers and cheers until another somebody waves a specially colored flag, and then whichever speedster barrels past the flag first wins. Folk dress in all manner of finery and wonderful hats to go and watch the races, but only if it's horses doing the barreling that day. This, at least, is understandable, for horses, in secret, love hats more than any other creature. It is a horse's tragedy that they can never properly wear one.

To my mind, Fairyland races are much more sensible. The racetrack is the size of the world. Racers may barrel anywhere on any steed—over the Candelabra Desert or the Tattersall Tundra, across the Perverse and Perilous Sea, through the Worsted Wood, to the tops of the Pickapart Mountains or the Peppercorn Pyramids, down to the bottom of the Obstreperous Ocean where the Octopus Assassins lie in wait, even into Fairyland-Below or up to the Moon. And instead of racing a horse against a horse or a car against a car or a lady against a lady, Fairyland races ladies against chariots, centaurs against cheetahs, carriages against flying carpets, phoenixes against Dodos. You see, Fairyland long ago determined that Yetis were faster than anyone else and lost interest in races where the speediest always won. Now the race goes to the cleverest, the luckiest, the most reckless, and the most wanton. Nothing is banned, everything is allowed, and anyone with a crumb of wisdom to spare stays indoors until it is all over.

But wisdom is for owls and Oxford professors! Let us go to the races! You may wear your finest or your foulest, overalls or opulence. I believe I shall wear a hat, for I look splendid in them, but if they make your forehead itch, that's perfectly all right. Picnicking is certainly allowed and I should never let you go hungry. Folk sit anywhere they please to sip their lemonades and catch a glimpse of the race as it goes by. Perhaps we will snag a seat in the Tulipbulb Amphitheatres of the Springtime Parish, or the beechwood bleachers of the Autumn Provinces. Perhaps we might gather with the gargoyles on the rooftops of Pandemonium, lay out a nice comfy lawn chair on the banks of the Barleybroom, or pitch a tent under a staircase in Asphodel. This is the first way in which Fairylanders love to gamble on a race. The racetrack covers every part of Fairyland, and so do the grandstands. Everyone hopes they have staked a claim on the very patch of glowerwheat on which something exciting will happen, but who can say? Where you and I keep our wallets, there is only one way to gamble on a race. Who shall win? Who shall lose? Give the nice man your money, and maybe you'll get it back, but probably you won't, because most things in any world are tricks, whether they are horse races, elections, or books about faraway and unrealistic places. But in Fairyland, gambling is an ancient and revered art. Fairy bookmakers won't take gold or silver at all. They prefer something more personal.

Let us spread out a blanket at the starting line in Pandemonium. I've brought a great orange parasol so we don't get sunburnt, and plenty of fizzy drinks and sandwiches for all. You see, every race begins in Pandemonium. Once, the ifrits tried to start a Firebreak (which is something like a marathon, if all of the runners could fly, travel back and forth in time, and were on fire) in their home of Flegethon City. All the runners stood ablaze at the starting line on Fervor Street, their volcano-batons in hand—but the city of Pandemonium moves according to the needs of narrative. It cannot stay in one place when it has caught the scent of a story. Just as the Firebreak was set to begin, Pandemonium arrived, rudely jostling Flegethon City right out of its pleasant spot on the shores of Braisebottom Lake to get a better seat.

All races begin in Pandemonium, even if they do not want to, for Pandemonium quite refuses to miss one single second of excitement.

Come with me. We shall get to the race grounds first,

before even the maddest racing fan has thought to put the
kettle on and start looking for her lucky socks. We shall kick
off our shoes and stretch out our legs on the outskirts of the
city, on Gingham Green, right on the lawns of all the rich and
famous—they can't stop us. Narrators may go where they
please. We've got an excellent view of the Great Foulard, the
winding, twisting, curlicuing avenue that connects every
street and avenue and boulevard and humble chiffon alley in
Pandemonium. Just past the Ghostloom Gate, the Great
Foulard dives into the Barleybroom and comes up on the
other bank clean and sparkling and called Gadabout Road
instead. But from where we sit, we can see everything: the
gownstone houses of Herringbone Heights, the glittering
Angora Aqueduct, the silk balloon of Groangyre Tower. We
can smell the bakeries of Calico Common as they heap pastries and bread and cakes and pies onto carts and wheel their
wares into the Plaited Plaza, where they will sell every last
cheese pastry and luckfig tart and wish they had baked more.
And we can hear folk less industrious than we starting to
arrive at the Plaza, yawning, shaking the dew off their wings,
taking their morning constitutionals: changing into six or
seven animals just to get the blood going. In the center of the
Plaited Plaza, a fountain bubbles away happily in blue marble,
silver, and watered silk. The great splashing statues depict

Good Queen Mallow piercing the heart of Gratchling Gourdbone Goldmouth with her trusty needle while her sensible knit scarf flutters behind her. Already, a family of dryads have gathered to sit on the fountain's rim, kicking their cedar-bark legs into the air. They wave us over—plenty of room for all. But we've already snatched up the best spot for ourselves. From a narrator's picnic blanket, there's nothing you can't see.

The day of the Cantankerous Derby woke up with gold dust in its eyes and three lumps of sunshine in its tea. Garlands of lavender and rowan branches and great bright paper lanterns hung from the noses of all the gargoyles peering down into the Plaited Plaza. The Stoat of Arms paced back and forth nervously, reciting the rules of the race to itself and hoping it had not forgotten anything important, like its racing silks or the finish line. Bakers, spectators, souvenir sellers and book-makers crowded in from the side alleys and streets and the Great Foulard as it emptied its morning traffic out onto the flame-colored patchwork cobbles.

September, Saturday, and A-Through-L arrived first. September had felt that it might look tawdry if the Queen came dawdling in when everyone else already had their shoes tied and their various engines purring. She'd set the moon in her bedchamber to wake her long before dawn and crept out of the Briary before even the Zinnias had stopped snoring. Ell soared up into the air and gave a few mighty flaps of his scarlet wings the way a runner stretches on the grass by the racetrack. She wore her Watchful Dress and her emerald smoking jacket as though they were ermine and veils of gold. Saturday wore his best sturgeon-skin trousers and a little blue-white stone on a lash of leather round his neck. September had asked many times why he wore that funny old opal, but he would never say. The Marid's blue chest and all his marvelous tattoos shone darkly in the sun. Saturday and September, having become rather practical on the subject of adventuring over the last many years, filled a small suitcase with various trifles and pies and samosas and profiteroles from the carts. A pieman with round, friendly cheeks and round, friendly serpents where her hair ought to be insisted on slipping in a little almond-wood barrel of cider.

"The Queen shouldn't thirst while I'm on my fourth cup," crowed the pieman.

Next came the Once and Future Club, sauntering, swaggering, and staggering, for few of them had anything polite to say to a good night's sleep. Each of them came well equipped for racing: Madame Tanaquill led the way, riding a magnificent horse with eight legs, a mane of rainbow light, and two vicious, glowing red coals where a usual horse's kind dark eyes would be. Pinecrack followed by himself, as he felt quite capable of achieving top moose-speeds on his own four legs. The Knight Quotidian drove a sensible four-wing family dragon. Hushnow, the Ancient and Demented Raven Lord, flew an enormous Roc named Wenceslas down from the Herringbone Heights into the Plaited Plaza. A Roc is a great enormous carnivorous bird, bigger than a humpback whale and the color of the sun. Now, you might think a Roc flies faster than a raven, and that was why Hushnow chose one for his mount. But it is not so—Rocs are quite slow as fliers go, somewhere between a bit of dandelion fluff and a paper airplane of middling quality. Hushnow, the Ancient and Demented Raven Lord, was really and truly *fabulously* demented, much more demented than ancient, and he thought the Roc was a wonderful plan.

Cutty Soames strutted in in a captain's tricorn hat, seven gold earrings in each ear, and the polished wooden wheel of his ship, the H.M.S. *Chimbley's Revenge*. She waited at anchor on the Barleybroom docks. The Headmistress sat in a prim chair perched atop a magnificent brass school bell that bounced up and down on its clapper. She whacked her bell smartly with a riding crop. It whinnied, a little fearful trill of a ring. Charlie Crunchcrab rode in on a sea-goat with frightful horns like ships' anchors. He glared furiously at September and refused to speak to her. More came, thick and fast, on horses and gryphons and giant platypi, in carriages that blinked out in one place and reappeared in another, in complicated machines September did not think anyone could get out of without a team of engineers or possibly doctors. And then came the heavyweights, riding nothing because nothing could carry them: Thrum, the Rex Tyrannosaur, the First Stone, and Goldmouth the Clurichaun, his tattoos gleaming black in the sun, his magenta eyes burning with fury that he should have to lower himself to a footrace with the rest of them.

A sharp pain snaked up through September's right foot. She lifted her shoe; a tiny creature glared up at her with hatred, no bigger than a stone in a ring. She sat atop a hazelnut carriage roofed in grasshopper wings, whose wheel-spokes were long, slender spiders' legs. Whatever drew the carriage was so small September could not see them at all—the harnesses floated free, as thin as cobwebs, strung between empty collars made of bright, pale moonbeams. The carriage-driver was a lady caught halfway between beautiful and terrifying— her face so gaunt, her hair so wild, and her eyes so huge that she looked like an electrified dragonfly who had once asked to be made into a human girl for Christmas and almost, almost gotten her wish. She snapped a whip made of cricket's bone; its filmy lash cracked against nothing, yet the hazelnut flew forward. It barreled toward Madame Tanaquill, who was feeding her horse a lump of fire and making what she considered an extremely fine joke to Curdleblood, the Dastard of Darkness, who simply refused to understand it. He forced a smile and patted his mount, which appeared to be a long streak of the color black and nothing more. But when Tanaquill saw the little nut-coach and its fierce-faced driver, she went quite pale. Her hand fluttered to her iron necklace and the welt beneath it. Tears filled her eyes. And the Prime Minister of all of Fairyland dropped to one knee. She bowed her head, and then covered her face with her hands, letting the other knee fall to the ground, until she was simply crying on her knees like a little child.

"Queen Mab," she whispered.

September suddenly felt very self-conscious, standing on her own two feet. She knew that she oughtn't bow herself, being Queen, at least for the next little while. But she felt terribly cold and uncertain to see Madame Tanaquill shiver as she extended her long finger for Queen Mab to whip mercilessly. The Prime Minister shuddered; September shuddered herself.

She should have thought to bring a steed. Surely, the Briary had heaps of them. But Ell and Saturday had always been everything she needed. She could hardly run like Pinecrack or whip a bell into fighting shape. Ell could fly, but so could half the other racers—and it's very hard to balance on a Wyverary's back when he dashes through the clouds. But September needn't have worried. I would never abandon her so. I have been waiting for ages and ages to give her my coronation present—and here it comes, huff-puffing across the patchwork cobblestones with a burlap sack that reads AROOSTOOK POTATO COMPANY over its spare wheel.

Aroostook the Model A Ford sped blithely toward September and Saturday, almost preening in the sunshine. Mr. Albert would never have recognized his old farm car now—Aroostook's windows had all turned to stained glass, its wheel to a hard, bright green sunflower, its dash to tanger-ine scrimshaw, its levers to thin golden arms ending in cuff links and balled fists, its squeeze horn to a cobalt-and-white-striped phonograph bell. Since September had seen it last, the Model A had become even wilder. Not a trace of its old greenish-black paint remained. Now Aroostook's doors and wheel wells were covered in brilliant feathers and striped pelts. Its wheels had outgrown the need for tires and wrapped themselves up in storm clouds—all except for the spare, which, beneath the old burlap sack, was a long, thick cat's tail, curled up around itself in satisfaction.

September and Saturday ran to their old friend, patting its

engine, asking after its gas tank, exclaiming over its new body. Both tried to hug Aroostook, but it did not come out quite right, for you cannot get your arms around a windshield or a fender, and besides, all Fords are somewhat embarrassed by public displays of affection.

The Plaited Plaza filled and filled and then overflowed. The Club shuddered at the crowds. It seemed many people meant to race who had never met a snifter in their lives, and the Club did not approve. September hadn't seen half of them in the grand hall. Not Kings and Queens of days gone by, but fauns and bugbears and gnomes and spriggans who came with knapsacks full of ambition strapped on tight. But September didn't see the racer she worried about. *Perhaps she won't come,* September thought. *Perhaps she'll just lose interest and go learn to knit with the hamadryads.*

Oh, September. They always come. No one in the history of the world has ever been so lucky as to escape confrontations forever. Though, I must admit: The Marquess actually overslept on the morning of the Cantankerous Derby. When you have slept for five years, one stacked on top of the other like mattresses, it's very hard to convince your body that you're allowed to wake up again. But I woke her. I crept into her room in the Briary and brushed a lock of her hair from her lips. The lock flushed blue and she sat straight up, gasping.

You might think it wicked of me—why not let that awful lady sleep through to the end of time? But, darlings, I have many more stories than September's to look after, and I cannot neglect even one of them.

The Marquess stepped out of nothing—she just opened a piece of air like it was a door with a nice sensible handle and stepped into the Plaza with her son Prince Myrrh close behind her. The Marquess smiled at September. Her hair faded from black to deep rose-pink. She gazed up at the statue of herself battling the clurichaun. Goldmouth, his golden teeth as sharp as vengeance, glared at her from across the square. Prince Myrrh waved shyly at September. He had come to see his mother off—and then dash away to his own schemes and trials, for the Marquess had told him when she woke that children should dream greater than their parents' industries. Perhaps September and Myrrh might have found something to say to one another had the Green Wind not pounced upon another perfect moment and come sailing down out of the dazzling sky on the Leopard of Little Breezes—followed by Iago, carrying the Red Wind, her red coat flapping rakishly, her red pistols glittering. The Blue Wind came after, on her great giant puffin, and the Silver Wind on the Tiger of Wild Flurries, and the Black Wind, on the Lynx of Gentle Showers! And yet another Wind, the only one September had not yet met, the Golden Wind, riding the Jaguar of Soft Showers. A-Through-L roared in delight and flew red circles round them all.

"Green!" September cried, nearly beside herself. She jumped up and down as though no time at all had passed and she was still washing pink and yellow teacups in her parents' sink and had only just now seen a man riding a flying Leopard for the first time. "Blue! Red! You came!"

"Well, of course we came, my sour little blueberry," cried the Blue Wind, halfway between a sneer and a giggle. "How else am I going to steal a crown?"

"You're racing?"

"Oh yes," the Red Wind said. "Fairyland is far too important to leave it to the Unwindy. We've been lax. It's not your fault—you're stuck in one place. You can't see anything but what you've already stepped in."

"I can't let one of *them* win," said the Silver Wind, her fine gray hair wafting up round her head in a crown. She jutted her chin toward the other Winds. "Thieves and brawlers!"

"I'm not one of those," the Black Wind snapped, wounded. "I'll have you know I'm a perfectly respectable and responsible creature of the night."

The Golden Wind said nothing. September and his Jaguar stared at one another.

"And you, too, Green?" September said at last. She did feel a little hurt. Didn't he think she could manage a throne?

"Oh, I don't want to lord it over anything much more than my breakfast, but I thought: Why not? Winds always race—it's our nature!" The Green Wind landed softly. The Leopard of Little Breezes padded over to drink from the fountain.

"Hawthorn!" September waved, seeing him at last, marching in from the Great Foulard. "Blunderbuss! Tam! Over here!"

The Changelings rode high atop the scrap-yarn wombat. Blunderbuss wore her full armor, the very armor Tamburlaine had painted for her outside the Redcaps' cellar. She had once been little and dense and fierce as any wombat—but Hawthorn and Tamburlaine had made her gigantic, stupendous, a first-rate combat wombat. Her armor bristled, all thorny Steppe-grass lashed together like fiery whips, winding round and round her in pumpkin-colored ropes, braided tight. The grasses had thatched up into bright greaves on her legs, a belly-breastplate on the underside of her tummy, a curling orange saddle on her back with long, wheat-sheaf stirrups handing down round her ribs, and a brilliant helmet over her head, with grassy nubs for wombat ears and several splendid spikes. Her fuzzy face was made quite fierce and triceratops-like by all her finery. She tossed her armored head at the sky and hurtled her thrill at the spires of Pandemonium.

"What do you say to all this?" hollered the combat wombat. "Pretty flash for a game of tag!"

Hawthorn and Tamburlaine looked guilty—guilty and beautiful. Hawthorn wore the long-tailed cap Gwendolyn, his human mother, had knitted for him with polar bears and kangaroos on it and his father Nicholas's old leather jacket with Gwen's gold jewelry sewn all over it. He would never give those up if he lived to be as old as the alphabet. But underneath it all he wore the outfit he'd found laid out for him in their room when he woke up that morning: a fine troll's tunic woven out of obsidian and granite and shale (for trolls can weave stone into cloth stronger than marble and softer than a child's cheek—though it's very hard work and bruises the weavers all over). On his feet he wore the great and powerful Golden Galoshes, only they really were Golden, and embroidered with very probably some sort of enchantments. His hands were sheathed in the rare and precious Carnivorous Mittens, only they really were tigerskin now instead of scratchy orange and black wool, complete with hard silver claws. And over his tunic, the formidable Houndstooth Suit, which really was made of fierce hounds' teeth, thatched together like a coat of mail.

Tamburlaine's walnut-wood skin looked as though it had been polished over and over—she shone like something burned inside her. Her hair was in full bloom, purple and crimson flowers cascading down her back like a highwayman's cape. She, too, wore what the Briary had given her: a dress of thick canvas, belted with a length of green knives from the knife tree in her own forest. She'd fastened lionbone greaves to her legs and wore bear's claw rings on her fingers. On her back Tam carried a quiver of paintbrushes, and across her chest two bandoliers of paint-pots.

"Where's Scratch?" asked Saturday, looking for the gramophone.

Blunderbuss pawed the Plaza stones ruefully. "He's such a fragile little fellow, don't you know. He could snap a leg or a handle as easy as flipping his record. We snuck out while he was snoozing away, snoring out torch songs. He'll be safer in the Briary. The wilds are no place for delicate technology."

Tamburlaine frowned wretchedly, already missing her friend.

"We're sorry, September," Tam began. "It's only that we're Changelings. If only Changelings were in charge, nobody else would ever have to get kidnapped just to make the math work out. We think you'd be a lovely Queen, but we can't trust anyone who hasn't had to grow up in the human world."

"I grew up in the human world," September said crossly.

"It's not the same." Hawthorn sighed. "You don't know what it's like to always, always feel that you don't belong, to your family, to your city, or your school, knowing there's something different about you, something off, that you're not like the others, that you're an alien all alone."

September crossed her arms. "Hawthorn. *Everyone* feels like that."

But the troll shook his head. "You were human. You *matched*. You don't know what it's like to be stuck in your own body like a trap."

Oh, but Hawthorn, my best and dearest boy. Listen to September, who knows a thing or two about living in a strange body. Max could tell you, too, and Thomas Rood and Penny Farthing and even the boy named Humphrey who carved his name in your desk. You could tell him, and so could I. No one belongs when they are new to this world. All children are Changelings.

"We have to try," Tamburlaine said gently. "And we're not the only ones! That's Sadie Spleenwort over there, with the mushrooms in her hair." A girl with auburn braids was kissing a giant jackal on the nose and reaching up on her tiptoes to scratch his ears. "She'll probably beat us, actually. She's stubborn and sour and stupendous. And Penny Farthing, on the velocipede!"

September looked and saw the little girl she had met on the back of a wild velocipede the first time she came to Pandemonium. Penny was quite grown now, whooping and laughing on top of her steed while her mother, Calpurnia, sipped a coffee and grinned with pride.

"Ladies and Gentlemen and Everyone Else!" bellowed the Stoat of Arms. Several invisible horns sounded, shattering the merry noise into a hundred million pieces, leaving only quiet behind. "Welcome to the Cantankerous Derby! Let us all get this over with as soon as possible for I am already bored with every single one of you! Please behave yourselves while Mrs. Grandiloquent Cockscomb, the Royal Bookmaker, commences the Reading of the Odds!"

A gorgeous old basilisk wearing deep black sunglasses hobbled forward, carrying a book nearly as large as herself, which was no small feat, as Mrs. Grandiloquent Cockscomb was a scaly reptile the size of an igloo. Her orange-and-violet-feathered tail rose up even farther than her head, which looked very much like the head of a stegosaurus September had seen illustrated in one of her history textbooks.

"After conferring with the twenty-one members of the Society of Probability Paupers," began Mrs. Cockscomb in a reedy, raspy voice, "I am honored to recite to you, gloriously gathered Fairylanders (and Others), the Hallowed Odds. The

Paupers prefer to begin with the winners: We find Madame Tanaquill favored to take the crown at two to one, followed by the Marquess and Queen Mab at three to one. A surprising upstart rising up the rankings—Gratchling Gourdbone Goldmouth comes in at four to one, and old Hushnow close behind. Now, on to something more interesting! We are offering generous odds on Thrum being effervesced into his constituent atoms by lunch, the Blue Wind snatching the crown and hiding it for not more than three years, but not less than two, causing three-quarters of a revolution in Pandemonium, and that bloody great wombat unraveling completely before all is said and done. Please see myself or one of my Lamblers to place your bets. Gold and silver not accepted—today we are taking foreign currency only! Human dollars, pounds, rubles, drachma, et cetera, chimeric lodestones, kneecaps, or firstborn children, but only nice ones, let's not have a repeat of the Bleakness Cup incident!"

The Stoat of Arms sighed with relief. "Thank you, Mrs. Cockscomb. And now, may I introduce the Racemaster, who will, if everything goes swimmingly, make sure I never have to see most of you again!"

The horns sounded again. A-Through-L hid his head under one wing. September and Saturday clapped her hands over their ears—and when they uncovered them again, they were alone.

The Plaited Plaza stood empty, not a single long-dead monarch, waving dryad, or pastry seller remained. No Stoat of Arms, no Mrs. Cockscomb, no scrap-yarn wombat, nor even one solitary spot from the tail of a Leopard.

And no Aroostook.

The sun still beamed overhead; the fountain still gurgled pleasantly; the grass on Gingham Green still sparkled with yesterday's rain. But September, Saturday, and Ell stood by themselves in the middle of a suddenly silent Pandemonium.

CHAPTER VI

THE MAN FROM
BLUE HEN ISLAND

*In Which September Meets Babe Ruth, Acquires a Steed,
and Learns a Great Deal About What Lies Ahead*

"What's happened?" Ell bellowed, spinning in a great red circle on the empty cobblestones.

September squeezed her fists together. "Have we lost already? Is everyone else that much faster? Where's Aroostook? And Hawthorn and Tam and Blunderbuss?"

Saturday wanted to comfort her, but he had no good thoughts to offer. "Maybe we did something wrong," he fretted.

"Maybe we've been disqualified. Or the Marquess has done something awful to everyone."

"Ought we to just . . . start running? The Ghostloom Gate is open, perhaps that was the starting gun. How are we to know?" September took a step forward, but she was not at all sure of the step.

"*Races* begin with *R*," Ell said mournfully. "I much prefer Dances. And Fairs. And Ball Games."

An ear-battering smack of drums and firecrackers echoed through the air. A swirl of a thousand colors filled up September's eyes so that she could see nothing else. The colors whirled and spun round one another, spinning out in front of A-Through-L and up into the air. Finally, they unfolded and became an impossibly slender, pointed man made all of racing silks and checkered flags, in every color and every pattern, as though someone had ripped off a patch from the costume of everyone who had run a race since before the mile was invented. He did not seem to have hands or feet so much as the twisting silk of him came to graceful points at the ends of his arms and legs. His face was a marvelous origami—noble crests, green chevrons, black stripes, lace handkerchiefs given as favors in some long-forgotten joust, all folded tight together to make a sharp, clear face with searching, canny eyes.

Now, all races must have a Racemistress or Racemaster. To find an ideal Racemaster, first track down a school principal who loves nothing better than tricking students into misbehaving, unless it was coming up with the most joyfully complicated punishments. Make certain that she has studied all her life to become an expert in every sport and game, from poker to croquet to Arcanasta to Daemoninoes to the Royal Game of Ur, the way ninjas train to perfect every martial art. For the Cantankerous Derby, the Stoat of Arms would sooner have lived out its days in a petting zoo than chosen anyone other than the greatest Racemaster who has ever lived or breathed or fired a starting catapult directly in the ear of a Glashtyn—and just such a one floated nimbly before them.

The man made of flags bowed, flourishing his arms and bending his head. "Good morning, Queen September, I will be your Racemaster for the next many days. Years, possibly! But let's not get ahead of ourselves. My name is Ajax Oddson. By my reputation, you will know you are in hands both good and fair."

"I'm sorry, but I don't know a thing about you," September said cheerfully. She had long ago ceased to be embarrassed by not knowing a thing in Fairyland.

Saturday squeezed her hand. "Is there anyone in the human world who plays a game so well that everyone knows his name, so well that his name *becomes* the game, and you can hardly think of one without the other?"

September thought for a moment. "I suppose there's Babe Ruth. That's baseball. It's a bit like sword fighting and a bit like juggling but far less interesting to watch than either one."

"What a funny name!" said A-Through-L, his nostrils flaring. "Babies oughtn't play with swords, unless they are trolls." He rocked from one great red leg to the other. "If Fairyland has a Babe Ruth, then Ajax Oddson is him. I'm very pleased and also nervous to meet him. I *thought* we might. Who else would take charge of the most important race that's ever cried *on your mark*?"

The Racemaster inclined his head demurely. "You're too kind, Master Wyverary. Your Majesty, allow me to put you at ease. I had my education at the Home for Excessively Competitive Children on Blue Hen Island, where any child who loves to win more than he loves to eat or sleep or drink or have one single friend goes to be among his own kind. There we can be cared for by folk who understand our needs and wants and need-nots and want-nots. On our first day, we found a single blue poker chip lying on our pillows with the motto of the school stamped on it in gold. IN LUDO VERITAS. *In the Game Is Truth*. The day we turned that one chip into one thousand, we graduated. And my specialty has always been Derbies."

Ajax Oddson twirled around, his chevrons and checks and diamonds flying. "Now, I am a Dandy. You may think me large and grand and beautiful, but"—he leaned in and held one pointed silken hand to his mouth, sharing a delicious secret—"in actuality, I am no bigger than a bullfrog. I have short, thin, highly breakable legs—anyone could beat me in a race. My old headmaster, Babel Y. Hexagon, whom I could defeat at Go while underwater and half asleep, could gallop all the way round the world faster than I could crack the four hundred meters. I could not get much better, tiny as I was, without wings or any particularly pragmatical magic. Oh, I am a dismal magician. My only aptitude is for Odd Magic—I can feel the improbabilities of any event with an outcome as surely as I feel the swelling of my nose when I am sick."

"Improbabilities?" asked September.

"Oh yes. Even Magic handles the probabilities—whether or not a thing is likely to happen given this and that and the other thing. Odd Magic deals in *imp*-probabilities—which is more like gym class than math. The Imp-probable Master can look at that happening and tell just when and where to put his finger or move a teensy little stone or place a dinner plate in the middle of the road to send all those fuddy-duddy probabilities flying off in every direction, to cause the most trouble, the most chaos, the most *Unlikeliness*. But that's not much good to a soul who longs to play fair. My Odd Heart could only tell me how astronomically Unlikely I was to come out the victor, down to the last and loneliest and mold-iest decimal. So depressing! Knowing that you will lose is as disheartening as knowing that you will win. It's the *unknowing* that quickens the spirit and puts sweat on your brow! But the Derby!" The Racemaster leapt from the fountain to the awnings of the shops to the ledges of windows and back down to balance on the tip of Ell's wing. "The Derby is not just a race, it is a battle and a dance and a scavenger hunt. It is not won by the swiftest, nor the strongest, nor the creature with greatest lung capacity or slow-twitch muscle mass. No! The Derby is won by the cleverest, the most devious, often the most vicious, but sometimes the most kind, and always, always, by the seat of one's wits! For just as I was growing bored with the same old games, Fairyland was growing bored of racing with Dodos and tracks and linear thinking. It was, indeed, Headmaster Hexagon who invented the first Derby— for each Derby is unique, with its own laws and customs. Hexagon's Derby took seven years, flattened two separate villages, used up all the salt in the sea, and everyone still feels rather uncertain about who won. Isn't that just the best thing you've heard all week? Yes, in the Derby I found the grand love affair I had always sought. And I found myself. For when

Dandies come of age, we make new, fleet, nimble bodies out of whatever obsesses us, whatever we adore unreasonably. My mother is a creature of arrows and catgut strings and curving bows, my father a marvelous beast of folded sheet music. And I? I gathered together the racing flags of every Derby I won, and the proud silks of every opponent I defeated until I could stitch together the finest limbs anyone has ever made—a body of victory! After all, my darlings, the clothes make the man!"

The Racemaster spun round again and bowed. September could not help herself, she clapped without meaning to, and then felt quite silly.

"That's all wonderful, Mr. Oddson, it really is . . . but . . . where has everybody gone? Have we won already? Or lost?"

The Racemaster stroked his chin with one blue-and-green-checked hand. "Ah. Ah-ha. Stoatums did tell me one of you was a foreigner and wouldn't know a Derby from a dervish. Are you her?"

"I usually am," September said with a sigh.

Ajax Oddson smiled with the tips of two pink flags. "It's to keep the whole thing fair. If everyone could see where everyone else dashed off to first, then you'd all have a pretty good idea where to start looking for the Heart of Fairyland and there wouldn't be any sport in it. Besides, people tend to make a hash of the starting line. Pushing and shoving and stabbing and turning into turtles. As a courtesy, all racers have been enclosed in a small bubble of space and time. They cannot see us and we cannot see them, but I assure you they are all safe and sound and so are you. These bubbles will last for a few hours after the *Ready Steady Go* to ensure a fair start for all. It's a fantastically difficult bit of hexing, I'm told. Something about Wet Magic and Severe Magic and Shy Magic all at the same time and also a certain very expensive opossum. At the same time, all participants have been delivered to their individual and *individualized* Starting Lounges, arranged in a large circle around the city of Pandemonium, so that no one has an advantage. Some of them are quite near to us right now—but our little space-time opossum has provided this lovely peace and quiet before it all goes absolutely mad. Within their bubbles, each registered racer is at this very moment hearing this exact speech from their own personal copy of Ajax Oddson. The race will begin once everyone has heard the rules and asked whatever adorable questions they have in their back pockets."

"So you're not really here?" asked Ell uncertainly.

"Oh no, Master Wyverary! I am where I belong—at the finish line. It's all done with mirrors! And a dash of Hot Magic from a bruja named Quintuple Pod. She's a doppelgänger and my right-hand man. Got a cabinet full of copies of herself hanging up like winter coats. She can do this sort of thing while eating scrambled eggs with one hand and reading the newspaper with the other. Now, let's take attendance and make sure it's all gone to plan. It's not easy to coordinate mirrors and opossums and Quintuple, you know. We could all lose our heads. Or the spare change in our pockets. Is your team all present and accounted for?"

"No!" cried September. "No, they are *not*. Aroostook is gone."

Ajax Oddson unfolded his forearm and peered at the silk. "I don't have anyone registered under that name."

"It's my . . . it's *a* car. A Model A Ford with a burlap potato sack over the spare tire and a green sunflower for a steering wheel."

"Ah. Ah-*ha*. And by car you mean a carriage?"

"I suppose."

"Any carriages, cars, catamarans, or other conveyances are classed as steeds, my dear."

"Aroostook is not a steed! Well, it might have been, but it's been through a lot."

The Racemaster seemed terribly excited. "I have invented a number of thrilling, terrific, tremendous rules especially for the Cantankerous Derby, the most spectacularly important

Derby in the history of Fairyland, but this is my favorite. All Steeds Shall Be Collected and, at the Firing of the Starting Catapult, Redistributed to Racers at Random!"

Saturday frowned deeply. "What? Do you mean . . . someone else is going to drive Aroostook, and we'll get . . . what? Queen Mab's hazelnut coach?"

Ajax clapped his own hands in delight. "Yes, you've got it! Isn't it genius? No one will have the vehicular advantages they so carefully planned out or built or tamed or enchanted. It will be gloriously, brilliantly *fair*. Let's hope you don't nab the nut, though, eh? I shouldn't like to be in possession of anything belonging to Miss Mab. And no abandoning your steeds just because you got a rocking horse instead of a rocket! Anyone crossing the finish line without a mount shall be disqualified!"

"Poor Aroostook," September said softly. She did hope someone not too terrible got her beloved Model A. She shouldn't like to think of Tanaquill grinding the gears.

"Poor us," Saturday whispered back. "Did you see the magma skis Our Lady of Lava brought? Or the Knapper's gyroscope of daggers?"

"At least they didn't put me down as a steed," Ell sniffed.

"You rode round my neck once, Ell," said September, reaching up to touch his warm, scaly flank. "On the Moon, when you were small. So if you're a steed, then I am, too. No one had better call you one unless they're prepared to saddle me up alongside. It's not a very nice word, really."

Ajax clapped his silken hands. "Let's not hold up the whole Derby, boys and girls! Shall I tell you my second one-time-only special Cantankerous Rule? I shall! If You Should Encounter Another Racer, the Two of You Shall Be Said to Occupy the Same Square on the Playing Board and Shall Duel at Once. The Opossum of Space and Time will provide a Dueling Ground in which both fighters will have access to the same magic, no matter their species or education. Quintuple Pod and I Will Doppelgäng a Random Racer to Your Side Immediately to Officiate the Duel. Hopefully this will winnow down the numbers a bit. It's dash crowded out there."

"Duel to the death?" September asked. She would not kill anyone. She would *not*. How could she ever go home if she did such a thing? How could she ever stay? A death is too big to forget.

"We are not barbarians, madam!" Ajax Oddson held his hand to his breast, mortified. "No, these will be Duels to the Dodo! Well, to the Dodo's Egg, to be exact. The loser of the duel shall be considered Out of the Game. Disqualified, three strikes, offsides! They will find themselves safely returned to the Egg—to wherever he or she came from, be that the Moon or Nebraska or primordial chaos or the land of the dead. It's quite humane. After all, everyone was content in their own good homes or graves or prisons three days ago—no reason to fear such places now! No harm, no foul."

"And the . . . Officiants will be just like you?" asked Saturday. "We'll be able to hear and see them, but they can't touch us or harm us. They'll still be running the race, wherever they are. Or, I suppose, we will, if the lot falls to us."

Oddson steamed on.

"Deftly explanated, Mr. Blue! Any Cheating, Rule-Trampling, Duel-Tampering, or Belligerence Toward Myself will earn you a visit to the Penalty Box! Which brings me to my last invention: Halfway Through the Derby, Everyone Shall Switch Places According to Whatever Scheme I, Ajax Oddson, Deem to Be Most Hilarious at That Time. That is all! And I must inform you that everyone else has finished talking to me and seems quite anxious to begin! Are you ready to meet your steed and hit the road? Shall I fetch the starting catapult?"

September looked to Saturday and Ell. They'd been cooped up in the cellar so long. It would feel wonderful just to run and run and run together. And who knew? Perhaps at the end of all that running, she might still have her crown.

"We're ready, Mr. Oddson," she said firmly.

The Racemaster reached into his left sleeve, covered in zigzagging golden lines. He drew out a little catapult—and as he drew it out it grew and grew until it was bigger than Ajax himself, made all of obsidian and wolf-bone. The pocket overflowed with bizarre and mysterious objects, some colorful, some drab, some large and covered in spikes, some soft and small and well-worn.

"Ladies and lads and gentle-wyverns, Queens and Questers! I have packed my personal catapult full of items you would find incredibly useful in the running of a Derby, from Seven League Boots to salamander cloaks to Belinda Cabbage's new and untested Geographickal Engine! I have selected these objects with love and care and malice aforethought, to protect and guide you on your way. Let the Cantankerous Derby begin!"

A dagger flashed in Ajax Oddson's hand. He slashed through the Sauterelle's ropes. The catapult sprang forward and fired all those wonderful, useful things into the sky. They soared over the spires of Pandemonium and far away, so high and far that September lost sight of them long before they landed. The invisible horns sounded, fireworks exploded over the Plaited Plaza, raining confetti down into the Mallow and Goldmouth fountain. The Gabardine Gate raised up slowly, showing the road out of Pandemonium and the sparkling waves of the Barleybroom river.

The Racemaster seemed to deflate like a hot air balloon. His silks drooped to the ground, suddenly empty. His crisp points started to come loose, his cheeks and eyebrows unfolding and untying until there was nothing left but a great pile of old flags on the patchwork cobblestones. But no—not only a pile of flags. From the depths of all that fine, painted fabric, they heard several snorts, a furious squeal, and an indignant roar. Then the loud, horrid *rip* of silk tearing in half, and then in half again. Something was trying to come out from inside the rags that had, only a moment ago, been Ajax Oddson, Blue Hen Island's greatest student. September's stomach went cold. She remembered Tanaquill's dreadful horse, Hushnow's gargantuan Roc, Curdleblood's hideous shade of black.

"Get off!" snarled the silk-heap. "Get off me, you nasty old bedsheet! I'll bite you stupid! THIS IS THE WORST THING THAT HAS EVER HAPPENED I HATE YOU AND I HOPE YOU COME APART IN THE WASH."

An orange spike snagged through a flag showing a noble crest with polar bears rampant and a hobgoblin with spectacles on. Then another spike. Then a pair of chomping, gnashing, vicious teeth.

Wombat teeth.

Blunderbuss burst out of Ajax's racing flags, shredding them to stitches and tatters.

"TA-DA!" she bellowed. "Did you hear those snobs calling me a *steed*?"

CHAPTER VII

Everything Has a Heart

In Which No One Is a Steed, Cross-Referencing Proves
Unhelpful, and A-Through-L Proves Himself a
Librarian in Good Standing

September grabbed Saturday's hand. Her whole body shook with the need to go, go, go, run, faster, get ahead of the pack, find a shortcut, pound the road. The Marid looked up and down the Barleybroom for a ferry, for the other racers, for anything the catapult might have dropped. But the scrap-yarn wombat was in no such hurry. Blunderbuss stomped up and down the shores of the windy river. She snatched at the chinstrap of her grass helmet and tore it off, kicking it along the sunny grass like a ball that had greatly disappointed her.

"A steed! Me! A mount! And this is the second time, too! That dull battle-ax Tanaquill put me in a *stable*, if you can believe it. A stable! As if I'm nothing but a pitchfork! Don't I talk? Don't I know my multiplication tables? Don't I have my own tender ambitions? Don't I bite with conviction? I busted on through an apartment wall into Fairyland just the same as anybody else. I am not a Chevrolet! I am a stupendous splendid fantastic amazing combat wombat. I am! I'll steed *them*!"

A-Through-L stomped beside her, his orange eyes filled with sympathy. She was only somewhat smaller than the Wyverary—the ground trembled a little as they squashed it underfoot.

"My father was a Library," Ell said comfortingly, "and when I was young my family all lived together among his strong, sturdy stacks. Back then, my brother T-Through-Z used to say the world is divided into the riders and the ridden, and I always thought he was being pompous and grim because those are his favorite things besides roasting romance novels, but I believe him now. Half of everyone thinks I'm September's horse. As if *I* don't know my multiplication tables! As if I wasn't there when the Marquess fell! I know that I *can* be ridden, but I *needn't* be. I could ride somebody, if that somebody was big enough. It's not my fault I'm too heavy. It's their fault they're so little."

Blunderbuss sniffed a little. She tore up a patch of Barleybroom grass and clover and flax flowers and chewed resentfully.

"We were gonna *win,*" she huffed. "Me and Hawthorn and Tam. We were gonna do a double flip and land on the Briary with all our feet planted and a crown for each of us. I wanted to see the look on Scratch's bell! Now who've they got with them? Probably Sadie's mangy dumb jackal with his face stuffed full of biscuits. And *he'll* get to wear a crown while I get nothing! I never get anything!"

"*We* might win, you know," said Saturday, who certainly felt their chances were better than a couple of Changelings fresh from Chicago, wherever that was. If they won, September would stay. It was all he could think. You couldn't be a long-distance Queen. She would stay and he would never have to turn to say something to her and find no one there ever again.

Blunderbuss gave him a pitying look. "No offense, but your girl doesn't even want to boss Fairyland about. You can't win without a want boiling in your belly. Besides, my kids have magic leaking out of their ears. None of this would have happened without them."

"Oh yes," said September slyly. "Thank you, Hawthorn and Tamburlaine, for bringing Goldmouth back to life. A king so wicked there's a statue of him dying in the capital for everyone to wash their stockings in. I'm sure we're all terribly grateful."

"I wouldn't go talking about bringing ornery things back to life, Miss Egg. It doesn't look too good on you."

September laughed. She knew the wombat meant to sting her, so she laughed instead of blushing or sputtering, which never got a girl anything but rolled right over. It was a fair point, anyhow. She pushed her hair out of her eyes. The wind pushed it right back, hot and sweet and full of the best sorts of city smells. She took a breath and said the thing that had spent the last three days pacing all the rooms of her mind. "Maybe I don't want to be Queen, exactly. But if we don't win, then someone dreadful might. We've got to win, because we can't count on the Marquess or Tanaquill or Goldmouth losing. And . . . and I'd be a good Queen, I think. I wouldn't be *bad,* anyway. Maybe I could be the opposite of a tyrant, an un-tyrant, and Fairyland would be, well, like a story in a book."

And if I were Queen, I could stay, she added silently. *I could stay in Fairyland. I could be good at Fairyland, the way the Sibyl was good at guarding the entrance to the underworld and the Calcatrix was good at the magic of money.* A terrible longing for her mother pressed on her chest. Her mother would tell her that if there was ever a chance to do something extraordinary, it ought to be snatched immediately. *Only, if I stay, will I ever get to hear her tell me a single thing again? Perhaps . . . perhaps I could bring my parents through the Closet Between the Worlds and we could all be together here. Halloween brought my father to Fairyland-Below, and she's only my shadow. You're allowed to do that sort of thing when you're Queen.*

Darling September! That is why anyone wants to rule. Oh, they would never admit it. But at the bottom of their hearts, anyone who longs for power longs to have everyone and everything they love safe and happy forever in one place, no matter the cost. It's only what happens to those they do not love that makes it all go wrong-headed and hard.

Saturday stared out over the river, into the dry hills beyond. He could not quite tell where Pandemonium had settled herself. They had to get moving. If they won, she would stay. He whispered it over again in his mind like a song. "It doesn't matter. We've got to figure something out before the opossum's bubble pops and we're surrounded by the worst family reunion that's ever packed itself a picnic."

"I shall be honest," began September, pulling her emerald smoking jacket tight round her. "I haven't any little idea what the Heart of Fairyland is or where to find it. I had hoped someone else might."

Saturday, Ell, and Blunderbuss exchanged guilty looks. "We've been whipping our brains against it for days," the scrap-yarn wombat said. "I've only just got to Fairyland so don't look at me. I hardly know where the broom closet is! But if you ask me, anything important is in the Land of Wom, and if it's not in the Land of Wom, it's not awfully important."

"I don't know," said Saturday. "But I know where I would hide something, if I needed to. I would hide it way down deep at the bottom of the sea, snug under the weight of water and safe from all those silly toy monarchs who can only breathe air."

"*Hearts* begin with *H,* Ell," September said to the Wyverary. "I thought you might know where we ought to go. Where Fairyland hides its heart. Because Saturday's right. It's got to be hidden, or else the Derby would be over in a minute and a half."

The Wyverary fretted and clawed the earth. He wanted so to be useful. "But, September, everything has a heart! Well, mostly everything. I can tell you all about Wyvern hearts, if you want. Or Periwig hearts or Fairy hearts or

Marid hearts or even a little about human hearts. But you can't leave it all up to me! I thought *you* would know! It sounds like the sort of secret a Queen would learn on the occasion of her coronation, doesn't it?"

"Just try, Ell," coaxed Saturday.

The huge red Wyvern cocked his head to one side and spoke slowly, as if reading from a book. "Hearts: hollow pumping organs that move blood throughout the body or any similar thing. The center of a body. The part of a creature that feels and fears and wants and swells with courage. The important bit—*the heart of the matter.* A suit in a deck of playing cards. The shape of a Valentine with two round parts and one pointy part."

September grinned. "Cross-reference! *Heart* begins with *H* and *Fairyland* begins with *F*!"

A-Through-L scrunched up his snout. His long whiskers flicked and snapped. "The Dun Cow Café in Gingham Green serves a drink with melon chunks in it called the Heart of Fairyland. When Cutty Soames was King, he had a grand pirate ship built out of dryad bones and starlight and he called *it* the Heart of Fairyland. It's also the name of Queen Mab's sword, only it's not really a sword so much as a spindle. Oh, and they used to call the Moon the Heart of Fairyland, in the days before astronomy was born." The great Wyvern sighed.

"September, my father was only a little local Library. Worlds don't print their secrets in encyclopedias! I wish it were as easy as reading off the population of Pandemonium! I would have read the H's more carefully if only I'd known."

"Oh, Ell, don't worry! You know I can't bear to see you frown. Goodness, I wish I'd paid more attention to my lessons twice an hour!" She touched his scaly skin. It was so warm, as warm as Summer.

Blunderbuss gnawed at her own whiskers. "What's that bit about the center of a body?" she said thoughtfully.

"Oh!" exclaimed September. "Could it be that easy? Ell, what's the exact center of Fairyland? Where I come from, it's somewhere off the coast of Africa, I think. What's neither east nor west nor north nor south, but perfectly in the middle? *Center* begins with *C*!"

Ell did not even take a moment to consider it. "Why, Meridian, of course!" The Wyverary's voice grew quiet and full of awe. "The Great Grand Library lives there. The biggest and widest and deepest and oldest Library in all of Fairyland. My great-great-great-greater-than-great-grandmother. She hatched all the other Libraries. Even the Fairyland Municipal Library. Even the Lopsided Library on the Moon. Even my father, Compleat. Fairyland has a Library in the center of it— maybe the Heart is there! Maybe the Grand Library *is* the

Heart! But I suppose we would have a terrible time trying to carry the Grand Library to Runnymede Square. Still, even if the Library doesn't have the Heart of Fairyland, surely someone, sometime, wrote something about it! A thing is hardly real if no one's written about it. It's the writing that makes a thing proper and solid and true in the first place."

A-Through-L nodded firmly, agreeing with himself. Though the red lizard didn't know it, he had just spilled the first law of Dry Magic. It is true in our world, too, and this is why the first thing we do when a child gets born is write down her name and her weight and everything else we know about her.

"Does anyone know where we are, exactly? I've been trying to pinpoint us, but I can't tell," Saturday said. He added quietly to himself: "I can't smell the sea." It is very frightening for a Marid when he cannot smell the sea, or hear it, or see it glimmering in the distance. If he cannot smell the sea, he cannot find his way home. "I think those are the Handhills—but then that bit of mist over there might be the Inksop Marshes, except they should be west of the hills . . ."

"Oh, it doesn't matter," chirped Ell cheerfully.

"Doesn't it? I rather reckon it does, if we're headed toward your gran," groused Blunderbuss.

"But it doesn't. I am a Librarian! Well, Assistant Librarian.

And I haven't worked a shift in ever so long. But that's only because I was in prison! I wasn't *shirking*. So I should still be a member of the Catalogue in Good Standing."

"What does that mean?" asked September.

Ell beamed. "All Librarians are members of the Catalogue. That's what you call a coven when it's made up of Librarians instead of witches. Librarians have sorted and alphabetized all the magic that ever thought to put a rabbit and a hat together. Who do you think invented Special Collections? Severe Magic and Shy Magic, Dry Magic and Wet Magic, Umbrella Magic and Fan Magic and all the rest? Librarians, that's who! And of course they learned a thing or two along the way. The Catalogue connects every Library to every other Library just the same as if they shared one long hallway. No one wants to wait for *On the Criminology of Fairies* to arrive by stagecoach when you could just pop out of the Municipal stacks and into the towering shelves of the Crowdleian Library and have it back in half a wing beat! It's very necessary magic. I'm not meant to tell anyone—it's one of the High Secrets of Circulation. The Catalogue would turn me into a bookmark if they knew! September? Is this right? Is this the way to win the Derby? Should I take us to Meridian? Or Wom? Or under the sea? Only I think Saturday would have to manage that."

September squared her shoulders. She was the Queen of

Fairyland, if only for a little while. She had better get used to deciding things, even if the idea of getting it wrong frightened her all over.

"Yes, Ell. Take us. We won't tell anyone how you did it."

A-Through-L stretched out his long crimson wings to gather them all close in. Blunderbuss snagged a bit of her yarn on his talon. September tucked it back into place without a word, and at that moment, the wombat began to love her a little. Hawthorn would have fretted over it something awful, but September simply fixed her up without a fuss. The truth was, Blunderbuss hated to be reminded that she was made of yarn while everyone else was more or less made of meat or meatlike stuffs. September peeked under his wing at the deep, rolling Barleybroom. She remembered the first time she saw it, how wide and wonderful it seemed—until the Glashtyn came roaring out of it. What lived beneath now, she wondered?

The Wyverary danced from foot to foot. His orange eyes blazed with glee. He carefully laid one long black claw against his snout and whispered:

"SHHHHHH!"

And all four of them disappeared with a sound like a date-stamp clonking down, leaving behind a puff of dust that smelled strongly of dictionaries, first editions, and the complete works of everyone ever.

CHAPTER VIII

GREENWICH MEAN TIME

*In Which September Visits the Great Grand Library,
Is Threatened by Numerous Bears, and Consults
the Reference Desk*

I t is true that everything has a heart. The hearts of towns and villages and cities do not look very much like the heart of a person, but they have hearts all the same. Sometimes it looks like a train depot, sometimes it looks like a university, sometimes it looks like a castle, sometimes it looks like a river, sometimes it looks like a factory. A town must dream or it will die, and a town's dreams come from its depot or its university or its castle or its river or its factory. It longs for marvelous folk to come through the village center on a shining train and stay. It longs to make steel so strong it can build the whole of the rest of the world, or to see its river filled with great ships trading one thing for another until no one lacks any longer. It yearns to protect its villagers from the rampages of time and economics. It wants to make wisdom so bright it can keep the lights on for the whole of the rest of the world. If you look at the center of any city, you can see what it wants to be when it grows up.

The Great Grand Library did not know Meridian was the exact center of Fairyland when she settled there. She did not even know it was called Meridian, for it was not called anything at all yet. She was but a young and reckless hut whose owners had abandoned her during the first Fairyland Ice Age, which was caused by Hushnow, the Ancient and Demented Raven Lord, biting off chunks of the sun for his children to gobble up. This is why ravens are wiser and wilier than most other birds and some people, though it also covered Fairyland in green glass glaciers. But without the glaciers, there would have been no ice wyrms, so on the whole, it all comes out reasonably even. The sun sulked and moaned for a thousand years or so and then got over it. But the Great Grand Library knew only that the family of weremammoths whom she loved and sheltered had run off at the first sign of wyrms and left her alone with nothing more to her name than a candlestick with no candles, a porridge bowl with no porridge, and a single book without a bookshelf to keep it safe from the storms.

The Great Grand Library picked up her studs and her door frame and high-tailed it south, looking for a better life. Now, a hut, no matter how good-hearted and sturdy-souled, has little use for candlesticks (all houses, huts, shacks, and bungalows can see perfectly well in the dark, though mansions have a terrible fear of it). Nor does she need much in the way of porridge bowls. A house eats only evening hours, the smells of baking things, and wood polish. And even if she did decide to give food a go, she would not start with porridge, which is horrid. This left the Great Grand Library, neither great nor grand nor a library quite yet, with her single solitary book. She sat down to read it in a patch of poor raven-chewed sunshine, and when she finished, she read it all over again. By the time she had finished her fourth reading, the hut looked up and realized that a gnome had wandered into it and lain down to sleep. When the gnome awoke, it unpacked its belongings, which included two more books. When the gnome left for an exciting business opportunity in the brand-new baby city of Pandemonium, the hut hid all three books from him and kept them for herself.

And so it went. The hut prowled all over Fairyland, enticing Fairies and spriggans and hobgoblins and wights to move in and move out, and each time, the hut stole their books, and her collection grew. She read every last book and then started over from the first one, the were-mammoths' book, again and again. Finally, she got so heavy with the weight of her books that she could not prowl any longer, and the place where she plopped down at last is the place where she still sits.

The heart of Meridian is a hut that wanted to be a library when it grew up.

And that is just what September and her friends saw when they appeared, rather suddenly and with a loud *chuh-chunk* stamping sound, in the middle of the Great Grand Library. They landed in the Mystery section, which had once been a tiny kitchen where were-mammoth children had laughed and refused to eat their greens and gotten porridge all over their antlers. Now it had a ceiling like an overgrown cathedral, tangled up in flying buttresses and skylights and study desks zooming and darting to and fro like warplanes. But there were still a number of sinks and china cabinets and sideboards and tables with dinner plates laid out, though they had no beef or cheese on them, only more books, piled forty volumes high. The Mystery section is also the theatre district—for all of the town of Meridian is contained within the Great Grand

Library, safe and sound and snug behind a wall of book-shelves, just as a medieval village bunkers down within a wall of bricks.

Ell could hardly stand still—so he didn't. He leapt into the air, soaring up the stacks past the buttresses and the spitfire study desks with their green lamps blazing.

"Wait!" called September. They had to stay together—who knew how far Tanaquill and the others might have gotten by now?

"Looking for clues!" he shouted down while he darted all round the tip-top shelves, where there are precisely no books on the Heart of Fairyland. Human novels are kept on the top shelves of the Mystery section. The Great Grand Library did not have many books from the human world. She had to wait until some traveler who happened to bring along a paperback dropped it or traded it for a fourth wish or left it carelessly on a bedside table—with the spine split and pages dog-eared! The Library's spies could never stand such abuse. Whenever she heard a book cry out in vain, the Great Grand Library sent someone to liberate it on the double quick. This is just what happens when you cannot find the book you were only just yesterday eagerly reading.

"Agatha Christie!" Ell cried. "Jules Verne! A whole mess of people called Brontë! I've never heard of *any* of these! They definitely sound magical. September! Are these friends of yours? Do you know them? Oh, I want to read all of them!"

But September could not answer. She was busy being glared at with cold ferocity by a gigantic brass ball. The ball, greened over with age, had two suspicious eyes carved into it and a narrow, pinched mouth. Numbers, both Roman and regular, were etched all over the rest of it, framed by a fan of hour hands from an antique clock like a peacock's tail. It could raise and lower itself on a long brass pole in the center of the room.

"Do you have a library card?" the ball hissed down.

"N-no?" September called up.

"Then you are not allowed! Intruder! Brigand! Tourist! Begone or I shall set the book bears on you! Vandal! Hoodlum! Critic!" The brass ball spun furiously round his pole. "Ooh, I'll bet you scribble in the margins, don't you? You fiend! You devil! I can see it in your beady little non-spectacled eyes! You're just the type of monster who uses an innocent book to prop open a door or straighten a table with a wobbly leg. Or maybe you only read magazines? Savage!"

"Oh, get off yourself," barked Blunderbuss. "I've eaten more books than you've shelved in your whole weird pinball life and I enjoyed every last one, thanks very much."

"EATEN?!" screeched the brass ball.

"Yes, eaten! How else do you think a wombat reads? I never trust my eyeballs. I trust my *belly*. Chomp, chomp, chomp, ooh, the vizier did it, what a surprise! Yum, yum, so that's how you build a transistor radio! Bring on the poetry for dessert! Now quit your wheezing and introduce yourself like a civilized person. Ball. Thing."

The brass ball shot down the length of his pole to get a better glaring position. September and Saturday might once have shrunk away from his outraged gaze, but they stood up straight to him.

"I am Greenwich Mean Time, thank *you* very much, Guardian of the Great Grand Library, Overdue Books Reconnaissance Officer, and Chief Babysitter to the Prime Meridian. That's Latitude and Longitude's strapping lad. They go out on the town so much these days—and they'll leave their boy with me until he learns to stop pulling the Equator's tail. I'll ask you not to make any sort of ruckus, or you'll wake him from his nap. And I will also thank you to *leave,* for you have no *card,* and therefore you are *trespassing,* and therefore you are my *enemy*!"

September stepped forward and refused to be shamed. "My name is September, this is Saturday and Blunderbuss. We do not use books as doorstoppers nor scribble in the margins, and we came with a Librarian, a member of the Catalogue.

He's just up there, the bright red fellow scarfing up Jane Austen." September pointed toward the ceiling, where Ell was flipping pages at speed with one delicate claw. He looked up, chagrined, blushing orange. "We are racing in the Cantankerous Derby, and we need your help. Or somebody's help. Where might we find the Reference Desk?"

As Ell descended through the Human section, past Biographies, Autobiographies, and Crypto-Biographies, past Histories, Lies, and Assorted Trickeries and back down into the Mystery Kitchen, one of the airborne study desks detached from its unit and zoomed down after him. An Oxtongue Fairyish Dictionary lay open on it, the pages riffling like propeller blades, its green pull-chain lamp flashing like the lights on the tips of aeroplane wings. They landed neatly side by side.

"No, no! Bad desk!" screeched Greenwich Mean Time. "They don't belong! Don't answer their questions! Get back up there and get ready for Re-shelving Maneuvers!"

But the Reference Desk did not budge. It tilted upward at A-Through-L, thought for a moment, and then purred, rubbing affectionately against his great scarlet leg. A-Through-L reached up under to the patch of rough fur that covered the place where his wing joined his body, where they'd secured their little bit of luggage for the race, since Ell could carry a giant's suitcase and hardly feel a thing. The Wyverary, after a moment's fiddling, produced a large copper shield on a heavy chain. He whirled it round his neck in one practiced movement.

"*I* have a card, Mr. Greenwich," said the Wyverary proudly, "and I am quite sure you will find my account current and in the black, with not so much as a whisker overdue."

The brass ball scowled at Ell's shield, which showed the sharp crescent of Fairyland's Moon resting on its side, full of books, surrounded by a ring of all the letters in the alphabet.

Greenwich sighed flamboyantly. "Oh, very well. I did *so* want to throw someone to the bears today. It's a thankless life I lead! Fine! If you must insist on speaking to me and being alive and wanting things and all that rot, so be it. As I have said, I am Greenwich Mean Time. I safeguard the Library's Time. I am the most precise, the most exact, the most correct timepiece ever born! I was the first colt sired by Piebald, the Stallion of Time, and I came of age in the harsh climes of the Hourglass Waste. I hunted wild chronologies and drank from the Ticking Stream, which turns the wheel of the Bygones Mill. Christopher Wren himself lassoed me while I slept and brought me to Meridian to look after the Library. I hate him for it and love him for it by turns—this is a loving century, but soon I will spit at his portrait again! I keep the Watch. I set the Due Dates and the Hours of Business. My precise and impeccable calculations determine how long any one person with jam on their fingers is allowed to spend in the Special Collections Pantry. My left cheek is tracking the time for the Cantankerous Derby as we speak."

Saturday leaned forward eagerly. "How are we doing? Has anyone won yet? Are we behind or ahead of the pack?"

"Won? Aren't you an impatient little inkblot! There's plenty of time yet for winning and for losing. I would say you're a little behind the pace, though I'm not meant to tell you any such thing. But I do like folk to *know* when they're failing. But I won't say more! No! I alone hold the time! All Fairyland clocks take their measure from me!"

"*All* clocks?" said September sharply, recalling a room in the Lonely Gaol crammed to the ceiling with clocks of every kind, each clock belonging to a human child in Fairyland . . .

"ALL. And don't think your Hourglass has stopped, young lady. *Plink, plink, plink* go the sands!" Greenwich Mean Time laughed cruelly. His clock-hand tail shook with delight.

"I don't know why you need to be *quite* so mean," Saturday scowled defensively.

The brass ball grew serious and quiet. "All time is mean, young man. It takes and does not give, it rushes when you wish it would linger and drags when you wish it would fly. It flows sullenly, only in one direction, when it might take a thousand turns. You cannot get anything back once time has taken it. Time cheats and steals and lies and kills. If anyone could arrest it, they would have time behind bars faster than you can check your watch."

September felt very hot in the dim light of the Mystery Kitchen. *I got something back from time,* she thought. *But it's all jumbled up. When I was old I felt young, I felt myself, as I am now, and whenever I looked into a mirror I got a shock like a bit of lightning in my cheeks. But now that I am young again, I feel old, I feel myself, as I was when I was the Spinster, quite grown up.*

Yes, September. We have all of us got it jumbled up. You never feel so grown up as when you are eleven, and never so young and unsure as when you are forty. That is why time is a rotten jokester and no one ought to let him in to dinner.

"We need to find the Heart of Fairyland," September said. "We thought it might be here, in the middle of everything."

"Well, you're wrong," snapped the brass ball. A bit of the green verdigris on his forehead crumbled off. "Isn't it fun to be wrong? No, it is not. But it *is* fun to watch someone else be wrong."

But the Reference Desk looked up at Ell with its large, innocent green lamp shining. It closed the Oxtongue Fairyish

Dictionary with a heavy *thunk*. When it opened the ponderous book again, it was no longer a dictionary of any sort, but something called *The History of Fairyland: A How-To Guide*. It looked very old but very well cared for, the kind of book that would spend most of its time asleep in a glass case.

"Oh, you vicious little flirt!" breathed Greenwich Mean Time. "They don't even have gloves on! You put that back." The Reference Desk straightened its legs, refusing to be shamed. "Young lady, if you so much as dream of putting a bare finger on one page of that volume I shall have the book bears on you before you can footnote!"

"What are book bears?" said September irritably. "You seem to be very fond of them."

"No one is fond of them," groaned Ell. "When I worked in the Lopsided Library I learned to be vigilant! Once, I stayed up for three days and three nights, armed only with my flame and my claws, to keep them out. All the while I could hear them scratching at the door, fiddling with the window locks, trying to scrabble down the chimneys! I roasted one just as he was ruining a thesaurus."

"But what *are* they, you great red slowpoke?" growled Blunderbuss.

The Wyverary lowered his head so that his dancing orange eyes could get right up close to September. "September, have you ever been reading along in a lovely book, impatient to get to the next exciting bit, when out of nowhere you noticed that some word or other was spelled entirely wrong? Or the quotation marks faced the wrong way? Or came across a scene where a fellow's eyes were suddenly blue, when they'd been green up till now? Or perhaps you wanted very much to know what happened to the lady in plaid from Chapter Three, but the author seemed to have forgotten all about her and you never found out?"

"I suppose," September answered slowly.

"Well, that's all the book bears' fault! All books are born perfect, you see. Sometimes they stay perfect, but really, rather more often than anyone would like, the book bears get to them. They're tiny bears the color of pages with a million teeth and clever claws. They sneak in at night and chew through the pages of a book, gnawing and munching and gulping. They nibble a letter or two out of words and leave behind . . ." Ell shuddered. "*Typos.* They dig into the paragraphs and mix up details so that the fellow with green eyes wakes up one day with blue ones. They chew through plots until the story doesn't hang together quite right anymore. They're a menace! And once a bear has gotten to one copy of a book, they can just tunnel right through to all the other copies, leaving their messes all over the place for poor copy editors to clean up! All Librarians gird themselves against book bears like doctors wear masks to keep out the plague. I've had nightmares! I dream I'm covered in them, and they keep chomping off the letters in my name until I'm C-Through-J and I don't even know what the Barleybroom's called anymore!"

Greenwich Mean Time nodded approvingly. "Quite right! But the Great Grand Library came to a truce with the bears long ago, and now the bears of Meridian only devour our enemies—the untidy, the tardy, and the careless! At one word from me they will swarm over you, gobbling up your continuity, carving up your history, scrambling up the letters of you until you forget how to spell your own soul! I've got a cave full of them in the Satire Cellar and they're *very* hungry."

"We'll be careful," said Saturday, and bent to *The History of Fairyland: A How-To Guide.* "Could we see the H section, please?" he asked the Reference Desk politely. The pages flew. "Hags, Various. Hats, Notable. Hallowmere, Halloween— look, September! You're in here!" September leaned over to see a beautiful illustration of her shadow in the deepest of black inks, dancing on the fields of Fairyland-Below. She blushed, feeling both proud and caught in the act of dabbling with history, which surely carried *some* penalty, somewhere along the way. "Happenstance, Harrowing, Hart, White. Hart, Black. Hart, Red. Hart, Motley. There are a lot of harts in here. I thought they were extinct. Ah. Heart."

September didn't know what she'd hoped to find. A full-color illustration, along with a map, a train schedule, and a packed lunch? Maybe a note congratulating them for being so clever as to look it up in the Library rather than skipping all over deserts and fens prying up rocks to peer under. But the ancient book offered none of these. The entry was short. It had no pictures. Saturday read it out loud:

"Once upon a time, there was a young and beautiful world called Fairyland. Fairyland lived all alone and liked it that way, for it meant she got to go to stay out dancing with the galaxies as long as she liked, eat any travelers she wanted to without cleaning up after herself, and leave the magic on night and day and no one could tell her otherwise. But though Fairyland lived alone, she had many friends: the Sun and the Moon and the Stars, the many Winds, the Four Directions and their cousins the Seasons, Time and the Sea and Fate and Death and Chaos and Physicks and Luck. Each and every one of these loved to get dressed up in their finest costumes and come round for visits. The Sun would sit on the sofa devouring seed cake. Chaos would drink up all the milk while East and West and North and South played cards. The Moon would dance with the Sea and whisper in her ear, and the Winds would dance with Physicks and Death and Fate would argue until their arguing started to look like dancing, too. Time would always try to behave himself, but Luck always got him to laugh. In this way, Fairyland lived happily for eons upon eons, and all she ever worried about was whether or not she had made enough biscuits for all.

"But one evening, Fate brought a guest to meet Fairyland—another world, like herself, but not very like herself at all. The new world was a good guest, and brought presents: a beautiful basket with Change inside. All night long, Fairyland talked to her new friend, asked if his cup needed filling, impressed him with her wild ways and her rough manners and her clever schemes. They danced together on a carpet of snow. Everyone watched, and everyone worried for Fairyland, for this new world was surely a bit of a rake, or else Fate would not have made friends with him. But they felt silly the next morning. For a long while yet, all went along as it always had. Fairyland lived more freely and lushly and joyfully than ever. The new world visited her often, always with gifts, and whenever Fairyland saw her suitor, she smiled and the whole of heaven and earth burst into flame and flower.

"After an epoch or two, however, the new world began to visit less often. When he did come, he was sullen and sorrowful. Finally, Fairyland asked what could be the matter. And he answered:

"'Must you keep your gravity so untidy? It's all rumpled and uneven. Every day I see folk flying about who should walk on the ground! Anyone could shoot up into the air or dive down through the earth at any time, and there's no rhyme or reason to it!'

"'I *like* my untidiness and rumpledness and unevenness!' replied Fairyland, and would not discuss it further. After another era had passed, the new world sighed and said:

"'Must you allow Physicks to run rampant the way you do? It's a ruffian, I tell you, a delinquent! It does what it pleases and obeys no sensible law!'

"Fairyland drew herself up proudly. 'Physicks is my friend, and I love to watch him play. If he vandalizes a thermodynamic or two, what's the harm? They're prettier when he's done with them, anyhow.'

"The new world shook his head and tried to eat his seed cake, but he had lost all his appetite. At last, after a long age in which many things happened, including dinosaurs, Atlantis, and several uninvited comets, the new world tried to coax Fairyland round to his way of thinking once more.

"'Oh, what is it now?' said Fairyland crossly.

"'It's your biology, I'm afraid. I can't bear to see it lying about in lumps and tatters! You've got people with the bodies of horses or dragonfly wings. You've got folk who can grow to great heights and shrink down to nothing anytime they need to reach something from the top shelf. You've got talking rocks and underwater horses and lions with eagle wings. It's unseemly! Please, you must make it listen to reason.'

"Fairyland grew so angry that six new volcanoes twisted up out of her northern reaches.

" 'You are a rake and a rascal and a boring old dunce. How can a world as young as you have such a fusty mind? You cannot order my darling gravity, my beloved biology, or my dear dashing Physicks to do as you say. Have it your own way in your own home, and let me have it my own way in mine. I shall never listen to you on these matters. Go away and never come back!'

"And so the new world slunk away and tried to forget about Fairyland. But he couldn't. He spent most of his time collecting pictures that reminded him of her and telling stories of their adventures to any folklorist who would listen. Nor could Fairyland, proud as she was, forget her old friend. She missed his funny, stick-in-the-mud ways and the way he danced when the harvest came in and all seemed golden and good. As the ages turned ancient between them, Fairyland began to sneak out at night to spy upon that other world.

Occasionally, she would steal a rose from his garden or a nail from his door or even, every now and again, a sunny-faced child who wandered too far from the gate. And in their sleep, each world would sometimes turn over and reach for the other's hand, interlacing their fingers like two sets of forever-turning gears. But when they woke, their hands were always empty once more.

"Fairyland lives happily, but she has never lived quite alone again. This is the sorrow of the human world and the Fairy world, who cannot get along, but cannot part."

Saturday finished and stood back.

"What does all that mean?" asked Blunderbuss.

"It means Fairyland's Heart is broken," came a cool, crisp, disapproving voice.

September spun round to see the Headmistress standing behind them.

CHAPTER IX

I PUNISH, YOU PUNISH, HE OR SHE PUNISHES

In Which September Learns a Spot of Latin, Fights Her First Duel, and Is Banned from the Library for Life

"What are you doing here?" Ell demanded sharply. "No one could have gotten here faster than me!"

The Headmistress rolled her eyes. "You are not the only member of the Catalogue in good standing." She had lost her enchanted school bell at the firing of the starting catapult, of course. But she seemed entirely disgusted with her replacement—a cloud of colored bubbles in the shape of a large and friendly butterfly. It kept trying to wrap its pastel wings around her and nuzzle her ear.

"Ugh! Get away from me, you overgrown cupcake!" the Headmistress snarled. She tried to beat the wings back but the butterfly just snuggled in again to hold her. "It's utterly useless. It belongs to the Happiest Princess—have you met her? She's got hot cocoa for blood and whipped cream for a soul. She's just full of joy and wonder and merriment and she ruled with an army of sherbet ponies and buttercream giants. Oh, but everyone loves her! I tried to bring a little *discipline* and *order* to this bucket of lunatics. I had them up at a decent hour and working toward reasonable personal goals. I got them to eat sensible meals and go to bed early! I gave out detention slips only when *absolutely* necessary and all anyone wants is to go back to Macaroon Mondays and infinite slumber parties! I think she calls this thing Treacle. If I didn't need it to finish the race I'd have set it on fire."

Treacle patted her head with one bubbly wing.

"I am a serious person!" the Headmistress wailed. "I do serious things! This is intolerable!"

Ajax Oddson's voice filled the Mystery Kitchen. A few thrillers trembled from inside the cabinets.

"Do my little eyes spy a pair of Cantankerous Contenders occupying the same square? You know what that means!"

A thunderclap echoed through the Great Grand Library and a number of purple fireworks went off high above them, spelling out the words:

The Wonderful World of Duels

The Reference Desk frantically stamped out any stray bits of violet flame before they could singe a single book. When the sparks faded, a handsome oval frame hung in the air, the sort you might expect to hold a very fine mirror or a portrait of someone whose name no one remembers anymore. This frame did not hold a portrait or a mirror, but rather, Hushnow, the Ancient and Demented Raven Lord. Or at least a doppelgänger of him, sent with love by a nice lady in Mummery named Quintuple Pod. Hushnow squawked loud and long. He appeared to be struggling mightily with his new mount, which September recognized as Penny Farthing's velocipede.

"Curse all bicycles and little girls!" screeched the birdking. "I ate the sun! I'll do it again if I get peckish, just you watch!"

"Hush now, Hushnow," chuckled Blunderbuss, nosing at the cover of *Detective Mushroom and the Case of the Peculiar Pooka* to see if it seemed tasty. Greenwich Mean Time gave her a look so dark even the Ancient and Demented Raven

Lord clammed up. The scrap-yarn wombat let Detective Mushroom lie. "You're meant to referee, you daft parrot!" she yelled. "On you go!"

"Oh! Er. Yes. A duel. That's a fancy word for wedding, is it? All right, all right, don't get your feathers mussed." He cleared his throat. "We have gathered here together to join together the Headmistress and Queen September in holy matrimony . . ."

"No!" cried everyone all together.

"We're meant to fight each other," September said, and not without a spark of fear singeing her voice. "Though I really would rather not. I've never had a duel before, unless you count Martha May at school back home, and I didn't come out well in that."

"Right!" cawed Hushnow. "No one cares! As Officious Officiant, it is my duty to choose your weapons so that neither of you can stick it to the other by picking Complaining or Pulling a Gormless Face or whatever human girls excel at. And I choose—"

"No!" roared Greenwich Mean Time. "No dueling in the Library! Don't you dare! Books are flammable, drownable, rippable, stabbable, and explodable! And very easily shocked! The whole Mathematicks section faints dead away at the sight of blood."

But the Ancient and Demented Raven Lord quite ignored the spluttering time ball. "I choose . . . Latin Conjugations! Turn back to back and walk off ten paces!" Hushnow shook his feathers and eagerly puffed up his chest.

"But that's not fair at all!" protested September. "I don't know any Latin!"

The Headmistress smiled coolly and turned round, showing the back of her gray bustled gown. "But I do, my dear. After all, Latin is a dead language, and I have been dead for ever so long. We've learned to get along terrifically over the centuries. And if I can come back to life, why can't the Roman tongue? I think it's a perfectly fair choice. Hushnow is such a level-headed fellow."

"He's fixed it so you'll win," Saturday glowered.

"If you say so," said the Headmistress, who, after all, cared only for the rules that tipped their hats her way.

"Paces!" squawked Hushnow. His screeching echoed up to the high ceilings of the Mystery Kitchen. "Turn around, you daft monkey! I can't dawdle all day. I'm having a spot of manticore trouble at the moment and this idiot bike is no help at all!" A growl sounded faintly in the distance. Wherever Hushnow was, he was not alone.

September turned around. The Headmistress stood only a little taller than she. Their shoulders touched briefly, and then the Ancient and Demented Raven Lord began counting to ten. "One for sorrow, two for joy! Three for the bites I gave the Changeling boy!"

"But I have no weapons!" hissed September. She could feel it all closing in on her. The duel, the race, the walls of the Library, everything. She'd thought she left feeling helpless behind long ago—only we never leave *helpless* behind. It is a country in which we all hold passports. *I am going to lose,* she thought. *I am going to lose quickly. Though at least I'm unlikely to be killed by a verb.*

A-Through-L arched his long spine. His eyes twinkled at her. "September, I have known you since the only thing you wanted in the world was a slice of cake and I have never once seen you without weapons. At the very least, you always have me. You don't need to know a lick of Latin! I know plenty! *Latin* begins with *L!* Just say what I say!"

September walked back toward her friends, counting her steps. *Losing only means going home, doesn't it? Back to where I came from. I would see Mother and Father and Aunt Margaret again. I would sleep in my own bed.* But a hot desire not to lose stole through September. It burned out everything else. The Headmistress was a tyrant. She'd said so. You stand up to tyrants. That's what all her father's books said.

Did she know any Latin at all? City Hall had a Latin

motto on the front of it. September wracked her memory searching for it. All that she found was that it started with *F*. Saturday and Blunderbuss very much wished they could help, but neither of them had actually heard the word *Latin* before and could not begin to guess what would happen next, except that it would probably be over quickly. Saturday twisted his opal necklace fretfully. He could not even enter the dueling grounds. The air around September and the Headmistress had gone hard as glass.

Hushnow cawed out: "Ten for the crown I'm going to prance around in while you all blubber and moan, see if I don't!"

The Headmistress whirled around, her gray skirts flaring, showing fiery-colored petticoats beneath. Treacle, the butterfly, hovered behind her, and for a moment it looked as though the lady herself had a pair of bubbling wings of every color. She drew a quill pen from her hair and leveled it at September.

"Amo, Amas, Amat!" the Headmistress thundered.

The air before her quivered, then sizzled, then snapped open. Three knights appeared, slender and short and dreamy-eyed. They wore rose-colored armor with blazing hearts painted on their helmets and their shields, for the words the Headmistress had flung at September were *I love, you love, he or she loves*. One carried a sword, one carried a poleax, and one carried a lance. They each had their names engraved upon their magenta-and-gold breastplates: AMO, AMAS, AMAT.

Ell whispered urgently—September did not understand a word he said, but she repeated after her Wyverary, beating her voice into shape, hammering it into something strong and bold and fierce. She'd never made a battle cry before, but she did her best.

"Exsarcimus, Exsarcitis, Exsarciunt!" she cried out. The flying Reference Desks above startled and snapped into formation.

The air before September quivered, then bulged, then parted like a theatre curtain. Three fellows marched out, all very grubby and muscly and ruddy in the cheeks. They wore armor, too, but theirs looked like steel overalls with blazing hammers and needles etched on them, for the words Ell had given September were *We fix, you fix, they all fix.* One carried a pair of screwdrivers, one carried a saw, and one carried a wrench not unlike September's own. They each had their names embroidered on a patch above their hearts: EXSARCI-MUS, EXSARCITIS, EXSARCIUNT.

The soldiers flew at one another. Amo skewered Exsarcitis with his poleax. Exsarciunt fenced Amas deftly, sword against saw. They ranged all over the Mystery Kitchen while Greenwich Mean Time raged against them, flying helplessly up and down his brass pole. Finally, they managed to break each other's defenses at the same instant, and both fell. Exsarcimus twirled her screwdrivers like six shooters and leapt onto Amat, piercing him through the heart on his pink breastplate. All six of them vanished into smoke where they collapsed, no more alive than the dust on an overdue book.

"Castigo, Castigas, Castigat!" screamed the Headmistress.

This time there was no quivering of the air. Her army of verbs seemed to fly directly from her fingers—three soldiers all in black. Their shields showed an awful crest: a child standing in a corner with his hands over his eyes, for the words the Headmistress had parried with were *I punish, you punish, he or she punishes.* One brandished a ruler for the rapping of knuckles, one held a wooden paddle for cruel spankings, and one hoisted a quiverful of forks for the suppers wicked children had to go without. They each had their names pinned to their chests: CASTIGO, CASTIGAS, CASTIGAT.

Ell paused for a moment, thinking furiously. Then, suddenly, he laughed, and the laugh of a Wyverary, terribly pleased at his own cleverness, bouncing off the walls of a library is a wonder to hear. He whispered his magic words quickly into September's ear. This time, he only needed two.

"Vincam! Vincemus!"

Twin warriors burst into thin air. They wore crowns, one of gold and emeralds, one of laurel leaves. They had forged their armor from shining trophies and medals. Garlands and sashes hung from their necks and their shields bore the sigil of a prize ribbon with dozens of ruffles, for Ell's fighting words were *I will win. We will win.* Yet their weapons were nothing like swords and maces. One took aim with a tiny glass dart, dancing with blue light. The other took off her gauntlet to reveal a silvery mechanical hand. They each had their names stitched onto glorious long cloaks: VINCAM and VINCEMUS.

The crowned pair looked pityingly at the Headmistress's punishments. Vincemus did no more than waggle her finger at Castigo and Castigas. Green fire flowed out from her metal knuckles in a thin, sharp jet. *I punish* and *You punish* fell instantly to the ground. Vincam tossed his dart casually, as though he had only dropped it, silly him! But it caught Castigat between the eyes and he vaporized before he could throw a single fork.

A-Through-L had used the future tense. His duelists brought weapons no one would get bored enough to invent for a hundred years. Vincam and Vincemus bowed, first to each other, then to September, shaking her hand, then Saturday's hand, then patting Blunderbuss on the head and punching Ell playfully on the knee. They saluted, clapped each other on the back in a brotherly fashion, and disappeared in a golden fire burst.

The Headmistress had gone both red and black in the face. Tears streamed down her cheeks. "You're a nasty little cheat," she snarled between the hitching of her tears. "You copied off your classmate there. Everyone saw you. You *fail*. You will be held back for eternity! See me after class!"

"Don't be a bad sport, Olivia," crooned Hushnow, the Ancient and Demented Raven Lord. "It's not her fault you don't have a second. Nobody makes friends with the strictest sourpuss in school."

"But I just got here," the Headmistress whispered, whose name was indeed Olivia. Once, long, long ago, before she ever heard the word *Fairyland,* she taught in a very famous school. If I were to tell you what it was called, you would be shocked out of your shoes, and I should get a very stern talking-to from the administration. "I don't want to go back. It's lonely when you're dead and you've only got Latin to talk to."

And we might feel sorry for her—September certainly did. She had gone to the underworld herself, after all. But if only Miss Olivia had decided on a sensible retirement in the

Autumn Provinces instead of trying to become a terrible tyrant once more, then we would instead be telling the story of the kind lady who does her crosswords every morning by the window and likes mugwort cakes for tea, instead of the woman in the gray bustle crumbling before them like the pieces of a shattered eggshell. Tiny dark shapes ran toward her, hurling tiny growls and roars before them. The book bears dove into the Headmistress, trying to get a bite of her narrative before the Dodo's Egg took her back completely, snatching at her syntax and her orderly punctuation until nothing remained but her quill pen lying on the floor of the Library.

September looked away. She could not help it. Even if the Headmistress had only gone back where she'd come from, the sight of it made her want to cry, and she did not want Hushnow or Greenwich to see her do it.

"You've got to take it," cawed the Raven Lord. "The pen. It's your proof of victory. They'll want to count up at the end."

"I don't want it. That's ghastly," September said evenly, quietly.

Hushnow worried his feathers with his long black beak. "Everything good is also ghastly. Your lovely roast chicken dinner was once a live rooster singing up the dawn. Your toasty woolen jumper was cut off the back of a happy sheep.

Even those pretty books I can see behind you—most of them got written by someone as dead as dust and you spend your afternoons dog-earing ghosts. You can ignore the ghastly, but it doesn't go away. Might as well enjoy the good. Even the demented know that. And it's such a nice pen."

September knelt and picked it up. Its feather was deep indigo, its nib silver. She wanted to leave it where it lay. She wanted to go find an empty bookshelf to curl up in and forget the sight of the Headmistress fading to nothing. But instead, she put the quill in her pocket and stood up straight.

"Ta, then!" chirped Hushnow, and his image puffed out like a film ending.

Saturday sighed in relief. His breath ruffled, ever so slightly, the pages of *The History of Fairyland: A How-To Guide.*

"Ow!" he yelped, and snatched his thumb to his mouth.

A book bear rose up on its furry hind legs on the edge of the Reference Desk. It licked its chops, hungry for another chomp of Marid.

"What did I tell you?" sighed Greenwich Mean Time. "You've only yourself to blame. No breathing on the books!"

"It's all right," whispered Saturday. "It's only a little bite. Good luck to that bear if he wants to start chewing through my history. He'll never find his way out again! But, September, we have to go. We can't stay. If the Headmistress got here so quickly, the rest must be far ahead."

If we win, she will stay, the Marid thought desperately, and told no one how his thumb throbbed and hurt.

INTERLUDE

Abracadabra

In Which Aunt Margaret Shows Off

Parents never take quite the same path as their children through any country at all. This is good and right and proper, though it does make for heated arguments on holidays.

Aunt Margaret did not take Susan Jane and Owen through the Closet Between the Worlds. Nor did she lead them out into the wheat fields and cause them to trip over a stone wall into the Glass Forest. Nor did she show them the place in Mr. Albert's weathered fence where the world gets thin and you can hop right through. She did as she had always done: twisted the silver rings on her finger into place, counted to three, said *Abracadabra,* and disappeared. Only this time, she was holding her sister's hand when she did it, and her sister was holding her husband's hand, and though they did not notice in the least, a small and amiable dog was chewing nervously on their shoelaces.

Strictly speaking, Margaret didn't *need* to say abracadabra. She didn't need to say anything at all. But she liked a little dash of theatrical flair in everything she did. She'd said it the first time she traveled under her own steam, and the second, and then never given it up. What our Miss Margaret did not know was that she'd been saying abracadabra as a joke for so long that it had become a magical word. It is certainly possible that, after all this time, the magic that took her to Fairyland had gotten so fond of her joke that it would refuse to let her in without its favorite password. For its own part, the word *abracadabra* very much enjoyed being taken seriously for once. It had had nothing to do but make rabbits go into and come out of cheap top hats for ever so long, even though it came from a language called Aramaic, and therefore had an extremely ancient and noble pedigree.

But Margaret had always said abracadabra and she said it this time. All four of them—Margaret, Susan Jane, Owen, and the dog—faded gently away from the farmhouse outside Omaha, Nebraska, and faded gently into an extraordinary forest throbbing with colors. The trees rose overhead in shades of crimson, tangerine, aquamarine, glittering gold, opal-black. One of the tree trunks was covered with little gloved hands politely offering pots of maple syrup. Bloodred and blood-purple butterflies swarmed over another. Wide, curious green eyes stared from the backs of their wing. Some of the trees burned with a beautiful scarlet fire, and from the flaming trees flaming birds burst up like peacocks startled into fireworks. One even had a Sunday dinner in its branches, porkcones glistening caramelly brown, its cornbread branches oozing butter and honey and mushed peas, its plum pie blossoms dripping crust onto their heads.

"Well, this is new!" exclaimed Aunt Margaret. And it was, for a young girl called Tamburlaine had painted it alive only a little while ago. "This whole forest used to be the very edge of the Tattersall Tundra. I always come out here. How alarming for my poor puppies! They're used to eating nothing but mice and moss. I'll bet they've gotten fat." She put two fingers in her mouth and whistled.

The small and amiable dog felt personally insulted by this remark, and yelped indignantly. Now, it is far past time for me to tell you the dog's name, so I shall do it now and the poor beastie will not have to spend any more pages feeling desperately unimportant. Fenris is a very ferocious name for a pug with a curly tail. But September had given it to him out of her book of mythology when he was a pup and he was very proud of it. There—we'll have no more sad eyes from you, Fenris!

"Oh, Fenny," said Susan Jane, and picked him up, which he liked much better than sitting down in the mud where he could get stepped on. Owen scratched the pug behind his ears. Both September's parents tried not to look too agog at the Painted Forest. They had been to New York City. Owen had seen London and Paris. They were not country rubes. They could handle a tree full of thin Italian daggers. They could handle two moons in the sky. And of course, every girl wants to look just as cosmopolitan as her older sister, even when she is thirty-nine years old and her older sister is forty-three. Susan pocketed a few of the daggers off the tree, for she was a practical woman who liked, better than almost anything, to be prepared.

They could even handle Margaret's puppies—almost.

A team of six hippopotami pulling a grand sled behind them crashed through the brightly colored woods. Yet not a one of them could be called a proper hippo—one was made all of lavender leather with gold stitching, one all of twisted glass and wire, one of hundreds of brass buttons with flowers and anchors stamped on them, one of tarnished silver with a hinge along her back like a scruff of fur, one of deep red cake with white icing, and one that was all over pictures of bones and muscles and diagrams of knee and elbow joints. They bounded toward Margaret and tackled her in a heap, licking her face and making happy, contented hippopotamus noises. The sleigh managed to keep itself out of the mud, but only barely.

"Maggie," September's father cried out. "Are they hurting you?"

September's mother laughed. "Mags always made friends with monsters. Once she found a scorpion hiding in the mailbox and named it Oscar."

Margaret snuggled all the hippos and kissed their noses. "I do miss Oscar sometimes," she said, laughing. "But these aren't monsters. I made them." Margaret could not help feeling proud that her family could see at last that she was not the barmy old scatterbrain they took her for—though Susan had never really thought that at all. "An old thaumaturge named Thimbleneed taught me how. Thaumaturges change things into other things, by and large. But you can't make something out of nothing. There aren't so many laws here, but that's one. And all I had were the things in my school satchel when the Golden Wind brought me over on his jaguar. I named them all after the most mysterious and forbidden things I knew at the time—the bottles in Papa's liquor cabinet." She giggled as though, somehow, she still thought it was a bit naughty. She patted the hippopotamus made of lavender leather. "Vermouth here I made out of my old diary. She's got a lock on one side, see? I cut all the brass buttons off the wool coat Grandmother sewed for me to make Beefeater, who is such a worrywart! I always come back, love, and I always will. Blackstrap is my glasses—Mama was so angry when she thought I'd lost them! But I could hardly say I'd turned them into a hippo. Old Kentucky is quite the fiercest one of the lot—I conjured her up out of a slice of your seventh birthday cake wrapped up in wax paper. I'd saved it to eat after school. Do you remember my old silver locket? I kept a little painting I'd done of you and me and Mama inside. Well, that's Schnapps here, with the hinge on her back. And I suppose it's time to admit I stole Papa's anatomy book. I was fascinated by it. All the pictures! They looked like black magic to me. And in the end I turned it into my darling Pálinka."

The hippos seemed enormously pleased to hear their names and even more pleased to see their Margaret. They rumbled and cooed and whined at her, and she rumbled and cooed and whined back, for Margaret was entirely fluent in hippopotamus. They sniffed Susan Jane's and Owen's hands and Fenris barked a great deal and in a moment or two they were all packed into her sleigh and ready to be off.

My daughter has been here, Susan Jane thought. *My daughter has been here and survived because she is brave and smart. I shall be, too.*

"Where are we going?" asked September's father.

Margaret smiled. "There's a Derby on. We're going to Mummery." She snapped her fingers. "Abracadabra!"

Vermouth, Beefeater, Blackstrap, Old Kentucky, Schnapps, and Pálinka sprang up and dashed out of the forest faster than clouds across the sky.

CHAPTER X

Journey to Mumkeep Reef

In Which Saturday Goes Home, Leaves a Wombat and a Wyverary Alone, Though on a Very Nice Beach, While September Meets Both a Bathysphere Named Fizzwilliam and an Alarming Number of Octopuses

Blunderbuss dug in her woolly heels.

"Nope. No, thank you! Not an inch farther till we eat! I know it's a race but we won't go far if we start skipping meals. Top athletes eat more than anybody, that's the truth. If you don't have dinner, you don't have anything!"

Reluctantly, September and Saturday laid out their

supper under the hundred million stars of Meridian. They congratulated themselves on their practical planning as they set out the plates, the salt and pepper, the bowls and the cups. They'd packed a blanket as well, so that nothing got damp or dirty. For A-Through-L they had a basket of good bitter radishes and a number of lemons, alongside a cold joint of mutton swiped from the Briary stores. Saturday helped himself to a luckfig bun and a parrot pie from the Plaited Plaza carts. September dug through their satchels until she came up with some oranges, arugula, and cinnamon biscuits for Blunderbuss, who also helped herself to most of the clover and nodding little bluebells growing round their picnic blanket.

But for the Queen of Fairyland, for the Engineer, there was only roast legislamb cutlets, gruffragette salad, and somewhat lukewarm regicider. In the early hours before the Derby began, September had filled a hamper with her royal suppers and breakfasts, each wrapped carefully in wax paper or poured into small, sturdy flagons that would not leak. She still wore the crown—she hardly even felt it anymore. But as long as it stayed on her head, she had to make certain the Greatvole and the Wickedest Whale kept dreaming away and not doing whatever dreadful things they waited so eagerly to accomplish. If those meals had ever tasted nice, they certainly did not once they'd gone cold and traveled a thousand miles by

Library Catalogue. September sighed and chewed on her rather tough, rubbery cutlets.

"Is your thumb all right, Saturday?" September did not want him to see her worry, for when she was afraid, he got afraid, which made her more afraid still, until they both had to go and sit down in the sun for a while so they did not egg each other on so much.

"I'm sure it's fine," the Marid said, and neither did he show a wick of worry on his face. "It doesn't hurt. It was only one bear, after all. I expect I'll suffer no worse than a stray exclamation point dangling off my name. Saturday! Sounds rather bombastic, doesn't it?" But it did hurt. It burned in the dark.

Blunderbuss rolled one of her oranges between her paws playfully, wriggling her haunches. She lobbed it over to Ell, who nudged it back bashfully. "So Fairyland has a broken heart. Poor poppet. But what does that mean for us? Is the Heart in pieces, then? Off crying in different corners, playing sad saxophone music and writing poems? Two pieces? More?"

September sipped her regicider and made a face. It tasted thin and sour. "I think it might mean just that, Blunderbuss. If it means anything."

Saturday sat up, rubbing his bare blue arms with his hands. "But there has to be a solution—there has to be a

Heart to find. Ajax Oddson would never cheat. I'll believe trickery of anything in Fairyland, but Oddson wouldn't put his hand in if there wasn't a way to win. And I had an idea, while I was reading that story in the Library. An idea about where to go next. Only—" The Marid's shoulders slumped in the starry shadows. The Wolf's Egg rose over his beautiful shoulders. "Only it's a little bit selfish. And maybe I'm wrong. Maybe I just want to go home. I can't tell if I'm on to something or I'm just homesick. We haven't got much time for mistakes."

"Home?" asked Ell.

"In the story, one of Fairyland's friends was the Sea. The Moon danced with the Sea and whispered in her ear, remember? And I thought perhaps . . . perhaps the Sea knows where Fairyland's hid her broken heart. Perhaps Fairyland hid her heart down there. Because you can hide anything under the ocean. The Sea knows more secrets than any of us will keep if we lived to be as old as longing. And the Sea's mysteries aren't just words or books or locks of hair tied with a ribbon. They're a place. Mumkeep Reef, down deep in the dark blue barrens of the Obstreperous Ocean. Whenever the Sea finds something she likes, in a pirate ship or a hurricane or a nereid's hideaway, she makes off with it immediately and stashes it in Mumkeep Reef. I've never spoken of it to a . . . a dryhair.

That's what we call people who don't have the good sense to live in the ocean. Or the good gills. Mumkeep Reef is the kind of secret that secrets hope to be when they grow up. You can't ever tell anyone I told you. Even if we don't give it another thought between us. You can't even say the word *Mumkeep* to a dog."

"We would never!" cried Ell, quite offended at the idea.

"When I was a child, my mother took me to see it. She let me stay and play there for days and days. In the turtleshell vaults and the captains' chests and the safes with the hexacoral locks. The crabs and the starfish and the shipwrecks and the leviathans whispered with me until I fell asleep and my mother carried me home. What I mean to say is, we could go there. I could take you there. It's the best place to keep a secret. Meridian is not so far from the ocean. I can hear it. I can smell it. The waves are laughing. But I could be wrong! I could be wrong and we could end up so far behind and the Marquess probably has the Heart by now anyway. I don't want to be wrong. Not when it's this important."

September watched Saturday talk. She loved to watch him talk—the way his eyebrows moved when he meant something sincerely, the way his mouth twitched when he knew something he wouldn't say, the way he tugged on his topknot when he felt too shy to interrupt but so badly wanted to interrupt that he felt his thoughts coming out of the top of his head. Once, he could hardly get through a sentence without apologizing for it. But you can't stay bashful once you've joined the circus, and he'd learned his voice on the high trapeze.

Still, it was easy to forget that Saturday was not simply a human boy with blue skin. That he had never seen a blackboard or a snowplow or an office building, just as she had never seen a shipwreck or a leviathan or a reef. He was far stranger even than Ell or Blunderbuss. For Marids lived in every direction at once, like the currents and eddies of the sea. A Marid might meet his future or his past walking down any street on any morning, whether or not he had had his coffee yet. They had met his older self on the Moon once, and September had felt as though she might shake apart at the sight of Saturday standing beside himself as though nothing at all could be the matter. They were almost the same age, but even when she had been the Spinster, Saturday had always seemed so much older and so much younger than she.

"Your home is near Meridian?" she said softly.

"Well, if you mean the place where I was born, no. Not even a little. Do you know when we got closest? It's funny. When the Marquess locked Ell and me into the Lonely Gaol, I could hear the seals barking in my old neighborhood. But look—can't you see? The silver light where the land meets the sky. That's the ocean. It's only a few miles. And if we can get to the shore without too much trouble, I can summon a Bathysphere in two clicks of a dolphin's tongue. But if I'm wrong, it could cost you the Derby and you'll never be Queen and you'll vanish again, like all the lights going off."

Saturday put his blue hand over his mouth. He hadn't meant to say all that. But he wasn't sorry he had. So he smiled, to show he was glad of having told the truth.

"I'm just sure I'm wrong all the time," September said softly, and she put her hand on his knee. "But I always do it anyway. It's a good plan."

Death herself could not say no when Saturday smiled.

Meridian lies in the warm, wafty lands below the Tropic of Scorpio. Winter snow only comes once every five years, and when it visits, you cannot imagine a more cheerful, polite guest. It brings gifts of ice and Christmas pudding, tidies up after itself without having to be asked, and never overstays its welcome. The moment anyone begins bellyaching about shoveling the walk, Winter has already fetched its hat and coat from the rack in the hall. So the beach that Saturday sought was not a stony, gray, and frozen bluff, though that would have been very romantic in a certain sort of way. They flew through the night, rather than lose time walking over the miles of berry brambles, mango forests, and chartreuse sand dunes. September clung to Ell's back while Saturday gripped Blunderbuss's woolly flanks with his knees, and everyone felt very clear on the point that none of this made anyone a steed, it just made them sensible with their resources and admirably efficient people.

The morning sea rolled in, blue and violet with little sharp eddies of pink and green sizzling along through the breakers. Waves crashed and rippled onto a beach that had only once felt cold, in a nightmare when it was young. Coconut trees bent low with fruit. Thirsthorn thickets crowned high dunes like unkempt golden hair, their fruit sloshing with fresh water. Crystal floatberry bushes grew as close as they could to the surf. The first floatberries grew in the rich cumulus fields of Cloud Cuckoo Land, carefully tended by clockwork falcons. The rest of them are always trying to get back home, twisting and curling drifting up into the air, joyfully drinking up the sea mist. The black sand beneath September's and Saturday's toes crumbled so soft and fine it felt like walking on top of a chocolate cake. September could not help reaching down and running her fingers through it.

Saturday bolted into the waves, leaping up in the air, spinning round twice, and plunging into the foam and the tide. He stayed down for ages and ages, far longer than September could, even on her best day at her best swim meet. When he finally came up again, he looked quite different. September realized that in all the time she had known the Marid, she had never once seen him at ease. Not really. Now that he had his ocean around him, every tiny part of him relaxed. He matched the ocean world like one shining button in an endless, flowing blue coat.

"Watch this!" Saturday grinned. He crouched down, balancing on the pads of his bare blue feet. He made a little coaxing, shushing, trilling noise in the back of his throat. "Come on, then," he said gently, sweetly, as though calling a kitten stuck up in a tree.

The Marid stroked the sand softly—and seashells sprang up under his fingers. Hot-pink scallop shells shone wetly against the jet-black sand. Turquoise cockleshells rose up, too, and lemony-bright hermit crab shells, spiny tangerine conches, little spiraling brindled snail shells, spotted cowrie shells, and big bronze geoduck shells. (A geoduck is a terrifyingly large and opinionated clam that lives both in Fairyland and, curiously, in the part of the world where your intrepid narrator was a child.) Saturday clapped his hands, pleased with himself, for he had felt just the teensiest bit uncertain that it would work. He hadn't done it in so long.

Saturday pressed his fingertips against the shells like the keys of a very odd piano. His hands flew over them, tapping in some sort of order that September could not guess at. Each shell yelped when he touched it, but their yelps sounded like whale songs and buoy bells bonging away together. When he finished, the waves began to churn and froth and bubble. Something glassy broke the surface, and kept on breaking until it broke free.

"What did I tell you? A Bathysphere, scrubbed up and ready, just for us."

It was a bathtub.

A burly, walloping bathtub, bronze and deep and wide, with fierce claw feet. The back of the thing rose high up so that you could rest against it, and a curving glass dome closed in the Bathysphere so that dryhairs like September could ride inside and not drown.

"We won't fit in there," Blunderbuss said doubtfully. "And anyway I'm made of wool. If I go swimming, I'll shrink. And I like being big! I've gotten used to it already because it is the best and I am also the best so I ought to be big."

A-Through-L nodded vigorously. "Shrinking is the most dreadful thing," he said from experience. "It feels like disappearing. You lose yourself, inch by inch. Don't do it, Buss."

"We'll stay," the scrap-yarn wombat said firmly. "You go paddle about in your supersecret lair of secretness and we'll just lie out in the sun and discuss Agatha Christie and eat coconuts—ALL THE COCONUTS."

"Are you certain you'll be all right?" September said. "I don't want to leave you! Awful things happen when we're apart, Ell. What if one of the other racers comes and you have to duel?"

The wombat and the Wyverary leapt up into the sky together, circling, jostling, bonking their heads together, and tumbling back down laughing. The ground shook. "Look at us! We'd knock down the sun if it gave us the side-eye!" Blunderbuss rolled around in the sand, kicking her stubby feet into the air.

Ell shrugged down their traveling bag so that September could pack herself the royal supper, just in case. "Besides, you're the racer, September. If Tanaquill or Crunchcrab come whinging by, we'll just wave and have another coconut. If you're not here, Meridian's an unoccupied square."

I have read a number of stories in which the hero strides boldly and bravely into the next adventure, never once turning to look back. September looked back several times. Over her shoulder, over the lip of the Bathysphere, once or twice turning completely around and opening her mouth to speak, to say that she'd thought of some way to cram them all in—but she hadn't thought of it, and couldn't say much of anything. This was their only lead. If they didn't go to Mumkeep Reef, they might as well give up and go see what was playing at the cinema in Pandemonium.

"Please be here when we get back," September whispered instead.

A-Through-L beamed at her, flaring his crimson wings in the sunshine.

"I am always here when you get back, small fey. Haven't you learned anything?"

The Bathysphere picked up its clawfeet like a prancing stallion and clopped into the rippling water. It was quite roomy enough for September and Saturday to sit side by side. Each of them could reach the controls—a bank of bronze brush-handles, soap spigots, hot and cold taps, squeeze bulbs like the ones on old-fashioned bottles of perfume, and several dials showing depth, water pressure, distance to destination, and temperature.

Without thinking, September reached out and picked up two polished pearl soap dishes. She held one to her ear and spoke into the other:

"Mumkeep Reef, please."

Then, she pushed the down-bubble-bath brush forward, slowly but confidently. The Bathysphere surged over the continental shelf of Fairyland and sank pleasantly into the free ocean.

"What are you doing?" cried Saturday. "I haven't told you how to drive it yet! You could have grabbed the wrong nozzle! I'm sorry, I'm sorry, I don't mean to snap," he said hurriedly, and caught her hand up in his. "You frightened me, is all! You were made for the sky and the grass and the open plain—the Sea can hurt you so much more than she can hurt me. How did you know what to do?"

September stared at him.

"The Bathysphere told me. Didn't you hear?"

"I didn't hear anything, Tem," Saturday answered, and he did not like his answer one bit. His eyes filled up with worry like tide pools. September had always been so wonderfully bullheaded. She didn't imagine things or make jokes at his expense. "Perhaps the Derby is too much, the pressure of it . . . perhaps we need to sleep."

But September refused to nap. She stared hurtfully at him. The moment the glass dome had closed over their heads, a clear, bright voice had spoken and explained everything. It *had*. She wasn't hearing things.

"Well, the Bathysphere wished us a good morning, told

us to keep our hands and feet inside him at all times, and asked where we were off to this fine day. Also his name is Fizzwilliam. He comes from a large family in the P&P— that's Perverse and Perilous, I'd guess. He's the middle child, but he got quite a lot of love from all sides. He lost a sister in the mer-wars and thinks of her every year around this time. Oh, and he likes jellyfish for his suppers and his favorite color is yellow, but not that nasty sickly yellow some sea sponges have, the smashing bright yellow of bananafish."

Saturday frowned deeply. "September, Bathyspheres don't talk. Marids invented them—so we could invite friends to tea without killing them. Marids have a terrible habit of falling in love with dryhairs." He blushed, a deeper blue.

"Sure they talk! Or this one does! Saturday, I sat down and Fizzwilliam piped up at once! And then I looked at the controls and it just made *sense* that the dishes were meant for talking back to him and the down-bubble-bath brush was the one on the left. You brake with the handle on the right and reverse with the one in the middle, and you steer with the hot and cold taps. Am I right? I *am* right. How would I know all that about Fizzwilliam's family if he hadn't told me?"

What did it matter, if they were speeding on ahead? If she was happy, and trying to win, trying to stay? But Saturday could not help arguing. Some people must always argue, or they don't feel right in their skin. "You could have made it up. To tease me."

September gave him a pointed look. "When have I ever fibbed to you, Mr. Suspicious? I even told you the truth about my First Kiss, and I didn't have to do that at all. I always tell you the big, snagged-up truth."

A cloud crept into Saturday's eyes. "Your First Kiss? When was that?"

September punched his shoulder playfully. "Ha-ha. Your shadow kissed me without asking when I met him in Fairyland-Below. You must remember. I gave you my Second Kiss right away. You got my Third Kiss, too. But you asked. You wrote on a little card in blue ink: *I should like to kiss you if you want to be kissed, and you like me in a kissing kind of way, and not only in an adventuring way.*"

"Yes, of course I remember," Saturday murmured, and rubbed the tops of his arms, as he did whenever he got nervous. "I was very careful with my penmanship." But he didn't sound certain about it at all.

September sighed and looked out into the bubbling turquoise water, growing deeper and darker blue as they sank, streaming ahead toward Mumkeep Reef. "I do wish we could go faster! The Derby will go on without us up there and I'll bet the Rex Tyrannosaur can run frightfully quick. Oh!

Fizzwilliam says that if we look out the port side, we can see the county of Ys, which used to cozy up to the east coast of Fairyland, but got in a quarrel with the Pickapart Mountains and huffed off to have its own fun on the ocean floor."

"Bathyspheres don't *talk*," Saturday repeated stubbornly.

"Well, maybe you just never bothered to talk to them," September said, more snappishly than she would have liked. But she *could* hear Fizzwilliam! His voice sounded fresh and clean and warm, with a little saucy lilt to it, as though Fizzwilliam had seen many things in his life, and most of them shocking. She heard it as loudly as Saturday's. She stared out the window at the lights of Ys, a shimmering web of street lamps like miniature castles, marquee lights in the theatre district advertising the opening night of *A Midsummer Night's Bream*, and well-dressed lanternfish strolling to work with important papers tucked under their fins. Both of them brooded separately, until September decided to change the subject so that they could brood together.

"You talk about the Sea in such a familiar way. I can hear you put a capital letter on it!"

"Well, she is my grandmother. She's all Marids' grand-mother. I suppose you know your grandmothers well?"

September picked at the hem of her emerald-colored smoking jacket. The jacket did not mind. "One of them. The other one died before I was born. It must be nice, to have a grandparent who can never die."

"She's not all warm currents and friendly whales. The Sea is very old and very set in her ways and very . . . particular about her housekeeping. She's a terrible hoarder. She steals everything she can get her waves on and she won't let go of even one doubloon, so it gets terribly cluttered. No one's ever dared to try to take anything out of Mumkeep Reef."

"The grandmother I know, that's on my father's side, she hates anyone touching her things. She doesn't trust the banks anymore, so she keeps all her money and anything else valuable in a tin box under her bed and she says if anyone tries to swipe it she'll tie a sheriff round their necks and throw them in the river. I do miss her awfully. And my father. And even the teacups in the sink."

"That's just how it is with mine," said Saturday, all happiness again, eager to change the subject.

"Do we mean to take something, then?" September asked.

"If there's something to take. I'll apologize at Abyssmas dinner. We've always been her favorites, we Marids. She'll forgive me. Probably. I should bring her a box of corsairs. They're her favorite."

"Will it be difficult?"

"I don't know. I've never stolen anything before." And Saturday gave her a circus-boy grin, a *hey-watch-me-do-a-trick* sidelong something that September loved best of all his hundreds of smiles.

September sat up very straight. "Fizzwilliam says he loves us and wants us to be safe and also he has sighted several unsavory creatures below us, port and starboard. He does not love *them*."

Saturday sighed. "That will be the Pieces of Eight. I didn't want to say. I thought they might have gotten lazy and would just let us steam past. I didn't want you to worry. It'll be all right! They're only mostly furious."

"What does any of that mean?"

"The Pieces of Eight guard Mumkeep Reef. The Octopus Assassins. A very ancient guild. Masters of the Octopunch and the Luminous Eight-Armed Thrill-Throttle. They're actually nonapuses—nine arms. But when they pass their initiations, they always come out of the Grueling Grotto with eight. No one knows the fate of the ninth arm. It is one of their marauding mysteries."

Saturday reached forward and pressed one of the bronze soap spigots on Fizzwilliam's dash. It was all over before September could ask where Saturday was going: a hatch opened in the glass dome, Saturday snatched one of the pearl dishes, shot up out of the Bathysphere and into the open sea, and the hatch sealed up again, leaving September alone and only slightly drenched.

She pressed her nose to Fizzwilliam's glass dome. All below her, spread out across the ocean floor, lay Mumkeep Reef. Coral branched and braided and knotted and sprawled, forming itself into a maze of staircases and grottos, spires and catacombs, peaked huts with the lights on inside, pits and vaults and great fields of waving anemones like a siren's long hair. On every prong or shard of coral September saw a ship skewered, galleons and skiffs and dhows, even a few Bathyspheres like theirs. And everywhere else lay rusted boxes teeming with barnacles, bottles crammed full of unread messages, steamer trunks packed long ago with love and lost at sea, lockers and safes and cabinets and caskets. And treasure chests, the very kind every pirate draws in his notebook while his teacher tries to get him to agree that *i* comes before *e* except after *c*. Saturday darted and dove above the reef, swimming as easily as September could laugh.

But in and among all these locked-up, gnarled, crumbling wonders, she saw hundred of glass jars. Jar after jar after jar, every one open and every one aimed at them like an angry cannon.

And every one filled with a furious octopus.

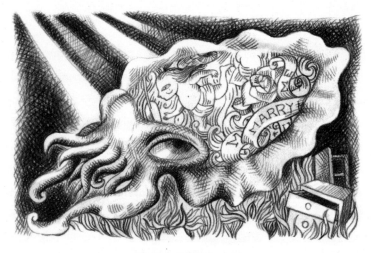

CHAPTER XI

THE TATTOOED PENGUIN

In Which September and Saturday Tell a Lie to Avoid Death by Octopus, Meet an Out-of-Work Cuttlefish, Take in a Show, and Get Matching Tattoos

Four Pieces of Eight fired themselves at Saturday, exploding out of their jars, cannons of fiery-colored, tentacled hate.

"HALT!" trumpeted the lead octopus, a stream of bubbles punctuating her sentences.

Saturday came up short, floating in the deep blue sea, everything lit by the unearthly glow of Mumkeep Reef.

"Not you," the Octopus Assassin sneered. "I have no quarrel with you, Marid. Enjoy your visit to Mumkeep, leave a donation in Anne Bonny's skull—you'll find it over by the wreck of the *Revenge*." The octopi fell into formation around September's Bathysphere, flaring their fiery limbs, ready to drag her down at one word from their captain. "Her. How dare you bring a dryhair here? I can smell the dirt on her from here. She does not belong! She's already seen more than any dreary two-arm should!"

The others snapped their sharp cerulean beaks at her. They fanned out, whipping the water into white foam. The Bathysphere clanged and shuddered as an octopus lashed its tentacles around the glass dome. Another wrapped its arms around the bronze bottom of the tub. They began to drag Fizzwilliam down, down, down to the sharp crags of Mumkeep. September yelped, gripping the broom handles, trying valiantly to pull up. All she could hear was Fizzwilliam's terrified, chattering cries as he tried to jerk free of the marauders.

"Drown her!" one hissed.

"Crack that tub like an abalone!" bayed another.

"If she can breathe water, she can stay. If not? Too bad!"

"Pull her out and give her the Luminous Eight-Handed Thrill-Throttle!" They all agreed.

The Bathysphere crunched into the plain of anemones.

September could feel Fizzwilliam's bruises and bent clawfeet. "We'll get you free and safe again," September promised him. "You'll see your brothers and sisters again and they won't even notice the dents!" Fizzwilliam assured her in his gleaming voice that it was not in the least her fault. He should have asked for anti-octopus modifications for Abyssmas.

The leader swirled over the top of the Bathysphere. She snapped her tentacles together and flung them out again in fury. "I am Hugger-Muggery, High Assassin of the Pieces of Eight! I personally throttled Scylla, Charybdis, and Mr. David Jones and they thanked me for the privilege! You have but two choices, biped! Come into the open water and show me you are a creature of the Sea, even though you've got dirt and drought written all over you, or let me in." She coiled and uncoiled those flame-bright tentacles to show that September would not enjoy it if she chose the latter.

"She will do no such thing," Saturday said.

"Don't make a ruckus in your grandmother's house, Marid!" Hugger-Muggery's huge, round black eyes narrowed in her bulblike head. "She likes her quiet. She does not like clumsy cows chewing on her china!"

"I'm not a cow!" September said finally. It is very hard to get a word in edgewise with octopi. They love to talk. Only manatees love it more.

Hugger-Muggery dismissed her with one tentacle. "All dryhairs look the same. Cow, cheetah, wallaby, who cares?"

"September has every right to visit Mumkeep," Saturday continued as though no one had said a single thing—though September could hear the tremble in his voice. "She is my wife. By law, she owns half my secrets. I have brought her to meet my grandmother. Isn't that what a good grandson does?"

September held her breath. She was not anyone's wife, thank you very much. But the way Saturday said it, *wife* sounded like something exciting, something daring, something a bit scoundrelly, like *pirate* or *bandit*. And they were bandits, of course. Come to steal the Heart of Fairyland.

The Pieces of Eight stared in at September. "She's not your wife," Hugger-Muggery finally said. "Where's her tattoos?"

Saturday rolled his eyes to show how little he cared for the objections of octopi. "She can't get tattooed without the cuttlefish's approval, you soft-headed bully. We've only just wed. In the Autumn Provinces, in the Worsted Wood. I put a wreath of kelp round her neck, and she painted her name upon my eyelids. She wore green; I wore blue. We danced for three days, my wife and I—along with a Wyverary, a wombat, a Dodo, a family of trolls, a matchstick girl, a gramophone, a whole gang of shadows, a Yeti and his dog, a talking lamp, Winds of every color, a wairwulf and both his wives. Seventeen versions of me were there, along with her parents and mine and a pooka and Ajax Oddson, the greatest Racemaster who ever lived. We told each other our true names and fell asleep among our friends, covered in moonlight and the silver comfort of the right ending. She is my wife and I am her own and you were not invited. Leave us alone."

September's heart shook within her. The way he spoke sounded strange to her. It did not sound like a lie. It did not sound like a clever trick played with sly glee. It did not have his circus grin peeking out on one side. It sounded just the way it did when her father told someone how he had married her mother. It sounded like a memory. But it had never happened. Of course it had never happened! They'd never even met a troll before Hawthorn came galumphing into the Redrum Cellar. She would remember painting her name on anyone's eyelids, let alone Saturday's delicate blue lashes. But she knew his voice like her own, and somehow, she knew he wasn't lying to the furious eight-armed assassins. And September remembered the little girl they'd seen that long-ago night on the Gears of the World, the girl with pale blue skin and a mole on her left cheek. Saturday had called her their daughter, come to visit them in the past as Marid children always do. September could hardly speak.

"Did you truly marry a saber-toothed tiger?" the Octopus Assassin asked Saturday incredulously.

"I'm not a saber-toothed tiger," said September through gritted, non-saber teeth.

"Close enough!" snapped Hugger-Muggery. "If you're hitched, she won't mind letting the cuttlefish ink her properly."

"That's why we came," Saturday lied boldly.

"Only take us quickly," September said. "We haven't much time."

Hugger-Muggery narrowed her watery eyes. "What's the hurry, hm?"

The Cantankerous Derby, September thought. *My crown running away from me.* The thought surprised her. *She touched the circlet of jeweled keys on her head. If it is my crown. Maybe there is someone better, in all that crowd in the Plaited Plaza. Hawthorn and Tamburlaine, or Sadie Spleenwort, or the Green Wind. Oh, I wish I were back in the Redrum Cellar! I couldn't leave, but I knew what was right and what was wrong!*

But she lied along with Saturday: "No hurry! I'm just . . . eager to meet a real live cuttlefish!"

The Octopus Assassin snorted bubbles. "Dryhairs. We will escort you, obviously. I never trust anyone with greater or fewer limbs than myself. How can I? I see the world in eights—eight directions, eight seasons, eight virtues, and eight deadly sins. Eight is holy! Eight is supreme! Who knows how a bear like you sees? In twos, for your weak arms? In fours, for arms and skinny legs together? Your ugly hard head makes five extremities, but then you have ten fingers and ten toes. In your murky mind, are there ten seasons? Twenty directions on a compass rose? There can never be peace between us! The best we can hope for is . . . curiosity. I have only felt curiosity for one dryhair in my life—Woofwarp, the Spider-Monk of the Torii Orchards. He was the boiling hot green of an emperor tetra fish and his venom could lay waste to a thousand fugu! I taught him our ways and he taught me the devastating Flying Snowstorm Spinneret Strangler. We saw the eights of the universe eye to eye to eye to eye. But I had to abandon him. He would not leave his rickety orange gates for the excitement of Ys or even the mysteries of Mumkeep. So what? I don't cry about it! Only dryhairs cry. When they feel hurt, they stop fooling themselves that anyone can truly survive on land and the Sea pours out of them. It's beautiful, but they forget quickly. Dryhairs come and go like punches in the wind! Only the Sea lasts!"

Hugger-Muggery shot forward through the water like an eight-armed orange bullet. When she drew up her tentacles, she looked like a flower. When she snapped them back again, she became a spear. The other Octopus Assassins dragged the Bathysphere along behind, even though September kept trying to explain that Fizzwilliam would be more than happy to provide his own propulsion. They ignored her with the kind of brute force only an octopus can muster.

September could see a hundred things she wanted to investigate pass by on the ocean floor below. How could so many ships have wrecked in the whole history of the world? After half so many, September thought people might have considered giving up the naval life. Strange fish moved between safes and lockers and sunken chests of drawers. Their snouts and gills glowed in brilliant shades of purple or yellow or electric blue, but they wore robes spun from rough brown kelp, belted with ropes from the riggings of all those dead ships. Fizzwilliam gave up on convincing the Pieces of Eight to let him drive his own self. He told her that the creatures in robes were monkfish. They tended the vast loot of Mumkeep Reef, kept an accurate count, and formed a number of societies to discuss the best pieces and what they might mean, as well as to drink a great deal of brine brandy and tell jokes about squid.

"We ought to talk to them," September whispered. "Surely, they'd know where to look for Fairyland's Heart."

Fizzwilliam laughed. When a Bathysphere laughs, it sounds like water trickling down through a golden drain. He would not explain what he found so funny, but I shall tell you. The idea that a Monkfish would answer any question put to it is quite, quite absurd. They speak only in riddles—well, that's fine enough! Most monks do. But a Monkfish speaks only in the *answers* to riddles, and this makes them intolerably annoying. All wise fish avoid them.

The cuttlefish lived in a dark, pitted corner of Mumkeep Reef. Dragon-eye coral twisted up into sloping, pointed shapes very much like a certain opera house in Australia that would not be built for many years yet. (All coral in every world think of Australia the way that you and I think of Mesopotamia—it is the ancestral paradise of their civilization and they send it Valentines each February.) Orange cup corals held little scraps of light like lime peels. Peach-colored staghorn corals snaked out into shelves, ladders, and baskets full of glass pots of green-blue cuttlefish ink. Inside the coral opera house rested a gargantuan cuttlefish, her great sad W-shaped eyes rimmed with incandescent ultramarine like spectacular eyeliner. But cuttlefish eyes only *look* sad. It's the shape that does it. But they are secretly the happiest of all cephalopods—only no one believes it, for they always look as though they were about to burst into tears from the weight of all the sorrow in the world. But truthfully, they were probably just thinking of an especially rude joke.

Unless you are a sushi chef or a marine biologist, you have probably never seen a cuttlefish. September certainly hadn't. Up till then, she had thought orca whales or perhaps the Portuguese man-of-war she had seen in one of her father's books were the prettiest things that lived in the sea. In one second, on the far north cropping of Mumkeep Reef, she changed her mind.

A cuttlefish has a head like a particularly soft, glum, toothless crocodile. Really, they've got a great lot of short tentacles for a face, but that frightens people and puts them off their dinner, so they hold them all together to look friendlier when company happens by. A cuttlefish has a body like a lovely colorful teardrop-shaped blanket with graceful veils running all round the border. They've got stripes like zebras, three hearts, and best of all, they can be any color they like at any time. The skin of a cuttlefish is like a screen in a cinema, and they can show anything they please on their big, silky backs. (In fact, it's on account of an encounter with a cuttlefish that the Marquess acquired her kaleidoscope hair—though it was terribly embarrassing for her and she made me swear not to tell.)

We have cuttlefish in our world, of course. But they all came from Fairyland, just the way your restless narrator came from the west coast of her country, but made her house on the east coast of it. Nothing like cuttlefish can happen without magic. Cuttlefish are extremely intrepid explorers, and they came to our oceans seeking newer, ruder jokes and found they liked it quite well. September thought something that handsome ought to have a fancy name, like the Reef and the brass ball in Meridian and even she herself did. But a cuttlefish is such an astonishing thing that giving them a frilly title would be as silly as a peacock wearing a ball gown.

A Monkfish with a face colored like candy canes walked peacefully among the coral. You'll notice I did not say he swam. He used his brawny tail to walk in a shuffling fashion, the way human monks sometimes do. He had once been told by a fisherman that it was much holier to move that way. Honestly, that fisherman had gone a bit mad. But if you squint, you can see it his way: Whatever is hardest is often holiest.

"Hello," September said shyly. Radiant things made her shy in the same way that selfish things made her cross. Probably the cuttlefish couldn't even hear her inside Fizzwilliam.

The cuttlefish answered by rearranging the lights on her lovely striped skin into a glimmering image, all fuzzy at the edges: an ultraviolet child running up to a neon yellow child and leaping into their arms so hard they both fell over into an absinthe-colored puddle. *Hello.*

Saturday smoothed his topknot without quite knowing he'd done it. Everyone wants to impress cuttlefish, which is perfectly all right because cuttlefish love to be impressed. She turned her glittering, mournful eyes to the Marid. He longed to stroke the creature and tell it all was well, really it was. "I want you to meet my wife, September," he said in a voice too soft to bruise the sensitive creature any further.

How far will we have to go with this? September thought. *I've only just made it back to seventeen years old—I don't want to accidentally trip and fall and get up married.*

The cuttlefish's skin flushed pale, erasing the leaping neon children. Several images flickered by: a vermilion hand with a ring on the left finger, a coppery Fairy leaping over a broom, an azure arm with tattoos snaking around it. *Weddings are nice.*

Hugger-Muggery tapped her tentacles impatiently against the staghorn coral. "Get *on* with it! Poseidon save me from the slowness of hedgehogs. She came to get inked."

September rolled her eyes. "For crying out loud, I'm not a hedgehog. That's not even close!"

The Octopus Assassin squinted her bulging eyes. "Are you sure?"

"Yes!"

The other flame-bright octopi released the Bathysphere from their snaking arms. Fizzwilliam floated free. September could feel his relief tingling in her hands and feet. Saturday kicked his long legs twice and drew up close. He put his cobalt hand on the glass of the Bathysphere.

"If she accepts you," he said, "then the Sea accepts you, and you'll be part of the family. Able to share all we have, so long as you share what you have. We make our lives into a potluck dinner—everyone brings their best with lots of pepper and no one goes hungry. Or lonely."

September searched his eyes for a conspiratorial glint. *Show me we're only playing,* she thought. *Wink at me. Raise your eyebrow. Tug on your ear.* But she could see only Saturday, as he always was, earnest as the North Star, without a lie in his bones. September winked. *See? Reassure me.* But he only pointed at a bronze shaving cup on Fizzwilliam's control board. The bottom of it had a fine mesh. A handsome shave brush with a wooden handle and lionfish-spine bristles rested inside. September picked it up. She had seen her father shave many, many times. She knew how it was done. But she could not think what the purpose might be. She hadn't any whiskers. And the lionfish spines looked quite poisonous, all striped like a copperhead snake. She sighed. *In for a penny, in for a purple cuttlefish. Whatever's gotten into Saturday, he would never do anything to hurt me.* But as she reached for the brush, September remembered Saturday's shadow, pushing her into the Sea of Forgetting, not sorry at all, watching her sink down into the black.

Just as she had watched her father do in the upstairs bathroom, September swirled and squooshed the brush in the cup. *Father, are you all right without me there to record your temperature and read to you when your leg hurts? Oh, please be all right!* A bright foam slushed up from the spines, the color of the inside of an avocado, if it had caught on fire. She looked at Saturday questioningly. He only nodded at her—and there it was. A little wink. A wink that said: *We will trick our way to the finish line, octopus by octopus.*

The foam smelled of hot, unripe fruit and sizzling seeds that would burn your tongue. Mercifully, Fizzwilliam's fresh, soothing voice filled her ears, telling her not to be a Suspicious Sue, that everything that made a Bathysphere run was squeaky clean and pure as a bar of soap milled on a summer cloud. Lionfish spines are only venomous when they're attached, the Bathysphere explained. They have to want to poison you. It's the wanting that makes the poison.

September felt a wonderful calm. She didn't know why she hadn't always consulted machines whenever something troubled her. They had such a comforting way about them. She gave the brush one more fatherly *swish-swirl* and blinked back tears of missing him and daubed it all round her chin and her chops and down her smooth, slender neck. She made sure to get her upper lip, for she had a horror of mustaches. Her father had grown one when she was four and she'd cried for a week because a stranger with a slug on his mouth was sitting in the good chair. One evening in the Redcaps' Cellar, they had played Truth or Truth (you cannot dare much in prison) and Saturday had confessed that he could not grow a mustache or a beard, for Marids are part dolphin, and their skin will not cooperate. She had felt secretly joyful, and poured him a cup of red rum with extra cherries in without telling him why.

Tropical green foam dripped from September's face. She looked down at the cup and the brush. Fizzwilliam began to tell her what to do, but somehow, she knew before he got four words out. She held the cup over her mouth and knocked three times on the bottom with the knob of the shave brush. At once, the foam hardened a little and the cup softened a lot. They flowed together and rippled out over her face in fine, sparkling trickles, like tears flowing upward. For a moment, fear stiffened September's body like cold lightning cracking open every vein at the same time. The ooze crept up over her mouth and her nose, then into her eyes and her ears. She didn't want to breathe it in, she would surely choke—but it gave her no choice. September breathed in—and she could breathe in quite well! She breathed in and felt the gunk toughen up, growing stiff and glossy. The wreckage of her first shave covered her whole head in a hard shell. She wore a beautiful copper-green mask sculpted into a perfect likeness of her own dear, familiar face, down to the mole on her left cheek and the last curls of her hair.

Fizzwilliam lowered his glass dome and the Sea spilled in, filling up his tub and swallowing up September as fast as a hiccup. The water rushed over September, colder than she expected, and heavier. It felt nothing like the rivers and lakes back home, and nothing like the Perverse and Perilous Sea, either. The Obstreperous Ocean held on to her tight. It felt like nothing so much as her own mother, holding her with firm hands in the public swimming pool when she was hardly more than a baby, keeping her safe and buoyant in the sun, showing her the marvelousness of water without letting her know how deep and dark such a brightness could get. The mask let her breathe like a Marid, and September had always been a wonderful swimmer. She frog-legged out of the Bathysphere and into Mumkeep Reef, feeling the salt water against her skin. The emerald-colored smoking jacket did not greet getting dunked with quite so much delight. It spoke urgently to the Watchful Dress, and the pair of them sleeked themselves down into a tight, smooth suit like sealskin, stretching to cover both fingers and toes.

The cuttlefish watched September turn a somersault in the water, just for the feeling of doing it. She played all her colors across her skin, making mystic patterns of unguessable meaning, tsunamis of gold and rust and indigo, luminous galaxies containing all the wisdom of the infinite universe bursting open and drifting apart, then knotting together again into thick electric fists. September stopped her somersault and stared in awe. Tears rose beneath her mask. It was like looking at a star writing its last poem. Saturday's chest ached for the endless, profound sorrow in the cuttlefish's W-shaped eyes.

"I'm just kidding," the cuttlefish said, and laughed uproariously. "I can talk! I just love to put on a show. You can take the cuttlefish off the stage, but you can't pry the stage off the cuttlefish, am I right?"

September felt quite glad of the mask just then. A mask cannot show disappointment. "But the lights . . . ," she said. "The tsunamis, the galaxies . . ."

The cuttlefish preened, ruffling the veils along the sides of her body. "Pretty good, aren't I? Would you say 'a boffo performance'? What about 'a tour de force'? Maybe 'a star-making turn'? I don't want to put words in your mouth. But I do *need* the love of the critics! The piping hot ardor of the audience! The generous salt of *approval*!"

"It brought the house down," September said generously, though she still felt a bit cheated. But that is the way of theatre, girl. It is everything, and then the curtain comes down and all you've got left is a program and a half-eaten chocolate. But September did so love to give somebody what they wanted. Most of the time, it was much easier than holding it back.

"I'll take that and live on it for a year, young penguin!" The cuttlefish smiled. This involved opening up her a face into its many thick, short tentacles and waggling them vigorously. It is rather hideous.

Hugger–Muggery leapt at the chance to prove herself the smarter of the two tentacled monsters present.

"She's not a penguin! Even I know that."

The cuttlefish oozed out of the coral a little to get a better look.

"She is flightless, can only breathe underwater for short intervals, and stands upright. I say penguin! And what I say goes. Young penguin, I am Sepia Siphuncle, at your service. Once, the greatest comedienne under the sea, star of the cephalopaudville stage! Now ridiculously retired tattoo artist living by her lights. You can call my Monkfish there Brother

Tinpan. He was my stage manager in the good old days—days so good you only appreciate them when you're old!"

Brother Tinpan inclined his head toward them. "Time," he said courteously. Bubbles drifted up from his seaweed cowl.

Sepia rolled her sorrowful eyes. "Meet the Mysterious Monkfish, Only Two Bits! Forgive him. Conversation with a Monkfish takes some problem-solving skills. They don't really talk, they just answer riddles, so you have to work backward and figure out the riddle he's answering before you can get a spotlight on what he means to say. So *time* will be . . . 'Until I am measured, I cannot be known, yet how you will miss me, when I have flown!' He's pleased to meet you and can tell you're a jolly sort he'll miss once you've gone and left him alone with this old pun-and-punchline girl again. Any great actress learns to speak the special language of stage managers if she wants her fins lit right!"

Saturday put his head to one side, his posture full of longing. "I miss it, too," he said.

"Oh! Are you also a refugee of the stage? A mummer, a mugger, a knockabout rogue? Tell me, what did you play? Clamlet? Oedipod Rex? Tuna Tartuffe? Quayrano de Bergerac? No, wait! I want to guess! A quick-change act? A song-and-dance man?"

"I was in the circus," Saturday said. The pride in his voice was a wild trapeze singing through the sea. "I only ever had one review, though. In the *Almanack Tribune*. Page twenty-two, bottom-left corner. In very small print."

"No matter, no matter! It's the *praise* that counts, my lad, not the page! Let's have it!"

Saturday reached up to the blue-white stone he wore round his neck. He put his fingernail against one side and it popped open—a locket! Inside, a scrap of newsprint nestled safely under glass. It read: *A promising newcomer.* The Marid grinned jubilantly. His fingers shook a little as he closed up the locket again and let it fall where it belonged, over his heart.

The cuttlefish rippled happily. "Magnificent! Tip-top stuff! Ah, the circus! How stupendous. The circus is pure, I've always said. Nothing but spectacle. No squirrelly little words getting in the way of the rings of fire and the dancing bears. Were you a clown? I would so dearly love to talk shop with another practitioner of the comic arts! We could debate the rule of three or the horrors of improv!"

Saturday's eyes dimmed and filled with shadows. He shook his head, his topknot floating upward in the seawater like a question mark. "I . . . I was . . . not a lion tamer. I don't think. I have a fear of lions, you know. No!" Relief washed over his face. He'd caught the ragged edge of the answer as it tried to get away. "No, I was a trapeze artist! The trapeze. I flew through the air with the greatest of ease."

September stared at him. How could Saturday forget his trapeze, even for a moment? He loved the Stationary Circus almost as much as the Sea itself. Almost as much as her and A-Through-L. How could he let it slip from his mind when he carried his only review in a locket round his neck? September remembered every job she'd ever done. Fixing Mr. Albert's fence or battling her own shadow in the underworld—any of it sat at the tip of her tongue, ready to perform a death-defying leap of truthfulness as soon as anyone asked. But he had remembered, in the end. Perhaps it was only the excitement of coming home at last.

"Ah, well, never mind. It does my three hearts good to meet another thespian, whether or not he knows a catchphrase from a callback. Now, you say you've married this penguin. Come closer, birdie, let me get a look at those flippers."

September swam down to Sepia Siphuncle, breathing easily, though the air tasted salty and thick. The cuttlefish's spangled eyes roamed over her. She lifted her veils and ran them along September's arms.

"Before I get started, princess penguin, tell me: What do you call your mother's sister?"

"Aunt . . . Aunt Margaret!"

"Bzzz! Wrong! Aunt-Arctica!" Sepia guffawed. Her zebra stripes flushed a dazzling lilac. "You can clap now," she allowed. September and Saturday did, politely. The Octopus Assassin glowered darkly and refused.

"Fair enough, one-liners are a chump's game, after all. Like scrounging up pennies to pay for lunch. You may get what you need, cent by cent, but dollars fill you faster. Give me a role again! Let me be a *protagonist* once more! Let me trade alliterating insults with a squid for all seasons! Give me a script and I'll give you anything you ask. A part, a part, my kingdom for a part!"

"Wheel," Brother Tinpan admonished gently.

The cuttlefish wriggled and writhed. "Wheel? Oh, which one is that—no, I know it, just give me a moment. Ah-ha! 'I go round in circles, but always straight ahead. I never complain, no matter where I am led.' Well, that's not very nice, is it, Tinny? He means to tell me you'd prefer I get my inks going and quit talking about myself so much, but you've got the kind of stubborn manners that won't let you tell me to stuff my own tentacles in my mouth and jump off the continental shelf. You're such a cynic, Tinpan! Trying to saw my audience in half and make them disappear. Fine. I'll make her the greatest wife ever to trod the aisles. But you have to listen to my new jokes for a full hour tonight. Not a minute less! And if you complain, the hour starts over again!"

"I think you're tops. Honest! A-list material," September said slyly, though she meant it, really. You can be sly and sincere at the same time, though it takes practice and if you're not careful, you will throw out your back. "A one-cuttlefish show not to be missed. It's only that we're running a race, and I don't have the faintest idea what's happening on land, or to whom! It took some time to get here. I've an awful worry in my stomach that it's all slipping by up there."

"I understand completely," said Sepia Siphuncle. "The curtain goes up on time, whether you turn up or not. The show must go on. Even if the show is mostly a chase scene. Pull up your sleeve and give me your flipper, pretty penguin. Left or right, doesn't matter. Whichever one you like best."

September held out her left arm. She'd never given any thought to liking one more than the other. But she wrote with her left hand and used left-handed scissors and strummed her aunt Margaret's funny old mandolin with her left hand, so it seemed to her that her left arm liked *her* best. The sleek sealsuit the emerald-colored smoking jacket and the Watchful Dress had made together parted along an invisible seam. The cuttlefish wrapped her tentacles around September's fingers, then her wrist, then swallowed her all the way up to the fore-arm. It didn't hurt—Sepia's suckers rested on her bare skin like kisses. Her glitter-ringed eyes locked on to September's, deep within her diving mask, black into copper, cephalopod into primate, W into O, sea into land.

September felt something hot and thick running up her arm. *I'm bleeding,* she thought frantically. *She's bitten me and I'm bleeding! Oh, it's so much! I can't live without that much blood!* But she didn't feel woozy or weak. In fact, she felt strong, really *fantastically* strong, as though her left arm could battle a hundred Octopus Assassins before her right had even woken up in the morning. She tried to lean back carefully and get a look at what Sepia had done to her. The way she felt just then, she thought that if she raised her arm up, she'd just lift the whole huge cuttlefish up over her head.

Rivers of black ink began to creep out of Sepia's mouth onto September's skin. Not the usual flat sort of black that comes in a paint can, or even the rich, bottomless, gorgeous sort of black that the sea knows how to make in the moonless Winter. This was cuttleblack, traced in speckles of electric blue and green like Sepia's W-shaped eyes, stippled all through with feverish, dancing drops of gold. Five bands of ink wound around one another like serpents in love, chasing one another, but slowly, deliberately, up September's arm, past her elbow, surging for the shoulder. They made graceful, curving lunar patterns on her skin. The patterns seemed to move the longer she watched them—now like waves, now like briars, now like stars parading down the streets of the sky. They weren't the same as Saturday's lovely tattoos that she had spent so many days memorizing. These were her own, but they would look very pretty next to his. September thought them so beautiful that she didn't think about whether or not they were permanent and she'd be stuck this way and have to explain it to most everyone she met until much later. Sepia Siphuncle, star of stage and reef, let September go. Her left arm looked like a map of heaven.

"Fire!" screamed Brother Tinpan. "Fire! Fire!"

Saffron ripples of irritation flowed up and down the cuttlefish's body. "Can't you let me take my bow at the end of a performance without making it all about you, you, *you*?" She sighed. "The penguin was about to give me my review! I need it! I'm starving for it! I don't even know that one. You've never yelled 'Fire!' before."

Hugger-Muggery, who had fumed in silence all this while, snapped to attention, her tentacles locking into position as straight and tense as an arrowhead. " 'I am always hungry, I must always be fed. The finger I touch will soon turn red.' Someone is coming! Arm the alarums! Assassins, to me!"

Someone *was* coming. A black beast hurtled toward them out of the deep salt blue of the sea, a shadow in the shape of a tremendous sea horse.

Ajax Oddson's voice filled every nook and cranny of Mumkeep Reef, gurgling happily, like children do when they try to pass messages back and worth under water.

"I say! What do I see in that sea? Why, it's two Derbymen about to obey my decree! It's that time again!"

Far beneath the surface of the Obstreperous Ocean, purple fireworks erupted into a shower of flame, spelling out:

Everyone Loves A Duel!

CHAPTER XII

A School of Saturdays

In Which September Turns into a Bear, Saturday Swims
Up the Time Stream, a Pirate Loses His Temper, and
an Army of Undead Princesses Is Summoned

The shadow sea horse drew closer. Its warlike snout pierced the water. Its spine curved down like the neck of a violin. It was made for battle. It was sure and easy and vicious.

And it was not a sea horse.

When its bony black tail ran aground on a crag of Mumkeep Reef, sending a school of scarlet fish scattering in all directions, September saw right through into the soul of the sea horse, which contained a small man with a lumpy face and a glorious cravat. The sea horse's eyes were not eyes, but two glass bubbles. Its snout was not a snout but a cruel cannon. Its tail was not a tail, but a rudder. Cutty Soames, Captain of the Coblynows, spun the wheel of a submarine made of shadows, and he looked quite beside himself with wrath.

A porthole opened up in the water just above them, growing slowly like a soap bubble until it popped—leaving a bolted ring of brass hanging in the sea. A pane of glass separated the Obstreperous Ocean from the Dueling Officiant: a grinning young lady all in blue, wearing silken indigo trousers and turquoise opera gloves and sapphire-colored boots with crisscrossed icicle laces all the way to the knee. She smirked at September and buttoned her long, beautiful sky-colored coat, trimmed in wild, woolly fur from some impossible, blueberry-colored sheep. Her long, azure hair lay over her shoulders in a serene, glossy style, topped off with a furry cobalt cap with an ice-spike like old pictures of the Kaiser. She chomped on the end of her churchwarden pipe, and blew a great pyramid of smoke into their faces, only it blew apart when it hit the porthole glass, so it did not quite pull off the devil-may-care effect the Blue Wind had hoped for.

"Girl, ho!" the Blue Wind called.

"Wind, ho!" September answered happily. She did not trust the Blue Wind any further than a rabbit trusts an owl, but she had missed her, all the same.

"HALT!" screamed Hugger-Muggery. Many more than four Pieces of Eight fired themselves out of their glass jars all over Mumkeep Reef. The water churned as its tentacled army took flight. "Yes, you! You, Cutty Soames! Cutty Crudheart! Soames, the Slime of the Sea! Captain of the Courageless Cockroaches of Snotropolis!"

The Blue Wind and Sepia Siphuncle broke into wild applause. The Blue Wind whistled through her teeth.

"Top-shelf stuff!" the cuttlefish hollered. "No one really straps a good insult on these days, it shocks the matinee crowds! Brava!"

"Shut up!" snarled Cutty Soames from within his submarine sea horse that wasn't a sea horse—or a submarine, either. It was, in fact, Curdleblood, the Dastard of Darkness's steed—a fiendishly clever shade of black. Cutty had nearly set fire to the Barleybroom when he found his prize galleon replaced with a miserable puddle of paint. But when he tried to stab it with his trusty cutlass, the Captain of the Coblynows discovered that a clever bit of black has a thousand and four more uses than a galleon. The Night Wagon, for Curdleblood had given it that name when he found the poor thing hiding in an art gallery, bored out of its wits, had learned to roll itself out into any kind of transportation the Dastard of Darkness wanted, so long as it did not have too many moving parts. The Night Wagon could do you a burnt-black horse as quick as turning the downstairs lights out. A charcoal carriage? An ebony velocipede? A shadow-fueled hot air balloon? Too easy. Once Curdleblood had fancied a coal-souled locomotive to take him in style to visit his mistress, who lived in the Bootbat Forest. This was the Night Wagon's favorite, up until the sea horse submarine. A locomotive engine has more parts than a horse or a balloon. It almost gave up when it got to the steam pipes and piston rods. But it did love Curdleblood, Dastardly though he was. The Night Wagon longed to please. When it rocketed through the countryside, it felt so black it could burst.

Cutty Soames, suddenly shipless, had needed the Night Wagon's help. It listened to the pirate king's many, many complaints, which he beefed up with plenty of curse words and just plain curses, and rolled itself out into something useful and splendid and deeply, profoundly, magnificently black. Together they had already dueled both Hushnow, the Ancient and Demented Raven Lord, and the Knapper. They'd won handily, both times, for the Night Wagon always took care to brush in a few fire-spewing extras when it did itself up for the evening.

"Shut up!" Cutty Soames spat again. September rubbed her sleeve on the eye of the black sea horse to get a better look.

The Coblynow had a rather handsome face, though it was all eyebrows and cheekbones, and much bigger than a face ought to be, considering he hardly came up to September's waist. He'd slicked his hair down with good red mud and put a few ancient coins in it for that touch of flash for which all pirates have a weakness. He wore a salamander-skin cravat, too, pinned with a polished musket ball—and the name tag Hawthorn had given him, still stuck to his grand coat. "If there's anything I hate more than an octopus it's having to talk to one! Yes, yes, I'm a terrible naughty wicked gob of mud and everyone hates me. Good! Fine! I am a pirate. I liked doing pirate things when I was alive the first time and I like it now. I never wanted taxes or treaties! I want to steal your gold and potatoes! I don't want to dance at the fashionable balls! I want to do that thing where you cut the rigging in just the right spot and shoot up to the crow's nest! I don't want to be loved by my subjects! I want them to build barricades and enchant their street lamps into angry giants with candles in their hair so that when I sack their ports, it's at least a *bit* of a challenge! That's the trouble, of course, once you're King, nobody conjures up gaslight giants when they see your sails on the horizon anymore. They just try to scrape together half of their everything down to their dinner rolls and hand it over with stoic fortitude. Barnacles and bunions! It's enough to depress the sunshine out of Spring."

September scoffed at him. "Good grief, then why bother racing in the Derby? I'm sure we'd all rather you stayed home and whittled a plank or something. If I end up Queen when all this is over, I shan't steal anyone's potatoes or sack their ports! Cutty Crudheart, indeed!"

Cutty Soames straightened his cravat and dropped his sea-weathered hand onto the hilt of his cutlass—his only true friend, until he'd gotten hitched to the Night Wagon. "Girls must girl and pirates must pirate. If they held an election, I'd spend it down the pub burning it to the ground. But let me win something, let me beat someone else to it, let me swipe it when everyone else has gone to sleep? I can't help myself any more than a kid can stop wanting the gun-toting dolly in the window."

"The Derby? Are you running in the Cantankerous Derby?" Hugger-Muggery said. Her voice changed in the tiniest way. A tremble crept in, like a mouse balancing on the handle of a spoon.

"Yes," Saturday said slowly, caught out. They couldn't hide it now. EVERYONE LOVES A DUEL still hung in the dark water like burning birthday candles. "We didn't want to say. Grandmother doesn't like anyone putting on airs. This is September. She's the Engineer. The Queen. Ruler of Fairyland and All Her Kingdoms."

Hugger-Muggery, Sepia Siphuncle, and Brother Tinpan tried to scrub the shock off their faces, but they'd gotten far too used to life in Mumkeep Reef, where they never had to worry about what half-cocked expression hung around on their faces, to manage it.

"I formally apologize for my behavior earlier, Madam Engineer," the High Assassin of the Pieces of Eight said stiffly. "You, of course, have every right to visit any benighted corner of your kingdom, from the Hourglass Waste to Mumkeep Reef and anywhere else. You may cut off my tentacles now."

September's copper mask made her look severe and unmoved. Very like a Queen, though she couldn't know it. Inside the mask, her real face wrinkled up in horror. "I will absolutely *not* cut off your tentacles! What a gruesome idea! Please don't let anyone else do it, either! I'm not really Queen yet. It's only been a few days and if I don't win the Derby, no one will remember that I wore the crown at all."

"But if I keep my tentacles, I will one day forget how shamefully I insulted the Queen—I mean, the Engineer! I will do it again! I must be reminded!" wailed the Octopus Assassin.

"Good! Wonderful!" September cried. "Insult away!" She felt very silly all of the sudden. Her cheeks burned. All their subterfuge and careful creeping and they could just have told everyone she was the Queen and had their pick of Mumkeep's plunder! Now she had a tattoo and might possibly be married when all she had to say was *I'm the Queen, give me what I want.*

That's all right, my girl. Don't fret. Power is a coat that's always too small. It takes time to wear it in, to feel like it's really yours, to fill up the pockets with your own lint and house keys and slips of right and wrong with cat's fur hanging off them. And for people with hearts as quick and raw and hungry as September's, that coat will never fit quite right.

"If you'll excuse me," said the Blue Wind, tapping a wrist with no watch on it. "I'm rather busy with a rabid cloudicorn just now, so if we could speed things along, that'd be swell, thanks. Another heist or two and I'll have the Heart in my hands."

"You're lying," September said hopefully. Could they be so far off track? No, no, there was something important here. There had to be. The Blue Wind winked at her and shrugged. *I might be. I might be Queen already.*

Cutty Soames stomped his foot twice, and then again, as

doing anything only twice always left him feeling unfinished. "Name the weapons, you half-boiled robin's egg! By lime and vinegar, I've met doldrums quicker than you."

The Blue Wind stroked the ends of her azure hair and thought. She took her time, but only because she knew it galled everyone something fierce. She'd chosen before Cutty called her an egg. Just after the octopus called the Coblynow's beloved robber's paradise, Port Pelerine, by the perfectly delicious name of Snotropolis.

"Very well!" The Blue Wind raised her sapphire-ringed hands inside her porthole. "Hold on to your parasols! I choose . . . Insults! That way at least I'll get a giggle out of it. And the cloudicorn may overhear and start feeling bad about herself. Without their bottomless cauldrons of scalding self-esteem, cloudicorns have no power."

September grimaced in her mask. "Can't it ever be anything I'm good at?" She knew it wasn't Queenly to complain, but she didn't feel particularly royal just then. But then, what would that be? Sailing a raft with a dress? Singing? Competitive automotive tinkering? Infuriating the upper class wherever she found them?

"Nope!" the Blue Wind said cheerfully. "Where would be the fun in that? Come on, September, you can't always be so nice all the time! Get ill-tempered for me! Show me irascible!

Or are you just a fluffy little dandelion seed waiting to be huffed and puffed into nothing by a drunken field mouse? See? It's easy!"

The Night Wagon came about, turning the broad, bony breast of its sea horse body to September, who suddenly wished she hadn't gotten out of Fizzwilliam's nice, safe, very *metal* tub. The Pieces of Eight bolted back into their glass jars like a flock of fiery rare birds who had just sighted a man who works for the city zoo. Sepia and Brother Tinpan shrunk down into the coral opera house. The cuttlefish went dark, snuffing out all the lovely lights under her skin.

Cutty Soames got a good gust of breath up under his lungs. He boomed out: "Go pick lice off your mother's backside, you lazy, saucepan-headed ape! You couldn't rule a side of steamed carrots, you unbearable, unremarkable, un*magical* sack of giggling baby toys!"

September recoiled as though he'd shot her in the chest with his flintlock. Part of her, the part that had been the Spinster, thought he could have done better than *lazy,* but the rest was quite good stuff. But the part of her that had always been September felt herself right back in school, staring at Martha May, a girl with red hair who'd just slapped her for no reason but that she could and no one would punish her. Hearing all the whispers of Martha May's friends rising up like a nasty cold tide, filthy with words like *freak, crazy, nitwit,* and *weirdo*. She'd run home and got down on her hands and knees, trying to scrub those words out of her mind. But it never worked. She could always still see them, no matter how hard she scoured. She couldn't think of anything to say to Martha May that day, even though it would have felt so good to lash out with something unspeakably clever and devastating. She'd reached for words to use like armor, but found nothing there. *She was right. I am a freak. I am unremarkable. Everything that's happened to me has only happened because of other, more interesting, stronger, more wonderful people. I'm nobody.*

The waters of Mumkeep Reef bubbled as though they meant to come to a boil. But they didn't.

A squadron of gorillas and orangutans bubbled up into the ocean from nowhere at all. They wore diving helmets hammered out of saucepans, having no friendly Fizzwilliam to help them to a shave. They shrieked and hooted and giggled out their primate war cries. But the helmets made them look like hideous, monstrous astronauts. Their faces were invisible behind metal grills, long, hairy arms beating back the water, bearing down on September and Saturday. The diving apes brandished baby rattles and dollies with buttons for eyes and dynamite for hair. One swung a baby's mobile full of painted sailboats in one fist and a knitted blanket in another like a trident and net. Another twirled a wooden train round his head like a ninja's flying wooden sticks.

Saucepan-headed ape. Sack of giggling baby toys.

September could almost have laughed, if she weren't about to be thumped soundly by an underwater gorilla wearing a saucepan on his head and pointing a toy fire truck at her face.

September turned to Saturday. "I can't think of anything!" she whispered.

"Of course you can," Saturday reassured her. "I heard you call Sir Sanguine a great talking punch-bag with rum barrels for ears in the Cellar."

"I know! But Sir Sanguine's my friend. It's easy when you're friends. Then it's just like a hug that's got its love on backward. But he's right, he's right. I *am* an unremarkable ape."

Saturday ran his hand over the carved copper hair of her breathing mask. She could not feel his dear fingers, but she could feel their comforting weight. "Don't say that. Never, ever. You are my remarkable ape. Don't go beating yourself up before the gorillas get a chance." He clapped his long blue hands and gave her a playful push. *If we win, she will stay.* He had to get her to fight. "Let's get mean! You can do it! Everyone's got a big hot sour lump of everything hateful they didn't say because their manners outboxed their cussedness.

I know you can be a grumpy, ornery, bitey old bear. Pretend you've only just woken up in the morning. What did you call me last Sunday when I tried to rouse you by seven?"

"A vicious rotten blueberry," September said, and blushed shamefully. She never meant anything she said before ten in the morning.

"See? You're a natural. But you'd better be quick with your blueberries, or else I think we'll both get a rocking horse to the head."

The army of undersea gorillas and orangutans had gotten their sea legs under them. They'd be on her in nothing flat. One orangutan the color of rust on a steamship aimed his pale pink rattle with lavender bows painted all round it directly between her eyes. September thought the ape meant to taunt her, but six quick bolts of lightning fired out of the rattle. Three forked off harmlessly into the deeps, one pranged off a jagged shard of coral—and two caught September squarely in the face. One scorched her left temple; the other charred her right cheek. If not for Fizzwilliam's shaving-cup mask, September would have burnt out like an old lamp. She smelled baby powder as the smoke cleared, the way you smell ozone after a thunderstorm. *You just got lucky,* September thought. *What if he'd aimed for your chest? Say something! Anything! Come on, self, hit back!*

September dug deep for muck to fling at Cutty Soames. But all she found were *freak, crazy, nitwit,* and *weirdo* lying around at the bottom of her heart like skinny old rats in a cellar. But no—something else glinted out from under her pride. She kicked backward suddenly, swimming well free of Saturday, a maniacal adrenaline grin aching on her face.

September poked herself in the chest and lashed her voice up into a stern whip. "September, you are nothing but a grumpy, ornery, bitey old bear! You can't even boss Sunday morning around, what do you want with a crown?" And it was true, it was true—if she couldn't even tell off one solitary undead pirate, how could she manage the giants and dragons of ruling Fairyland?

The waters of Mumkeep Reef closed in on her, black and blue and heavy. It felt like slipping into one of the expensive fur coats down at the Brandeis & Sons department store on Douglas Street. She always knew she oughtn't—her mother could never afford one of the long black minks or the custard-colored beaver-fur capes. Those were for fancy people, not for them. *Oh, Mom, if I come through this I will find a way to get you all the capes in the world. I will.* How she'd loved to hide in the coats, closing them up until only her little nose peeked out. Now, at the bottom of the ocean, September felt a thick, stout, white fur button up around her. This time, not even her nose showed.

September was a polar bear.

The roar came all the way from the pads of her shaggy paws, up through her powerful snowy haunches, her huge, fleecy belly, slurping loudness from her bear-bones and her bear-blood all the way up. She'd never owned something so big as that roar in her life. It was as big as an ice floe, as big as a fat, tasty, unsuspecting seal asleep on the snow, as big as Aunt-Arctica. September swung her great furry arms wide, slicing through the water with her fabulously vicious claws, and roared like every bear who'd ever tried to sleep through five more minutes of winter rioting all at once. The ape army recoiled. A gorilla threw his dolly at September. It bounced harmlessly off her strapping fuzzy chest, exploding meekly when it hit the reef, quite embarrassed to have even made the effort. September roared again. Roaring was really the most perfectly excellent thing in the world. She told herself to do it more often.

September banged her front paws together. When she pulled them apart, fiery balls of sleepy morning sunshine skewered themselves on each black claw. The ape army charged the sun-wielding polar bear. They swung their wooden trains against her and fired their rattles. Her fur smoked where she took her hits, but they only annoyed September, like bees buzzing in her ears. She flung her little morning suns at gorillas and orangutans alike, whanging their saucepan diving bells around, setting their fur on fire, roaring all the time, roaring fit to deafen a thundercloud.

The apes vaporized into seawater bubbles. The September-bear lunged to chomp the bubbles in her snout and pop them with her claws. A giggling polar bear is a very disconcerting sight, let me tell you. It is probably for the best that as soon as the last baby rattle disappeared, her bear-head fell back like a hood and her shaggy chest split down the middle. September stepped out of her bear-skin just the same way she stepped out of the coats at Brandeis & Sons when her mother found her at last: a little chagrined, but not in the least sorry to have done it.

Cutty Soames let out his own roar on the bridge of the shadowy sea horse. September might have been frightened, had he done it five minutes earlier. But now she just laughed.

"You should work harder on your roar," she said breezily, still giddy with bear-ness. "Use your diaphragm! Really give it some proper breath, you'll get a much deeper pitch."

The Captain of the Coblynows gripped the hilt of his cutlass until his knuckles looked like they might make a run for it. His red eyes smoked like coals in a furious hearth.

"I'm going to hang your bones from my mainsail, you ladle-brained peasant! You've got the brain of a sunburned badger, the courage of a bowl of porridge, and the grace of a giant with a head injury! You prancing, marshmallow-hearted *cow*!" Cutty'd run out of breath by the end of it, but he yanked out that last with a hoarse belch.

"That's the second time I've been called a cow today." September sighed. "I don't know what's so horrid about being a cow. Mrs. Powell's cow is called Marjorie and she's well behaved and very useful. But I suppose I did jump over the Moon."

September talked slowly to buy herself time. *He called me an ape,* she thought furiously. *That's all right, humans evolved from apes, it's nothing to be ashamed of. Don't get sad, get smart! Think! Coblynows evolved from . . . I think Sir Sanguine said chimneys? There ought to be something juicy there . . .*

The waters of Mumkeep Reef roiled and glugged again. A gang of giants with bandaged heads galloped out across the ocean floor. They wore peasants' rags and rode majestic, ice-hoofed cows with horns forged from beaten plowshares. Marshmallow bells hung from the beasts' necks, skins crinkling black, as though roasted by an invisible campfire. The deep water slowed them down, but they did not wait. Each giant hoisted a monstrous ladle aloft and whirled it round his head like a mace. Every time the ladles came round, they lobbed boiling black porridge at September, Saturday,

Sepia, Brother Tinpan, the Pieces of Eight, anything they could see through their bandages. The dark globs ate through whatever they landed on like acid with butter and brown sugar on top. A mob of flaming badgers wove in and out of the cows' legs, scampering across the dueling field, their fur burning the water around them into acrid steam and smoke.

September tried to get a roar going down in the bottoms of her feet, but it would not come. The giants hollered out battle songs in the old tongue. She took a deep breath through the mouth of her mask.

"Go eat an anchor, you soot-addled pile of bricks!"

It wasn't bad. She put a nice, solid sneer on it. The Blue Wind clapped her hands in her judge's frame—she always wanted September to learn to sneer properly. And it did genuinely hurt Cutty's feelings. But all she got for her efforts was a shower of chimney-bricks floating down to her like flakes of fish food dropped into an aquarium. They mortared themselves neatly into a wall any garden would love to bring home to meet the tomatoes. September and Saturday crouched quickly behind it, but the wall could do nothing more for them than be the best wall it knew how. So it swiveled round and circled them safely, mortaring up its own seam quick as oats.

"I tried!" September insisted. "It's hard enough to think of something cutting without having to make it something that's good for battling as well."

"Go again," urged Saturday. "He got about twenty in one breath, surely you get more than one."

"That was the best I had!"

September felt a small hand tug at her recently tattooed wrist. It gave her such a startle she nearly vaulted over the wall and into a gaggle of giants. She turned to look what had her by the arm, her heart bouncing all round her insides like a lost pinball.

A small boy squeezed her hand. A small blue boy. A small blue boy with a topknot and the very beginnings of a long, lovely tattoo that would one day look like curling waves breaking over his shoulder blades. It was Saturday, when he was young and small, a Marid in his natural habitat: out of time and out of order, popping out of the past to pull on her sleeve.

"Hullo, Bear Lady," said this new Saturday. He was no more than four or five, his little black eyes quick and mischievous. "I saw you be a bear so that's what I'm going to call you."

Saturday blinked at his younger self. Then he laughed, really rather loudly, as though he'd only just understood a joke he'd heard years before. "Hiya, Little S," he said, and tugged affectionately on the boy's much-shorter topknot.

Four-year-old Saturday hopped up on his own blue feet. "Hiya, Big S! I came to help! I'm top of the food chain when it comes to name-calling." He put his hands on his hips. "Slights, mockeries, slanders, cheap shots—if you want someone to run home crying, I'm your fish."

"Saturday!" September gasped. "That's not you! You wouldn't curse a storm if it flooded your house!"

The older Marid shrugged, half embarrassed, half proud of the pixyish little hooligan he'd once been. "I wasn't always quiet, you know. Before I got locked up in a lobster cage and wrestled every day for wishes, I ran wild through the Sea. Marids are all orphans for a while. We live in jumbled-up order—what Papa could keep up? I told you I met my mother on a beach when I was twelve and she was twenty-four. I gave her a dune daisy. But all the versions of me before I turned twelve still had to have something to do while they were waiting to be born. Some of me sold cockleshells, some of me played high-level hopscotch with the narwhals, and some of me picked pockets and ran with the rougher schools of mackerel and mermaids."

"You said you'd never stolen anything before."

Saturday laughed. "Well, only some of me has. It wasn't

really a lie. Don't be angry." He turned to Little S. "I remember being you. It was fun. Before the Marquess's nets came down."

Little S didn't seem too worried about the nets or cages in his future. A Marid lives all at once, like sparkles of sunlight darting through moving water. Why wear yourself out gnawing on the rind of the future? Right here and now, Little S meant to call some giants nasty names, which was the most fun he could imagine. "Let's not tell our life stories when we've got a pirate to put down and flaming badgers to put out!" he scolded them. "I'm small, but I have a big mouth. You have to, on the mean old Seas! Grammy doesn't like it when I swear, and she won't let me drown anyone because it makes a mess, but I can do you at least a hundred bang-up taunts and five or six scorchers without breaking her rules. This is gonna be a day for my scrapbook!" The boy bent down and kissed September's hand quite gallantly. He deliberately twinkled his eyes at her. "I'm gonna love you some day, Bear Lady, so I wanna get started on impressing you."

Little S put his foot into a crack in the brick wall. The wall dug out a row of handholds for him and he scrambled up, sticking his nose up over the ledge.

"Oy! Bilge-rat!" he shouted. The Night Wagon came about sharply, pointing its sea horse nose at the cause of this new ruckus. "Yes, you! Bilge-rat! You scurrilous scurvy-sore!

You preening putrid princess! Why don't you come out of that gloomy-two-shoes merry-go-round pony and scrub our bricks like the filthy chimney brush you are?"

Cutty Soames, Captain of the Coblynows, fixed the boy with a stare like a walked plank. Shall I tell you what lay smoldering behind that stare? Duel or no duel, he meant to murder that child. The worst lashings come from a truthful whip: Thousands of years ago, the Coblynows had indeed been born from chimneys, bound to them like a dryad to her tree, forced to keep house for people with no personal hygiene at all. When Cutty took the helm of Fairyland, he and his boys smashed every chimney in the kingdom, broke every brush over their knees, rubbed every slovenly Fairy's nose in soot until they promised to clean their chimneys twice a year as they'd repeatedly been told. It was the greatest day in Coblynow history. Cutty forbade anyone to speak of the Brick and Mortar Years forever after, and the Coblynows took to the high seas, where they could live in the open air and never let the fires of their plundering go out and never pick up after themselves or anyone else again. And no one had spoken of those dark days since. They hadn't dared. Until this miserable brine shrimp of a lad.

"You heard me!" the little blue guttersnipe brayed again. "Who's a fussy 'fraidy-crab who won't get his toesies wet? It's you, sir!"

But not the same guttersnipe. This one was seven or eight. The one who'd called Cutty a bilge-rat was still thumbing his nose over the top of their pathetic brick wall. The one calling him a 'fraidy-crab was flashing in and out of the arches of Mumkeep Reef like a tropical fish.

"Boiler-brained grog-for-guts!" giggled another child, much older, nearly twelve.

"Spoiled spaniel of the seven seas!" hooted a fourth, a bouncing three-year-old Saturday with seaweed in his long hair. He didn't even have a topknot yet.

"Lime-loving lackspine buccane'er-do-well!" howled yet a fifth tittering, mocking blue nine-year-old Marid backstroking casually through the current. Cutty found that one particularly unnecessary. He had to love limes or else lose his teeth to scurvy! How was he to help the plain facts of naval life?

September crowed delight. They were surrounded by a school of Saturdays, darting, flashing, firing through the brine like blue arrows. Some were younger than the first Little S, hardly more than babies, some were old enough to have grown their topknots long, though none older than twelve, the age when Saturday met his mother and gave her a daisy. All the Saturdays her Marid had ever been, all coming out of time to help her like an army of love.

Words came on in September's head like cinema lights. She'd heard them as she was falling asleep at a play her mother took her to see long ago. A girl wore a boy's clothes and spent most of her time running around a forest not knowing anything about anything. She'd not thought of the words in years. She'd liked them because they had *thou* in them, which she thought the fanciest word anyone could wear, and still did. And with all the Saturdays wheeling about, spitting gobs of derision at the pirate king, they shook themselves awake in her head.

September climbed up to the top of the wall and yelled: "Thou art like a toad; ugly and venomous!"

The Sea seethed. Froth churned; the sand convulsed. The bandaged cow-riding giants and their burning badgers ceased banging away at the brick wall and skittered back as Little S's army came leaping out of every ripple of salt water. Great black, mostly toothless bilge-rats stampeded out of the sandbars wearing tricorns and long velvet coats and dashing rapiers on their hips. They held their tails like cat-o'-nines at the ready, thin and whippy and covered with scurvy sores. Behind them came the archers: well-brushed spaniels with curled ears and silk ribbons in their tails, notching chimney brushes into crab-claw crossbows. The pups remarked to their brothers in arms that their breakfast bones had not been *quite* so thick or so many as yesterday, but that Mumsy had promised they could all sleep on the bed tonight, so they might forgive her if she gave up some table scraps. And finally, the cavalry made their entrance. Out of the shipwrecks of Mumkeep Reef climbed a regiment of putrid princesses, skeletons in ragged, rotten gowns and tall, pointed hats covered in starfish and musketball holes. Their sea-slime hair oozed down their backs in oily braids. They wore sea slug rings on their bony fingers and sea cucumber necklaces round their bony spines. The princesses whistled to a herd of dejected merry-go-round ponies with grog-barrel cannons strapped to their saddles. The ponies sighed and bounced to their mistresses, using their carousel poles like pogo sticks. The ponies accepted their fates. What was the point of it all? They'd never know. The princesses mounted up, drawing cutlasses of their own, plundered from their own ships for one last charge.

A bilge-rat lifted a golden boiler-valve to his lips and blew through it like a hunting horn. The giants roared; the demonic cows threw themselves against the scurvy rats. The spoiled spaniels let fly a volley of chimney brushes that pierced badger after badger as they fell, the dogs howling and congratulating one another on each palpable hit. The princesses galloped full tilt, singing a ghostly war shanty, swinging their blades at giant knee and cow throat and badger snout without a care which was which.

In the midst of the fight, one last warrior hopped onto the field: a toad as big as a siege tower, its violet-and-green skin oozing exotic poisons. It fired its long pink tongue at the knees of one of the tallest giants, wrapped it round twice, and hauled him down onto the seafloor with a tremendous crash. The toad then turned and hopped back into the darker waters beyond the dueling ground, dragging her catch triumphantly behind her. In the wake of the toad, the furious waters went white with action. September could see nothing in the fizzing, boiling brine.

When the thrashing foam cleared, not one slimy braid off the skull of one putrid, valiant princess nor one bandage off the head of a giant remained. The round was a draw.

"No!" cried September. How could anything stand against rats and dogs and princesses and an incredible venomous toad? All those Saturdays had come—they ought to have won it. They were meant to have won it. Whenever another Saturday had turned up before, they'd always been on the right path.

But the Little S's were all gone. So was the kindly brick wall that had looked after them so well.

"That's how we are," Big S said with a sigh. "Now you see us, now you don't. Their time only swam alongside ours for a moment. Like ships passing overhead. They tried. I tried. We tried."

"It's all right," September whispered, and pinched Saturday's chin as they sometimes did when they didn't know what to say to make things seem good again. "I have to do it myself. That's what a Queen does. She saves herself."

"You're a grubby cheat," Cutty Soames gloated, sure they were spent. He pulled the levers of his black sea horse so he could get a closer look at his winnings. What burned behind his gaze now was victory. He didn't even bother calling her something outlandish. It was over. The wench had nothing. He had won. "Nothing but a silly little girl playing dress up."

A dress appeared in the water, swinging over an invisible clothes hanger. A frilly, lacy, poufy dress that looked like a cupcake had fallen icing-first into a drawer full of fake plastic jewels. A custard-colored beaver-fur cape hung over its shoulders. Slowly, menacingly, the dress unwound its strands of plastic jewels. It drifted toward September, taking its time.

September shook her head. She gave several strong kicks, rising up to the bubble glass eye that looked right into the Night Wagon's cabin. The dress flounced after her.

"Am not," she called to Cutty Soames, and laughed in his face. "Not silly, not little, not playing. Look at me, you old tyrant!" September held out her cuttlefished arm. "I've got a tattoo! I'm a *freak*. I'm a weirdo. I'm the crazy, nitwit Queen of Fairyland! So go soak your head."

And in that moment, she did want to be Queen. She wanted to be Queen so that no one like Cutty Soames could ever steal a potato or call a girl names ever again. The lace dress never got near her. The waters of Mumkeep Reef spun into a whirlpool, and out of the eye of the whirlpool flew a straitjacket. The kind of awful coat you only wear if you are Harry Houdini or a patient in the sort of dreadful places they sometimes put girls who cannot behave primly or properly. This one wasn't hospital white, though. It had tattoos inked all over it: hearts with arrows through them, mermaids, anchors, hula dancers, five-pointed stars, roses, dragons, and, in big block letters, the words *Mom* and *Dad* and *Victory*.

The straitjacket unbuckled its clasps, unlocked its locks, and swept up the lace dress into its long arms. It squeezed tight, tighter, tighter still, until the dress-up gown disappeared in a puff of old perfume.

. . .

Brother Tinpan brought September what was left of Cutty Soames, Captain of the Coblynows: a weathered, ancient coin with a star on one side and a ship at full sail on the other. A sevenpence coin from Cutty's own reign. September took it, but she didn't like it. Just because he was a tyrant didn't mean she felt happy about sending him back to Fiddler's Green or Davy Jones' Locker or wherever Fairyland pirates stashed their last treasure. Saturday leaned his head on her shoulder. September finished the dregs of her regicider, for it was surely nearing dinnertime on land. She nodded to the Monkfish, who regarded her with soft black eyes.

"I feel foolish, just asking after all this ruckus like I'm wanting directions to the general store. But I've got to, so I'm asking. Brother Tinpan, is there a piece of Fairyland's Heart in Mumkeep Reef? It was broken a long time ago, and I've got to gather it all up again, but I haven't even found one measly shard of the thing, and it's getting rather late in the day."

Brother Tinpan touched September's hand with his candy-cane-striped fin.

"A rainbow," he said, and swam back to Sepia Siphuncle and the hidden wonders of Mumkeep Reef, still hidden.

"I'm rubbish at riddles," September said, sighing, flipping the coin over her fingers a few times, a trick she'd learned from her father.

Saturday looked up through the miles of water, toward the sun and the shore and the rest of everything. "I like them. The one he meant goes *It's red and purple, orange and green, and no one can touch it, not even the Queen.*" He said nothing for a long time. "I was wrong. And now we're so far behind."

CHAPTER XIII

INSPECTOR ELL AND THE CASE OF THE HIJACKED HEART

*In Which September and Saturday Are Reunited with Their
Friends, A-Through-L and Blunderbuss Become Detectives,
and Everyone Gets Eaten by a Vole*

Fizzwilliam let them off just where he'd found them and
bid a fond farewell. He bent his front clawfeet forward in
the surf, bowing at the knee like a dapper parade horse. His
farewell sounded like a hot bath filling up to the brim, though,
of course, only September heard it. She left her diving mask—
now an unassuming shaving cup once more, on the captain's

seat. The Bathysphere disappeared beneath a cresting wave. The girl and the Marid looked up the beach strand, searching for a big red shape and a big orange shape somewhere in the shade of the green palms.

They didn't have to look long. It's not so hard to find a Wyverary and a giant wombat. Even if they were no bigger than a boy and a girl, you need only make a beeline for who- ever is making the most wholehearted hullabaloo about some thing or other they have just set their love on.

"Halloo!" A-Through-L called down the sand. He lay on his back under a canopy of palm and papaya and breadfruit trees, his wings stretched out lazily, one powerful leg crossed over the other, surrounded by a small mountain range of coconut shells and papaya skins and breadfruit crusts with jam still freshly oozing out of them.

"What time do you call this?" Blunderbuss growled. She meant it to sound endearingly mum-like, but wombat mums are very growly, so it came out rather ferociously. She didn't notice anything the matter. To a wombat, a growl sounds like love. "We've got to keep moving, you two!"

September and Saturday clambered up the black sand beachhead. Neither Ell nor Blunderbuss got up to greet them, being very full of fruit and very caged in by the remains of their lunch. The scrap-yarn wombat stretched out, hoisting up one of Ell's scarlet wings with her left forepaw to make a beach umbrella for herself. September kicked her way past the mounds of coconuts and fruit peels. She followed that long Wyvern tail until it became a Wyvern—a Wyvern wearing the most astonishing contraption on his familiar, friendly face.

"What . . . what are you wearing, Ell?" asked September, not wanting to offend if her friend had decided to try a new look.

The Wyverary had found two large pieces of sea glass and wrapped them all round with floatberry briars so that they would sit more or less straight on his muzzle. Leftover lengths of vine drooped down among his whiskers while the berries bobbed in the air at the ends of their curly stems like butterscotch-colored balloons. He'd also tied a length of brandybean vine round his waist like a bathrobe belt and hung a plump purple turnip from the thing. Ell peered over the rims of his new spectacles, looking entirely pleased with himself.

"It's my pince-nez! All great detectives wear them, you know." Ell grinned toothily. "Essential for Seeing Through Subterfuge and the Art of Observation!"

"It's my turn, Ell," yipped Blunderbuss. "Hand over the nosepincher and let me have a go! I've got a theory about that Oddson fellow. Top to bottom suspicious, wouldn't you say, monsieur?"

"Indubitably, madame," Ell replied gravely. He waggled his whiskers, curling them up like a waxed mustache. "But I think you'll find I've got another ten minutes!"

"We can't spare ten minutes," Saturday said miserably. "We didn't find anything at Mumkeep Reef. We're no better off than when we started. I bet Charlie Crunchcrab's got farther along than us by now."

"You found a tattoo," Blunderbuss chirped approvingly. She shook off the peels and shells and started stomping up the beach. "Nice!"

September squeezed a last bit of water out of her hair, running after the wombat. Ell thundered behind.

"Where are you going? We haven't decided our next move!"

"Our next move is to move. Can't stay in one place! Ell and I hashed it out while I had the pince-nez and we agree: next stop, the Worsted Wood. Where you got your wrench! That casket makes the Queen's sword, stands to reason it's necessary for becoming Queen. Maybe it's a piece of the Heart of Fairyland! And if not, the spriggans might know. Ell says they have a university, and that's where people keep their smarts."

A-Through-L picked September up in one claw and twisted round to put her on his back. Then, he snatched up Saturday in the same fashion. "It's far, but we can make up time if we don't stop to sleep, or for anything else. From this minute, no stopping till spriggans! We saw Goldmouth run by with a bundle under his arm—we hid, because he is dreadful, and I think you would be upset if you came back and found us bleeding. Though we would win, of course, in a fight! But we would probably get very bruised." His turnip banged against his knees as Ell ran.

September wrinkled her brow doubtfully. "Detectives? The Worsted Wood? What on earth are you two talking about?"

"We only left you for a few hours," marveled Saturday.

"If that's what you call 'all day and all night and half the next day,'" Blunderbuss grumbled. "We had to slap up some sort of fun. And lucky for you we did!"

"We've been reading!" Ell whooped. He pointed his nose toward their luggage. A small blue book peeked out from beneath the lid. A mightily abused dust jacket clung on to the cover for dear life. It showed two men in blue uniforms looking very concerned about a lovely young lady lying on a blue sofa. Above their heads, September read:

THE MYSTERY OF THE BLUE TRAIN,
BY AGATHA CHRISTIE

Ell rattled on as they ran. "Well, I have, mainly. Buss wanted to eat it, which I have tried to tell her is a completely wrongheaded way to go about literature-ing. She said I was being culturally insensitive and a complete dunce. But one of her favorite dunces, so that's nice."

The scrap-yarn wombat hid her face in a heap of papaya. "Aw, don't be sore, Ell. I'm only rude to my nearest and nearest. Anyway, I should've remembered. *Wombats* start with *W*. You gotta learn our p's and q's the slow way."

"We agreed the fairest fix was for me to read aloud. After all, if Buss did it her way, there wouldn't be any story leftover for me. So I did and we loved it so much I read it all through again and then we had a long discussion over our fourth dinner about the themes and imagery and metaphors—"

"Don't trust metaphors," the wombat snorted. "If you let things start claiming to mean other things, there's no limit on how many things they can mean! Madness! I am a stonking big knitted wombat, Ell is part Wyvern and part Library, and that's *that*. We don't mean anything but us and I'll fight anyone who says otherwise!"

"*I* mean lots of things, thank you kindly," the Wyverary said, without the littlest spot of anger in his voice. They had clearly got their teeth into that argument many times in the night. "Anyhow, the point is, we've talked it over, and we've decided to become detectives."

Blunderbuss nodded her woolly head enthusiastically. "We're on the case! The Case of the Hijacked Heart!"

"So you don't have to worry anymore! We've learned so much I feel dizzy! We are *much* more interesting beasts than when you left us. Now we know all about Mysteries, Deduction, Motives, Mistaken Identities, Jewel Thieves, Belgian People, Steam Trains, Red Herrings, Heiresses, Chloroform, Ballerinas, Cigarettes, Rubies, England, Femme Fatales, and Boy Femme Fatales Though There Doesn't Seem to Be a Word for That but There Should Be. Honestly, September, you never told me half of what your world gets up to! I told you all about mine, but you kept all this fantastic stuff in your back pocket. It's not fair. But it's amazing! I want to know more! Do all human men have splendid mustaches, or is it only Monsieur Poirot?" And he gave her a jaunty smile, curling his whiskers once more into a perfect, bright orange petit handlebar mustache.

September bit her lip. "Ell . . . did you steal that book from the Great Grand Library?"

The Wyverary let his whisker-mustache drop instantly. His eyes filled up with hurt. "How can you ask me that? September! I would *never* steal a book! I wouldn't even take a book from a cabinet marked Free Books unless I could track down the owner and make sure I was really allowed to. I would especially never steal a book from my Gigi!" Ell blushed. It went all the way up his cheeks and over the top of his head, turning him cantaloupe-colored as it went. "She said I could call her that," he whispered. "It stands for Great Grandmother. I know I ought to have come as soon as I heard Greenwich Mean Time sounding off at you, but I couldn't stop looking at the Human section. So many books I'd never heard of! So many titles I couldn't understand? What's a *Wuthering*? Why is it Important to Be Earnest? I am *always* earnest. Why would anyone not be? I tried to skim a few of them even though I know they're Special Collections and I oughtn't go grubbing them up without a librarian present, but I was *so* excited, and I was *very* careful, and claws aren't nearly so grubby as fingers and I just wanted to find out about the House of Mirth so *badly,* because it sounds like a *wonderful* place. And just as I was about to find out what was so great about Mr. Gatsby, a great huge candlestick with no candles in it leaned over and rested itself against my shoulder in just the gentlest way. Like when you lean your head against my shin sometimes. And the Great Grand Library whispered to me, because that's any library's favorite way of talking. She said . . ." A-Through-L had to stop for a moment. Turquoise tears swam up in his eyes. "She said I was a good librarian. She said my father would be so proud of me if he could have seen my alphabetizing and my powerful *shhh* and the size of my tail. She said I could visit her anytime I wanted and call her Gigi and next time she would make me cookies and let me use the Old Stamp. That's the first one Gigi ever had. Christopher Wren made it for her out of mushroom. It's her way of saying she trusts me, you see. The Old Stamp is very delicate. And I am very big." Blunderbuss sopped up his tears with her paw. She understood all about this sort of thing. She wanted the boy who made her to be proud of her, too. Ell made a sound between a laugh and a hiccup. "And then she said that as she'd missed all my birthdays, I could take one book to be my very own. My book. I've never owned a book before. A library's books belong to the library, not the librarian. She said I could have any one I wanted except *The Canterbury Tales,* as that one's her favorite."

"Why on earth did you pick Agatha Christie?" asked September, who thought murder mysteries were a little ghastly, though whenever her mother finished one, she snatched it right up.

Ell toed the sand bashfully. "Well . . . it sounded very exciting. And it had a lot of exclamation points in it, which is one of the signs of an excellent book. And I didn't like how Mr. Gatsby talked to people, when I was flipping through it. But mostly, *mostly* everything was blue on the front. And I like blue."

The Wyverary looked fondly at Saturday, who smiled uncertainly back.

"Don't even try to get it off him. You'd think it was his egg." The scrap-yarn wombat munched resentfully on a fresh coconut.

Ell raced on. "But don't you see? We know how to solve a mystery now. We know the method. We know the rules. We've taken the case, Buss and me, and we mean to solve it. We'll find the Heart of Fairyland before you can say denouement! It's all in here." He tapped the cover of *The Mystery of the Blue Train* with one claw—but gently, so as not to damage the dust jacket. "I've got everything we need: the pince-nez, the mustache, the patent leather shoes—well, I don't know what patent leather is, but my claws are black and shiny and at the ends of my feet so I think that's good enough, and I managed to make up for it with the turnip pocket watch." He displayed the purple turnip hanging from his belt, which he'd sliced so that it could open on a hinge and stuck a piece of coconut shell into the meat of the turnip as a sundial. "That part seemed odd to me, but I was very careful to do just as Monsieur Poirot does. When it comes to magical talismans, you can never tell which bit does the heavy lifting. You can never leave anything out."

September had never had a watch of her own, so she

couldn't tell her friend that people used to call certain kinds of pocket watches turnips on account of their shapes, and because turnip is more fun to say than watch. But let's keep that to ourselves, shall we? Ell did his best—and I couldn't bear to break it to him. Could you?

"We take turns with the talismans," Blunderbuss said pointedly. "One of us might catch something the other missed."

September shook her head in disbelief. "All right, I give in. What have you deduced, Mr. P? Where is the Heart of Fairyland?"

Blunderbuss and A-Through-L looked eagerly at each other.

"If we examine the evidence," Ell began.

"And retrace our steps," continued the wombat.

"The Marquess has it," they said together, and with finality.

"What?" September cried. "She can't! It's too soon! I didn't even get a chance! Do you know where she is? Can we get it back from her?"

Saturday blinked slowly in the sun. He hadn't said a word for a long while. The Marid shook his head from side to side like a dazed bull. He sighed, sat down on the black sand, and put his hands in his lap. And then he said an awful thing:

"I'm sorry, I don't understand. Who is the Marquess?"

September's eyes widened and a whole rush of words scrambled over themselves to get out of her first, but she didn't get a chance to say any single one of them. The black sand beneath them tilted sickeningly. The coconut trees began to swing wildly back and forth. Then the thirsthorn hedges burst into showers of fresh water. Then the floatberry brambles snapped and rolled down the beachhead. Ell and Blunderbuss began to run, and then lift off into the air. Whatever was coming, they did not want it to catch them!

A great dark shape broke the sands like a whale's back breaking the waves. September could not think of anything to compare it to. *As big as the Briary. As big as the Jarlhopp's mines below the world. As big as a newborn moon.* Chunks of hard, sharp red crystal covered the shape, a red so deep it looked black until the sun hit it and sent a dizzying dance of maroon prisms bouncing through the air. But beneath the red-black diamond nuggets, soft, sleek fur stuck out like grass breaking through cobblestones to grow in the sun. The shape shuddered and disappeared beneath the sand.

When it rose again, the Greatvole of Black Salt Cavern seized them all in its impossible mouth and dove deep down into the earth.

CHAPTER XIV

A Detour Through Voleworld

*In Which September Rides a Greatvole under the World,
Saturday Cuts His Hair, and Blunderbuss Loses Several Toes*

You and I have traveled together often, to places both odd and outlandish—and sometimes spectacular. We are no strangers to the underground! We have run headlong down to Fairyland-Below and learned to like it there! We danced in the capital and had tea with a Minotaur. We have no fear of the dark or the deep! I'd wager you didn't even gasp when the Greatvole snatched up September and her friends and dove beneath the sand! Instead, you clapped your hands and said:

Oh, I am glad! Fairyland-Below is a very exciting place and I shall be happy to see it again!

But voles, even Greatvoles, do not live in Fairyland-Below.

Let us think of Fairyland as a staggeringly magnificent cake, one with three layers and far too many frosting flowers and glacé strawberries and fondant ripples and flaming plums all over it. Let us take a great swaggering knife between us— it will take both our hands—and slice it open to see what we can see inside. For that is all a story is, my dears: a knife that cuts the world into pieces small enough to eat.

All that icing and candied madness on top is the land we've wandered through so far, Pandemonium and the Autumn Provinces and Meridian and even the Whelk of the Moon. Below that we should find a scrumptious dark slab of cakey chocolate earth where folk can plant their carrot seeds and pear trees. If we cut deeper, we should find another slab, thick and moist and full of shadowy sugar and delicious adventures, and that is Fairyland-Below. Further and farther than that, we should at last come to the last morsels of cake: the rock and magma and the very sort of hot, spinning core you've seen in your geography classes. Of course, in Fairyland, the core is not only a superheated ball of magnetized metals, but also the Nickelodeon, a red-hot city of lavalings living the lavish life.

Perhaps you have now realized that voles and other creatures of the Digging Class would not dive all the way down
to the sparkling cities of Fairyland-Below. They chew through
the earthy cake where seeds sprout and worms and beetles and
pill bugs and ants and grubs and anything else that loves to
crawl crawls their best. The Greatvole of Black Salt Cavern
swam through the earth like a cuttlefish through the water.
Her paws paddled gracefully through the loam and the clay.
Her tail swept back and forth with the powerful rhythm of a
shark. The Greatvole moved so fast you and I would hardly
glimpse her passing, the way subway trains clip by in the dark
so quick that all you catch is a long stripe of light. And so
September opened her mouth to scream—and only got a single horrid gulp of dirt before the dark, wet mud vanished and
they could all see and breathe quite easily again.

For you cannot bake a three-layer cake with nothing at all
to stick them together! Between those wonderful layers of
Fairyland's geographical trifle lie ribbons of berries and syrup
and still more frosting: the secret caves and grottoes of
Voleworld.

Voleworld is a paradise for all who love to dig—wide
enough and high enough for any bulldozing beast. Friendly
work lamps twisted into chandeliers light the shadows into a
warm, homey glow. Mudpaintings of great diggers dot the

walls: Grundler the Mad Mole, Electro-Hare the Holy Holer, Whistlepig the Grandhog, Spadeheart the Bombastic Bilby Rat. Here is where the diggers come to rest. You'll find a thousand taverns made of shovels and picks battened together, bathhouses hammered out of gold pans and roofed in dud dynamite sticks, and drill-bit dance halls playing all the underground hits on a dirt bottle organ. And, most importantly, Voleworld lies beneath the whole of Fairyland, connecting each acre with each county. Get down into Voleworld and you can get anywhere else you like quicker than an earthworm's wriggle. Which is why the devoted diggers tell no one about their home, and make certain that no exit or entrance is labeled sensibly.

September, Saturday, Ell, and Blunderbuss opened their eyes to see everything I have just told you streaming past on either side. The portrait of Electro-Hare, the Shovel and Headlamp Inn, the Ruby Rake Night Club, the tunnels leading every which where which wheres can wind. All four of them had the same urgent idea at once: Somebody else's mouth was no place to be. The Greatvole had September by the back of her emerald smoking jacket, Saturday by his topknot, Ell by his turnip pocket watch, and Blunderbuss by her little fuzzy woolen tail and one hind leg. The emerald-colored smoking jacket split hurriedly down the back so as not to be the cause of its owner's death. Coats have a strict honor code, and any one failing to protect its owner from rain, snow, hail, or ravening rodents shall be made into overalls at once.

September scrambled up the Greatvole's onyx teeth and over the top of her nose, grappling onto the red-black crystals to haul herself up. Saturday made no time for a first, second, or third thought: He whicked out a little pair of scissors from his trousers and cut his splendid topknot in half, climbing up after September. Ell looked worriedly at Blunderbuss. He could bite off his watch fob, no problem. But where would that leave the scrap-yarn wombat? She didn't have any scissors, but even if she had, the loss of a leg would hurt her pride so. The Wyverary twisted round so that his snout poked right up against the greatsnout of the Greatvole. Ell had not met many folk bigger than himself, and if it were not *very* urgent, he'd sit his red haunches down for a long chat. But it was very urgent, and so the Wyverary took a short, shallow breath— enough to scald, but not to roast—and blew a bubbling burp of indigo flame straight into the left nostril of the Greatvole.

The creature roared indignantly and opened its mouth to give whatever had bothered it a good, deep bite. Ell and Blunderbuss flew up and over those smoking nostrils in a flash of orange and red, tumbling over the Greatvole's eyebrows and skull, down her neck and black salt spine, and into a shallow space between her shoulder blades where September and Saturday sat on their knees, catching their breath. The emerald smoking jacket had already seamed itself back up into a fetching short emerald-colored bolero jacket, so that September could move about freely and not get a sash snagged on any vole parts. Two large, pearly tears dropped from Saturday's eyes as he felt back for his proud topknot and found only a ragged, sawed-off ponytail. All September wanted to do was shake him until he explained why he couldn't remember the most important things that had ever happened to them, but there was no time, no time. And the wombat was on fire.

September leapt forward and batted at Blunderbuss's hind leg, which smoked and crackled like a broiling Christmas ham.

"Watch where you aim that fire hose, you great red lunkhead! Clodhopper! Donkey! Sir Oafington of Oaf Hall!" the wombat hollered and hawed, trying to stub out her paw on the Greatvole's back like a cigar. Ell's whiskers drooped. Saturday sniffled and puffed out his cheeks, then blew a ball of glittering sea foam at the half-cooked wombat-shank. September had seen him do that from a trapeze platform once, with a smile on his face that would blind every star in the sky. But now he did it with no more pomp than a winter's cough. The foam sizzled as it hit blackened wool, but the embers died out, leaving only steam. Saturday fell back against Ell, exhausted, curling into a little blue ball.

Blunderbuss waggled her hind paw, trying to get a look at the damage. September could see stuffing coming out, but she didn't want to embarrass Blunderbuss by saying anything. Then the wombat saw A-Through-L's miserable, embarrassed eyes, pleading forgiveness with every long eyelash.

"Oh, come on, don't be such a Sensitive Susie! I've called you worse over the question of Poirot's mustache! You know I never mean it. You're my Sir Oafington and I like you better than all the clowncakes in Oaf Hall. In the Land of Wom, that's just how we talk to our families! You gotta be nice to strangers even when they are the worst, because they don't know you well enough to understand how *shut your big face* can mean *I've missed you more than the whole world can know.* Come on! Call me something! You can do it!"

A-Through-L stared at his feet. He did try. But all that came out was "You have very nice eyes."

Blunderbuss blinked her very nice eyes. "Ooof. Don't worry about it, not everyone's got the knack. Thanks for the escape, Inspector Ell-O. Now where the devil is this ripsnorter taking us?"

September wiped her hands on her legs. The Watchful

Dress, though currently shaped like sensible work trousers, did not appreciate it. Mud came off her palms—they were all quite grimy, really. But little black crystals tumbled free as well, pieces of the huge dark rough-cut gems crusting over the creature's mammoth body. September picked a little crystal up and tasted it gingerly.

"Salt!" she exclaimed. And then understood. "Oh . . . oh no. I thought we'd only been gone a few hours! But you said . . . you said we were under the sea all night and into the next afternoon. I didn't have my breakfast! I didn't eat my flapjacks or my cordial! This is the Greatvole of Black Salt Cavern and she's woken from her thousand-year slumber!"

"My name is Brunhilda," the Greatvole rumbled, like continents crashing together. "If you wouldn't mind shifting, I've got a nerve just there, and you're pinching it."

They scrambled to move out of their little shallow between two shoulder blades, farther up so they nestled against the nape of her neck. The ride was much rougher up there. September clung on desperately as the Greatvole stretched her long-sleepy muscles.

"Are you . . . are you going to devour the world and chew on its bones?" Ell asked carefully.

The Greatvole snorted. The roofs of Voleworld's taverns and inns fluttered with the force of her breath. "Not today, if that's all right by you. Worlds give me heartburn. They stick in the gullet something fierce. But thank you for assuming the worst, it's not at all painful to be wakened by ignorant prejudices!"

"I'm sorry! It's only that I read all about you when I was a hatchling. You start with G! And all the encyclopedias in my father's stacks agree that you nearly destroyed Fairyland with your terrible digging and chewing and tunneling, until the Rex Tyrannosaur hit you over the head with a mountain and sent the honeybees of Wallowdream to sting you to sleep."

"Such a lot of fuss over a few earthquakes! Nobody talks about how beautiful my new mountain ranges looked, or the new ski resort opportunities I opened up every time I broke the surface and shoved up fresh slopes, or how nicely a bottomless chasm goes with any city, no matter the style. Or all the jewels and gold I spat out when I got done chewing through a desert! Or the absolute *fact* that without me, Fairyland would still be a big flat boring nix and naught full of crabgrass and dust, fit for nothing but lawn chairs! I tunneled out everything here! S'why they call it Voleworld and not Rabbitworld or Meerkatworld. Every time you relax in a lovely valley or tightrope between two towering crags, you ought to thank your lucky geography for Brunhilda the Greatvole! But no! Instead, they all whined and bawled like a bunch of babies because good design takes risks. Because I erased a few rough drafts when anyone could see farming villages just don't *go* with tundra ecosystems! Let me be a lesson to you, kiddies—keep your dreams small. Build your own house and they'll praise you staircase to windows. Build your own world and you'll get all the thanks a mouse gives a snake. So yes, then Thrum the Rex Tyrannosaur sent all those bees after me and I'm sure he had a grand old party with all his Uptop friends, telling vicious vole jokes and congratulating themselves on getting a spanking-new topography for the bargain price of a vole's pride. Maybe he's still lording it on his Cretaceous Throne, guzzling bone-beer and admiring the swanky cave I made for him."

September frowned. All the while the Greatvole had been complaining, she'd been carefully, quietly fetching her flapjacks and cordial from their luggage. She paused with flask and plate in hand. "I don't think so," she said slowly. Whatever Thrum was doing at that moment, she felt sure it had nothing to do with bone-beer. "You've been asleep for a thousand years." It seemed safer on the whole not to mention to a resentful behemoth that Thrum had come back from the dead along with everyone else and was therefore huntable and findable, so long as he had not had any dueling mishaps yet.

"Perhaps," September said, hoping to sound both polite

and commanding, "you might take us to the Worsted Wood? We need to move quickly, or I wouldn't ask. You seem terribly fast and strong. If you took us under the ground instead of over it, we might make it in time to win the Cantankerous Derby."

The Greatvole of Black Salt Cavern slowed and stopped. This took many miles, for anything as large as a Greatvole cannot go from top volespeed to zero in less than seven leagues.

"Oh," Brunhilda said, her voice clogged up with sorrow. "A thousand years? Why didn't anyone wake me? I suppose erosion will have spoiled my best work by now. The sea and the wind and the heat and the snow will have taken the edges off my crags and the colors off my canyons. A thousand years is a long time to go without basic maintenance. I meant to keep it all tidy and fresh, once I'd finished. I meant to *finish*."

September did not think. She acted, and thought about it later, and had a little quiver, because the Greatvole could have eaten her and everyone she loved and asked for dessert. She tapped Ell's knee. The Wyverary flew her gently down from the skull of the Greatvole, with Blunderbuss and Saturday following behind. She steadied her heart and strode up to the salt-jeweled beast's huge face. *You can stop up hurts, if you are Queen,* she thought, and her heart beat madly in her chest.

"Brunhilda, Greatvole of Black Salt Cavern, I am September, the Engineer. Which is to say, Queen of Fairyland and all Her Kingdoms. It is my duty as Queen to send you right back to sleep with no supper. In fact, I am the only ruler of Fairyland in a thousand years to fail to keep you conked out. And I have to get you back to bed, because otherwise you're going to start erasing villages again, and I daresay villages like to stay where they're put."

The Greatvole started to growl again, but September held up her hands. Her eyes shone with the strange feeling of knowing the right thing to do. If she'd only known it, she looked very like a certain Changeling troll had done on a playground in Chicago, talking to a boy who wanted very much to hit him.

"Brunhilda, *thank you*," September said, and into her voice she put all the warmth she'd ever heard from her mother and her father and Ell and Saturday and Aunt Margaret and Aubergine and the Whelk of the Moon. "Fairyland is the most beautiful place anyone could want. I love it awfully. I love the Candelabra Desert and the Worsted Wood and the Perverse and Perilous Sea and every island in it. I love the Barleybroom and Pandemonium and the way you can follow a mountain road all the way to the Moon. I came across the whole universe just to see it. Most of the time, it's so wonderful, it stops me missing my home and my family and everything I ever loved before I met Fairyland. Most of the time. "

"I made that mountain," the Greatvole said shyly. "It was so hard to get the curls of her hair right."

"I know you did." September smiled, though she didn't know that mountain had curly hair, for she'd never seen it from far off, only from its peak. "You did so well. But just now, Fairyland is in the middle of a rather sprawling mess, and if you start fixing up your work like I know you want to, no one will understand that you're only trying to make it perfect. They'll send the bees after you again. Now, I don't want to put you to sleep. I hate the taste of these dry flapjacks anyhow. But I shall have to unless you do as I ask."

The Greatvole gnawed on a bit of tunnel and waited.

"Let Fairyland stay. Brunhilda, it *is* finished. It's finished and wonderful and none of us want it any different. Even the bits that the sea and the wind and a lot of revolutions have worn off and broken off and blown off—Fairyland wouldn't be quite as lovely without her broken bits. So don't sleep— just rest. Enjoy some bone-beer of your own. And when this is all done I promise to call down to Voleworld and you can come up and start a new geography in some place that hasn't got a village yet. We'll pick it out together. No bees, no bears, no one to tell you what fjord to put where. And before you rest, take us where we need to go, so that I can keep my crown and my promise."

The Greatvole gnawed some more.

"Fine. But I hate fjords. Snap off one of my whiskers—the smallest one you can find or you won't be able to fit your little hands around it. Take it and when you want me, when it's time for my triumphant new archipelago . . . or maybe a chain of volcanoes . . . well, just stick it in the ground and call my name."

The whisker was as long as a black crystal sword in September's hand. She slid it into a sudden sheath in the Watchful Dress and looked at a clutch of dark tunnel entrances in the wall of Voleworld. The Greatvole bored happily through the earth up ahead of them, leaving them to their choice. Each had a neat wooden hatch with large, well-made words burned into it:

TO WIN THE DAY
TO WIN THE HAND
TO WIN AGAINST ODDS
TO WIN THE WAR

September did not have to think twice.

THE HOURGLASS WASTE

*In Which Lions Attack, Songs Are Sung in French,
and Everyone Misses Something Deathly Important,
Except for the Dog*

It is always difficult to believe that while we are having our own adventures, others are behaving with just as much der-ring-do and flash and swashing of the buckles as we. It is especially hard for children to believe that their parents might be off performing their own astonishing feats of Grown-Upedness whilst their little ones are battling ferocious octopi under the sea. But it is true. The Land of Parents is strange and full of peril.

September's family sped through Fairyland on a sleigh drawn by six hippopotami named for her grandfather's liquor cabinet. Aunt Margaret's hippos were much faster than the kind you and I have seen in the zoo. They are much faster than cheetahs or hawks, and a bit slower than the newest and most modern of trains. They flew through the Inksop Marshes and the Candelabra Desert, through the Worsted Wood and the Springtime Quarter where the Marquess had slept for years. They spent a night in the shadow of the Peppercorn Pyramids. Susan Jane made a respectable campfire out of a few of the daggers from fallen redcroak branches, and a bit of black, crumbled pyramid. They sang one another songs and Fenris howled, for he longed to be included. Owen sang them a lovely French song he had learned at the front, though it made him sad and Susan Jane had to hold him tight until he fell asleep.

In the night, they were menaced by two blue lions, grown thin and rangy without anyone to feed them. September's father socked one in the jaw. September's mother flung one of the daggers she'd squirreled away from the dagger-tree at the other's shoulder. But when the lions saw Aunt Margaret, they whined and shook their heads and backed away, their blue tongues lolling.

"Madame Pearl," they whispered in terror, and bolted back across the meadow.

"Is that what they call you here?" Susan Jane said as they tried to go back to sleep.

"Yes. *Margaret* means 'Pearl' in Greek, you know. I thought it sounded very romantic. And at the time, I was living on the Moon, the great big Pearl in the sky."

"It must be nice to give yourself a fancy new name," September's mother yawned. "I always thought I could do with something grander than Susan."

In the morning, the galloping liquor cabinet pulled them past Flegethon City where the ifrits live and burn. When the suburban flames died out, they found themselves in a vast, pale, barren wilderness. The land thirsted, the stones were tall and thin, the color of snow. The air grew hot and still and heavy all round. And everywhere they saw hourglasses filled with sands of darkest red and green and blue and violet—some tiny, wedged between boulders, some so huge that a mountaineer might think them a proper challenge. Greenwich Mean Time was born here, in the Hourglass Waste. Margaret seemed suddenly very sullen and sour. She begged her hippos to run faster. *Over the next hill there's water and glowerwheat, my loves, I promise!*

Soon enough they did top the next hill and down into a valley full of wheat with little gas flames burning at their tips. The sun began to set, turning the sky a wild scarlet. Susan Jane and Owen looked up at Fairyland's Moons rising in the east. *One's so much smaller than the other,* September's father thought. *How strange!*

As they left the Hourglass Waste behind them, a gust of

wind billowed through two chalky crags. An hourglass slosh-ing with pomegranate-red sand lay snugly between them, half buried in the white dust of the Waste. The breeze blew the dust away from the glass and the wood and the crags, up and into the sunset and over the glowerwheat.

The hourglass had a brass plaque on it. Neither Margaret nor September's parents nor the hippopotami saw it. Fenris did, but he could not tell anyone, though he yipped valiantly. The plaque read:

SEPTEMBER MORNING BELL

And its sand had nearly run out.

CHAPTER XV

THE BRAVE AND THE BONKERS

In Which Blunderbuss Goes Home, Everyone Eats and Yells a Great Deal, and September Jousts a Dinosaur on Wombat-Back

They climbed out of the earth into a hot, tangled, green-golden valley. The sun crackled and popped on the oddest plants: fire-colored flowers shaped like great thick stacks of ice cream scoops, whippy vines heavy with ripe, black-skinned passionfruit oozing seeds, long, hot pink blossoms hanging like tongues from the branches of macadamia trees, big glossy quandong fruits dropping softly now and then from ashy, squat trees, skinny orange yams pushing up half out of the ground. September and Saturday put their hands over their noses.

"But this isn't the Worsted Wood at all!" cried September. Her frustration felt like a bellyful of boulders. Would they never get on the right track? She reached back for Saturday's hand.

"If we win, you will . . ." But he couldn't think of how to finish.

September touched his face. "Just hold on, Saturday. We'll find out what's wrong."

A-Through-L howled. "There's no woolly trees or pumpkin pies or anything! Where are we?"

Blunderbuss opened her nostrils wide and sucked in the scents of the place that was decidedly not the Worsted Wood.

"Slap my bony rump if that's not the best whiff I've ever gulped! What's your problem? Come on, you dags! Open your mouths and huff! Chew on that *air*! Each breath's as good as a meal! You don't know, it might be the Wood! Maybe the spriggans have redecorated since you last popped by. I'm sure it is! You said the Worsted Wood was beautiful—isn't this beautiful?"

Blunderbuss wasn't wrong. The smell of the place was wonderful—rich and sweet and savory and sharp. But it was so *strong*. September felt faint, as though a bushel of apples had pummeled her head. The scrap-yarn wombat scampered on ahead.

"Are those blue tongues? Ell, you gotta try these! They turn your tongue blue, see?" She dove headfirst into a thicket of electric-blue berries and came up sticking out her scrap-yarn tongue, stained ultramarine with juice. Ell adjusted his sea-glass spectacles and checked his turnip pocket watch.

"It's quarter past that rotted bit there," he fretted. "Hadn't we better figure out where we are and get back to the Derby? Someone could cross the finish line anytime and we wouldn't even know unless Ajax sent us a note! We have to *go*!"

"I know! I know!" Blunderbuss danced from paw to paw, hardly able to contain herself. "But . . . but we're here. Now! What if we never find it again? Even though you won't let me have my turn with the specs, let us DEDUCE the STUFFING out of it, mon ami! Whaddowe got? Quandongs?" She snarfed a big red one off a bush. "Check. Macadamias? Check. Passionfruits?" She ripped a dozen off their vines and gobbled them down. "Huge spanking check! Emu apples, golden wattles, blue tongues, warrigal greens? Cram 'em in your face! Top-shelf digging dirt? Oh yes, we have some right here! And if that's not enough, look, look, follow me!"

The scrap-yarn wombat leapt out of the brush and scurried up over a hill covered in blue tongue berries. Her paws left wet prints full of smashed cerulean fruit. They scrambled up after her. Blunderbuss was already crowing and jigging and spinning around three times in excitement. She bent down and bit the earth, to show that she liked a thing, and that she thought a thing was delicious, and that she thought it was hers.

"We're in the Land of Wom!" Blunderbuss roared.

September got herself up to the top of the hill, slipping on berries all the way. She looked down into the north end of the valley. A village spread out as happily as a cat in a sunbeam. It was a shantytown, full of clapboard houses and peeling board-walks and rusty nails and swinging signs. Warm wind whistled through the slats of the buildings. But the slats and boards and posts and roofs were all painted like the night sky. Deep black and blue and burning stars, white comets and tiny, twinkling red planets. *I've never seen painting like that,* September thought to herself. *Even that fellow in Rome couldn't make that bakery look so exactly like the Milky Way.*

"I'm home! Me! Blunderbuss! The Great Chicago Wombat! What are the odds?"

September smiled. She thought of the door she'd chosen and was glad for Buss. But she'd chosen to win against odds— Oddson. She'd thought it would take them right where they needed to go. But why would the Heart of Fairyland be hiding in the Land of Wom? This couldn't be right. "Buss, if you're from Chicago, how do you know we're in Wom?"

Blunderbuss puffed out her chest proudly. "When Hawthorn asked me to come to life, he specifically said: *Please wake up right now this moment and be alive like Scratch and be a real wombat and be able to talk and walk and bite and do marvelous things like firing passionfruits and horseshoes and whiskey bottles out of your mouth at our enemies and singing the ancient songs of the Land of Wom, which we both know is the most beautiful Land that ever was a Land.* He's a very polite boy and he thought of everything and now I am HOME and HOME means BITES, FOODS, and OTHER WOMBATS. Last one to Wom is a kangaroo!"

"Wait, Buss, we can't stay! Wait!" September protested.

But off she ran, and off they all ran after her. They couldn't leave her if they wanted to—if they got to Mummery without their steed, they'd be disqualified anyway. Saturday laughed madly and spun around a few times of his own on the way into town, without a care. September was all care, but she resolved not to show it. Not yet. *Everyone deserves to go home and feel happy about it when they get there,* she thought. *Everyone. Queens shouldn't worry or whine, should they? We can't be so badly off. It's not halftime yet. Ajax said at halftime we all swap places.*

Blunderbuss tumbled into the center of town, her huge-ness throwing shadows up against the night-sky shacks.

"Whoa there, cobber!" a handsome, furry wombat hollered from a twilit rocking chair on a starry porch. The sign over his head read PUDDING-FOR-ALL GENERAL STORE. He wore a smart waistcoat and small, round sunglasses. "Slow yourself down, how about that?"

For a moment, September thought Blunderbuss was going to cry. She scrunched up her diamond-shaped magenta button eye, and then her thick brass button eye. She wrinkled up her nose and shook her head bullishly from side to side. She got so choked up she couldn't say a thing, which was certainly a first. The scrap-yarn wombat had never met a claw-and-fur wombat before.

The other wombat pulled a carrot-cob pipe out of his waistcoat pocket and lit it without a match. He had a bit of Wombat Magic and didn't mind showing off. "No need to go thundering about like your arse's on fire. Ruddy tourists. No respect for anyone. Go on, get your postcards and be on your way, thank you!"

Blunderbuss finally found her voice. "I'm not a tourist, I'm a wombat!"

"Oh, come off yourself, you are not," scoffed the furry fellow.

"I am so! Look at my teeth!" Blunderbuss bared her cloak-clasp teeth, which only seemed to make the other wombat uncomfortable.

"If you're a wombat, I'm a cockatoo!"

"She's the most wombat I've ever known," A-Through-L said with all the sternness any Wyvern can command. If only he had not had a turnip tied round his waist, even a mountain would have cowered.

The wombat spat onto his veranda. "You're made out of yarn *and* you're the size of a rhinoceros. I know wombats are the greatest animals ever invented, and it's only natural you should *want* to be one, but you're embarrassing yourself, mate."

Blunderbuss gritted her teeth. She strode proudly over to the Puddings-For-All General Store and pointed one fuzzy lilac-colored paw at the wombat in the rocking chair. "You listen here, Little Lord Much-a-Much. I am from Chicago and in Chicago, *all* wombats are made of yarn and the size of rhinoceroses! Is this how you say how-do to out-of-town cousins? I always heard the Fairyland branch of the family were nice as raisins, but you're just a cheeky little runted bear cub and I shall tell everyone so when I get back." She was, of course, quite right. Being the only wombat in Chicago, all wombats in the city looked just like her.

The wombat creaked back and forth on his spangled rocker, puffing on his pipe. Then he burst out of the chair and off the porch, giving Blunderbuss's paw a great, solid bite. Buss didn't yelp. She grinned like Christmas.

"You should have said! I've always wanted to meet a Batty from . . . Chicago, was it? Well, I'm a mad old duffer, ask anyone, but I own up when I'm wrong. Of course you're one of us! No one but a wombat could disrespect me so lovingly! Welcome! I'm called Conker, this is my store—Oy, Bluestocking!" Conker yelled into the shop. "Come meet the biggest Batty you'll ever see! Now, there's not room for you inside, I'm afraid, and you do seem to have a *lot* of friends, and that one's a bit . . . well, he's a bit all over Wyvern for my comfort, but you won't want to stay out in the sun and roast. Let's get you into the Night-Barn! It's where we have our after-dinner dances and our pre-lunch layabouts. Hurry now, you great hippo, you'll want to meet everyone!"

"Not everyone," whispered September. "Please. The Derby."

"Just let me have a minute," pleaded the wombat. "A minute at home. Don't you want a minute at home?"

September suddenly felt so tired she wanted to lie down in the road and pull it up over her like her bed under the Briary. Home. Home, with Mom and Dad and oranges and a cake in the icebox. Home.

"I'm starving!" said Saturday, and bolted off toward the barn. "The Derby will keep! Just a bunch of silly running around anyway!"

Where was her Saturday? What had happened to him? They should never have gone to Mumkeep Reef, September thought, and that was the truth.

They walked down the wide wombat road, past star-spattered signs that told them all about Dog's Breakfast Bakery, the Happy Shovel Tool Repair (A Happy Shovel Is a Dirty Shovel!), and Bustnose's Fine Joolery, a cozy moonlit inn called The Courageous Quokka attached to a less cozy but much larger pub called The Querulous Quokka (known jointly as the Brave and the Bonkers, for no one had time to say all that mess together), Tugboat's Terrific Tobaccos and Constitutional Law Shoppe, and dozens of little sturdy black and blue houses gleaming with constellations. The great glittering barn at the end of the road opened up invitingly, full of shade and the bustle of wombats. Long garlands of macadamia flowers hung on the walls, fine cool dirt covered the floor, and the stars on the rafters lit it all in soft silver. As she stepped through the door frame, September touched the barn-boards with her bare hand—and snatched her hand away as though it had scalded her. The Night-Barn had no wood in it at all. The slats were slick and hard and blisteringly cold. She could feel the frozen winds of space howling through them, the winds she had felt tearing at her on the Moon. She almost thought, if she leaned too hard, she would fall into the ragged, beaten boards and tumble into the naked black sky.

The wombats had built their town out of the night itself.

"Are Chicago wombats nocturnal?" Conker asked politely. "We figured a ways back it made no sense to confine your loafing, feasting, digging, and dancing to the nighttime! You lose fifty percent of your fossicking time that way! S'why we built our little town of Nightgown, so we could have our comfortable dark all round anytime we liked and not lose a moment of puttering and prattling. Best village in Wom, no competition! Plus, when you think about it, if you're nocturnal, you can only have supper, dinner, a nightcap, and a midnight snack. Really limits your gorging options, yeah? Stick around in the daytime and you get breakfast, lunch, tea, and afternoon nibblies as well!"

"But when do you sleep?" asked Blunderbuss, who had never heard that she was meant to be nocturnal in the first place.

"We wombatnap now. Screamingly efficient. Fifteen minutes an hour will keep you sharp!" Conker hopped up, grabbed a rope hanging from a big, dented bell, and swung back and forth, ringing the thing within an inch of its life.

Wombats banged open their doors all over town, wriggling their soft noses in the wind and trotting on down toward the barn, laughing roughly and growling and biting one another as they came.

"Here we go! Here's our mob! Blunderbuss—and what a great big chomp of a name that is!—this is Shilling, she's our candle maker, and here's Meatpie and Snagger, our glassblowing brothers, Bluestocking, my wife, the mudbrained buffoon of my heart, Oatmeal, our tinker, Banjo, the town poet, Chicory, our dressmaker, Fair Dinkum, the town beauty, Watchpot, our soup maker, Gregory, well, Wom only knows what you do around here . . ."

And on and on they came, each large and bright-furred and loud, each terrified for a moment of Blunderbuss and A-Through-L, then rambunctiously affectionate once all had been explained. September and Saturday and Ell said more *Hello*s and *How Do You Do*s in a quarter of an hour than they thought they'd said yet in their life.

Conker crooned in delight as a particularly robust wombat wearing a powdered judge's wig made her entrance. "And this, Blunderbuss, *this* is Tugboat, our Tobacconist and leader of all the nations of Wom! We'll show you how we do our governmenting after tea."

As the scrap-yarn wombat was busy impressing everyone

by telling them she already knew of the Fair and Just Tugboat and how she chewed up the laws suggested by the wombattery at large and spit them at the wall, keeping what stuck and chucking the rest, Conker and Meatpie and a bright yellow wombat named Lollygag made the tea. They stuffed pawfuls of tea leaves into tin buckets, filled them with hot water from an enormous simmering pot at the back of the barn, and holding their waistcoats out of the way with one paw, swung the pails around their heads frightfully fast to get it all steeping.

"How do you choose a Tobacconist?" Saturday asked. He popped a gooseberry into his blue mouth.

"Only because in Fairyland proper they apparently do it by running all over the place like a madwoman's laundry," Blunderbuss said with a giggle, munching on a heap of golden wattle-flowers.

"Eh," yawned Conker as he poured the tea into a long starry trough so they could all drink as equals, "she wanted to? And no one else minded?"

Tugboat laughed gruntingly. "These bludgers don't like the taste of the laws. Oh, they're nasty, they taste like sour nuts and bitter old stinky fur and being responsible for things! Waa, waa, waa! Gnawknuckle over there took one lick of the Law for Fair Distribution of Gravy and sicked up all over the place like a picky little baby. They taste fine to me! Fine as a yam in a pot that says ALL FOR TUGBOAT on it!"

"I like the taste of anything," Blunderbuss gruffed happily.

"I bet you do, you great fat Sunday roast! Ah, but that's the trait of a true wombat. Good to know even the Chicago mob shares our values! Unconquerable Bellies! Mighty Bities! Stiff Upper Pouches! That was my campaign slogan, you know. Pickiness is for mammals! We are marsupials! And you can't make a marsupial without soup, and it is time for my soup, and I want my soup. Watchpot! Soup me!"

The Tobacconist of the Land of Wom trundled off to the soup barrels.

"Did you hear, September?" whispered a breathless Blunderbuss. "She called me a great fat Sunday roast! Tugboat the Tobacconist called *me* a fat glob of meat!"

"Congratulations?" ventured September. "Can we ask the way to the Worsted Wood? Or is that only polite after tea?"

"I swear, you lot never listen to a word I say. That means she thinks I'm beautiful and wonderful and practically her *daughter* and I should definitely, *definitely* come round for All Bowls Day this year—that's in November. You can come, too, I'm sure she won't mind—"

A vicious, booming roar crashed through the Night-Barn. It rang in September's ears. Ell groaned, digging at his. Saturday spun to defend himself, drawing his scissors and holding his breath. The wombats of Nightgown lifted their noses and snuffled at the sound, mildly interested.

"Just knock, how about that?" Conker hollered. He waddled over and flung the barn doors open.

Outside stood Thrum, the Rex Tyrannosaur, his teeth out and his eyes blazing. His green-black scales shone darkly in the sunshine.

"Thrum! What are you doing here?" September's ideas of what was sensible and what wasn't shoved her right out of being scared. "What could you *possibly* be doing here? *We* didn't even mean to come here! Did you actually come looking for the Heart of Fairyland in a wombat town?"

The tyrannosaurus looked a little shamefaced—but only a little, for dinosaurs would rather drown in tar than admit they're wrong. That unfortunate attitude played a key role in their extinction. Naturally, they have steadfastly refused to own up to it, so I cannot tell you where it all went reptiles-up.

"A Heart is meat," Thrum said stubbornly. "No one knows more about food than wombats. They *might* know. *You* don't know anything!"

September laughed in his face. "Wow, you really have no ideas, do you? And I thought *we* were bungling the whole thing!"

Ajax Oddson's voice filled the air above Nightgown. "My, oh my! What have I got in my sights? A couple of brawlers raring to fight! Let's all get our napkins for . . ."

"See what you've done now?" September sighed. She had had enough of dueling, and dueling a dinosaur was just ridiculous. Absurd! Her sense of sensibility would not accept it. But the green and violet fireworks burst into the sky once more, showering the Night-Barn with sparks that reflected in the deep sky of its beams. They spelled out the words:

The Duel du Jour!

"A duel?" said Conker. "In Nightgown?"

"Like a boxing match or with swords and that?" asked Meatpie. "Or a joust?"

"Who cares?" Tugboat yelled. "Looks like my shop's got the best seats! I've got corncakes and pepper pies for all! And a jug of sunshine!" Sunshine is what wombats call their local home brew. It would knock all of our grandfathers clean over with one sip.

Conker and Bluestocking hurried back to their own

porch. The Nightgown mob rushed to safe cover—so long as the safe cover offered a good view.

"We've got prime front-row rump-space!" Bluestocking called out in her best hawking voice. "Sunshine and sausages! A cup for sevenpenny, a link for two Tugbits!"

The familiar judge's frame shimmered into the air a few feet above the dusty road. Wreathed grasses and gooseberries braided up into a ring around a terrible pale face covered in tattoos. Vicious magenta eyes glowed with hate. Gratchling Gourdbone Goldmouth opened his mouth and screamed wretchedly at them. His gold teeth, his gold tongue, his gold lips reflected the black night-boards of the town.

"Well, hello, you old worn-out baseball!" chuffed Blunderbuss. She turned to the stands confidentially. "He got turned into a baseball and sixth graders hit him with sticks. It was excellent." Tugboat and Conker tittered on their porches. "How are things? Horrible? Good, good. We've got a drawer we can forget you in if you're feeling homesick!"

"Is it time for physical education?" he thundered at them, and his voice held none of the uncertainty and fear it had when he asked Hawthorn and Tamburlaine that question in the moments after he'd dragged them all into Fairyland. Now it was simply his own brutish joke. "I choose now, yes? You have to pay attention to me now. You have to do what I say.

You can't just stand around sniffing your own rot and pretending to ignore me! You will obey me, and I will eat up your obedience, because after all these years I am starving for it, you whining, breakable *nothings*."

September felt her stomach give up stomaching and crawl into her toes to die. For the first time, she thought she might have gotten lucky, only having to deal with the Marquess when she first came. What awful had that creature done when he ruled? Who could ever have defeated him?

"It's a duel, not a lecture, Goldmouth," the Rex Tyrannosaur growled. "We ignored you because you *always* do this—you drone on about yourself for hours and then start eating people. I eat people, too, I'm not saying I don't! But I have *manners*. I don't dominate the conversation with my own problems. I listen. I let them talk about their lives, their fears, their new poems, their clever little ways of organizing their desks at home, and *then* I eat them. And that? That there? That's what you call class, King Baseball."

But September could see Thrum's massive legs tremble a little, his long tail twitch. Even he was afraid of Goldmouth, the great dinosaur lord. But if he showed his terror, that would mean admitting he was weak, and that was far too much like admitting he was wrong to be borne.

Goldmouth flushed with rage. He lunged forward, trying

to break out of the doppelgänger's frame and into the Land of Wom by sheer force of will and weight of skull. But he could not. "I am going to set you on fire, lizard. Once you kill that tiny girl. I am going to set you on fire in Runnymede Square and all the mammals will cheer." The clurichaun turned his monstrous head to September. His voice grew so low and grinding that she could feel her bones bending under it. "For weapons, weakling, I choose Biting. *Eating.* Gnashing." September looked at the tyrannosaurus rex standing across from her on the road. He grinned, showing teeth like jagged arrowheads. Goldmouth laughed and the laugh of Gratchling Goldmouth sounded like the death of hope. Then his laugh died and he spoke just like all the insipid gym teachers he'd had to suffer through during the years of his imprisonment in the school bag of Thomas Rood, the Changeling boy who now called himself Hawthorn the troll. "Good luck, try your best, and don't forget to have fun!"

September shook her head. The sheer unfairness of it prickled her skin into goose bumps, ever so much worse than a silly Latin verb. She ran her tongue over her small, flat teeth. They wouldn't even leave a mark in Thrum's hide.

"I'll roast him!" Ell offered.

"No," said September feebly. "We can only use the chosen weapons—I don't even know if your fire would work on the dueling ground. Magic gets all turned around in here."

CHAPTER XV

The Wyverary took a deep breath and tried a gout of flame—but nothing came. Ajax had given much thought to armoring his dear, treasured rules.

"Just run," begged Saturday, though he knew she wouldn't, that she barely knew how anymore. If he didn't know much, he knew that. *If we win, she will . . . what was it?*

September looked up at the sun, the bright clouds, the night-sky shops of Wom, the blue tongue berries growing on the hillsides, her wonderful, beautiful Wyverary, her beloved Saturday. She looked at all the round, sweet faces of the watching wombat mob.

"I'll only go home if I lose," she told herself. "Oddson said. Back to wherever I came from. It's just the most painful bus ticket home you can imagine, that's all." She drew the Greatvole's crystal whisker from its sheath and tested its sharpness.

"I don't want you to go home," Ell said miserably, brushing her cheek with his scarlet muzzle. "I want this to be home. I want us to be home."

The Rex Tyrannosaur clawed the earth with his razor-tipped feet. Saliva dripped from his teeth. "You'll be old again. You only got young when the Dodo's Egg broke and when you lose, everything goes back into the shell. Everything. You'll go home and you won't be able to come

310

back and you'll be old and used up and no one will even know your face."

His words hit her heart and snapped against it. And somehow, her fear snapped in half, too. The dinosaur towered over her. He could swallow her in one bite. His claws could rip her apart without so much as a wink and a wave. And all he could think of to threaten her with was getting old in her own home.

September laughed at the tyrannosaurus. She saw him flinch. Her laughter was as good as a weapon, sometimes. She could hold it in front of her and it would stop even the lizard king. "Forty's not the worst thing to happen to anyone," she said, pointing her whisker at his eye. "And if I turn forty again today, then that makes today my birthday, and on my birthday, I get whatever I want."

She turned and kissed Saturday's lips, Ell's nose, Saturday again. And again. The tattoos along her arm felt hot and alive.

"I love you," she said. "I love you and I'm not sorry for anything and nothing could ever be as good as us again in all the worlds that ever were. I'll find a way back. I will. We saw our daughter, after all, didn't we? On the Gears of the World. That means it's not over."

For a terrible moment, September looked into Saturday's deep black eyes and knew he had no idea what she was talking about. All she saw there was a keen and interested boy about to watch a duel. But he kissed her back, and it was a kiss full of their history. The sun must have slanted strangely, that's all. Oh, but, September, it wasn't the sun, and a kiss may hide a thousand troubles.

Blunderbuss nosed up behind her, grabbing her by the scruff of the neck and tossing her up onto her own broad, woolly back.

"Buss, you don't have to. You'll get hurt. Let me down." September stroked her ear, though. She felt very warmly toward everyone, now she was certain to lose.

"Don't be stupid, Lady Stuff-Up! Without me, you can't even reach his kneecap. You will be an actual, no-fooling ankle-biter. This is my moment to shine like yarn never shone before! And it doesn't break any rules because I'm just your bloody steed, aren't I? In the Land of Wom, we bite to show we like a thing. And that we don't like a thing. And that we think a thing is delicious. And that we think it is ours. Because anything you bite is yours, everyone knows that. We bite when we are angry and hungry and joyful and excited to go home and frightened of wild dinosaurs and because it is Tuesday but also because Saturday and Ell are watching and especially when we are DELIGHTED but NERVOUS. Nothing says I am having feelings like a bite." The scrap-yarn wombat leaned round and, ever so softly, bit September's toes. She hoped Hawthorn would not be too jealous.

September blinked and blinked, but she gave up and admitted she was crying. "This doesn't make you a steed," she said, and steadied her whisker-sword in her fist.

"I know that, goofball. I will NEVER be a steed. But I am a COMBAT WOMBAT and I bite for Wom!"

Blunderbuss charged the Rex Tyrannosaur at full speed, hollering ancient Wom battle songs that brought tears to the eyes of Tugboat, Conker, Bluestocking, Meatpie, and even Gregory. Thrum bent his huge head and thundered at them, kicking potholes into the road and roaring fit to wake the hills themselves. September hoisted her whisker like a jousting lance. *Maybe it's not teeth exactly, but it'll bite when I stick him with it,* she thought desperately.

Perhaps if she had jousted a dinosaur five years ago, September would have closed her eyes at the last moment. But she kept them open now. Some things are so big and frightening you've got to get big to face them. *Don't be afraid, don't be afraid,* she thought to the rhythm of the wombat's gallop. *Home to Mother and Papa and home to the teacups and the dog and school and you'll find a way back someday. Someday, someday, someday.*

September kept her eyes open and her sword straight and she rammed that whisker right into Thrum's thick, scaly hide, a perfect hit, in the middle of his narrow breast. It bent against his ribs and vibrated out of her hand. The tyrannosaurus howled and snapped at her with all the strength of his primordial jaws—and missed. Blunderbuss dodged and careened and jogged off past the great lizard with a whisker sticking out of his chest.

"Brilliant job, Rexy! You fight like a fossil!" said the wombat madly, laughing, the battle riding so high in her heart that she did not notice the long wound in her flank where Thrum had caught her. Stuffing puffed out. Yarn began to unravel. She didn't even slow down, swinging round for another pass.

September drew her wrench from the depths of the Watchful Dress. It gleamed in the sun as it had the day she pulled it from the casket in the Worsted Wood. Blunderbuss sang out the ancient Wom songs of defiance, which roused the hearts of Oatmeal, Snagger, Shilling, Watchpot, Banjo, and even the beautiful Fair Dinkum to bursting. *Home,* September thought, to the beat of Blunderbuss's mighty paws. *Home to Aunt Margaret and my own bed and oranges for breakfast and algebra and the daisies under the kitchen window where the Green Wind came.*

This time, when the Rex Tyrannosaur tried to slash at her with his jaws, September swung her wrench back like a bat and brought it crashing against his snout. Several teeth went flying into the sunshine, twinkling like broken glass. The jarring blow shook her wrench out of her hands. It went tumbling across the dirt. Thrum roared in agony. Goldmouth roared outrage from his judge's box. Blood showered the dry earth. The wombats roared from their night-porches.

"A cracking cart-wheeler!"

"What a drive! Full points!"

"Ooh, she's got an arm on her!"

Blunderbuss cackled. She skidded around, not feeling the new cut on her rump in the least. Stuffing puffed behind her like steam from a train engine. "Home run!" she yelled. "Get yer peanuts, get yer popcorn, get yer souvenir dinosaur teeth! Come on, girl, don't stop now, just one more go and we've got him!"

"I don't have any more weapons, Buss!" September hissed. But they all heard her. The Watchful Dress had only a pair of short bandit's daggers to offer, no use at all against dinosaurs.

"It's all right, it's all right," the scrap-yarn wombat said, stalwart and bold. "You've got me. Only I feel a bit funny in the tum. Uff. And if I go in for the bite he'll get me good and I probably . . . I probably . . . well! Never mind!" And she warbled out one last ancient and sorrowful song of Wom, full of longing and stubbornness and hunger.

"Right!" cried Tugboat, the Great Tobacconist of Wom. She leapt over the rail of her porch. "Are we going to let a measly T. Rex come in and bash up *our* family?"

"NO!" snarled the nation of Wom as one.

"We are wombats! We bite! We claw! We dig! AND NO ONE INTERRUPTS OUR FAMILY DINNER!" Tugboat got her paws under her, hurtling toward the Rex Tyrannosaur at furious speed. Behind her rode a hundred wombats snorting the glorious anthem of the Infinite Mob as they made their town shake. Tugboat screamed to the skies: "FOR WOM! FOR CHICAGO! FOR MOB AND FOR NIGHTGOWN! FOR BLUNDERBUSS THE BRAVE AND SEPTEMBER THE BONKERS AND FAIRYLAND NEVERENDING!"

The wave of wombats slammed against Thrum and swarmed over his legs, his haunches, biting into his belly, gnashing his tail, climbing up to the top of his ponderous skull and dragging him down, down to the dust and the street and the legends of Nightgown ever after. Goldmouth bellowed powerlessly, beating his red-threaded fists against the doppelgänger's spell, cursing viciously, swearing all their deaths.

But when the Rex Tyrannosaur hit the earth, he was nothing more than the dry bones he had been before the Derby ever dreamed of beginning.

September dismounted and pulled the Greatvole's black whisker from a long, petrified rib. As she slid it back into the Watchful Dress's sheath, Ajax Oddson's voice bonged out through the streets of Wom like the bells of a church no one ever asked for. September could barely hear him over the cheers of the wombats and A-Through-L and Saturday and her own relieved, giddy cries, which she wanted to stop making, for they surely sounded silly, but could not, because she was alive and an alive thing wants to make noise.

"The old Cretaceous tango plays out like always! Mammals: on top! Reptiles: boo-hoo! Now, I think you've all had far too easy a time of it! I'm falling down on the job if you look so pleased with yourselves! Are you ready for a taste of the old Blue Hen double-cross? It's Halftime! ONE, TWO, THREE! Everyone switch places!"

The Land of Wom disappeared around them like a curtain falling.

CHAPTER XVI

A Troll in the Hand Is Worth Two in the Bush

In Which September Woos an Alphabet, Answers a Riddle, and Judges a Duel, While Charles Darwin Rides to the Rescue

They landed hard in a chilly meadow, nothing like the wild, thick tangle of the Land of Wom. Soft green hillocks flowed all around them, full of wild violets and clear rivers and sturdy stone bridges. Rather a lot of rivers. Rather a lot of bridges. In fact, the meadowy hills seemed completely crosshatched with brooks and streams, and each one had a strong stone bridge over it that looked as though it had stood since the invention of both stones and streams. Everywhere that did not have a river running through it or a bridge arching over it was peppered with odd clay cones sticking up out of the ground like toadstools. One pair of cones had a sign leaning against it:

WELCOME TO SKALDTOWN

"Come here, Blunderbuss," September said. She had found a curved twig among the violets. She bent it against her finger to bend the end into a tighter curl.

"What? No! I don't want to." But the scrap-yarn wombat lay on her side in the grass, horribly wounded, panting with pain. Her stuffing puffed out in a dozen places, her foot half burnt off, yet still she whined and protested. "What's that you wanna stick me with? Don't let this whole Queen idea get lodged in your head, girlie. You're not the Queen of me. I don't like sticks. They snag on me and unravel bits."

"You're already unraveled to bits. I want to help. I can help. Please let me?" September said sweetly. "You helped me, after all."

The scrap-yarn wombat lumbered over to her and plonked down on the grass.

"I did good, didn't I? Praise me, please. I want to be

praised. Did you hear them say my name? Yours, too. Oh, I feel bad. Is it bad? I'll never not feel bad again! I think I might throw up."

September went round to her hind foot and gathered up the loose yarn. She pushed the half-scorched stuffing back into Blunderbuss's paw and began to crochet up the wound with her new wooden hook. She'd never crocheted a thing before—her mother knitted. But suddenly it made perfect sense. She looked at Blunderbuss's leg and knew loads of stitches and tricks, like she'd always known them. When she finished with the foot, she began on the long slash through poor Buss's flank. That was harder going, as she had no spare yarn to work into the split stitches. The emerald-colored smoking jacket gave it a serious think and slowly spooled out some of its sash into a long green thread. September took it up gratefully and knotted it into place. The smoking jacket winced, but felt proud.

"Can someone tell me what's going on?" Saturday asked plaintively. "You were talking about somebody called the Marquess before that vole nabbed us. Who is that? And why is there a wombat here? Why don't we ever get any time just the three of us?"

September and A-Through-L exchanged glances. She began working on the gouges Blunderbuss had taken on her other side. She packed in the stuffing without a word, and only gasped a little when she saw the muscle of the scrap-yarn wombat's heart peeking through: a rolled-up piece of note-book paper that read *Dear Blunderbuss: Please be wild and wonderful* . . . She covered it with an extra half-treble stitch, and then a bobble on top so no one would ever again see her secret core.

"How can you forget the Marquess, Saturday?" September said, hoping her voice did not shake. "She caught you and locked you in a lobster cage so you could grant her wishes. She put you in the Lonely Gaol and I had to get you out. You know who the Marquess is. You've always known. Better than me."

"I don't know what you're talking about," the Marid said stubbornly. He kicked something away with his foot. It skittered through the grass.

"Come on, Mr. Blue," Blunderbuss coaxed. "You know me! We stayed up all night playing wrackjack our first night in the Briary, when Miss Important over there went to her little club meeting. I won best of a hundred and one. You had to give me your earring. You asked me what a wombat wants with a single earring and I said same thing anybody wants: to look gorgeous and dangerous at the same time!"

Saturday looked at her blankly. September knotted off the wombat's new foot and chewed off the yarn-end with her teeth. Blunderbuss waggled her ear, shaking off a most annoying buzzing thing.

"Saturday," whispered A-Through-L. His orange eyes swam with tears. "Oh, Saturday. We went to the Moon together. Just you and me. When she left us and there was no one else. Blue and red forever, you said. Forever."

"I'm sorry," Saturday whispered. "I don't . . . did I go to the Moon?"

"But you remember me, don't you?" September said without much hope.

The Marid squinted at her through the dazzling sunlight. He tugged at his shorn topknot. "Yes," he said finally. "September. We rode a bicycle."

"A velocipede," September corrected, her eyes filling with tears. Something nuzzled against her calf.

"It's the book bear," Ell whispered. "He got bitten. At the Great Grand Library, remember? He touched *The History of Fairyland* and Greenwich Mean Time sicced a book bear on him. The bite has been chewing through him, through his memory and his history. It's mixing up his continuity. Mangling his words. Eating up his narrative. His story. What's a boy without his story? No one. In another day he won't know his own name. We've got to get him to a copy editor before it's too late."

"Well, you won't find one here!" a voice hissed from under the nearest bridge. "Go fall apart somewhere else! I don't want my sequence of events unsequenced or my vowels disemvoweled or my consonants disconsolate!"

A-Through-L got down on his belly and peered through the grass under the bridge, quite terrifying the troll who worked there. A large red lizard face appearing suddenly at your office window would put anyone off their day. The troll wore a long, mulled-wine-colored magician's cloak and a sleeping cap with gleaming symbols stitched all over it. His face was nearly all nose and moss, and his strong shoulders could have out-lifted Atlas. The troll yelped and waved his huge hands in front of his face.

"Who's that trip-trapping on my bridge?" he tried to bellow, but his heart wasn't in it. He hadn't started right, and now the whole rhythm of the thing was ruined.

"Me!" cried the Wyverary. "A-Through-L, if you please. But I don't trip-trap. I sort of *boom-crush* and *pound-smash*."

"Very well, but please no crushing, this is a family bridge and I don't want it pounded. My name is Hemlock and you must answer my riddle if you wish to cross my bridge!" The troll cleared his throat and spoke with elaborately trilled *r*'s. "Until I am measured, I cannot be known, yet how you will miss me, when I have flown!"

"But I don't want to cross your bridge," began Ell.

"Time!" September didn't look back as she called Brother Tinpan's answer over her shoulder. She touched Saturday's face gently.

"You can't forget," she whispered to him. "It's all too much to forget."

She reached down to flick something off her ankle—an ant or a moth or a bit of dandelion fluff. Spring was coming in Fairyland. It had gotten almost too hot for a jacket, smoking or otherwise. But the little creature crawling up her leg was not an ant or a moth or a bit of dandelion fluff. It was a tintype letter *S,* and it was snuggling up against her and purring contentedly.

Hemlock sighed, wholly unaware that a little block of tin with a raised letter *S* carved on it in a rather Gothic style was trying desperately to make friends with September. "Tourists are getting too clever," the troll groaned. "I remember the days when a top-shelf conundrum like that would get you written up in the folktales. Now everyone's heard your best before you get out of bed in the morning. My brother Monkshood got so fed up with losing the game he's started asking for state capitals. My wife says we oughta switch over to differential equations. But I'm a classicist, me. I'll still be singing the golden oldies when the worms are trip-trapping over my head. I like it when the answer is *Time.* It always is, anyway." The troll rubbed his boulderlike nose with one mossy wrist. "That was the riddle I asked the day I lost my son. I ask it once a day so he knows I still love him, even though everyone knows the answer. I'm a weepy old billy goat when you come down to it. That's the trouble with being a troll. You can't forget any ruddy thing, any more than a rock can forget its own hardness."

The tintype letter *S* hopped up onto September's hand like a parakeet. It danced a happy tinny dance. Its fellows, seeing *S* had got an in with the long-haired lady, came bouncing through the grass on the corners of their blocks: a wooden letter *T,* a bronze *B,* a silver *F,* a stone *Z,* and a gleaming golden *E.*

"You've got an infestation," Blunderbuss said.

"What's wrong with them? What are they?" September chewed on her lip. *You oughtn't show your fear when strange beasts come round.* The letters *Y, K,* and *V* rolled up her arms under her hair. *I shan't be afraid of a bunch of letters! A Queen wouldn't be afraid of anything—oh, but if that's the size of it I shan't ever be Queen. But a great lot of letters are just words, and I like words. The bigger and longer the better.* *H, C,* and *M* clattered into her lap.

Hemlock chuckled. "They're an alphabet! They run wild round these parts, always have. Some grow enormous, up in the higher elevations. Ideograms and hieroglyphics as tall as a horse's shoulder. But here in Skaldtown we mostly get the wee ones. Italics and umlauts and the like. Aren't they precious? I found a little nest of Cyrillics in my rafters last week. Tufa, that's one of the three Primeval Trolls, hunted one down in the beginning of the world and taught it to turn into language. Nowadays they don't need to be taught—though you get more slang than proper sentence structure. Huh. It likes you. That's funny. I've only ever seen alphabets cuddle up to trolls before. Little traitors," he added fondly. He narrowed his eyes. "What did you do? Did you use a big word or a lot of subclauses in your sentences?"

"*Velocipede*." September shrugged. "I don't think that's *such* a big word."

Suddenly, all the sound in Skaldtown snuffed out. September couldn't hear A-Through-L listing off his best words or Hemlock applauding, nor Blunderbuss snuffling at her crocheted foot, nor Saturday asking if someone couldn't please tell him what a velocipede was. It was on the tip of his tongue, only he felt so tired.

No, all September could see now was Ajax Oddson, the Dandy made of racing silks, floating in front of her.

"The Cantankerous Derby cordially requests the presence of September at a duel currently in progress! Get your judging wig on, my gallant girl, my shrew of shrewdness! It's time for . . ."

And September saw a glittering purple ocean spread out before her, lying over the grassy hills and stone bridges of Skaldtown like a movie projection. A glorious galleon at full sail sliced through the surf toward a sun-colored Roc named Wenceslas. Above them all, green fireworks shot into the air, exploding into the words:

A Duel Delights Forever!

Beneath the flickering image, September could see her friends leap up and call her name frantically—but their lips moved without a sound.

"I'm all right!" she yelled back, hoping that they could hear her. "I've got to judge a duel! Maybe it'll be quick . . ."

Ajax's voice rang all round her head like broken church bell. He sounded so excited, September had to laugh. *He really loves all this,* she thought. *This is the best day of his life.*

"Today our swashbuckling scrappers are hashing it out on the Perverse and Perilous Sea! On the giant red bird we have Charles Crunchcrab the First! Looking resplendent on the Coblynow flagship, the H.M.S. *Chimbley's Revenge,* meet the Changeling Squad of Hawthorn and Tamburlaine! Oh, but I *do* think you've already met!"

September waved joyfully at Hawthorn and Tam. She

could see them quite clearly if she turned toward their ship, as though she'd stood on the rail herself. They leapt about on the deck of the *Chimbley's Revenge,* wearing Cutty Soames's fabulously feathered tricorns and his best rapiers. Scratch danced out behind them, wearing his pirate's hat jauntily askew on his gramophone bell.

"I thought you left him behind!" called September.

Tamburlaine laughed and wound his crank. Scratch sang out in the voice of the siren who sang the greens back at the Briary:

> *Can't keep a good devil down, sweetheart*
> *Can't keep a good devil down!*
> *The more you try to make him frown*
> *Clip his wings and take his crown*
> *He'll roar right back and paint the town*
> *No, you can't keep a good devil down, my love*
> *You can't keep a good devil down!*

"He stowed away, the rascal!" Hawthorn cried. He looked happier than September had ever seen him, his cheeks whipped red by the wind, his hair tangled and mussed, his eyes glistening and giddy. "We've been doing fantastically, how about you? We beat Piebald *and* the Knight Quotidian—he was dreadful, you'd never believe it. The soul of a scrub-brush and the mind of a to-do list!"

"Well, you won't beat me, you little turncoats," groused Charlie Crunchcrab.

The old ferryman wore his old thick goggles and his wild thick hair billowed over his barnacled ram's horns. He still wore his name tag. Hawthorn's own handwriting, reading *Charles Q. Crunchcrab.* The former King of Fairyland glowered at her from the back of his Roc, clearly airsick and homesick and competition-sick, which Ajax would call a terminal illness. "You were meant to work for me! My personal spies—and now you dare aim those cannons at your King?"

"Well," said Tam. "You're not our King. She is." The fetch pointed one long wooden finger at September. "For now."

"And you hired us to find a way to make you not-King anymore. Which I think we did smashingly! Go us!" Hawthorn grinned.

"I was wrong," Crunchcrab said simply. "One minute, everyone looked at me like I mattered more than their own mothers. The next, no one looked at me at all. You try taking that drop with a smile and a curtsy! I will be looked at! I will be seen! I will *matter!*"

Ajax Oddson's voice chimed in her ear like a boxing bell. "Choose weapons quickly—time is shortening its reins! The endgame approaches!"

"I'm sorry, he says I've got to choose weapons," September called to the *Chimbley's Revenge*.

"You better choose fair, missy girl," Crunchcrab scowled. "No stacking it for your friends!"

September turned on him, her heart blazing in her chest. "You know what, Charlie? I have had enough of you. You were only ever nice when you had your wings locked down and your family all turned into pitchforks and typewriters. What's fair? Handing over Changelings to Tanaquill? Letting Fairies run roughshod over everyone's faces again just because they could? Making me a Criminal when my biggest heist ended up turning you into a King? You were a *rotten* King and you oughtn't be in charge of anything bigger than a gumdrop. You only want the throne because somebody came and took your toy away and, even though you were quite done playing with it, now you're pitching a fit. I used to think Fairies would be wonderful, glittering miracles but you're really just the worst lot of brats I've ever met. I'll choose what weapons I like! And do you know what I like? A troll gave me the idea. It's awfully good. I choose—State Capitals!"

And September laughed in the Fairy King's face, for she

knew quite well that Hawthorn and Tamburlaine had gone a long way through the Chicago Public School system, and would be able to swing a Springfield without batting an eye. *It's only this once,* she told herself. *I'll play fair forever after. But just this once I want to pull out somebody's rug like they're always pulling out mine.*

It was over so fast September choked on her own breath. Her duels had gone on and on, round after round. She'd thought they all would.

Tam rubbed her hands together. "Phoenix, Arizona!" she screamed, and at the same moment, Hawthorn hollered: "Baton Rouge, Louisiana!"

Crunchcrab sputtered and stuttered, trying to remember that the capital of Cockaigne was Blancmange or that the Buyan courthouse was in sunny Kvass or even that the Queen of Fairyland-Below ruled from Tain. But Charlie had never traveled much in his life nor wanted to. Travel only got you blisters. All he could think of was his home.

"Pandemonium!" he yelled with what he hoped was gusto.

The waves chopped and rose between the Roc and the galleon. A mad minstrel spun up from the surf, the bells on her hat jangling, her doublet and hose flashing dark rainbow colors, juggling fire and knives. Her hair flew wild—and

September stared, for she could see all at once that the minstrel was made of a million tiny Fairies and sprites and pixies, all jumbled together into a writhing, glittering minstrel-shape. She remembered A-Through-L telling her about Pandemonium the day they met—*Population is itinerant, but Summer estimates hover around ten thousand daimonia—that means spirits . . .*

"And *pan* means all," September breathed, just as she had then.

The mad minstrel burst into flames.

A great phoenix swooped down from the clouds, its body all one burning ember from beak to tail feather, glowing black and red as a December hearth. In its charcoal talons the bird-inferno carried a long red spear hewn from a bayou cypress—for that is what *baton rouge* means in French. The phoenix hurled his spear directly between the eyes of the mad minstrel of Pandemonium, who exploded into a million burning sprites raining down into the steaming sea. The phoenix cawed triumphantly and beat his wings against the sky.

Hawthorn and Tamburlaine lost no time. "Lansing, Michigan!" fired the troll. The fetch put her lovely flowering head to one side and laughed. September knew that laugh, for she had made it herself, when she'd thought of a wild and winning play. Tam squared her shoulders. "Darwin, Northern Territory! Australia!" she added quickly, in case whatever magic made a duel got confused between the countries.

Charlie Crunchcrab tried to think. *Tanaquill told me. So did the Stoat of Arms. The old Stoat made up a song so I could remember. But whoever needed to know such a stupid thing? They always treated me like a schoolboy. They were* my *states, they'd have whatever capital I told them to have! How does it go?* Charlie sang under his breath.

"Old Brocéliande is a lady fine, her foot's a shady forest and her head is . . . Myrtlewine!"

But it was far too little and late. Useless myrtle flowers spread dumbly over the sea while Charlie howled and a man mounted the flaming phoenix. The man had bushy brown muttonchops with the gray just coming in and a sad, but wise, look in his eye. He wore a velvet coat and a cream-colored cravat and carried a book under one arm. In the other, he hoisted a long tortoiseshell lance fletched with songbird feathers. The man had worn-out boots and sea-worn hands and his name was Charlie Darwin, all sudden-true. The phoenix soared up with one stroke of his wonderful wings, then shot down toward Charlie Crunchcrab. Charles Darwin's eyes grew keen as he threw his lance.

"It's the survival of them that's best at nicking things, my boy!" the great scientist thundered, and his lance took the Fairy King in the chest.

"Well, if that doesn't just top the tart," Charlie said with a sigh.

Charles Crunchcrab I looked down. He shivered. And an extraordinary thing happened. A dragonfly buzzed out of his fine peacoat. Then a little brown nightingale flew out of his trouser leg. Then Crunchcrab the Fairy wriggled and writhed and vanished. A pile of peacoat and flying cloak and the most delicate and lovely shoes you ever saw lay on the broad back of Wenceslas the Roc—as well as a cow, an antelope, a goat, and a very confused-looking ifrit with a smoky tail. All the creatures Fairies had evolved from, which is to say all the creatures they had stolen the best bits from, just as Charlie had told September so long ago. *Wings from dragonflies and faces from people and hearts from birds and horns from various goats and antelope-ish things and souls from ifrits and tails from cows and we evolved, over a million million minutes.*

Wenceslas grumbled over the extra weight of a sudden cow, but he persevered. He would get them to shore—the Roc could see it in the distance, a beach full of golden scepters and crowns and jewels and necklaces. Inside the left sleeve of Crunchcrab's peacoat hid a very handsome frog. The frog's name was Charlie and he knew if he came out from his sleeve the other creatures would be very angry with him. So he stayed where he was. Where he was felt good and safe and, most important, easy. No one would ask him to rule the sleeve or know its capital. No one would tell him he was sleeving wrong. No one would bother him at all. And I will tell you the truth: That frog looked happier than any ferryman ever born.

"Jolly good!" Ajax Oddson congratulated all of them. Hawthorn and Tamburlaine hugged each other while Scratch danced a pirate jig on the upper deck, singing into the wind. But the Racemaster had not finished. "Now, it's come to my attention that certain rules have been broken! Certain bad behavior has gone without punishment! Certain cheaters have prospered! Is this so? Not on my watch! Queen September, I sentence you to Lose A Turn! To the Penalty Box with all cheaters, rogues, and silly little girls!"

September banged on the edges of the frame as they went up around her like steam. "What are you talking about? I didn't cheat!"

The Perverse and Perilous Sea grew cloudy and dark in September's vision—and so did Skaldtown, still sunny and bright beneath the image of the distant dueling ground. So did Ell and Blunderbuss and Saturday and Hemlock the troll.

Hawthorn waved his hands in the air as he melted away, trying to catch her eye.

"September!" he called out to her, but his voice faded, too. "September, don't forget about the name tags!"

Hemlock the troll stared, dumbfounded, at the empty chimney cones of his village. Only a moment ago, he'd been chatting away to a wyvern and a wombat and a Marid. And then that girl the alphabet loved had gone all thin and misty and there'd been a pirate ship and a ruddy great Roc where she'd been standing. Hemlock had a horror of pirates—always had and always would. Nothing could be worse in this world than a pirate come to take what you loved and then sing a shanty about it. Hemlock had tried to look unafraid—and then there'd been a lot of yelling and exploding, and now they were all clean vanished: wyvern, wombat, Marid, girl, alphabet, pirate ship and all.

But he'd seen the captain of that ship. The moment the image of it sailed across the hills of Skaldtown. A troll. A troll in a funny coat with a nose like a boulder.

"That's my son!" he'd gasped to that absurd wool wombat with her button eyes. Why the beast looked like he'd just told her it was her own birthday he hadn't the faintest.

CHAPTER XVII

A PRACTICAL GIRL

*In Which September Finds Herself Alone
in a Strange House, But Not for Long*

September opened her eyes and knew three things: She was very far from Skaldtown, she was cold, and she was alone.

A little country house nestled itself just so on the shore of a caramel-colored whiskey lake. The long, stove-black trunks and warm cream-colored leaves of trifle-trees, heavy with ripe raisin and soursop tarts, bent low to frame a peaked thatch roof and snug stone walls. Someone had planted a kitchen garden: Green luckfig vines and loveplantain creepers chased sage and sweet basil and parsley up toward lattice windows. It needed weeding, but the first tomatoes were already coming in, and the peapods looked so awfully crisp and fat that September's mouth watered. Three cast-iron ducks waddled and quacked cozily between the brussels-sprout stalks, snapping at ladybugs. The door to the country house stood open. The smell of tea steeping and fresh cut lemons drifted out.

She was exhausted, hungry, and the chill peat-fog coming off the whiskey lake had already sunk into her bones. All she wanted to do in the world was run straight into that house, shut the door, climb into the warm sheets of the deep plush bed that surely waited inside, and never come out. But September hesitated. She had read far too many stories not to hesitate. When a girl finds a strange and perfect house in a wood, whether made of candy or on chicken legs or puffing smoke roses from the chimney, as this one did, she should never rush inside. The house usually wants to swallow her whole. And this was, presumably, the Penalty Box. She would find the table inside set for punishment. September drew the Greatvole's crystal whisker from its sheath and held it before her.

The lady of the house leaned out of the pretty cedarwood door. A rich, clean perfume wafted out into the garden before her, for the woman was carved entirely from soap. Her face was a deep olivey green Castile, her hair a rich and oily Marseille, streaked with lime peels. Her body was patchwork: here strawberry soap with bits of red fruit showing through, there saffron and sandalwood, orange and brown. Her belt was a cord of hard, tallowy honey-soap, her hands plain blue bathing soap. On her brow someone had written TRUTH, though the bold teacherly handwriting stood no longer so deep and sharp on her forehead as it once had.

Relief flooded up from September's toes all the way to the top of her head.

"Lye!" she called out, and ran up the neat flagstone path to fling herself into the arms of the soap golem. One of the awful secrets of seventeen is that it still has seven hiding inside it. Sometimes seven comes tumbling out, even when seventeen wants to be Grown-Up and proud. This is also one of the awful secrets of seventy.

"Hello, September," said Lye in her slow, soft way. Warm, soapy bubbles drifted out of her mouth when she spoke. "You've grown so since I saw you. Welcome to the Penalty Box."

"Oh, Lye, a million million things have happened since I saw you! I hardly know how to tell you!"

"Don't worry, child. The gossip in Winesap is of the very best vintage. That's where you are—just outside the village of

Winesap Station, in Meadmarchen County. Nowhere near any part of Fairyland you've met. But I have made my friends here. I keep their courage scrubbed and clean and they keep my know-how and my know-who fresh and bright."

The soap golem's face glowed with something like pride. When September had met Lye long ago in the House Without Warning, the poor lady had carried such a big sadness that she never once smiled. September didn't know what to make of the gleam of wicked delight on that green-soap face, or the tiny points of foam that rose up where a person might have a high-red blush.

"I made Ajax Oddson bring you here," the golem confessed without looking the least bit sorry.

"What? How? You can't bribe a boy from Blue Hen Island! What did you do?"

"I didn't bribe anyone," smirked Lye. "Mr. Oddson needed my help. He wanted to use the House Without Warning as his headquarters, and that is my house and that means I can leave the door locked if I don't like who's knocking. Mallow said that, and she was right. I told that Dandy I wanted to be paid and I thought I might faint when I said it for you know I never ask anything for myself even when I need it but I got my suds up under my bravery and it turns out demanding works very well. The Racemaster said he would make my bathhouse famous all over Fairyland. I would never run out of bathers for all my days. I said I was already famous. Anyone going to Pandemonium for the first time must come through my House. I have no need for advertising. The Racemaster said he'd give me a bucket full of emeralds and I told him I did not eat or drink or wear clothes and I owned my bathhouse and many books already so what use could I have for money and jewels? And the Racemaster thought and planned and laid out his racing blueprints on the tables of the House Without Warning and when he puzzled over how to move his racers when the time came to mix up their positions, I asked for my payment. That I should get to run the Penalty Box, all so that *this* racer"—Lye touched September's long brown hair—"should sooner or later come *here*. After all, why not here? Winesap Station is only a village not near anything much at all, and this is only a little country house where I come to think, and no one could get a strategic advantage out of either of us, and it cost him nothing. I am sure he thought there was a cheat in it somewhere, but he could not find it, and no soap-flake dolly could ever get one over on a boy from Blue Hen Island and so he spit in his silks and shook my hand and I won something, I won something for the first time in my whole life, and it felt like every bubble inside me popping at once."

"How did you know I would end up in the Penalty Box?"

Lye laughed and soap bubbles came dancing from her mouth. "How could you not? Everywhere you turn you bump into rules and knock them off their tables and break them on the floor. You trample half a dozen rules on your way from bed to breakfast. Oh! I am meant to say to you . . ." Lye straightened her back and made her voice as loud as she could, which was not very loud, but she did try. "September, you have been sent to the Penalty Box without supper for the breaking of Dueling Conventions, vis-à-vis having a great lot of wombats do your dirty work for you instead of biting Thrum definitively with your own teeth and/or other sharp stuff. You may commence being ashamed of yourself."

Lye let her body relax again. "I don't think you have to be ashamed and I knew you'd find your way to me, but, oh, September, the folk I have had to suffer waiting for you! The First Stone broke my bathtub and Pinecrack, the Moose-Khan, soiled my garden and Curdleblood filled up all the wood boxes with despair and burnt toast. Madame Tanaquill has been here four times already and I've had to listen to her tales of the Old Days four times because she never remembers me because I am not important, I am a bar of soap. She told me that and then told me how in her day everything knew its place and no slip of used-up soap would dream of putting on such airs as to speak to her or take her coat or prepare her tea but you know she drank up all my tea anyway and I didn't have anything left for the dinosaur and I am glad you bit him because he ate my laundry. I had to hide the tea I brought for you under a hearthstone."

"Poor Lye! I shall try very hard to be a better guest. Only how long does a penalty last? What's happened to Ell and Saturday and Blunderbuss?" September looked round for the eleventh or twelfth time, hoping they would come suddenly crashing out of the woods, full of tumbling words. But the woods only rustled with the mist and the wind.

"I do not know. I asked only to be the Penalty Box so I could catch you up in my house. You can't leave until Ajax sounds an Oxenfree Horn for you. I will be sorry if you want me to be sorry. It was only my first try at a conspiracy and I am not practiced at it yet. I have not even asked you inside so please come inside and drink the tea I have made for you specially and forgive me that I let you stay in the mist so long."

The cast-iron ducks followed September into the achingly cozy house. The kitchen had started modestly and grown to take up nearly the whole of the downstairs. Everything hung smartly in its place. A rack of well-used copper pots hung from the rafters, freshly spun wool hung over the stone hearth. Sheaves of lavender and thyme and hot peppers hung drying over the doorway—along with an old iron horseshoe. September glanced at it and put it away in the pockets of her mind to take out and take apart later. Whose house was this? No Fairylander could have hung that shoe. They were allergic to iron. Lye had laid out tea on a spicy-smelling wood table covered in a handsome black lace tablecloth. She'd made luckfig and pea-shoot sandwiches, lemon and loveplantain pound cake, hard-boiled peacock eggs. Deep magenta dishes dotted the table, filled with sugar cubes, lemon slices, pots of honey, cinnamon stirring sticks, and fresh sweet cream. But it was not tea for two—it was tea for five. Five cups, five saucers, five little spoons.

The soap golem's cheeks glowed. "You cannot have a conspiracy of one. The others have far to come and we did not know when Ajax would play his trick and some of us have strict rules governing where we can and cannot travel. Sit and drink and eat and be yourself and do not worry about your friends because they are very wonderful people who can do wonderful things with and without you and sometimes when all our friends are close round we cannot be ourselves as com-pletely as when we sit alone in a little house in the country where there are ducks and a garden growing. Now I would like to make you tea even though we ought to wait for the others but I am proud of it because I had it sent through the post and it took weeks."

September sat gratefully at the table. The ducks nosed at her feet for crumbs. "But I'm not alone, Lye. You're here."

"I am not a person but thank you for calling me one. It makes me feel very real."

September thought this a strange thing to say, but she let it lie between them on the table like an unfolded napkin. Lye pulled a copper kettle down from the rack and set it on a great black gas stove. It sat smugly in the corner of the kitchen, assured of its place in the center of the world. I have told you that everything has a heart, and a kitchen is the heart of its house. All the best holidays and feasts and gossip and midnight confessions and schemes and intrigues and biscuits and pies come from the kitchen. And the stove lords over the kitchen, for it makes the feasts, and there is nothing so good for hatching a plot as stirring a pot for hours. That is why witches do it so often.

Lye turned one of the black dials and lit a matchstick— but the stove did not light. She tried again and sighed.

"It is my fault. I do not come to Winesap often enough and a lonely house will break for attention if no one minds it and pets it and tells it it is a good house," Lye said, deeply embarrassed.

"Let me try? Perhaps I can fix it," suggested September.

She gave the black range a good long stare down. It glared mulishly back at her, and if it had had two big metal arms to cross over its chest, it would have. September cocked her head to one side. She opened the cold oven and peered inside.

"It's simple enough," she said with a little grunt, dropping to her knees, reaching her fingers in, and feeling around for what she wanted. "Her name is Mrs. Frittershank and she's got so many nieces and nephews she can't count them but she does try and once she had an ambition to cook something French but she got so busy with other things that it just never happened for her. She fell in love with a woodpile once but it ended badly and if she's honest she's never quite gotten past it and she's very cross with you, Lye, I'm sorry to say. She says you don't know goulash from guacamole—well, Mrs. Frittershank, I'm not sure I do either! And you only use her to boil up the bathwater and she will go on strike if she doesn't get something interesting to do and also she has a bent thermo-coupler."

Lye, being made of soap, thought nothing so odd about a talking stove, even if she couldn't hear it. She couldn't hear lots of things. "I am as full of sorry as a golem can be," said Lye, and folded her hands before her, staring mortified at the well-polished floor.

September could hear Mrs. Frittershank as clear as a blue flame lighting. She could hear where the stove was broken in the lilt and tilt of her voice, and how she stopped in the middle of words like a burner clicking on but not catching fire. "I've almost got it!" she reported from deep inside Mrs. Frittershank. Her voice echoed a bit.

Soft, dark laughter rang in the doorway like a shop bell. "If only everyone back home could see the Queen of Fairyland face-deep in an oven! Are we making Queen-pie? I'll want ice cream on mine!"

September smiled as she popped the thermo-coupler back into place. She knew that voice. She couldn't help but know it, for the voice was her own. She pulled her head and arms gently out of Mrs. Frittershank, stood, and struck a match. The flame lit without complaint and she put the kettle on before turning around, quite blackened with carbon and grime.

"Hello, Halloween." September looked fondly into her shadow's eyes.

Halloween, the Hollow Queen, Princess of Doing What You Please and Night's Best Girl stood under the lavender and the thyme and the horseshoe, carrying a present wrapped in black paper with a black bow. She wore a shadow of September's orange dress and a shadow of her smoking jacket, and on her head a crown of autumn mist with a pumpkin-colored jewel floating in it like a harvest moon. Like September, she had grown older. Unlike September, she looked quite well rested and top-full of secret delight.

"How nice of you to dress up for our little party, September. I love your tattoo," the Queen of Fairyland-Below said, and glided forward to kiss her grubby cheek.

September's shadow sat at the kitchen table with the ease of someone who has visited many times and has permission to get herself biscuits from the cabinet whenever she likes. But she had not come alone. Another shadow darkened the door. A thinner, more nervous shadow, with violet and blue and silver slights flickering in the depths of her skin. She wore a lacy shadow-dress, with thick shadow-petticoats underneath it, and elegant shadow-gloves and shadow-stockings and shadow-slippers. And the shadow of a very fine hat.

September knew her name—but even if she hadn't, Mrs. Frittershank was weeping all over the inside of her head, calling it out over and over: *Maud! Maud! Maud!*

The Marquess's shadow had brought a small black pot with a lid on it. September reached out to take it.

"Hello, Maud," she said softly. "I hope you're well." And she did mean it, for the Marquess's shadow was gentle and kind in all the places the Marquess was sharp and unyielding.

Maud held the pot to her chest. "Oh, I'm sorry! I should

have thought! But it's not for you. It's a *pot de crème*. *Chocolat*. For Mrs. Frittershank. She always wanted to cook something French, you see . . ."

Maud took the whistling kettle off the burner and replaced it with her pot.

"How did you know about Mrs. Frittershank?" asked September wonderingly. Saturday couldn't hear the Bathysphere. Lye couldn't hear the stove.

The shadow ran her finger along the oven door affectionately. She reached up to stroke the bottoms of the copper pots hanging from their rack. She lifted a tea towel with a black cat embroidered on it and held it lovingly to her cheek.

"Why, this is my house. I know everything about it. How could anyone not know their stove's name? Oh! And my ducks!" The cast-iron ducks hopped madly about her feet. She crouched down to let them up into her lap, whereupon they began the earnest work of nuzzling every part of her face with their bills. Lye stroked her hair with one cinnamon-soap hand. "I lived here when I was Mallow. Just Mallow. Not Queen Anything yet. I was happy here. I was a practical girl. I learned the magic of Keeping to Yourself. I ate coal-eggs and swam in the whiskey lake and became an expert in heaps of things. I had a friend who came round every Thursday. I think you met him. He has wolf ears."

"Shall we have our tea?" Halloween said, clearing her throat. "September hasn't got so much time as we do. Her appointment book is rather a monster. And gossip without tea has no bite."

"Is this . . . is this part of the Derby?" September asked warily. "Is this a trick, to keep me here until someone else has won?"

The soap golem shook her head so hard flakes of soap flew free. "It's not a trick. You played a trick. You cheated. You had wombat help. If anyone has tricked anyone, it's you. Oh, but we know it isn't. This isn't the Race. This is us."

And so September sat down to tea with her shadow and the shadow of her enemy. As well as a tall woman made of soap, who poured from a funny fussy little teapot with mauve roses all over it. It made September laugh—though not too loudly, as she didn't want to hurt Lye's feelings. But she had grown accustomed to everything in Fairyland looking outlandish. Whether she came across a bicycle or a train or a smoking jacket, they had always gotten tarted up in wild costumes and dashing souls. But this was the sort of teapot any old grandmother would have. Just squat and porcelain and slightly tacky, for no one in the world needs that many roses.

The soap golem looked toward the door. "But our fifth . . ."

Maud put her shadowy hand over her friend's pink Castile fingers. "Lye, she's on her way. You know her schedule . . . she never shows up on time. Too early or too late, you know. That's her."

The teapot poured a deep green tea into September's cup, a smoky red one into Halloween's, and a golden one into Maud's. Silken strings spiraled up and laid themselves softly over the brim of their cups, growing lovely parchment tea-tags as they came. September lifted hers to read on one side:

ILL-TEMPERED AND IRASCIBLE ENOUGH

She sipped it, and the tea tasted of a warm, sunny wind on her face, full of the smells of green things: mint and grass and rosemary and fresh water, frogs and leaves and hay.

"The Duke of Teatime made it specially for you. He calls it the 'Bishop's Best Gambit.'" Halloween sipped from her own cup but did not tell anyone the name of the tea inside, for she was a shadow, and shadows keep secrets out of habit, even when they needn't.

"I don't care for gossip . . . ," began September hesitantly.

"Oh, come now," Maud said, laughing. "You know it's only called gossip when girls do it. We mean to parley. We mean to share information. For example, you needn't worry about your friends. Oddson dropped them off in Mummery. He thinks you've had far too much help. They think the local pastries are dreadful. They'll be waiting when you get there."

"What about Saturday?"

Halloween fiddled with her tea-tag. "He's very sick, you know. My Saturday, Saturday's shadow, is sick, too. He doesn't remember me at all anymore. Calls me Dryheart. Or just Miss. When he calls me Miss he says it so cheerfully that I feel as though I shall choke to death on his smile. He remembers his own name, of course. It's only the story of us he's lost. And he's started pickpocketing in Tain. He's very rude to anybody who catches him out. But dear enough that no one asks for their wallets back."

September smiled sadly. "He was like that before . . . well, before you, Maud. Before the Marquess locked him up in a cage. I suppose if he lost that story, he'd have no reason left to feel shy. I'm sure if I can fix my Saturday I can fix yours, but I've no idea what to do. Do you? Is that what you've come to tell me?"

They shook their heads no.

"The Heart of Fairyland, then? Do you know what it is? Where it is?"

Again, the three women shook their heads.

"Then what is this all about?" September demanded. "What is the point of all this?"

Halloween glared at her. "We've gone to a lot of trouble, you know. You might act grateful! The *point* is survival. You might end up Queen, but have you seen the competition? You'll probably end up dead. I would prefer that you not die, September, as it would have the inconvenient side effect of *me* dying, and I like not being dead."

"I would also prefer to keep drinking tea and gossiping and looking after ducks and weeding my garden," said the Marquess's shadow. "But the trouble with villains is that they *do* tend to die at the end of the story. And if *she* dies . . ."

"Can't keep them around to make trouble," Halloween agreed. Lye whimpered softly. The Hollow Queen pushed the box wrapped in black paper toward September. She watched the sunlight glitter on the black bow.

"Did you grow up? When I did. When I was the Spinster. When the Yeti took my youth away. When I got lost in the rum cellar."

Halloween said nothing for a long time. Then she reached out and touched September's hair, her cheek, her long neck. "Yes," her shadow whispered. "It was frightening. But didn't we feel strong?"

September untied the black bow and tore open the black paper. She opened the box. Inside lay a green velvet cushion.

On the cushion rested the Rivet Gun.

Halloween, the Hollow Queen, grinned at September. "Okay, Nebraska. I want you to shoot me."

CITY OF FOOLS

*In Which a City Decides to Crash the Party, Resulting
in Many Reunions and the Fateful Firing of a Gun*

Long, long ago, I told you how to find Pandemonium—the
city moves according to the needs of narrative. When it
smells a good story, the capital of Fairyland nips up and runs
after it.

Mummery is not the capital of Fairyland, though it once
was. For Mummery came first of all the Fairy cities, before
Kvass or Blancmange or Myrtlewine or Almanack or Winesap
Station or Flegethon City or Pandemonium. In Mummery,

Fairies learned city tricks, to go along with their ancient country tricks of turning milk sour and beer flat and stealing away Changelings and turning shepherdesses into dragons. Alley Magic and Trapdoor Magic and Electric Magic and Loud Magic and Rubbish Magic and Takeaway Magic. But, like many oldest children, Mummery has always loved to tease and prod and play pranks upon everyone younger than it. (I shall leave you to guess whether your narrator got herself born first, last, or in the middle.) Pandemonium always struck it as an easy mark, too sunny and eager to please.

Mummery moves *against* the needs of narrative.

When the first Fairy city smells a good story, it cackles to itself and bolts off to break it. Should a young pixie need to rescue the gnome of her heart before the clock strikes midnight, Mummery will plant itself right in her path with a heavy mist on its streets so that she will be sure to lose her way. Should a unicorn seek vengeance against a gang of spoiled huntsmen who have a gentlemen's club in the chic neighborhood of Foolscap, Mummery will make sure to rush its most fashionable streets under those silver hooves long before the beast finishes her training, or hide away in the hills until long after she has given up.

And should a girl need to find her way to Mummery once she has seized the Heart of Fairyland for her own, the city will seize her first. It will lurk behind a toll road until it can spring out and catch her when she's got nothing but her wits to show for a long journey through the world. And it will pounce with great delight at having trod all over her third act and left muddy footprints everywhere.

Mummery lives to ruin the ending. And it has been very busy.

September came to town strapped for battle. She didn't mean to look as fierce as she did, but she didn't mean to come to town, either, so it hardly mattered. She carried the Greatvole's whisker on her hip, her cuttlefish tattoo on her arm, the Rivet Gun and her wrench crossed on her back—and her shadow behind her, cast long and tall on the ancient roads of Mummery.

The city threw out its best sea fog so that September wouldn't know she'd walked out of the woods around Winesap Station and into Mummery until she was deep in the high street of Foliotown. Only then did the sea fog begin to roll itself up like the awning over a shop in the morning. September looked out into a silent city. She knew it at once, without Ell to tell her, the way she knew how to drive the Bathysphere, the way she knew how to fix the gas stove. The thousand and four towers of Mummery loomed over her out of the mist. Curling jester's hats full of windows and balconies cast harlequin shadows on the narrow roads. Juggling clubs and staves leaned at every angle, with lights on in their penthouses. Topless ladders rose everywhere, up into the fog and out of sight. Aerialists' silks flowed from rooftop to rooftop to sword hilt to coin edge, connecting colored balls with tiled roofs and torches with shops in their tall trunks, concert halls within towers made of magicians' scarves and universities within chalices studded with fake glass gems, trick ropes coiled as high as clock towers filled with dressmakers and bread bakers, cathedrals inside giant double-headed cheaters' coins, blunted scimitars stuck in the earth of that fool's city, so vast their hollow blades could hold a hundred banks.

And all of them empty.

September walked the streets of Mummery, her blood beating madly in her brow, her nerves sawing back and forth over her senses. The unlit street lamps stared down unsettlingly at her—each one was a wooden club ending in a very nearly alive-looking carving of a fool's smiling or frowning or laughing or weeping face and gaudy hat. The mammoth juggling torches cast a fitful orange light through the haze. She thought she could hear voices, footsteps, but when she followed, she found only another alley ending with a locked door in a house of fortune-teller's cards or barred windows in the back of a gargantuan fiddle.

"I can't be the only person in a whole city," she said to yet another dead end.

Rustling sounds shivered through the sweeping silks overhead.

"Never the only," they whispered. "Never the only one, no one's alone, never the only one in a world so full."

Don't listen to that stage whispering, September's shadow whispered, trailing over the cobbles and curbs. She could hear Halloween in her bones, but the shadow's voice made no sound in the empty, echoing city. *Mummery is a bad old girl and she only wants to bruise you up a bit before she pounces. We pull this eerie act in Fairyland-Below all the time. I once made a gnome think she'd gone back in time to the Middle Evil era, just for fun. It's all just for fun. You* are *a naughty minx, aren't you, Mummers? Yes, you are! Who's a menace? Who's a creaky old slum?*

"Did you hear that?" September said sharply. She had heard it—Ell's flame popping and roaring into life. He always made a little gulping noise right before he spouted off, and she *had* heard it, down that street there. She darted off after it, running in the quiet, her own breath as loud as Wyvern's fire in her ears. The fool's-head street lamps seemed to laugh silently as she sped by.

But down that street there September found nothing but a bridge of shuffling cards, all aces, from a deck so old it had turned the color of a cow's eyes, without even lovely familiar diamonds and clubs and spades. Instead, the bridge riffled with scythes, nooses, vials—and hearts, for everything changes but hearts. The bridge arched over a river of mulled wine—but it ended halfway across, shuffling into the air, dropping aces onto the burgundy current. The cards drifted downstream like barges to market.

"Ell?" September called out. "Blunderbuss? I'm here! Saturday?"

A bolt of saffron-colored silk twisted and sagged between two wooden flutes with lace curtains in each hole. A familiar blue face popped over the side.

"That's me! I'm Saturday!" her dear Marid said, and gave her a brilliant smile. "Aren't you *beautiful*? What's your name?"

September felt all the blood in her prickle and turn cold like a million terrible needles. Tears flooded her eyes. It was only one little bear-bite. How could it take Saturday away from her so completely, as though none of it had ever happened, as though her whole life had been a dream that no one wanted to hear about? How could it take their story from them? But it could. It had.

"You can't forget me. You just can't," she whispered. "Everything else, but not me. Not us."

Oh, Saturday, whispered Halloween from the wall of the

flute where the torchlight cast her. *Look at us and remember when all you wanted was for her to come back. It's your turn to come back. But what can we do against invisible bears sent by Time to punish you?*

Saturday leaned forward at the waist and flipped over, winding the long silk behind him as he twirled slowly down to the street. "Why do you have that tattoo? That means you're married! My loss." He looked into her eyes, full of interest, without a care in the lines of his face, without the least pain dragging down his brow.

"I'm not married." September's throat got so thick she could hardly talk through it. "It was a trick we played on an octopus . . ."

"Octopi are very dangerous." Saturday whistled. "I'm impressed all over. How did you know my name?"

September reached out and touched his shoulder. She felt odd. If he didn't know her now, she'd no right to touch him as though he did.

"I knew you when you were older," she said softly. "We went to the Moon. We sailed the sea. My name is September."

"Oh! How wonderful, then. I look forward to becoming the Saturday who sails with you. Forgive me, I meet people out of order all the time—but then, you must know that, from our time on the Moon."

September clutched her elbows with her hands to keep from coming apart on that wet street in a strange city. "I do know."

The Marid clapped his hands. "Well, September-of-my-Moony-Future! We seem to have the place to ourselves, so what shall we do for a first date? First for me, I mean. I can teach you how to do a backflip into a double drop on the green silks back that way. Oh! I did see a mad wyvern with a turnip hanging off him and a very odd sort-of-knitted wombat thing? We should avoid them as best we can. When you meet mad folk on the road, some sort of story always starts up, and you've no control over how it goes."

September wiped her eyes quickly. "Where? Where did you see them? Can you show me? It's important. They're not mad . . . you will have known them, too, when you meet me." Verb tenses were always so difficult with Saturday, but now it was worse than ever.

"Oh . . . they're on the other side of the river . . . it's a long way round. Wouldn't you rather walk the tightrope between the Unseelie Unicycle and Big Bacchus? If you don't fall, you get a lovely pair of black wings."

September didn't want to smile. She didn't feel like smiling. But she knew this Saturday wouldn't know what she could do, and he'd be dazzled. She could never resist trying to impress him. She turned to the bridge of cards and moved her hands like she was dealing blackjack. It was a trick Sir Sanguine had taught her in the Redrum Cellar. That redcap could do anything with enough aces. The deathly playing cards shuddered and shuffled out, stretching to the other bank.

Saturday clapped his hands and to September's lonely heart it sounded like love. "Oh, September, I can't *wait* to meet you!" he cried.

Saturday took her hand and led her over the bridge of aces, down jackknifing streets, the angles of the alleys so sharp and steep that they tumbled down Mummery as much as they walked through it. And September heard Ell's gulping pre-flame sounds, and a refrain or two from an ancient fighting song of Wom, and they weren't phantoms—Saturday heard them, too. They followed the sounds and the cries and the song until they got close enough to hear another voice, a very familiar voice, bouncing off the high towers.

They burst, hand in hand, into a wide plaza ringed in immense marionette puppets without strings. They lay on their sides, sat cross-legged, stood bent over, their joined arms hanging down, rested shoulder to shoulder. They had doors in the soles of their shoes and lanterns lit in their eyes, shutters closed in their chests and old snow in the creases of their wooden hair. Under the gaze of the collapsed puppets, Ell and Blunderbuss fought for their lives.

September could hardly understand what she saw. A-Through-L spat his indigo fire at a girl in black. Blunderbuss fired passionfruits and horseshoes from her mouth, singing all the while. But the girl knocked both flame and fruit aside like bumblebees. She screeched back at them and fired arrow after silver arrow from her iceleaf bow. It was not a duel. It was a brawl, and the Marquess had already got an arrow through Blunderbuss's ear. The little block letters of the troll's alphabet danced around their feet. They saw September first and rolled toward her in a clattering wooden wave, beaming up at her with their *S* and *Q* and *E* and *W* and *B*'s.

Iago, the Panther of Rough Storms, lay calmly out of harm's way, behind the broad side of a tiger-striped, flower-wheeled Model A Ford with a burlap sack over its spare tire. For in the lottery of steeds, the Marquess had found herself behind Aroostook's wheel, and she had driven the length of Fairyland inside September's automobile.

"It's mine," the Marquess screamed as she nocked another arrow. "You nasty little thieves! You give it back! Give it *back*!"

September stared. Her mouth hung open. The Marquess was crying.

Now, whispered Halloween, the Hollow Queen.

"She gave it to *me!*" wailed A-Through-L. "You've no right! I hate you! I *hate* you! *Hate* begins with *H* and I've never used it once but I'll use it on you! I hate your lions and I hate your hat and I hate your horrible cold Gaol and I won't give you anything!"

"You're drunk!" Blunderbuss barked. "Go sleep it off!"

Now, hissed September's shadow. *Do it now, before she sees you!*

"You stole it from me. Just give it back and I'll let you go. I promise. It's mine. It's all I have left!"

The voice of Ajax Oddson filled the plaza of marionettes. Saturday, who had forgotten ever having heard it before, clapped both hands over his ears.

"What's this in my own backyard? Why, it's two old friends and all their secret scars! You know what that means!"

As soon as she heard the Dandy's booming voice, September cried out: "Now, Maud, now!"

Out of September's own shadow came a second, a shadow hiding in shadow. The new shadow wore lace petticoats and long gloves and a very fine hat. She peeled off the black out-line of Halloween's body and flew to herself, stretching out her hands with a terrible, eager love. The Marquess's shadow caught the Marquess up in her arms and whirled her round like a dancer at a ball. The Marquess looked into her own eyes in wonder and shock. Violet and green fireworks shot into the air above them. They began to spell out their words.

But before they could form into the *D* of *DUEL*, September unholstered her Rivet Gun from her back and shot the Marquess in the head.

CHAPTER XIX

THE GIRL WITHOUT WARNING

*In Which Many Secret Longings See the Light,
A-Through-L Loses His Treasure, and the Marquess
Gets Her Comeuppance*

A house snatched them all up out of Mummery in one swoop, as though it had been crouching in wait for hours and sprung out just when its cue had sounded. It looked much like a Spanish mosque—if a giant had firmly stepped on it. All the curly broken door frames and crumbling tiled mosaics lay in pieces and parts, each blue-green wall propping up the other. Fragrant stacks of red wood and pools of seeping black mud dotted the halls. Moss covered every shattered pillar.

September and her shadow, the Wyverary and his Blunder-buss, Saturday and Aroostook, the Marquess and her shadow, stood before a beautifully carved archway leading into a little courtyard where a shabby fountain gurgled valiantly as though it had never stopped since September last saw it. The arch read, as it always had:

THE HOUSE WITHOUT WARNING

Lye stood waiting for them, tears of liquid soap streaming down her face. All she could see was the Marquess, her friend, her Good Queen Mallow, Maud, the girl who ruled Fairy-land for a little while, and lost everything, and clawed her way back. And now the Marquess was riveted to her shadow once more. September strapped down her smoking Rivet Gun on her back. The conspiracy had done its work. Ajax could not touch them here, or make them duel. He had no power in Lye's world. That is what happens when a person lives alone for so long—no one else can change their ways.

"What have you done?" the Marquess whispered.

Her shadow brushed a strand of magenta hair lovingly out of her face. "I missed you. Lye missed you. You got so lost for so long."

The Marquess crouched down like a cornered wolf,

looking wildly from shadow to shadow to golem to girl to wombat to Wyverary to Marid to Model A. Iago licked his front paw.

"*She* didn't miss me," she said when her eyes fell on September.

"She did it for me," said Maud, her shadowy face moving against a crumbled wall. "We had such a lovely time together in the underworld. Oh, Mallow, don't you remember me? All the things we did together? Don't you remember Father's farm and the house in Winesap and Mr. Map? Our ducks and our magic and our friends? We defeated Goldmouth. We put a pot of cocoa on every table in Fairyland. We knew Yes Magic and No Magic and a hundred other kinds. We were so good, once upon a time."

"I want my book back," Mallow whispered wretchedly.

"What are you talking about?" asked Lye, hurt that her Mallow had not run into her clean green arms at once.

"The wyvern has it. He *stole* it. It's mine. Please, *please* give it back. You can do whatever you want to me, put me in a dungeon or put me back to sleep or drown me till I'm dead. I accept that I'm outnumbered. I won't struggle. Just give me my book back and you can have me."

Ell glared at her through his sea-glass spectacles. He clutched *The Mystery of the Blue Train* in his claws. September hadn't seen it in the chaos. It had a silver arrow through the cover. "But it's not yours! Not everything in the world is yours just because you want it. My great-grandmother gave it to me because she loves me and it's how I know she loves me."

Mallow sunk to her knees. Her shadow sank softly down behind her. "Wyvern, where do you think the library got it? A novel by Agatha Christie? Published in London and New York in 1928? Tell me, is Agatha a spriggan or a pooka? Or a dragon? It's *mine*. I had it in my satchel when I stumbled through into Fairyland from my father's attic. Most people don't think it's her best but I loved it. I used to sit up in bed in my little house in Winesap and read it over and over. I read my books of magic, too, and my neighbors' whole collection of Fairy romances, but I always came back to the jewel thief and the heiress and the wonderful train. I lost it when I moved to the Briary, after I cut down Goldmouth and sewed him up into a ball so he could never hurt anyone again. I searched for years, as Mallow, as the Marquess, but I could never find it. It was the only human thing I loved. It is the only human thing of mine left. If you don't give it back to me I shall start screaming and never stop."

A-Through-L gripped the book so tightly its boards creaked. But he couldn't bear to see anyone cry, in the end. He put it on the tiled floor and scooted it over to Mallow with his long black claw, unwilling to get very close to her. She picked it up with such care, running her hands over the cover and holding it to her cheek before she opened it like a knight opening a chest of treasure. Good Queen Mallow flipped through the pages, touching the story with her fingertips, the words that described the greatest jewel thief in the world and how he stole a ruby called the Heart of Fire and almost, just almost, got away with it. Her hand hovered over the master thief's name, a name that, when she was young and afraid, always seemed to her so full of power and mystery and strength that the letters could hardly contain it: *The Marquis*.

"It's how we found her," Blunderbuss grumbled. "The Marquis always tries to get off the train before the Inspector can figure out his game. We thought she'd try to head everyone off, too, and switch the Heart of Fairyland with a fake . . . well, assuming someone got it somewhere along the way and all trains end at Mummery . . . but she didn't have anything."

"Mallow," Lye said softly. "Mallow?" The Marquess did not look up from her book. "Mallow," the soap golem begged. "Please hug me. Please hold me. Please, oh, please. I have waited so many years to be hugged by you again and you said you would come back but you didn't, you didn't come back and I got older and I waited and waited and I don't want to wait anymore and I know you wouldn't stop loving me just because you got really busy with being a villain I know that's an awful lot of work but I am lonely and awful too so please hold me I have earned it."

Mallow looked up at the soap golem she had made when she wasn't much more than a girl, and everything was yet to happen to her. She held out her arms like a child and Lye fell into them. They sat that way for a long while.

"I don't understand," Mallow said finally, tugging her hat back down. "What's the purpose of this? Why bring me here? Why not just let us fight it out? I'd have won, Lye, I promise. That one's just yarn. Besides, September won't last much longer. She's almost out of time."

"What do you mean?" said Halloween sharply, hopping out of the water in the fountain. September jumped up guiltily and pulled out her Rivet Gun—in all the excitement she had forgotten their bargain. *You must let me free when it's done. No tricks. I won't be a shackled shadow again.* September held it behind her, against the place where she and her shadow joined. She thought of that day on the ferry with Charlie Crunchcrab and the Glashtyn when she lost her shadow the first time. It had hurt, then. September fired. Halloween leapt free, spinning on one toe with the joy of it. Saturday hopped up on a half-fallen wall. He chewed his nails, fascinated by all these strangers and their urgent whispers. It was better than the circus.

The Marquess tried to smile her old wicked smile, her triumphant smile, her smile of knowing something no one else knows. But it would not come quite right. With her shadow's hand on her shoulder and Lye's fingers stroking her cheek, with Iago trotting over to rest his great black head on her knee, she could not find her devilish smile in the cabinets of her heart. Her hair flushed a confused deep purple. She ran her fingers along Iago's sleek dark spine and drew up September's hourglass. The bottom bell was nearly full. Only a few grains remained in the top.

"It started going again when you got out from under the Fairies' thumbs. They break everything they touch, you know. But I suppose you and I do, too. I'm sorry, I really am. I'm sure you wanted to see how it would all turn out."

September gasped. Her hands clutched at each other, as though trying to keep herself where she was. "I'm not ready," she whispered. She held out one hand to Saturday, but he didn't take it. He couldn't understand why she was so upset. What wasn't she ready for?

"One never is," the Marquess answered wryly.

"No, no, no," moaned Ell. "This always happens and I always hate it." Blunderbuss bit his long neck comfortingly.

She didn't really understand, either. She'd only known Changelings before.

The Marquess wanted to rub it in, to tell the girl the worst of it: that no one was waiting for her at home. Her house stood empty in the still-chill May wind, among the fields shorn bald. Her parents had gone, even her dog had gone, and there would be no kisses on the forehead and tuckings in this time. Mallow couldn't see where they'd gone, but she knew they would not come back for their girl. She wanted to gloat. She wanted to say: *You'll find out how it feels to lose everything. You'll know how I felt. You'll do just as I did because it's the only thing anyone could do. In a few years it'll be the Engineer who is the terror of Fairyland's folk.* But it would not come out. She laced her fingers through Lye's and the words died in her.

"You know," Iago purred, "a real villainess doesn't do the expected thing. If the rules say she ought to grind her heel into the world and she straps on her best shoes, well, she might as well be a maidservant. So obedient. So mildmannered. Coloring inside the lines. Doing the drudge work of the tale with no thanks from anyone. Every cat knows how to keep his owner feeding them: You may scratch and bite ninety-nine times, but the hundredth time, you must leap into a lap and press your nose to their nose. Rules are for dogs."

"I am not a villain. Or an -ess," murmured the Marquess. "I was a hero. I *am* a hero."

"So save the maiden," the Panther of Rough Storms rumbled contentedly.

Three pomegranate-colored grains of sand remained in the hourglass. Two quivered and tumbled down into the lower bell. The Marquess's eyes found September's. Her hair blossomed orange. The emerald-colored smoking jacket held tight to its mistress's shoulders—it meant to go with her, if she had to go.

"We are so alike," the Marquess said. "It would break your heart how alike we are."

Mallow smashed the hourglass against the floor of the House Without Warning. Red sand flew in every direction. The last grain skittered across the tiles and came to rest against the lip of the broken fountain.

And nothing else happened.

September remained, standing much taller than she ever thought she'd be when she was twelve, her feet firmly on Fairy ground.

And she could not breathe. *You are never going home.* Her heart felt as though it had vanished from her body and left nothing but a hole. *You will never see your parents again.* September shut her eyes against her tears.

The soap golem led them to the center of the House Without Warning, which was really and truly a house now, with all the people Lye cared about inside it. At least for the moment, everyone the golem loved was collected within its long tiled halls and courtyards. All the crumblings and cracks looked suddenly charming and busy, covered in soft mosses and green with age. They began to build themselves merrily up again stone by stone. The soft smacking sounds of the golem's soapy heels against the floor were light, cheerful. Everyone walked quietly in a long train brought up by the softly grumping engine of Aroostook. Everyone was afraid speaking would spoil it and bring back the brawling they'd only just escaped. Finally, they entered a large courtyard. In the midst of copper statues and fountains shaking off their verdigris rested a huge bathtub, hollowed out of a single rough stone. The floor showed two winged hippocamps rampant in cobalt and emerald. The tub covered one of their hooves like a great horseshoe.

Lye pulled at Mallow's jacket and she wriggled out of it with a little laugh. She did not even seem to notice them watching her. She hesitated for a moment, then climbed into the stone tub, her skin flushing red with the heat. Her shadow eased in behind her, wrapping her long black arms around Mallow's thin, pale chest.

"Is this my punishment?" Mallow asked tremblingly. "Will you boil me alive?"

Lye snapped off her right hand at the wrist. It made a dull *chunking* sound, and September gasped. She had seen Lye break off her fingers before, but her hand was so much, so much!

"This is the bath for washing your anger," the golem said solemnly. She dropped her hand into the water. It fizzed up in bruised purples and reds and yellows. It smelled of dusty attics and the Briary gardens and the walls of the Lonely Gaol, of blue lions and black panthers and wooden spoons.

Mallow shut her eyes and shook her head. "You can't wash my anger, Lye. It's too big. It'll never come out. Never."

Maud, Mallow's shadow, dunked a bucket into the bath and poured the scalding water over her head. "When you are first hurt, your anger is fresh and bright and clean. It is hot and eager to defeat injustice. It makes you sharp and keen and quick, so that you can outrace your hurt and leave it lying on some faraway ground where it happened. This is why children cry so bitterly and scream until their faces go red at the smallest hunger or loneliness. They must get terribly, piercingly angry so that they can get out in front of all the little hurts of being new, or else they will never get free of them. But anger can go off like milk in the icebox. It can go hard and rotting and turn everything around it rotting, too. By the time you have made your peace, your anger has reeked up your whole heart, it's so gunked up with fuming. That's why you must wash your anger every now and again, or else you can't even move an inch."

September took the bucket from Mallow's shadow, filled it, and poured it over the girl who had been the Marquess's head. The cuttlefish colors all ran out of her hair. She wept and was Maud again, blond and young and running away over and over again. The girl who was once the Marquess clung to Lye. September felt she ought to turn away, that such grief was not hers to comfort, and so she did.

She walked over to Aroostook and put her hand on its hood. "What adventures you must have had!" September said, and was very glad the Model A had come through without a dent or a prick in her windshield. The engine warmed under her hand with recognition and tired happiness.

And then September heard Aroostook's voice in her head, just as she had heard Fizzwilliam the Bathysphere's voice and Mrs. Frittershank the gas oven's. It told her all about how it had escaped from Madame Tanaquill's impound garage and gone wildly wandering through Fairyland, changing whenever some old part of it felt wrong in this new place. It wanted stripes and scales and tangerine scrimshaw and a sunflower steering wheel and great gryphon feet so very badly. It had always had those things, Aroostook told her, even when Mr. Albert first bought it from the lot, it was only that no one else could see them. When September drove it through to Fairyland, it woke up, just as September did the first time she soared across the worlds. It would wake anyone up! And the more the Model A wandered, the more it yearned, the more it began to look on the outside as it had always known it should. Aroostook was a Terrible, Wonderful, Splendid Engine now! It fought a valkyrie and won! That was her helmet, there, in the desert-stone backseat! *Be proud of me, September, be proud of your Splendid Engine. Lift my hood and look at what I've made of myself! And tell Mr. Albert I'm sorry but I shan't ever be coming back, ever, ever.*

September popped the clasp on the Model A's hood and raised it up. Inside lay an engine all of glass and wildflowers and stalactites and bright sapphire cogs wrapped round with striped fur, all turning gracefully and sipping from the fuel tank still brimming with Ballast Downbound's sunshine-gas. It was a cave of wonders. And she understood it, just as she understood how to drive Fizzwilliam and fix Mrs. Frittershank. She understood Aroostook's workings top to bottom, and so she knew that if she lifted that ring of toad-stools there, she would find what Ballast Downbound, the stalwart Klabautermann who had helped her to the Moon, said lay inside ships and people and everything alive: ballast. *Anything that ever fascinated the ship, made it sail true, patched it or broke it, anything the ship loved or longed for, anything it could use,* B.D. had said. *It all just sort of sinks down and jumbles up together into something hot and heavy inside you, and the weight of everything you ever wanted in the world will keep you steady even when the worst winds blow.*

She lifted the ring of toadstools and moss and there it was. Small, because Aroostook was only a baby, really. But it lay nestled in the deep of her Splendid Engine—a little tight jumble of lunar rock and strands of Almanack, the Whelk of the Moon's hair, scraps of September's black criminal's silks, a stump of a candle from the Candelabra Desert where they'd been taken captive, a few chicken feathers from Mr. Albert's prize rooster, all wrapped around her carburetor, beating away like nothing so much as a heart.

The Heart of Fairyland

In Which Many Plans Find Their Ends

September stepped out of the House Without Warning and into a clanging, bonging, crashing, blinding riot of color and chaos.

Saturday giggled and swooped out behind her, soaring up to meet the madness, his blue limbs disappearing into the throng.

"I think we're late," A-Through-L said, his orange eyes widening to take it all in.

A twisted silver sign arched between two blazing juggler's torches, its letters spangling in bright, fogless sun:

RUNNYMEDE SQUARE

Below it hung a long silk banner painted red:

WELCOME RACERS!

Pinecrack, the Moose-Khan, antlers and all, rocketed through the air and slammed through the sign, sending pieces of RUNNY and MEDE showering down to the square below, onto the heads of a furious throng of would-be Kings and Queens. Curdleblood, the Dastard of Darkness, fired his onyx flintlocks at Horace the Overbear's roaring ivory-armored face. A woman with long, terrible teeth put her hands to her sides, screamed up to the heavens, and shivered into an enraged woolly mammoth, charging the Happiest Princess, tossing her tusks like a bull in the ring. Penny Farthing fenced the Ice Cream Man, whose pistachio epaulets hung in bloody tatters round his shoulders. Hushnow, the Ancient and Demented Raven Lord, darted in and out of the mob, pecking at heads and eyes and the odd fallen jewel he wanted for his new nest. Queen Mab chased Hushnow through the air in her hazelnut chariot, wrested back from poor Sadie Spleenwort who'd gotten it in the lottery. Sadie had only lost one finger to Mab's wrath, which both ladies considered fair. Sadie shot her sourbolt crossbow at Madame Tanaquill, but they only shattered into green smoke against the Fairy Prime Minister's back. Horace the Overbear had already bitten the Knapper six or seven times, but it didn't seem to slow the assassin-king down much. Half of them, comically, still wore the name tags they'd been assigned in the Briary grand hall. Winds of every color spun and sprang through the spires of Mummery on catback, whooping, hollering, blowing war-horns, shouting: *Behind you! Down below! Incoming emperor!*

And in the midst of it, Gratchling Gourdbone Goldmouth bellowed his fury at a troll, a wooden girl, and a gramophone. Scratch sang defiantly back at the clurichaun King in the voice of the Siren who once sang the greens:

Huff, puff, and howl, but I ain't afraid
Can't make a girl cower and a bird can't be swayed
Go on, turn out the sun, slap the moon up in chains
I'll just sit on my rock in the sea and the rain
Singin' these greens till the dawn comes again

Ajax Oddson danced above it all, the points of his racing silks bouncing from racer to racer to juggling club to torch to card-house to jester's cap to his own broad banner.

"Welcome, one and all, to The End!" he cried in his radioman's voice. "As none of you followed instructions and brought me the Heart of Fairyland, you'll just have to fight it out between you! It's one for the ages, yes sir, a Battle Royale to end them all! I, for one, can't wait to see how it shakes out!"

"I'll take the elephant if you knock Curdleblood into a primary color," said Mallow. She wore her old black dress and petticoats and splendid stockings, but not her hat. Never again.

September turned to her. "I didn't think you'd come. You didn't have to. I didn't ask."

"Do you see that red stitching over Goldmouth's shoulder? That's where I cut off his arm. You need me. You've come a long way, Susie One-Shoe, but I don't think you're the arm-severing type. This is my last fight. I wanted it to be a good one." Mallow winked at her and ran her hands through her short blond hair. It curled and thickened and lengthened and went black with electric blue ends once more. "I fought a cuttlefish for this hair! It's mine, fair and square." She mounted Iago and rode off into the fray.

"Up you go!" cried Blunderbuss, butting into September from behind and wrestling her up onto the scrap-yarn wombat's back. "Ready to bust heads?"

"I wish there were another way," September said with a sigh.

"There isn't!" Buss assured her. "Good thing you've got a combat wombat and a fire-breathing Library on your side!"

September shook her head. "No, no, Ell, you should go somewhere safe! You are not a combat Wyverary!"

The Wyverary nuzzled her with his red snout. "Are you suggesting that I would ever leave you, September? You might get squashed or roasted and if you get squashed I'll be squashed and roasted right along with you because we go together like two chapters, small fey. Besides, if I go, there's no telling which of those beasties will lock down my wings next. I can be very useful. It's the best part of being big."

September held up her arms and A-Through-L, half Wyvern, half Library, bent his neck low so she could climb up onto his back. Blunderbuss felt cheated for a moment. But she knew it was right and proper and she'd get to bite things anyhow. September lay flat against her Wyverary, feeling the heat of his huge heart booming away inside him. And now that she looked, *really* looked, she could see a history of balloon travel written on his wings, ever so faintly, in red ink on red skin.

They soared up into battle, gouting jets of indigo flame. Hawthorn and Tamburlaine snapped their heads up when the first tendrils of fire shot over their heads. It was the signal they'd been waiting for.

"September!" Hawthorn yelled up to her. He still wore his pirate's tricorn—and his leather jacket trimmed in gold necklaces. He grinned as wide as a troll can grin when they know an unanswerable riddle, and that is wider than continents. "Watch this!"

The troll drew his pencil from his coat pocket, held it over his head, and snapped it in two.

Half the contenders for the crown went stock-still and staring, their eyes bulging—the half with their name tags still pinned primly to their chests. They all began saying the oddest things.

The mammoth trumpeted in frustration. She struggled against her own words. Finally, she lifted her long, furry trunk and cried out: "There Is No Such Thing as Magic!" And shivered back into the long-toothed lady once more. She pointed a terrible finger at Hawthorn, and clearly she meant for some awful thing to come out and set him on fire, but nothing did.

Curdleblood, the Dastard of Darkness, threw his head back so hard his black minstrel's cap flew off and all his black hair came free. He screamed: "Go to Bed!" And fell down fast asleep.

The Knapper, whom September had not even seen, he'd busied himself so diligently with sneaking silently behind the Ice Cream Man in order to get his daggers into him, fell to his knees and wept: "Knives and Scissors Are Sharp, but Different from Swords, and You Can Only Use Them to Fight Cucumbers and Onions and Packages from the Postman!" He tried to make good on his sneaking, but his knives would not even pierce the Ice Cream Man's butter pecan cloak.

The Ice Cream Man himself was whispering: "There Are No Such Things as Ancient Enemies from Beyond Time," and as he repeated it, he melted slowly into the stones of Runnymede Square, being himself an Ancient Enemy from Beyond Time.

A giant by the name of the Ogre Underlord gritted his blue teeth and wailed helplessly: "I Am Not an Ogre! I Am Not an Ogre!" And then promptly disappeared.

The Happiest Princess looked up at Tamburlaine with a puzzled expression on her beautiful, cheerful face. "That Power Is Broken and All Go Free," she said, and laughed like a school bell ringing for summer vacation. She ran out of Runnymede Square and out of the story, for no spell, not Ajax's nor the Dodo's nor the Headmistress's long curse that would not let her grow up, nor even Hawthorn's, held her any longer.

Reynaud the Fox God twisted his long red tail in his hands. But he smiled his foxy smile. He'd been tricked—finally, after all these thousands of years of trickstering, he'd been tricked himself. What an extraordinary feeling, he thought to himself as he howled: "Go Play Outside!" and winked out of Fairyland altogether—out of our world, too. He reappeared somewhere far from any place I have ever written about or ever will, Outside Story and Tale and Song. Someplace new, where everything smelled like ancient jokes that hadn't yet been told, even once.

In the Outside, Reynaud began to run across hills beyond any rule of narrative.

But in Runnymede Square, Gratchling Gourdbone Goldmouth raked his claws down his own cheeks. His magenta eyes wept fire. He stared down at Hawthorn with a hatred beyond time and death and baseball. "I Am to Do as I Am Told," he growled.

Hawthorn the troll giggled maniacally. "Didn't anyone ever tell you idiots not to tell anybody your true name?" For he had written out all their name tags, their full and true names, on the backs of strips of paper torn out of Inspector Balloon, his beloved notebook. And the rules for human living he'd written out so that he could try to understand the strange world of school and his parents' apartment and Chicago that were still written in his powerful pencil on the other side of each one. Some more complete than others, true, but they'd done their work and bound these impossibly powerful Kings and Queens as surely as rope. It had worked even better than he'd thought. He hoped September saw it. She'd couldn't help but be impressed. It'd been ever so long since he'd gotten a good grade on something.

Hawthorn opened his mouth for his master stroke. He opened his mouth to tell his old baseball to drop dead. Goldmouth would have to Do as He Was Told. But Madame Tanaquill was faster. She brushed a shimmering pale lock of hair out of her face and said sweetly and clearly and quite calmly:

"All right, Goldmouth, kill them both."

The clurichaun was pleased as punch to do as he was told. He seized Tamburlaine in one colossal fist and brought her close to his burning eyes, baring his golden teeth.

"Tam!" Hawthorn shrieked. "No, Tam! Goldmouth, let her go! You Are to Do as You Are Told!"

But he was already Doing as He Was Told. He grinned at the wooden girl, the Fetch who had grown up fighting not to listen to the Changeling voice inside her that said she was made for causing trouble, for burning down human lives, for wrecking and ruining and never feeling bad about it. She'd loved her mother and her father, her flowers and his books, and because she loved them she'd strapped that voice down to the floor of her heart and never done a single bad thing.

"I broke your leg once," rumbled Goldmouth. He ran his hand over her head and snapped off every one of her plum blossom branches, letting them fall in splinters to the ground at Hawthorn's feet. "And now I'm going to eat your heart. Are you ready? You are the first meal of my new reign. And I am going to reign forever."

"*Tam!*" Hawthorn screamed, weeping and stabbing at Goldmouth's calves with Cutty Soames's cutlass. The clurichaun didn't pay him the slightest attention. "You can't, you can't, she's my Tam, I need her . . ."

"Hawthorn," Tamburlaine called down. "Hawthorn! Tom! Thomas!" She called him by his old human name. "It's all right, Tom. Remember?" She turned her eyes to his, grinning like a fool who has finally thought of a way to make the King laugh. "I *like* to wreck things. Nothing feels as good as the moment right before you break something."

Goldmouth shoved his tattooed fingers into her mouth, just as he had done to Hawthorn the day he dragged them into Fairyland. Just as he had done to countless folk when he ruled these kingdoms, reaching into her, searching for the tiny, hard nut of her soul, his favorite food, his only food. Tamburlaine's jaw cracked sickeningly, stretching as he scrabbled in her for the core of herself. *Just a little farther,* she thought as all the timbers of her body groaned and cracked. *Just a little farther, you ugly, useless baseball.*

Goldmouth moaned in ecstasy as his fingernails scraped against the blue match head in Tamburlaine's chest, the little talisman of her life his magic could distill out of a person if he could get his fingers far enough into them. He never knew what it would be, the surprise of it was half the point. Tamburlaine sighed and relaxed. She relaxed that part of her that had always struggled against her desire to wreck and ruin and burn and tear apart everything she touched. She gave in to it and it felt like eating a whole cake when she'd only had plain crackers since the day she was born.

Tamburlaine exploded. She went up in blue-gold flames that turned quickly to angry, bloody red. The flames of her engulfed the clurichaun, boiling away his tattoos, his scarlet thread, even the SPALDING on his back sizzled away.

Blunderbuss roared in depthless marsupial grief and bounded to Hawthorn's side. But together, Tamburlaine and Goldmouth burned to the ground, and when it was over all that remained was a blackened slab of wood shaped like a girl.

And a blue boy, singed out of the sky, lying in a crumpled heap in the center of Runnymede Square.

"Saturday!" It was September's turn to cry out. A-Through-L folded back his wings and shot earthward. She tumbled off his back to Saturday's side. The Marid did not move. She touched his forehead, his cheeks, his lips, his shorn-off topknot, the tattoos on his arms so like hers. She whispered all the things a girl can whisper when she bargains with what has already happened: *Please wake up, please be all right, please don't go.*

She looked at her love and she understood him. She understood the workings of him like the workings of Fizzwilliam and Mrs. Frittershank and Aroostook. And her mind leapt over itself to fasten everything together. She whistled softly.

The troll's alphabet came dancing toward her from their hiding places, for when they'd left the House Without Warning, they'd known at once this was no place for nice words. All the copper and tin and wood and silver and glass and bone letterpress type-blocks rolled toward her like kittens who've heard their mother coming.

Madame Tanaquill simply could not believe that she was being ignored. It had never happened to her before, not really. She found she hated it.

"If you're going to make it this easy for me," she scoffed,

and strode toward September with a long, old-fashioned sword in her hand.

"Don't you go near her," snarled Mallow. She put herself between the great former Fairy Queene and pointed a long, soup-beaten wooden spoon at her face. "If you take another step, I will take your breath from you and give it to the wind."

Madame Tanaquill tried to dazzle the girl who didn't even know she'd chosen a boy's title with her eyes. It was one of her favorite tricks with humans. She flared her wide, ultra-violet wings and made her eyes into planets of joy and despair in which any human mind would wander, mad, forever.

"No," Mallow said simply. It had always been her best magic. Her first magic. The No filled her up with its heat so completely that it left no room for anything else, let alone a Fairy's bedroom eyes. Tanaquill ignored her. She slapped Good Queen Mallow hard in the face, so hard her nails drew blood. "No," Mallow said. Tanaquill drew a slender sword. But Mallow waved her Spoon, and it melted away like ice. "No."

September stroked Saturday's scorched brow, the Saturday who did not remember her, even a little, whose memory had been cut away by terrible teeth. "I can fix it," September said.

"How can you fix it?" Ell whispered. "Oh, I didn't meant to say you couldn't, it's only . . . how?"

September knuckled away tears from her eyes. She looked up into the warm orange eyes of the first creature in Fairyland who ever loved her.

"I think it's because I called myself the Engineer. When they said I had to choose a title. I can see how things work—how everything works. And I saw how Aroostook worked, the ballast down inside it. And I can see how Saturday works, all the places he's broken. And Ell . . . I know what the Heart of Fairyland is."

She coaxed the type-blocks up onto Saturday's skin, smoothing them all right side up with her careful hands. September drew the Greatvole's whisker and held it at its tip like a long, black, crystal pen.

"The Heart of Fairyland is a story," she said, and she felt so warm and light and full of the rightness of it that she thought she might faint. "It's a story that gets told over and over, a million different ways, with a million different boys and girls and Marids and wombats and Wyveraries and trolls. It's a story that keeps all of us moving through the world like blood through a body. Like a race. Like a hunt. Like a Cantankerous Derby. We were always making the Heart. Under the sea and in the Land of Wom and in the Great Grand Library. And what do you need to make a story? What has Fairyland got where Aroostook has its ballast?" September

smiled up at all. "You need a pen"—she waved the whisker—
"you need words and letters and capitals and lowercases." The
letter blocks shivered with the pleasure of being needed. "You
need paper." She touched Saturday's blue chest with her shaking, exhausted fingers. A large, bold letter S hopped up to
cover the spot. "And you need ink."

September pricked her tattooed arm with the point of the
Greatvole's whisker. She cut deep, so there would be enough—
but she needn't have worried. The cuttlefish's ink, black and
green and blue and gold, flowed out of her arm, out of her
wrist and her elbow and her shoulder and her bicep, out of
every part of her that Sepia Siphuncle had painted. The ink
flowed down over the crystal whisker and dripped over the
letter blocks and onto Saturday's blue skin. But still, he did
not wake.

"It's not working," fretted Ell.

"Someone still has to tell the story, silly," September said.
She traced the whisker over and around the letters and whispered their story to Saturday.

"Once upon a time, there was a girl from very far away
and a boy who lived every which way at once . . ."

The tales lovers tell each other about how they met are
hushed and secret things. They change year by year, for we all
meet many times as we grow up and become different and

new and exciting people—and this never stops, even for a minute, even when we are ninety. I have told you September's every little secret. I have never held back even once. But I will let her have this last one, for you have heard already how the girl from very far away found a boy in a cage, and what they did after.

When September finished her tale, she laid her head on Saturday's chest. The ink smeared and ran and turned her face quite blue. She couldn't breathe or move. *I'm right, I know I'm right—aren't I?*

She felt a cold, hard hand on her head. As cold and hard as stones in the sea.

"Hullo, September," whispered Saturday. "I thought you'd never come back."

September sucked in her breath so fast she choked. She held her Marid as tight as anything. "Saturday! Oh, Saturday! I missed you so!"

"HELLO!" bellowed the First Stone of Fairyland, late to Mummery, sitting against a marionette and watching everything with great interest.

"Who cares?" Madame Tanaquill snorted. "The rest of us are still here, you know—the ones who didn't wander around like morons with a seventh grader's badge on their coats."

"No, they're not," September whispered. "No one's here

but us." She kissed Saturday just as though it was her First Kiss. And he kissed her back like it was his last.

"We won," the Marid said to her, touching her face all over now that he knew it so well again. "We won, so you'll stay."

"Yes. Yes. I'm staying."

But Tanaquill was right. The Winds still circled slowly in the sky along with Hushnow, the Ancient and Demented Raven Lord, and several other flying racers. A few still wandered about the fighting field, dazed. The fliers began to descend, seeing the clurichaun bonfire had burnt itself out.

Madame Tanaquill had not come all this way to be threatened with a spoon and a disgusting display of romance. She would not have it. She would not. She had been born to stand astride this world—and though she had done it for a time as a signpost, she knew who she was and she knew her destiny, which none of the clowns around her constantly throwing pies about and calling them great deeds ever had. Not the way she knew. And Tanaquill knew very well that the final act can only end with a wedding or a mass slaughter—and the way those two mewling simpletons looked, she didn't like her odds. But the Fairy Prime Minister had no worries to spend on it. You could always change the ending. Spoil it, rip it to pieces. Fairies loved to do it. They'd built their first city just to do it bigger and grander. It was easy. All you needed was the want—and a dart gun strapped to your thigh.

It all happened very, very fast.

Madame Tanaquill hurled her sword up and cut Hushnow, the Ancient and Demented Raven Lord, out of the sky before he could squawk any cryptic final word. She ducked beneath Mallow's Spoon and drew one of the Knapper's daggers from some poor sap's back and sent it flying into the chest of the Emperor of Everything, who toppled forward onto his face. He managed to squawk out a final word, but I shall not repeat it, or your parents would scold me. The Winds sped toward her in a rain of color. The Green Wind lead the squadron, the Leopard of Little Breezes roaring her own spotted war songs.

"September, are you all right?" Green called down. "Get down! Find cover!"

Tanaquill laughed. Her iron dress blistered her skin. Mallow swung her Spoon at her—and the Fairy Prime Minister shoved her away with a wave of diamonds that streamed from her hand like lace. Mallow landed on the far side of the square, half buried in jewels. Tanaquill bent down and yanked a lily-tangled crossbow out of Whipstitch, the Elegant Emperor's hand. It was going better than she had imagined it could. He tried to fight her, but Whipstitch had *If something is good, it is off-limits* written on the underside of his name tag, so for the moment, he could not touch anything he wanted to have at all. Madame Tanaquill spun round and fired the crossbow—and shot Ajax Oddson clean through. He crumpled to the ground in a heap of silks.

September gasped and leapt up. She could hear the gulping sound Ell made before his flame came bursting out. Blunderbuss lowered her head and got ready to charge the tart in the scrapheap dress, as she thought of Tanaquill. Saturday tried to get up, but coughed out smoke and staggered. The Green Wind landed and drew a green sword.

Tanaquill laughed roughly at him. "Oh, please. You're nothing but a bag of hot air." She unstrapped her favorite bronze dart gun from her thigh, its vicious dart snug inside. She held it up to her perfect lips.

September ran toward the Green Wind. She didn't say a thing. She didn't say *No!* Or *I won't let you!* Or *Don't you dare!* Or even *Stop.* She didn't think about it. She didn't think about home or Saturday or Ell or how much it would hurt. She didn't think about never seeing her mother or father again, or never finishing school, or never being Queen or anything else. She simply stepped between her friend and his death.

Tanaquill's dart took September in the throat. The poison spread through her like a quick green shiver and she fell.

The crown of Fairyland rolled off her head with a terrible clang, spinning across the stones, coming to rest against Blunderbuss's paw.

Only a moment later, sleigh drawn by a team of strangely colored hippopotami tore into Runnymede Square.

Susan Jane, Owen, and Aunt Margaret came just in time to see a crimson Wyvern throw back his head and sob fire into the empty sky.

CHAPTER XXI

DEATH COMES ROUND FOR TEA

In Which Not All Is Lost

September woke to the smell of mushrooms all around. It was a warm, comforting smell—and leaves, too, Autumn leaves, and deep, dark dirt. She opened her eyes: All round her rose tall black distaffs wound around with fuzzy silk and wool and fleeces, all colored as Autumn woods are colored, red and gold and brown and pale white. They crowded close together, fat and full, like pines and firs.

The moon peeked shyly out of the clouds above. Only one moon. September lay in a little clearing. Many parchment-colored distaffs had left their fibers all over the forest floor like pine needles. In the corner of the clearing sat a lady. September brought her hand to her throat, searching for her wound, but found only smooth skin. She sat up in the crisp night and looked into the eyes of a lady sitting on a throne of mushrooms. Chanterelles and portobellos and oysters and wild crimson forest mushrooms piled up high around her, fanning out around her head. September knew that lady. But this time she was not herself made out of mushrooms, but simply a vast, impossibly tall woman dressed in simple black—the last member of Lye's tea party, who only comes too early or too late. Death.

"Good evening, my lady," said September, as she had done long ago, when her death was small.

"Good evening, September," said her death. "I am sorry I could not make it in time for tea. But you seem to have done well enough without me."

"Not well enough. You know, I really thought I would win. I thought . . . I thought I would have been a good Queen."

"You would have been a good many things. I should know. The Country of Would Have Been is my home."

"You're so big," September breathed softly in the dark.

"I told you once: When I am distant and far off, I seem small to you. But when I am near, I look ever so tall. Would you like to come and lie in my lap? I will sing you to sleep, if you are tired."

"I'm not." But September walked over to her death anyway. "I'm not sleepy at all."

"I'm glad. It would be very awkward for me if you died just now," said Death, and folded September up in her arms warmly.

"What? I thought I *was* dead."

"And I thought I said I was *near*. Near, not *here*. Not certain. You know, I always think somehow people will listen when I talk, but they never do."

"But I felt the poison. I felt the barb in my throat."

"Do you feel it now?" Death's dark dress rustled in the Worsted Wood.

"Well, no," said September, touching her throat again.

"That should have been your first clue." Death chuckled. "I haven't gotten to do this often. Forgive me, I am enjoying it so much." The lady in black looked pointedly at September's feet. She followed the dark gaze of her own death.

September was wearing a pair of rich, soft green hunting boots. She had never seen them before in her life.

"What's happening to me?" She searched the face of her death and found only mischief there.

"I only ever got to see it once before. A man named Mabry Muscat. He gave his life for a girl he loved. King Goldmouth cut him down and I picked him up again."

September looked at her legs again. Now, she was wearing green jodhpurs. And green gloves. And a green dress. And her own green smoking jacket. And a green carriage-driver's cloak.

"The Green Wind told you: The new Blue Wind must steal something from the old one to take her place. The Red Wind must be bested in single combat. And the Green Wind . . . whoever gives up their life to save the old wind blows green and bright through the world on the back of a Leopard."

September laughed. She touched her long hair—it had gone a deep, wonderful green.

Death curled September into her great long arms, so long that they swallowed up all the green of her into shadow. And in the moonlit half-world of the Worsted Wood, Death began to sing September Bell awake.

> *Go to sleep, little skylark,*
> *Fly up to the moon*
> *In a biplane of paper and ink*

Your wings creak and croon,
borne aloft by balloons
And your engine is singing for you.
Go to sleep, little skylark, do.

Winds of Change

In Which Everyone Arrives at Their Destination

September opened her eyes. All she could see were clouds streaming by and a sky so blue it dazzled her. All she could feel was the beating of a Leopard's fierce, thundering heart beneath her.

"Hullo, Imogen," the Green Wind said to the Leopard of Little Breezes.

"Hullo, September," said the Leopard to the Green Wind. "I solemnly swear I will never bite you."

The Green Wind laughed. "I don't mind. I know a wombat who has quite a philosophy about biting."

"So do I," purred the Leopard of Little Breezes. "She's just down there."

September looked down and felt sick for a moment—she could see all of Fairyland racing by, every beach and mountain and long desert. And down by one particular sea and one particular shore lay Pandemonium, its bright woolen towers so achingly familiar and beloved, the green spike of the Briary gleaming in the sun. The two of them drifted slowly down past the clouds and the torches and the towers. The Leopard of Little Breezes took extra care not to jostle the landing. A handsome young man with a neat golden mustache and golden hair met them at the Ghostloom Gate. He wore a plain but very handsome maroon shirt and trousers.

"Mabry Muscat," he said, kissing her hand. "At your service."

And then he seized September up in his arms and spun her around so that her green carriage-driver's cloak and her green dress fanned out like sails. "Everyone's been waiting for you," he said. "I told them what happened—I couldn't let your mother worry like that! Seeing you sprawled out on the ground like a crime scene! My stars!"

"My mother?" September gawped. "What are you talking about?"

But Mabry Muscat only laid his finger aside his nose. "Wait."

"How long has it been?"

"Two days," answered the old Green Wind. "Enough for us to sort what needed sorting and you to get a new pair of boots, you clever cat. It takes time for . . . it takes time for a new Wind to stir up in the east and get herself huffing." He stopped and touched her long green hair. "Thank you, my daring darling. For saving my life. Such a funny tawdry thing to say. But it must be said or your father would never forgive me. And I shudder to think what your aunt Margaret would do."

"My father? *Aunt Margaret?*"

. . .

Let us say the world is a house.

We have said so many times. We have gone up to the roof together and watched the moonrise among lost baseballs and kites. We have gone down to the cellar with our lanterns and we were not afraid. We have gone rummaging through all the rooms and out into the garden. We have eaten well together and not washed up our dishes nor made our bed, for we had ever so much more important things to do.

A house shines its best when it is full. When all the people

who are wanted have come bustling through the door, laughing and talking over one another and checking to see who has
brought pie and who has brought fresh bread and who has
forgotten the apple cider.

It is quiet now, in our house. You and I have tidied our
bed and our dishes and opened the windows in every room. It
has been so lovely, making a house with you. We have done
everything just so. And in any long year to come, we may
always come back to this little house and see each other again,
just as eager, just as glad as we ever were to clasp hands and
sing songs and light all the lamps at once. This is my last
magic trick, the curious wizardry of narrators. Come close,
and I will whisper it, and then we shall have cocoa.

Endings are rubbish. No such thing. Never has been,
never will be. There is only the place where you choose to
stop talking. Everything else goes on forever.

I will always be here, in my old chair by the door, waiting
for you, whenever you are lonesome. Our little house will
always look just the same as when we first blew the dust off
the bookshelves, and the kettle will always be just about to
boil. Sometimes I will be young, and sometimes I will be old,
and sometimes you will be young, and sometimes you will be
old. But for as long as forever, I will keep a room for you. I
swear by the sparkle in my eye and the spring in your step.

It is time to start the feast. We have lit a fire in the hearth and put the kettle on. Company is coming, after all, and we have waited so long to see them smile.

In the most splendid room of the Briary, the Queen sat on her throne.

Dahlias and roses and macadamia flowers burst from the walls in brilliant colors and deep, rich chairs and sofas lay all round, no higher than the throne, piled up with pillows for comfort. On one chocolate-colored sofa sat a troll in a leather jacket, and on either side of him lounged much bigger trolls—a magician named Hemlock and an enchantress named Hyssop, with their son Hawthorn squashed in the middle, quite, quite beside themselves with wonder at having found each other. Hemlock had made sure to scoot the sofa close to the window, so he could look down at the Barleybroom docks and see the fine pirate ship on which he and his wife had hitched a ride after that ridiculous wombat told them to come to Mummery, they must come, they must, no matter what. In a raspberry-colored chair sat a wooden girl, quite burnt, but smiling. Bits of green wick curled from her fingers, her eyebrow, her knee. A tree may come back from the flames many times, and the Matchstick Girl thought she looked rather rakish with her crisped bark.

September's mother stood by the window. She wore a bright, lovely dress of orange brocade and her long hair was braided with gold. She wore a fur cape not so very different from the ones at Brandeis & Sons. She fidgeted, and though she hadn't told anyone, she still had her sensible jeans on beneath the gown, in case more running was called for. Owen, September's father, lay on a chaise so that his leg would not ache—though truthfully it felt better this morning than it ever had. He looked like he had only just come home from college. The color rode high in his cheeks. Aunt Margaret wore her favorite dress, trailing white silk with a belt of opals and a high fur collar. A rather pretty young woman with short dark hair sat sprawled in a blue chair with her feet up over the arm. She wore sunglasses and smoked a long churchwarden pipe.

A-Through-L stood at a long, empty bookshelf the vines of the Briary had thoughtfully made for him, set into the deep wall. He had put aside his turnip watch and got proper spectacles. He put *The Mystery of the Blue Train* on the shelf. He took it off again. He put it back. He could not decide.

And on the throne of Fairyland sat a proud and beaming scrap-yarn wombat, wearing a crown of blue tongue berries and silver stars. The throne was a new one, extra-wide and made of the same night-stuff as the shops of Wom. Good

Queen Buss surveyed all with a satisfied look on her woolly face.

"Hello," said September shyly.

The room erupted. Susan Jane broke several new land-speed records getting to her daughter and wrapping her in a long, hard hug full of worry and wonder and the old terror of a child's empty bed. Owen kissed his girl's hair and squeezed her tight.

"But how? How could you possibly be here?" September tried to say from under their squeezing. "Where did you come from? I thought I'd never see you again!"

"As if we couldn't find you, wherever you hid," said her father, kissing her hair.

"Mom, oh, Mom, I'm so sorry I didn't tell you, I'm sorry . . . don't be mad, please!" September was crying in big, breathless gulps. "I thought I wasn't ever coming home. I thought it was over. I thought you'd never know where I'd gone. And I'd never know what happened to you."

Susan Jane held her daughter. She laughed over her green hair. "We thought you were dead. We saw you fall. Your heart . . . you weren't breathing. Oh, Tem, adventures are well and good but do try not to get killed again! I couldn't bear it!"

September's father clung to his wife and his daughter,

laughing and crying. "How could we be mad? Look at everything you've done!"

"Everything?"

"My girl," her mother said proudly. Her father stood as straight as a man who had never been to war, and his leg didn't pain him at all.

"But how did you escape Tanaquill?" September protested. "Where is Saturday? Is that a *crown,* Buss?" And then the squeezing grew much heavier, for a Wyverary added his heft to it. They all said her name so many times she began to think of changing it.

Blunderbuss gave a little wombat howl of triumph. "Too right it is! I'm Queen! Good Queen Buss! Actually, I'm Tobacconist. Met that Jacquard lady, she let me pick and I wanted to be a Tobacconist so I am! I've already chewed up a few laws—the Spitting Ceremony's Tuesday! All of Wom is coming and most of Fairyland! Well. Not Mallow. Lye's got her for safekeeping. Forgiveness is forgiveness but I'm a practical wombat. They say they'll send their best luckfig tarts. She and Lye have got the ovens going again in that daft bathhouse of theirs."

"Oh, calm down you . . . you goofy-face," Ell said, blushing furiously. It had taken all of his strength to say *I love you* in Wom. "Technically, September, you won," A-Through-L explained. "Ajax said so, once he recovered from his shock. Oh—don't worry! He's quite all right. He's only little on the inside. A Dandy, like he said. Tanaquill only nicked him. You brought the Heart of Fairyland to Runnymede Square. You won the throne. But then you died. And Saturday had collapsed again—the smoke, you know, very bad for ocean-folk. And the grief. And I . . . I was in no state. I couldn't see anything but you being dead and *Death* begins with *D* but I couldn't bear it, I couldn't. So the crown rolled off your head and knocked up against Buss. Last wombat standing."

Aunt Margaret smiled and ruffled her niece's hair. She felt no need to make a fuss. She'd never been the least bit worried that Tem couldn't make her way. "I had to make a new throne for her, of course. Fortunately, I had excellent materials at hand." September stared. Beneath the macadamia flowers, the throne was made of twisted iron buckles and horseshoes, just the same as the Prime Minister's iron dress. Blunderbuss was all wool and cotton and silk, so it didn't hurt her any.

"You should have seen old Tanaquill beg!" crowed Hawthorn. "She went white as a surrender flag when your old aunt Maggie came hippo-ing in! Olly olly oxen free! I could live on that memory like a pantry full of potatoes!"

"Don't gloat so much, Hawthorn," said his mother, whose name was Hyssop, tugging on her own mossy hair. She actually thought gloating was devilish fun, but she had years of gentle scolding to catch up on.

Tamburlaine leaned forward. A new green wick peeked out of her cheek. "She's the one who did it to them. Your aunt Margaret, can you imagine? She turned the Fairies into tools all those ages ago. Time just runs around with its trousers on its head around here! They call her Pearl here. She's the one the Yeti told you about. The thaumaturge who punished the Fairies for using everyone so terribly by turning them into pitchforks and typewriters and signposts!"

September gawked at her aunt. She remembered the Yeti's tale of the great thaumaturge Pearl who appeared from nowhere and taught the cruel Fairies her awful lesson. Margaret made a little mocking gawk-face back at her.

"Don't you look at me like that, Missy. It's not like you told me what you were up to, either! Anyway, I think Tanaquill makes a fine chair! She always wanted the throne. Now she *is* the throne. And you are the Wind. Green suits you, dear."

"And you'll stay?" September said. "You'll stay. You see how lovely it is. You'll stay and be happy here, with me. You're not Ravished or Stumbled. You just came, because you were Needed."

They would. They all would. *If we win, you'll stay.*

"But . . . where's Saturday?" September asked. "And what about you, Ell?"

"I shall be Chief Librarian. I am starting a new library. It will have only books I love like brothers and sisters in it, so it will be the best library in the world. I've only got one volume so far, but you only need one, in the beginning. Mabry said you would be back, he promised us, and I didn't want to start till you got here, but two days is so long to wait. Now you're home I shall go and see my grandfather, the Fairyland Municipal Library, at last, and get his blessing. Oh, and I think I am King? Because of Buss and me, you know."

A-Through-L and Blunderbuss, being a Wyvern and a Wombat, had had to invent a new way of kissing. Love invents all kinds of things, and a new sort of kiss comes into the world whenever two people put their heads together. I think you'll agree theirs was quite splendid. Buss spat a passionfruit into the air between them and Ell scorched it with his flame. They did it all the time, until their guests grew awfully annoyed. And they did it just now, splattering roasted passionfruit onto the ceiling.

The Wyverary smiled with all his whiskers and teeth. "King consort, anyway. But you don't have to call me King! I'm your Ell. Perhaps Grandfather will like calling me King."

"The Marid will be along, the sneaky little brigand," said

the woman in sunglasses. She puffed a smoke ring at them. "You're only a little ways ahead of him."

"Who are you?" said September—though she looked awfully familiar, really.

"You might not recognize me without my puffins," said the old Blue Wind, who was hardly blue at all anymore, and certainly not a Wind. She was a young woman, pretty enough to be in the pictures, if she didn't have such a petulant look around the eyes. She'd forgotten her real name years ago, after she'd stolen a pocket watch from an old man and turned into something quite different from a young woman, pretty or not. She seemed quite put out. "What is the point of life without puffins, I ask you? Your little boyfriend swiped one of my littlest puffins while I wasn't looking. He snuck up on me in Mummery, the beastly thing! If there hadn't been a battle on he'd never have gotten away with it. And now I've got civilian life ahead of me and who's got a use for that? No one! And now your Saturday's got all my things, and my job, and my house, and I hate him."

"Hullo, Wind," said a deep, salt-sea voice. September whirled round.

Saturday stood in the window of the Briary, leaning against the viny wall, one leg crossed casually over the other. He wore indigo trousers with as much silk to them as a skirt with ghostly pale blue stars peeking out from the folds. He had on turquoise gloves and sapphire-colored boots with crisscrossed icicle laces all the way to the knee. A long, beautiful sky-colored coat hung like a dress from a heavy silver belt at his waist, swirling with aquamarine stitching, trimmed in wild, woolly fur from some impossible, blueberry-colored sheep. His long, glossy black topknot coiled out its full length beneath a cobalt cap rimmed in the same blue shag. The cap had an ice-spike on top of it, like old pictures of the Kaiser. In his hand, the Blue Wind held a little baby puffin, cheeping cheekily at them all.

September remembered the old Green Wind telling her how new Winds were made: The Red Wind had to be defeated in single combat, the Golden Wind had to be beaten in a singing competition—and you had to steal something from the Blue Wind. She laughed. Saturday leapt down from the windowsill and swept her into his arms. They kissed, and it was a new kind of kiss as well, for between them blew all the winds of all the worlds. Green and blue forever.

CHAPTER XXIII

EXEUNT ON A LEOPARD

In Which Nothing Is Over

Once upon a time, a girl named Rebecca grew very tired indeed of her parents' house, where she washed the same green and blue soup bowls and matching saucers every day, slept under the same patchwork quilt, and played with the same large and surly cat. Because she had been born in July, and because she had a mole on her right earlobe, and because her feet were very small and graceful, the Green Wind took pity on her, and flew to her window one evening just after her twelfth birthday. She was dressed in a green smoking jacket, and a green carriage-driver's cloak, and green jodhpurs, and green snowshoes. It is very cold above the clouds, in the shantytowns where the Six Winds live.

"You seem an ill-tempered and irascible enough child," said September. "How would you like to come away with me and ride upon the Leopard of Little Breezes, and be delivered to the great sea that borders Fairyland? I shall take you safely all the way there, past a comet, over several stars, and through a very cluttered closet, whereupon I should be happy to deposit you upon the Perverse and Perilous Sea."

"Oh yes!" breathed Rebecca.

Thank you for reading this book.
The Friends who made

THE GIRL WHO
RACED
FAIRYLAND
ALL THE WAY HOME

possible are:

JEAN FEIWEL, publisher

LIZ SZABLA, editor in chief

RICH DEAS, senior creative director

HOLLY WEST, associate editor

DAVE BARRETT, executive managing editor

RAYMOND ERNESTO COLÓN, senior production manager

ANNA ROBERTO, associate editor

CHRISTINE BARCELLONA, associate editor

EMILY SETTLE, administrative assistant

ANNA POON, editorial assistant